BY

JOSIE SILVER

A Winter in New York

One Night on the Island

The Two Lives of Lydia Bird

One Day in December

A

WINTER

IN

NEW YORK

A WINTER IN NEW YORK

New York

A NOVEL

JOSIE SILVER

DELL BOOKS
New York

A Dell Trade Paperback Original

Copyright © 2023 by Josie Silver

Book club guide copyright © 2023 by
Penguin Random House LLC

All rights reserved.

Published in the United States by Dell, an imprint of
Random House, a division of Penguin Random House LLC, New York.

DELL and the D colophon are registered trademarks of
Penguin Random House LLC.

RANDOM HOUSE BOOK CLUB and colophon
are trademarks of Penguin Random House LLC.

Originally published in the United Kingdom in 2023 by Viking, an imprint of
Penguin General. Penguin General is part of the Penguin Random House Group
of companies. Simultaneously published in the United States in hardcover by
Delacorte Press, an imprint of Random House,
a division of Penguin Random House LLC.

LIBRARY OF CONGRESS CATALOGING-IN-PUBLICATION DATA

NAMES: Silver, Josie, author.

TITLE: A winter in New York : a novel / Josie Silver.

DESCRIPTION: New York : Dell Books, [2023]

IDENTIFIERS: LCCN 2023021768 (print) | LCCN 2023021769 (ebook) |
ISBN 9780593722862 (trade paperback) | ISBN 9780593724934
(HC Library) | ISBN 9780593722879 (Ebook)

SUBJECTS: LCSH: Cooks—Fiction. | Food—Fiction. |
Family secrets—Fiction. | LCGFT: Romance fiction. | Novels.

CLASSIFICATION: LCC PR6119.I453 W56 2023 (print) |
LCC PR6119.I453 (ebook) | DDC 823/.92—dc23/eng/20230518

LC record available at https://lccn.loc.gov/2023021768

LC ebook record available at https://lccn.loc.gov/2023021769

Printed in the United States of America on acid-free paper

randomhousebooks.com

randomhousebookclub.com

2 4 6 8 9 7 5 3 1

Title page art from Adobe Stock

Book design by Barbara M. Bachman

*For Sally and Rose,
my inspiring friends*

A

WINTER

IN

NEW YORK

Valentine's Day

...

YOU KNOW WHEN A HIGH-OCTANE SCENE IN A MOVIE goes slo-mo for dramatic effect, and you hold your breath and ask yourself will the person on the screen leap the burning chasm between high-rise buildings or catch the priceless vase before it shatters into a hundred pieces? I feel like someone just pressed the slo-mo button on my life as I reach out to grab the final copy of the book I've been waiting on for the last year straight, and someone beside me makes the exact same move at the exact same time. I see their coat sleeve stretch out beside mine and I make an unceremonious lunge, a relay racer throwing out her arm for the baton because nothing but a win will do. My fingertips graze the cover, *actual* contact, but *no-no-no*, their—*his* arm is bloody longer and at the last moment I feel the book slide away from me into his hand.

"But I touched it." I can't stop the words from rasping out of my mouth as I panic-clutch imaginary pearls around my neck. That book was my Valentine gift to myself, and given everything I've been through, I think I deserve it.

His face is a mask of faux innocence when he turns to me.

"But I was here first," I mumble, like a crestfallen child who just got shoved off the last seat in a game of musical chairs.

He flips the book over to read the back. "I didn't see you, sorry."

He returns his attention to the novel, a clear signal that our interaction is over, and I look around for back-up, sure that someone must have witnessed the bookshop-crime that just happened here. You expect this kind of fight for the last glass of fizz at a wedding or the only remaining biscuit at the Monday morning meeting, but we're *book people*, for God's sake. We don't behave that way. Which must mean this guy isn't a book person, so maybe there's still a way I can win here.

"Excuse me." I clear my throat as if I'm about to make a loudspeaker announcement.

He looks my way again, dark eyes widening in question. I can't quite read his expression, but I think he might be trying to smother a victory smile and I really dislike him for it. Definitely *not* a book person.

"You probably don't want that one." I nod toward my—I mean, *the* book. "It's the third in a trilogy, it won't make any sense without having read the other two first." I cast a desperate eye over the bestseller shelf and reach for the latest Lee Child. "Try this instead. Everyone loves Jack Reacher. It's like the movie, you know, the one where Tom Cruise somehow manages to pull off being Reacher even though he's at least a foot too short for the role? Except this is better, obviously, because it's the book." I'm gabbling like a total idiot, and he looks from the book in his hand to the one in mine.

"Isn't that always the case, though?" He sighs. "The book being better than the movie, I mean?"

I slam my hand over my heart, blindsided by this undeniable truth. "Isn't it just?" I nod hard. "Every single time. I refuse to even watch *The Time Traveler's Wife*, you know, just in case."

He half smiles, polite, and I inch the Lee Child out toward him, a silent encouragement.

"So, you'd recommend I pick up the Jack Reacher series more than twenty books in, but not read book three of this series?"

"Yes, but these are all stand-alone stories." I tap the Lee Child and try to keep the annoyance from my voice. "You don't have to have read the others first to enjoy this one."

"But *this* one . . . ?" He turns the book over in his hands, cover side up.

An almost painful sigh rattles up my throat. I've studied that cover so many times online, looking for clues as to how the final story unfolds. The cover artists are fiendishly clever at hiding Easter eggs within the intricate illustrations—it's all part of the book's appeal.

"Massively complicated," I say. "One big sprawling story over three installments, not a hope of picking it up. It'd basically be like reading French."

"French, huh?" he says.

I get the sudden suspicion he's about to break into fluent French. "Or Dutch or Chinese or, I don't know, Swahili. Impossible, basically."

"Good cover, though." He looks closely. "Is that a rabbit?"

I can't help myself, I peer at it too. Damn it, he's right. I try not to think about what that might mean for the story.

"This one won't have rabbits." I flick the pages of the Lee Child like a magician fanning a deck of cards. "It'll be full of car chases and stakeouts and pithy one-liners." I give it the big sell even though I've never actually read a Jack Reacher to know what happens in them.

"*Lapin*," he says.

I tip my head to one side.

"French for rabbit," he says.

"Do you know it in Swahili too?"

"Wouldn't it be hilarious if I did?" he says. "But sadly no. What I do know, though, is that this rabbit will be more than just a rabbit." He taps the book. "It might suggest that Steph is going to discover a burrow of escape tunnels beneath the castle, or maybe it's more subtle, that she needs to leap into the unknown to save Estelina?"

My shoulders sag inside my winter coat as realization dawns. He's not putting that book down anytime soon. His victory expression is straight out of the David Rose playbook, smile tightly compressed as he nods, basking in his moment of glory. I offer a silent apology to Lee Child as I slide his book back onto the shelf. I think he can take the hit.

"You could always try the Jack Reacher yourself," he says. "I hear it's full of pithy one-liners."

I wish more than anything for a pithy one-liner of my own at that moment, but what erupts from me is far from concise.

"You know what? Have the book. Have. The. Damn. Book. It's fine. It's my life all over, in fact."

I sense him take a small step back as he passes his hand over his jaw, watching me. The shop lighting catches the gold of his wedding ring, incensing me further for reasons that are nothing to do with this stranger in a bookstore, but he gets it both barrels regardless.

"You take that book, which you probably won't even have time to open tonight because you'll be taking your wife out for a fancy dinner at the top of the Empire State Building or lying on a checked blanket in the back of a pickup truck looking for shooting stars or, I don't know, some other equally trite Valentine's shite."

My voice just hit unpleasantly shrill, and his expression stiffens as his eyes skim my mother's distinctive heart-shaped signet ring on my wedding finger.

"Well, I sure hope your husband knows better than to expect any *trite shite* from you tonight."

My Britishisms sound ridiculous in his New York accent, and I feel his judgment like a sharp slap.

"He's dead, if you must know, and I had just one crappy plan for tonight, which was to lie on my lumpy rental couch and read that book, and now, thanks to you and your bloody long arms, I can't even do that."

He looks mortified, understandably, apologizing in broken sentences as he pushes the book into the space toward me, but I've hiked too far up my moral-high-ground mountain to be able to reach down and take it. The air up here is so thin it hurts to breathe, so I huff one last furious time and stomp out of the store, hacking strings of paper love hearts out of my path as I go.

Shit. I made such a scene back there. Why did I say that? Shame sears me. It's one thing trying to life-hack my brain into believing Adam Bronson is dead so I'm not constantly looking over my shoulder, it's another thing entirely to say it out loud to a stranger in a bookstore. Because the exact truth is that while Adam's dead to me, he's still alive, was not ever my husband, and right now is no doubt being a monster to someone else back in London. I pull my blue-and-white-striped bobble hat down over my ears and bury my burning face in my scarf as I slip and slide my way along the slushy sidewalk toward home. I should have stayed inside today. I'm too heartsore for windows full of glittered roses and racks of lurid pink greeting cards. Valentine's Day pushes all the wrong buttons in me, a manufactured event that feels designed to remind me of all my bad decisions and their terrible consequences. I've been to hell and back over the last couple of years, spiraling downward from being a rising star of the London chef scene to a woman afraid of her own shadow. Or, being kinder to myself, to a lonely, grief-stricken daughter who found herself targeted by a controlling man who dismantled her life and all but imprisoned her in his home. It took Herculean courage to extract myself, even more to book a one-way ticket to New York. I landed here six weeks ago with all my worldly possessions shoved into a couple of bashed suitcases, clinging on tight to the last shreds of my dignity.

I don't actually want to stargaze in the back of a pickup truck or have dinner at the top of the Empire State Building tonight. I'm happy to leave that kind of cutesy stuff to unacerbic women like Meg Ryan. And yes, I know my eighties rom-com references are dated, that there are a million cooler films I could cite instead. I won't update my list, though, because memories of watching those movies with my mother while we ate our homemade gelato from her vintage pink melamine bowls are the glue that holds my bones together. Her beloved stories about this city have carried me here on a wing and a prayer, fanciful Sinatra-inspired nostalgia that if she could make it here, then maybe I can too. A fresh start in a new place, somewhere my dead-to-me ex can't trouble me. I sigh and decide to go easy on myself about that lie, making a silent promise to never say it again. At least it was to a total stranger.

SEVEN MONTHS
Later...

1.

"WAS I RIGHT OR WAS I RIGHT?"

Bobby links his arm through mine as we pass beneath the illuminated red, green, and white "Welcome to Little Italy" arch and find the place alive with street vendors, drumbeats, enticing smells and throngs of people as far as the eye can see.

My landlord-slash-best-friend has twisted my arm into spending the afternoon with him at the Feast of San Gennaro—an Italian food and culture festival that, according to Bobby, New Yorkers look forward to every year—knowing my love of food is just about the only thing strong enough to entice me from the safety net of my apartment these days. To say I've become a New York homebird since I pitched up on his doorstep nine months ago is something of an understatement. I arrived desperate for change, dreaming of the New York I knew only through my mother's favorite movies. It's laughable really, knowing what I do now, but I genuinely thought there was a chance I'd land a job filling pastrami sandwiches in Katz's Deli, or that there might be an Iris-sized hole waiting for me in the bustling kitchens of the Plaza.

Neither were hiring, as it turned out. I wasn't even brave enough to stick around at Katz's Deli long enough to ask—

the queue was crazy-busy and so long it was out the door and wrapping the block. The Very Tasty Noodle House was hiring, though. Bobby Han hadn't long inherited the entire building, from his swish top-floor penthouse down to the ailing noodle restaurant at the bottom, even though he'd never so much as touched a wok in his life. I like to think that my brilliant mother walked beside me in spirit as I trudged the darkening New York streets fresh off the plane, turned down by place after place. Blind instinct guided me along Chrystie Street and straight into the path of Bobby Han, who at that precise moment was sticking a CHEF NEEDED notice in the dusty window of his restaurant. Within the hour I'd accepted not only the job but the keys to the minuscule, old-fashioned apartment above, recently vacated by his ancient noodle-queen aunt. My pokey home is the buffer between the penthouse Bobby shares with his husband, Robin, and the ground-floor restaurant, a sponge to soak up all the noise and cooking smells so they can live in peace without the faint linger of peanut oil on their clothes or their Egyptian cotton bedsheets.

What I didn't realize back on that first day was that I'd also just found the biggest platonic love of my life. Bobby has turned out to be best friend and big brother all rolled into one gloriously loud, sarcastic package, human gold dust for a lonely girl starting again over three thousand miles from home.

This afternoon's rain-laden sky does nothing to dampen the atmosphere at the festival and there's an infectious energy and buzz in the air that carries people from stall to stall, tasting, savoring, collectively groaning in pleasure.

"You were so right," I say, drinking in the carnival of color and noise. "I want to try everything!"

We pause to observe the golden statue of Saint Januarius, patron saint of Naples, a brief tranquil moment before allowing the throng of people to carry us farther along the street.

"We need to start with sausage," Bobby says, steering me toward an impressively large catering truck bedecked with fluttering Italian flags. Rings of sausage sizzle on huge metal plancha grills, ready to be chopped and loaded into rolls piled high with slippery onions and peppers. I watch in fascination as an aproned guy behind the grill curls the sausage with fast, skillful hands, and another chops and fills sandwiches with the confidence of someone who has done it a million times before.

"Food of the actual gods," Bobby says, ordering two.

I'm so ready for it when I take it from him. It's how I imagined, only about a hundred times better.

"If I eat all of this I'll be stuffed," I say.

Bobby is already more than halfway through his. "But you're still gonna, right?"

I nod, not even sorry. The sandwich is smoky and rich, heaven in a bun. We walk and eat, soaking in the atmosphere, the low background hum of generators adding an air of fairground. People shout and laugh, a market-day-like jostle, and I feel myself relax into it, enjoying the change of scene. And what a scene it is. Glittered streamers and lights span the buildings over our heads, and everyone milling around below is here for the same thing—to feast. It speaks to my chef's heart in a language I understand, and it jolts me how much I miss creating new dishes and the joy of watching people eat.

Cooking up bowl after bowl of noodles is soothing in its own way, but I'm really just trying to imitate the authenticity of Bobby's aunt rather than pave my own path or come up with my own dishes. Being around all this creativity and culinary joy reminds me what drew me to kitchens in the first place: the heat, the urgency, the deep satisfaction. I miss it all viscerally, another piece of me temporarily lost because of Adam Bronson. There are lots of those pieces—my career, my self-worth, my confidence, the things that made me feel like *me*. I imagine them all lined up on the shelf of an emotional lost-property office waiting for me to reclaim them. I will. I am. Slowly, but I am.

We follow the sandwiches with sweet, ricotta-stuffed cannoli and I lean on Bobby, laughing as I swoon.

"This was your best idea yet," I say.

"I have lots of others," he says. "Just say the word."

I appreciate his unpushy nature a great deal, he's such easy company to be in. I know he worries I don't get out enough. He's probably right. In truth, the dentist is probably the social highlight in my calendar. It's not that I'm the reclusive type, per se, just that I was at rock bottom when I arrived in New York and it's taken some time to rebuild myself. Maybe that does look reclusive from the outside, especially against the bells-and-whistles backdrop of New York, but it's been restorative for me up to now. I've got Bobby and Robin, and there's Bobby's niece Shen too. She's the kind of nineteen-year-old who could run the world in her lunchtime if she so chose, but prefers to serve noodles to Bobby's customers between taking classes and dancing her way across the city every night. She's a pretty decent chef too, always happy to take over at the stove if I need a night off, which isn't very often. And then there's Smirnoff, who isn't technically my cat or Bobby's; he's lived in our building longer than either of us and seems to have full jurisdiction over where he parks his furry orange behind. Some nights he chooses my sagging green armchair, while other nights he's full stretch on Bobby's windowsill, watching the street shift down below. And then there are nights when he doesn't come in at all. I like to imagine him scaling the zigzag metal fire escape to prowl the perimeters of the building or visiting a glamorous Persian for a late-night booty call. In reality he's probably on someone else's sofa eating someone else's food—he's pretty shameless when it comes to taking what he wants. We should all be a bit more Smirnoff.

Music cranks up from loudspeakers just along the street, and Bobby tugs me by the hand to follow the herd, crooning an almost-impressive rendition of "That's Amore" as we go.

"You have to see this," he says, finding us a spot on the sidelines. "Meatball-eating competition."

The crowd parts as he speaks, clapping as they allow a line of waiting staff bearing huge silver trays of meatballs to march through the center toward a raised stand where a line of contestants sit ready for battle.

"I wonder how someone becomes an eating-contest champion," I marvel, gazing along the everyday faces of the men and women each about to consume enough food to feed a small village.

A sequin-clad woman gives a rousing rendition of "The Star-Spangled Banner" and then they're off, stuffing as many meatballs as they can into their faces, washing them down with bottle after bottle of water. The crowd goes mad for it, shouting encouragement, and I watch as the contestants eat with varying degrees of gusto, sauce on their chins and T-shirts. It's crazy, over-the-top and feel-good, a gluttonous celebration of this vibrant Italian corner of New York.

Afterward we buy bracing shots of limoncello and cardboard trays of hot, sugared zeppole, stepping off the sidewalk into the tiled doorway of a closed shop for shelter as the heavens open.

"I'll admit it. This was fun." I rest my backside on the traditional wooden window ledge. I'm warm inside my jacket, potent alcohol sliding into my bloodstream.

"I see you, Iris Raven. Food is the magic key to getting you out of your apartment." Bobby turns his back against the door. "I'll find more food-related adventures for us to go on."

"If it's anything like this, count me in."

I won't need to eat for at least a week, yet still I reach for another melt-in-the-mouth zeppole, brushing powdered sugar from my fingers. Bobby pulls his phone from the back pocket of his sprayed-on jeans, and as he bends to recover a pack of gum that has fallen out at the same time, I catch sight of the shop's painted glass door behind him. I go perfectly still and stare intently at it, my head to one side, because it's jarringly familiar. I've seen it somewhere before, I'm certain. I just can't put my finger on where.

"What is this place?" I say, cupping my hands to peer through the side window. It's in shadows inside, but I can make out the black-and-white checkerboard floor and oxblood leather stools lining the counter.

"Belotti's gelateria," Bobby says, not looking up from his

phone. "I'm surprised they're closed during the festival actually, there's always a line."

I shoot him a testy look. "Is it as good as mine?"

"How could it be?" Bobby's sigh is pure theater. "If I meant anything to you, you'd let me put that stuff on the menu in the restaurant."

"Never going to happen," I laugh, my eyes still lingering on that unusual door. Bobby is the person I like most in the world these days, but we're still not serving my mother's gelato in the Very Tasty Noodle House. Not in Katz's Deli either, for that matter. Nor in the super-swish dining room at the Plaza, not even if the head chef got down on his knees and begged me. My mum was a bohemian free spirit with an ever-playful glint in her eye, but she had one stone-cold serious rule when it came to her vanilla gelato recipe: it was a secret that I could never share with another living soul. It is the best vanilla on the planet and remains my desert island food. She made it for me as a small child and as a grown woman, served from her favorite vintage cotton-candy pink melamine bowls. And then when she became ill I made it for her, until it was the only food her body could stomach. Until it became more about the memories than the taste. She'd close her eyes as I held the spoon to her dry lips, the smallest amount enough to raise the ghost of a smile.

I click the camera open on my phone and snap a shot of the distinctive door, even though I almost don't need to because it's so memorable. Its slender old mahogany frame houses a bevel-edged sheet of plate glass, which has been hand-painted with a green-striped cup of swirled gelato topped with cherries and a neon spoon at a jaunty angle. The jewel colors pop from the glass as if freshly painted just yesterday, even though it exudes unmistakably stylish old-time ambience.

"I think I'm done," I say, taking one long, last glance at the door. "If I eat anything else I'll collapse."

"Home, then?" Bobby offers me his arm, and we step out into the crowds and duck our heads against the rain.

2.

IT COMES BACK TO ME IN AN ADRENALINE-FUELED RUSH as we make our way home, the door jumping out from my memories of a photograph I've looked at hundreds of times over the course of my life. As soon as we let ourselves through the peeling red side door beside the noodle house I make a garbled excuse to Bobby about grabbing a quick nap before evening service starts. I'm more wired than tired, though, as I slam the door of my apartment, my mind racing as I head straight for my bedroom, shrugging my coat off as I go. I drag my mother's scrapbook down from the top of the wardrobe and drop back onto the bed with it in my arms. I've looked at this stuffed-to-the-brim book countless times over the years, both with and without my mother by my side to fill in the blanks. It's a potted history of her youthful hopes and dreams, proof that she followed her performer's heart, even if things didn't work out quite the way she'd hoped in the end. Official publicity shots of her eighties band sit alongside more candid photos that pulse with gig-energy, cuttings from trade magazines, reviews from papers, the occasional ticket stub, the front of a cigarette box signed by all of the members of the band. I can't read their illegible scrawl and I don't recall their names, except for the confident red signature at the bottom belonging to Charlie Raven, the band's drummer. My father. He was my mother's on–off lover for several years, a physical relationship she always knew was destined to go nowhere. It ended the day she declined his offer to give her enough money to terminate her pregnancy. I have no memory of him at all; he died in a helicopter accident when I was six. My mother said she wasn't all that surprised when news reached her of his death, because he was the kind of full-throttle person who rarely lives to see old age. She didn't speak badly of him, exactly, just painted a picture of someone wild who blazed bright and burned out. She probably felt it was reassuring for me to hear I shared little in common with him except my surname, which she chose for me over her own anonymous Smith. My father's death has always just been a footnote in my story, someone who bears very little impact on who I am today. Charlie Raven, forever thirty-two.

Every page of my mother's album is full to overlapping, a tightly packed chronicle of the band's brush with the big time. But that isn't what I'm looking for right now. I flip quickly to the very last page. Just two precious things are pinned in place: a photograph and a torn, scrawled-on napkin. I peel back the protective layer and lift the photo carefully away, feeling the tug of age try to grip it in place. I stare at it now with fresh eyes, even though there's no question in my mind. Same mahogany frame, same brass handle, same striking paintwork. It's the same door. I've never known where the photograph I've looked at so many times was taken, with its faded summer look of a holiday romance, and my mother always declined to elaborate.

Turning the photograph over, I read her familiar script: *Santo, 1985,* a love heart doodled beside his name. Just seeing the loops and dips of her handwriting, so similar to my own, is enough to bring a lump to my throat. I flip it back to study the photo again. The young man gazes back at me. He's laughing, thick dark hair flopping over the hand he's raised to shield his eyes from the sun. The distinctive shop door is ajar behind him, sunlight refracting the colors in an arc across the image. Everything about the photograph is retro-stylish, from the hand-painted door to the guy himself, channeling *Breakfast Club* cool with his eighties leather bomber jacket, white T, and bleached jeans. I wrack my brain, trying to pin down any scraps of information I can pull out. There isn't much. She was a storyteller, my mother, but she always steered the conversation away when it came to this photo and the napkin alongside it, only ever going so far as to say that the guy was quite possibly the love of her young life. The mint-green napkin is torn in half, leaving just the second part of a gold printed logo visible: *otti's*. My mind connects the dots. Belotti's? I've never known before what the whole logo said, but I know by heart what's written on it in confident blue ink. Our beloved gelato recipe.

A quick internet search lands me on Belotti's homepage, a photograph of the shop basking in summer sunshine beneath a green-and-white-striped awning. Seeing that painted glass door on my screen is oddly familiar, like finding an old photo from your childhood of a place you've long forgotten. I don't know if my mother ever actually took me there as a child. I don't think so. I was born a couple of summers after she started touring, and we left America for good when I was three years old, far too young to recollect such specifics. How strange, really, that I should find myself living near to a place so important to her without realizing. But then, perhaps not so strange—moving to New York City felt like an obvious choice because my mother spoke so fondly of it, and recollections of her band memories and her early glory days nudged me toward the Lower East Side. My eyes linger for a moment on my wardrobe, my thoughts on the silver urn tucked away carefully at the back. There is a small comfort to be drawn from knowing she's here with me, that I've brought her to the place she first felt at home. Maybe one day I'll find the right time and place to let her go, to lay her to rest in the city she loved.

I look back at the photo again, my heart heavy and my head full of questions. I've always known that the guy in the photo was Italian, as of course is the recipe, but I just imagined the photo and the recipe came from a trip to Italy rather than from my mother's time in New York. Did my mother ever tell me that? I can't recall that she did, but then I'm not certain she didn't either. Maybe I've just lazily assumed it and over the years she allowed it to go uncorrected. And now here I am, a breath away from the place, reading the Belotti family website, unsure how on earth I have their recipe. They have a long, proud history in Little Italy stretching back to 1911, black-and-white photos of the gelateria spanning the decades, aproned family shots taken behind the glass-topped counter I glimpsed through the window earlier. I scan the website, digesting their story, struck by one recurring fact in particular: their famous and beloved vanilla recipe—the only flavor they actually serve, interestingly enough—is a closely guarded secret. So closely guarded, in fact, that only two members of the Belotti family are ever allowed to know it at any one time. My eyes track to the open scrapbook on the bed, to the recipe written hastily across that torn napkin. The

Belottis have fiercely protected this recipe for more than a hundred years, so why was it revealed to my mother? I understand now why she was always so insistent that I never share it with anyone—because it was never ours to share. Assuming it's the same, of course, which I guess is the next thing I should find out.

If I want to begin to unravel how my mother's life story overlaps with the Belottis, the first thing I have to do is taste their gelato for myself.

3.

MULBERRY STREET IS DECIDEDLY CALMER THIS MORN-
ing than it was last night with the festival in full swing, now
buzzing with a quiet sense of industry and anticipation for the
new day of feasting ahead. Chairs are being set out beneath
sidewalk café awnings as catering wagons crank up their
ovens; there's a similar feel in the air to when you take your
seat at a theater, the orchestra tuning up in the pits, that base-
level excitement as you wait for curtain-up. It isn't raining
today, but the chill in the air is enough for me to have layered
a thick woolen scarf over my denim jacket. One of Bobby's, I
think; he treats my apartment as an overflow closet for his
expansive clothing collection. Or his tester stock, as he calls
it, given that he owns three clothing boutiques across the city
and is on the brink of opening his fourth. The guy might not
know much about noodles, but he's a savvy businessman and
quicksilver when it comes to his professional life. He somehow seems to have more hours in his day than everyone
else—a businessman, a social dynamo, and a loved-up husband, yet still he finds unhurried time for me, especially if my
gelato machine has been on.

Pulling my phone out, I check the time. A little after nine.
I can see Belotti's coming up on the right and drag my feet,

unexpectedly nervous now I'm near. It's not as though anyone is going to recognize me. I bear a startling resemblance to my mother, but it's been more than thirty years since she would have been here. I pause and step to the side, imagining her making her way along this exact same sidewalk in the mid-eighties. What would she have had on her feet, I wonder, gazing down at my own apple-green Converse? Nothing, probably, if she could have gotten away with it. She'd have been much younger than I am now, eighteen or nineteen at most, shiny-eyed and full of ambition. My chest constricts as I think of her, even more so when I think about the fact that she isn't here anymore.

For a while after she died, I just couldn't wrap my head around the idea of a world without her in it. I still can't, not fully. My mother was always brimming full of bright, wonderful life, a human rainbow. Watching cancer systematically strip her of her colors was profoundly difficult, a dimmer switch turning in the wrong direction no matter what the doctors did to try to slow it down. I've never felt more hopeless than in those final days sitting at her bedside, desperate to keep her with me for one more conversation, one more reassuring clasp of my hand, one more smile. She insisted on staying in her flat, surrounded by her belongings and the memories that accompanied them, rather than going into hospital. At the exact moment she died, the large woven dreamcatcher hanging above her old cast-iron bedstead began to slowly twirl. Some might have said it caught on a wind from the cracked-open window, but I am my mother's daughter and I prefer to think that she blew on it just for me, to let me know she was safely on her way, and that it was time for me to be on mine too.

What would she make of my doing this, going to this gelateria that she seems to have intentionally kept me unaware
of? Why would one of the family members give her their
recipe? I've no intention of revealing her secret, of course,
but I yearn to understand how the pieces of her life then inter-
sect with my life now, to press a conch shell to my ear and
catch the echo of her across time.

Belotti's looks much the same as it did last night: no queue,
no sign of being open. I step inside the sheltered doorway and
study the freehand glass painting up close, noticing how fresh
the colors are, how carefully cared for it is for an aged piece
of art. I know from looking at the gelateria's website that
they've embraced the design as a central part of their unique
business fingerprint, recreating it on their aprons, menus, and
cups. I'm lost in thought as I examine it, so much so that I
don't notice the movement inside until the door opens, making me jump.

"Sorry, didn't mean to scare you," the guy says as I step
sharply back, startled.

I summon a smile. "It was my own fault, standing too
close to the door. I was just looking at the artwork."

He glances at it too, and then at me. For a moment I get
the same déjà-vu feeling as when I saw the door, as if I know
him already. Which is crazy, of course, because I don't, and
he doesn't look especially like the guy in my mother's photo,
so that can't be it either.

"Are you open yet?" I glance past him into the empty
shop.

"Not exactly," he says. "I'm just firing up the coffee machine, but there's no gelato."

I could leave now—the gelato is why I came, after all, but

coffee and a chance to step inside is better than leaving altogether if I want to know what this place was to my mother.

"Coffee sounds good," I say, and he lifts his shoulders and
moves aside to let me pass.

"You're early for the festival," he says, heading behind the
counter.

"Oh, I know. I was just here yesterday, actually."

He gestures for me to take one of the oxblood leather bar
seats at the counter as he turns his back to kickstart the coffee
machine into life. I watch him fill the bean hopper, observing
the easy confidence of his moves as he sets two cups on the
counter and adds milk to the foamer. I'm a coffee junkie, just
the sounds and smells are enough to relax my shoulders from
around my ears. I unwind my scarf and place it on the swivel
chair beside mine, taking in the old-school mahogany and
brass atmosphere of the place and the welcome glow of the
multicolored Tiffany-style glass lampshades. There's a small
upright piano in the far corner and family photographs fill the
walls, generations of Belotti men and women standing behind this same counter. The place has barely changed over
the years, which is, of course, all part of its charm. If it ain't
broke, don't fix it, and all that.

"So what brings you back again so soon?"

I pause as he places a simple white cup and saucer in front
of me along with a jug of hot foamed milk and a bowl of sugar
cubes. His own coffee is black; I appreciate that he's given me
the option. I stir in a little milk, using the distraction to decide how to answer the question.

"Coffee at Belotti's?" I say after a beat, throwing in a
smile and feeling stupid, but it's enough of an answer to suf-
fice.

"About all we're good for at the moment," he says, sighing into his coffee cup.

I look at him properly then and notice the dark circles beneath his eyes, the furrow between his eyebrows. Something is clearly troubling him.

"Will you be open later, with your gelato? I might call back. My friend said I really need to try it."

He skims his gaze to the ceiling as he shakes his head. "Honestly? Probably not."

Disappointment pushes through me, and I let the thoughts spinning inside my head come out of my mouth. "Is everything okay? I wouldn't normally ask a stranger that, but you look kind of wiped out."

He drums his index finger on the counter, as if he's trying to decide how to respond. "Isn't it my job to ask if the customer is okay and to offer to listen to your problems?"

"I think that's mostly bartenders, and it's too early for alcohol, even by my standards," I say. "Besides, you look more in need of a listening ear than I do right now."

He nods slowly, turning his gaze out toward the street, and I wonder if I've overstepped the mark. I sip my coffee, resisting the urge to jump in with both feet and apologize my question away.

"We can't make our gelato right now," he says, still not looking at me. "My papa had a stroke eight days ago. He's in the ICU and no one else knows the recipe."

I go still, my cup halfway to my mouth. "I'm so sorry to hear that. Is he going to be okay?"

His expression is carefully controlled. "We think so, but he's lost some parts of his memory. Not everything, like in the movies—he still knows he's Santo Belotti and who we all are, but some other things are gone, for now at least. The date he married Maria, the name of his grandparents' hometown back in Italy. Our gelato recipe."

"Gosh, that's tough," I manage, quietly reeling at the sound of Santo's name—the name on my mother's photo. "Is he likely to remember everything again in time?"

"No one can really say for sure." He looks down at the glass counter, gesturing at the empty metal gelato containers below. "My whole life this counter has been full. This place has been full, people even waiting in a line outside to get in."

He raises his eyes to mine, dark and troubled.

"Is there no one else who knows the recipe?" I ask, remembering that their website mentioned two Belotti family members always know the recipe at any one time. For this precise reason, I guess.

A noise leaves him, somewhere between a huff and a bitter laugh. "Technically, yes. My father *thinks* he has it written down somewhere, but he can't seem to find it."

I frown, thrown by what he's said. "Sorry, I thought you said Santo was your father?" I say, trying to keep the story straight in my head.

"He's actually my uncle, but I call him Papa. He raised me as one of his own because my father was never around when I was a kid." He shrugs. "He still isn't. He's in Australia now, and it was Japan before that. On to Europe in a few weeks if I remember right. He's a musician, travels light—so light he can't keep track of a damn recipe, apparently. I guess it's easy to be careless when you're never the one left behind to deal with the fallout."

"Oh," I say, a totally inadequate response. He speaks of Santo with great affection, and of his actual father with deep exasperation. I understand that feeling, because Charlie Raven never made any effort to be a father to me. "That's a bit crap."

"You can say that again," he says, scrubbing his hands over his face. "Over a hundred years in business, and the first time I'm left in charge I can't do a thing to help keep us from going under."

It's my turn to study my coffee, conflicted. It dawns on me that I, unlike the man standing in front of me, *can* help here. But in doing so, I'd be opening up a whole other can of worms. Santo, the man from the photograph, is still here, but he's married to someone called Maria. So then why did he share his family's precious secret with my mother all those years ago? Family loyalty and pride is engrained in every inch of this place, they've traded on this famously secret recipe for over a century. What would it do to them if they knew of his indiscretion?

"Have you tried to recreate it yourself?" I say, still thinking.

"Day and night," he sighs.

"That explains the dark circles," I say.

He shakes his head. "I can't believe this has happened. Papa was on the verge of retiring. He only comes by to load the machines in the morning."

The most fragile of ideas begins to form in my head. "Look, I'm not saying I'd be able to even get anywhere near to it, but I could try to help, if you'd like me to? I'm a trained chef. Well, I used to be, in London. Here, I toss noodles, but I still have my skills and anything's worth a go, right?"

He looks at me, blinks a couple of times in that way people do when they're not sure what to say or do.

"I have some gelato in the freezer," he says. "What was left over on the day of Papa's stroke. You could try it? It won't be perfect since it wasn't made fresh today, but it's —"

"Better than nothing," I finish, and he nods.

"Who are you?" he asks, a question that feels overdue. "I don't even know your name."

"I'm Iris," I say.

"Iris," he says. "Like the Goo Goo Dolls."

"And my mother's favorite flowers," I say.

He studies me. "Have we met somewhere before?"

We look at each other across the counter, and I feel that prickle of déjà vu again. Vibrations of the past, possibly, or maybe he's a noodle kind of guy and has been by the restaurant. It's not impossible. I briefly wonder if he's seen a photograph of my mother, the way I have of Santo, but I can't imagine why there would be any record of her here.

"I don't think so," I say softly.

"Giovanni Belotti," he says. "Gio."

We regard each other. Iris and Gio, no longer strangers.

"I'll go get the gelato," he says, disappearing into the back.

Alone in the gelateria, I slump into my seat and sigh. Am I doing the right thing? Would my mother want me to interfere? There's nothing but the hum of the coffee machine and the muffled sound of the outside world. Belotti's feels like the kind of place a time-slip could occur in a movie, a secret doorway to years and people past. How dearly I wish that could be true, that I could open that painted door and see if my mother sat on this exact same seat. I place my hand on the low back of the chair beside mine, the smooth grain of the polished red leather supple beneath my fingers. There's an inexplicable feeling of safety in here, a sense of timelessness and peace.

Gio returns and sets a small silver pail down in front of me. "Best to give it a little while to come up to temperature."

I nod. "Looks good." What I actually mean is it looks exactly the same color as my own gelato.

"We're usually busy with the festival right now," he says, shaking his head. "I hate that we're missing out this year."

I'm not sure what I can say that's helpful. "Is it seasonal, generally? Gelato, I mean?"

"Yeah, it is." He pauses, nods. "Obviously spring and summer are our busiest times, and March through September we run five mobile carts around the city and supply events—parties, weddings, that kind of thing. It gets quieter after San Gennaro, and people start to come more for coffee and pastries once the weather turns, but if I can't work this thing out soon . . ." He trails off, but I hear the words he doesn't want to say. If he can't work the recipe out, Belotti's gelateria might not see next spring.

"Maybe Santo will remember soon," I say. I don't add that his globe-trotting father might find his copy of the recipe, because I get the impression there isn't a hope in hell.

His smile is thin. "Maybe."

I watch the gelato soften around the inside edges of the metal, wanting and at the same time *not* wanting to taste it. Until I know for certain, there's still an outside chance I'm wrong.

Gio cups his hands around the cold metal.

"Help it along a little," he murmurs.

I half smile, imagining Bobby's face if he was here. He

always grouches about the metal beaker I make gelato in, says it takes his fingerprints off whenever he holds it. I notice Gio has capable hands and look away quickly. I'm a bit weird about men's hands. It's just my thing. Some people go weak for a peachy bum or bulging biceps, but for me it's all about strong hands. And shoulders, for that matter. Watching Gio warm the gelato for me with his hands has me unexpectedly flustered, so I pick up a spoon and suggest it might be time.

He looks into the tub, assessing, then stirs it to amalgamate the milky edges with the middle before pushing it toward me, raising his gaze to mine. I'm nervous out of nowhere, prickles of sweat breaking out along my hairline.

"Okay," I say, sliding the spoon into the smooth gelato. "Here goes."

I instinctively close my eyes when I put it in my mouth, concealing my reaction in case I give myself away. It's just as I knew it would be. Elevated a little from being scaled up and diminished ever so slightly because it's not freshly made, but the oh-so-familiar taste throws me back to all my yesterdays. I'm a toddler with dirty hands digging for treasure in a rental-house back garden somewhere in the north of England. I'm eleven years old in London, doing my homework at a table, which has one damaged leg propped on a stack of books. I'm fifteen in Cardiff, crying over my first broken heart. I'm twenty in Birmingham, celebrating my success at catering college. I'm twenty-nine in London, trying not to show my absolute panic as I listen to my mother telling me of her bleak diagnosis. I'm all of those versions of myself, accompanied every time by our—by *Belotti's*—secret recipe vanilla gelato served in a pink melamine dish. This gelato and that dish were the only constants in the ever-shifting landscape of my childhood, and tasting it here throws up a whole gamut of unexpected emotion.

I open my eyes to find Gio staring at me, fragile flints of hope in his worried eyes.

"It's . . . it's really something special, isn't it?" I say, struggling to keep my voice steady.

He nods. "My great-grandparents' recipe, never deviated from." Picking up a spoon, he helps himself, then sighs deeply. "It's not possible to recreate, is it? It's too special."

I take a little more. "I don't know, Gio," I say. "Let me have a think, play around with some ideas." I wrap my scarf around my neck and he loads one of their green-and-white-striped tubs with gelato.

"For the journey," he says, adding a spoon and a cherry on the side.

"I'll come back again tomorrow," I say, sliding down from the stool.

He nods, and I pick up the tub, noticing how it's the painted door come alive in my hands.

"I'll be here." Gio lays his hands flat on the counter. "I always am."

Vivien

...

"VIV, OVER HERE!"

Vivien turned toward the sound of her name, shouted loud enough for her to hear over the bohemian crowd packed into the late-night, smoky, backstreet club. She squinted into the gloom and caught sight of a grinning, shirtless Charlie Raven, both arms raised over his head to catch her attention, a lit cigarette dangling between his long fingers.

She wound her way toward him between writhing bodies, protecting her wineglass as best she could from spillages because she couldn't afford to buy another drink on the pittance Louis had paid her so far. Not that she was about to ask for more. The fact that she was here at all felt like pure magic, that of all the people in all the world, Louis Brockman had happened to walk out of Hammersmith Underground station and hear her busking in the rain. He'd stopped in his tracks, raindrops running from his slick hairstyle to gather on his eyebrows, watching her until she'd finished for the day, buying her coffee afterward and changing her life in the course of an hour. *Come back to New York with me,* he'd said. *Sing in the band I manage,* he'd said. The original singer had got return-to-college last-minute cold feet but Louis already had dates booked across the United States for the band. *Give me a year and I'll make you a star,* he'd said, and Vivien had believed every word. And she still believed him, even if the reality was proving far less glamorous than the picture he'd painted for her back in that steamy café in London. Not that Viv needed glamour. Louis had thrown her a rope and hauled her from the cold soup of London, living the fraught existence of a girl fresh out of the care system and loved by precisely no one, and she planned on clinging to it until her palms bled.

"Got you," Charlie said, reaching out and catching her hand to pull her toward him. "We're over here in the corner."

He turned away, still holding on to her hand, pulling her behind him as the crowds parted more easily for him than they had for her. She kept her eyes on the python tattoo slithered around his neck and between his shoulder blades, its head disappearing into the low-slung jeans tight on his skinny hips. He was the drummer in the band, louche offstage, wild the second he landed behind his drum kit. In the few short weeks since she joined the band, she'd already noted the way girls flocked around Charlie Raven, his mischievous energy and crooked smile difficult to resist. She was attracted to him herself, but not enough to get involved. This was her one shot, no guy was standing in the way of that.

She glanced at the stage as they passed by, swallowing a mouthful of wine as fuel because they were due up there in half an hour. Charlie's drum kit was already in place, Felipe's battered blue guitar leaning against a speaker. She wasn't nervous. She simply couldn't wait to get up there. The sensation of being front and center felt like being fired into the sun from a cannon and she craved it with all of her being. The Lower East Side club was the last one in a succession of similar small-time venues Louis had lined up for them in the city, all of them late night and packed out, all of them undercut with tension and pulsatingly, knife-edge sexy. Back in London, Vivien had eked out an existence from scant busking funds, a stone-cold bedsit and no one to turn to. Here she was part of something glorious, needed for the first time ever, and she threw herself into it headlong.

Charlie let go of her hand once she was among the band. As usual there were various hangers-on: Madonna-inspired girls in mesh vests over ballgowns and pearls, punk rock boys in leather and eyeliner, everyone high on cheap booze and marijuana and the rebellious wind of change blowing through the city.

Felipe, the band's lead guitarist, caught her eye and touched his fingers against the rim of his fedora, looking at her wineglass over the top of his mirror shades.

"What are you drinking?"

She bit the inside of her lip, feeling gauche. "White wine."

He rolled his eyes and reached for her glass, upending it on to the floor.

"Have a proper drink. We're doing Bloody Marys."

He refilled her glass full to the brim from a pitcher on the table, the contents dirty red and gloopy when he handed it back.

Viv sniffed it. "Smells like tinned tomatoes."

"Come on, Vivien," Felipe said, leaning against the wall. "Get with it."

She tasted it, a small sip, and wrinkled her nose at the

sharp hit of vodka followed by the unexpected savory twist of Worcestershire sauce, all awash in thick canned tomato juice. In years to come she'd learn to embrace a well-made Bloody Mary, but this wasn't that, and she all but gagged trying to get it down.

"You like it?"

"I do not," she said, shuddering as she took another huge gulp.

Charlie looked across and smirked, cupping his hand around a half-smoked spliff to relight it. "If you puke that lot up onstage it'll be fucking spectacular."

These guys were the people she'd spent most of her time with since arriving in New York, either practicing or performing, and they were forming a bond, of sorts. She couldn't say she actually liked them much yet, but there was comfort in the familiarity of their presence at least. She figured they'd probably save her in a fight, grudgingly, something which never felt more than an exciting breath away in the grungy, anything-goes backstreet clubs they spent most of their waking hours in.

Felipe laughed as he refilled Viv's glass with more red sludge. "It would look like you're actually fucking dying, internal organs splattered all over the front row."

"My kind of show," Charlie said, holding his smoke to the waiting lips of a girl leaning against him. "Hey, isn't that your brother?"

Felipe followed the direction of Charlie's nod and lifted his hand in greeting. Viv took advantage of the distraction to tip the disgusting contents of her glass into a huge potted plant behind her and then turned back to find herself face-to-face with a stranger.

"This is my brother, Santo. I got all the looks, obviously," Felipe said, droll. "Santo, this is Vivien. She's from London, don't you know?" He delivered the last line in a terrible English accent, making Viv sigh and roll her eyes as she stuck her hand out on impulse.

"It's just Viv," she said, gazing up into Santo's face and liking what she saw there.

His surprised gaze held hers as his fingers closed around her hand, and Viv floundered for something else to say as she registered the warmth of his touch, the slant of his cheekbones, the dimple in his chin when he smiled.

"Hi, just Viv," he laughed and glanced at her empty glass. "Can I get you another drink?"

Relieved to find Felipe had already turned away to talk to someone else, Viv nodded. "I'll come with you to the bar."

SANTO WASN'T A FAN of these kinds of places. He'd made an exception to come and meet Felipe's latest band since they were playing so close to home, even though he knew he'd feel awkward the entire time among the groupies that hung around them like cigarette smoke. It was neither his fault nor Felipe's, they were just very different people. When the Belotti family gene pool had been divvied up, Santo had been handed steadfastness and loyalty while Felipe got flippancy and skittishness, his calm and serious approach to life serving only to highlight his brother's caprice.

"What would you like?" he said, turning to look at Viv, already feeling like he'd phrased the question too formally. He'd happily take a little of his brother's ease with girls right now, for sure.

"White wine, please," she said, shooting him a shy smile.

He ordered himself a beer too, and then he didn't know what to say or do so he just met her smile with one of his own.

"I've never met anyone with bluer eyes than you," he said, without thinking. "Like the sky on the brightest day of summer."

She stared at him. "That's the best thing anyone has ever said to me."

He found that hard to believe. Viv was one of the most arresting people he'd ever laid eyes on in his life. It wasn't just those bluer-than-blue eyes and her unusual heart-shaped face; she was a good foot shorter than him but seemed to crackle and fizz with more than her fair share of energy.

"Are you younger or older?" she said, nodding across the club toward Felipe.

"He's two years older than me," Santo said. "Not that you'd guess, huh?" He gestured down at his short-sleeved striped shirt. He'd tried to wear his coolest stuff and still wound up feeling like someone's dad when he'd made his way through the club in search of his brother.

Viv tipped her head on one side and studied him. "I like it. It reminds me of a deckchair on Southend beach."

He wasn't sure what that meant, but the fact she'd said she liked it was enough.

"How about you?" he said. "Brothers, sisters?"

She knocked back half of her wine and shook her head. "Just me on my lonesome."

"Your mom and dad must miss you a lot," he said, thinking of his folks back at the gelateria, how much they missed Felipe even though they had Santo around to take the sting out of their eldest son's wanderlust. "Although sometimes Felipe makes me wonder if I might have preferred to be an only child too," he said, a laugh in his eye and a teasing grin on his face.

Viv drank the rest of her wine and slid the empty glass onto the bar, then looked up at him with a ponderous expression on her face.

"Felipe is nice enough, but he was wrong earlier," she said. "He didn't get all the looks."

Okay, so that was an unexpected turn. He liked that she kept him on his toes. "Another drink?"

She shook her head and laughed, her dark hair bouncing around her jaw. "Better not, Louis will kill me if I forget the lyrics."

Stunned as he was by her, Santo had somehow forgotten she was in the band. "Do you ever get nervous before you perform?"

She shook her head. "Never. This is what I love to do, and I do anything I love with my whole being. Will you stay to watch? This is our last show in New York. We head out for the rest of the tour in a couple of days, so you should help send us off with a bang."

He'd actually planned to duck out before the show because it wasn't his sort of music, but he was surprised to find himself wanting to hear her sing, to stay in her addictive orbit a while longer. He thought of Maria, the girl from down the block he'd been dating for the last few weeks, who'd let him kiss her at the movies just three nights ago and had invited him to lunch this coming Tuesday with her mother. He'd never been someone to lead girls on—that was Felipe's ball game. In truth, he hadn't had many girlfriends, he was always too busy at the gelateria, but Maria was starting to feel like someone he could see a future with. Still, no promises had been made, and now his head was full of blue-sky eyes, his palm still electrified from the touch of Vivien's hand.

"Sure, I'll stay," he said, as if there had been any chance he might not once she asked.

Across the room, Charlie Raven leaped up on to the raised stage and held his drumsticks aloft, spine arched, his head thrown back as his body soaked up the adulation from the undulating crowd.

"I think that's my cue to get over there," Viv said, watching Felipe step up and loop his guitar strap over his shoulder.

They pushed their way through to the stage and Felipe reached a hand down to haul her up beside him, touching two fingers to his forehead in silent salute to his brother before turning to give a wild-eyed, bare-chested Charlie the good-to-rock nod. Santo leaned his back against a concrete pillar, his breath stuck in his throat. He'd come here to see his brother, but he couldn't take his eyes off Viv.

He wasn't the only one—the energy in the place shot off the scale as soon as she opened her mouth, the smoky old-soul sound of her voice perfect for the Pat Benatar cover they opened with to get the crowd going. And, boy, was the crowd going. Viv's eyes roamed over the thrusting bodies as her words rang out, a call to action, to sing, to move, to be a part of their gang. Santo wasn't a dancer. He'd like to have been, but his natural reserve held him fast against the graffiti-covered concrete pillar, the hard beat thumping through his blood. He watched her command the stage, the slick sheen of sweat on her limbs as she moved, the amount she gave of her-self to the strangers around her. She caught his eye every now and then, and he felt water-cannoned against the wall by the sheer weight of her sudden undivided attention. Did everyone else in the place notice their connection? How could they not? She was effervescent, holding the club—and Santo himself— in the palm of her hand as she whirled and laughed at the end of one of the band's original tracks. He'd never seen anyone like her in his twenty-three years. He was smarter than to think he could hold on to a lightning bolt without getting burned but, man, did he want to give it a try.

"DIDN'T YOU ENJOY IT?" Viv jumped down from the stage, ignoring the many hands reaching out for her as she made a beeline straight for Santo. "You didn't dance."

"You were amazing," he said, and his expression told her how much he meant it. She appreciated that about him—he had an open, sincere sort of face that couldn't lie, unlike most of the people she'd encountered in her life so far. From the care agencies she'd been handed round as a teenager to the various retail bosses she'd worked for since she was fifteen, everyone had their own agenda and it was never in her best interests. Even Louis had his own agenda, but right now she was willing to let that ride because his agenda suited her too.

"Are you hungry?" Santo said.

"God, yes," she said. "Starving."

"I know a place," he said.

Viv grinned. "Let's go then."

"You sure?"

She considered it, and found she was. Santo wasn't a stranger, he was Felipe's brother. Her gut told her he was someone she could trust, and over the years she'd learned to rely on her own intuition. She wanted to spend some time with him, more than she could remember ever wanting to spend time with anyone else in her entire life.

"I'm sure."

Out on the street, Santo put his leather jacket around her shoulders and steered them a couple of blocks over to a late-night diner. They ate pie and drank espresso, and in the space of the next two hours they fell as much in love as it's possible to with someone you've only met for the first time that night. She sensed his loyalty and deep dependability, and he admired her free spirit and lust for adventure. They saw in each other things they felt were lacking from their lives. "Don't you mind having to stay in this one place forever?" she asked, having heard how he was next in line to take over the family gelato business.

"My place is behind the counter at Belotti's." He sounded surprised she'd even consider it as a negative. "It might not be for everyone, but it suits me just right."

"But not Felipe?"

Santo laughed, a deep roll in his chest that made Viv want to lay her head against it. "What do you think?"

"That he'd have the place closed down within a week," she said. "He'd go out and leave the gelato machines unmanned until the entire place overflowed with it, and then the entire street, and then the entire city would disappear under a gelato flood. And all the kids in New York would have to come outside with spoons and eat and eat until it had all gone again."

"I quite like the idea of the whole city blanketed in Belotti's vanilla," he said.

"And strawberry, and chocolate, and banana," she said.

He shook his head as he stirred his espresso. "We only make vanilla."

She sat back on her bench seat. "Ever?"

He nodded. "Yes, ma'am. The best vanilla you'll taste in your whole damn life, good enough to be the only flavor you'll ever need."

She sat back and crossed her arms, still wearing his jacket. "I guess I better try it for myself, hadn't I?"

"Come tomorrow," he said. "First thing."

"Rock stars don't do first thing," she laughed. "I'll come after lunch."

AND SHE DID. SANTO spotted her at the end of the line snaking out of the painted glass door the next afternoon and hurriedly untied his apron, begging the rest of the day off from his father as he filled a tub with vanilla and grabbed neon plastic spoons. His father didn't object; Santo never took a sick day or asked for time off, and frankly he was pleased to see a flash of spontaneity from his youngest son. Maybe he'd have thought differently if he'd known the reason behind Santo's sudden departure; he and Santo's mother held Maria and her family in high regard, and although it was early days, they were all hopeful it would be a match, in time. As it was, Santo disappeared out of sight and presented a laughing Vivien with the tub of gelato, much to the disgruntlement of the rest of the line.

"Rock stars don't stand in line," he grinned, steering her quickly away down Mulberry Street.

She held the gelato up and studied it. "Am I about to have my mind blown?"

Santo watched as she dug the translucent lime-green spoon into the tub and took a huge mouthful. No half measures for this girl—he'd realized that much last night as he'd watched her perform, and then again afterward when she made fast work of her slice of pie and most of his too. Life at full tilt was not a pace he was accustomed to, and he'd been in a constant, joyful tailspin ever since she'd taken his hand in the club last night. He watched with pleasure as her eyes rounded and she came to an abrupt halt on the sidewalk.

"Bloody hell! Santo," she gasped, then laughed, delighted. "You were right. Flood the city with this stuff, New York needs you."

He shrugged, thrilled that she loved it. "I told you it was the best."

She ate another huge spoonful, then held some out to him.

"I already know what it tastes like," he said, laughing and shaking his head.

"Yeah, but not when I feed it to you," she smiled, holding it out with her head on one side.

Santo saw the challenge in her blue eyes, the intoxicating boldness of her, and after a moment of hesitation leaned down and took the gelato from the spoon. She slid it slowly out of his mouth and watched him swallow.

"Well?"

"I didn't think our secret recipe could be improved on," he said.

She raised her eyebrows. "And now?"

"Now I know there's one thing in the world that makes it even better," he said slowly, enjoying her answering smile.

"You're cute, Santo Belotti," she said.

He felt a flush climb his neck. No girl had ever called him cute in his entire life, and his name sounded brand new in her English accent.

"Want to go see a movie?" he said.

"Now? In the afternoon?"

"Sure, why not?"

She frowned. "I don't know," she said. "Because movies are for best?"

"For best? You mean, like, for a special occasion?" Santo laughed, surprised. "Movies are for any time."

He noticed clouds cross her eyes as she thrust the half-eaten gelato back into his hand. "Maybe for you."

"And today, for you too," he said, trying to understand what he'd got wrong. "My treat."

"Can we watch *St. Elmo's Fire*?" she said.

He pretended to deliberate, even though he was always going to say yes. He'd have watched paint dry for the chance to sit beside Viv in the cinema for a couple of hours.

"As long as we can get popcorn."

She wrinkled her nose in the way he was already coming to recognize as one of her little quirks. "Go on, then, you're on."

NEITHER VIV NOR SANTO paid much attention to the movie. Santo spent most of the time sneaking sidelong glances at Viv, wondering how he could have known her for less than twenty-four hours but feel as if he'd known her forever. Viv spent the time trying to follow the story but also wondering if Santo was experiencing the same burgeoning, awkward, delicious feelings in his body as she was in hers. She couldn't say what it was about the boy that drew her to him; he exuded an aura of serenity she wanted to bask in, like spending a lazy summer Sunday afternoon floating on your back in the shallows of the Med with the sun toasting your limbs. Not that she'd ever been to the Mediterranean. She'd never been farther than London until Louis, the most unlikely of fairy godmothers, had offered her a golden ticket to perform on grubby stages across the United States. She'd had casual boyfriends in London, but Santo was the first person she'd ever connected with like this, instantly and out of nowhere, and as Emilio Estevez dipped Andi MacDowell backward to kiss her in the snow, she turned to him and found him watching her.

"I think I might love you, Santo Belotti," she said, startling them both, and then she leaned in and kissed him over the unfeasibly large bucket of popcorn. Neither of them saw anything else that happened up on the screen, they were too wrapped up in breathless, trembling first kisses and the swooping, exquisite wonder of first love.

THEY BOUGHT WARM PRETZELS from a street cart outside the movie theater for a buck each, pulling them apart with their fingers as they reeled along the busy sidewalk.

"This is my first ever street pretzel," Viv said, feeling all kinds of sophisticated as she drank in the sights and sounds of the street, still bustling in the early evening heat. Objectively, it wasn't any more glamorous than London. If anything, it felt more dangerous, but there was something entirely addictive about the grime, the graffiti, the eclectic swell of noise and endless visual drama. "She looks like she's on a TV ad," she said, watching a woman in a fur coat lean against a burnt-out car to light her cigarette.

"What would she be advertising?" Santo said, handing her some of his pretzel because she'd already finished her own.

"New York City, baby!" Viv laughed, spinning around, making his heart jump. "This place is crazy, I want to stay here forever!"

Her words reminded him of the thing she'd said to him earlier, in the movie theatre. *I think I might love you.* Had he misheard her? He knew these streets like the back of his hand but saw them afresh through her pretty blue eyes, noticing beauty in the street art sprawled across the frontages of the closed-up stores and buildings, feeling the restless energy like a heartbeat pulsing beneath the sidewalk. Did she really want to stay here forever? And what would that mean for him, if she did? They were questions he couldn't believe he was asking himself, but she brought out something in him that he hadn't known was there, and she made him feel more himself than he ever had before.

"COME INSIDE, EVERYONE'S GONE home," he said, pulling the keys to the gelateria from the back pocket of his jeans.

"Cool door," she said, running her fingertips over the painted glass as she followed him inside.

"Sit down." He gestured to the oxblood leather seats lining the counter as he moved behind it. "Let me make you some coffee, serve you like my favorite customer."

She grinned, smoothing her ruffled tartan miniskirt over her thighs as she perched. "And gelato too? Vanilla, of course," she said.

He shook his head. "There's none to be had—we make it fresh every day, and it's all gone."

"You don't have tubs in the freezer?"

He laughed. "I told you. Secret recipe. Fresh every day."

Her eyes shone with mischief as she leaned in, her elbows on the counter. "I love secrets. Do you know the recipe? Will you tell me?"

"Of course I know it, and no, I can't tell you. There's only ever two of us in the family who know it at a time, and the only reason two people know it is just in case something happens to one."

"In case one of you falls off a cliff or something," Viv said, laughing.

He shrugged. "Something like that. It's me and Papa now."

Viv noticed the pride in his voice, and her eyes scanned the framed photos on the wall behind him, many generations of Belotti men standing behind this same counter. How very different his life had been from her own foundling beginnings. She was a blank slate, the gold signet ring on her wedding finger her only link to the mother who had abandoned her.

"You're lucky to have all of this, you know. A place, a family, a history."

"I know," he said.

"And they're lucky to have you too," she said. "Because otherwise they'd have to rely on Felipe."

"True," Santo said. "He hardly comes here. I sometimes wonder if he feels guilty."

From what Vivien had seen of Felipe, there wasn't much in the way of guilt going on, but she spared Santo that knowledge.

"You make an excellent cup of coffee," she said, sipping from the small white cup and saucer Santo pushed across the glass counter.

"I've had a lot of practice," he said.

She wrapped her hands around her drink. "Have you had a lot of practice with girls too?"

Santo's easy expression faltered. "Not so much," he said.

There was clearly more to that story, but Viv found she didn't actually want to hear it, so she slid from the stool and walked slowly around the gelateria, trailing her fingers along the chair backs and wooden table edges.

"You have a piano," she said, pleased. "Can I play it?"

"I don't know," he said. "Can you?"

She laughed softly, taking a seat on the piano stool near the window.

"Excuse me, sir," she called, craning her neck to look at him over the piano top when he took a seat at a table with his coffee. "Do you have an admission ticket for this concert? It's very exclusive."

He patted his jean pockets and pulled out his cinema ticket from earlier. "Right here," he said, laying it on the table.

She nodded, flexing her fingers. "Any requests?"

"You choose," he said, and something in the way he held her gaze turned her stomach in slow somersaults.

"Okay," she murmured, placing her fingers on the keys as

she mentally flicked the pages of the songbook in her head. *Ah, of course.* Biting her lip, she closed her eyes as she began to play, and she kept them closed as she sang the opening lines of Madonna's "Crazy For You." It wasn't the kind of song she sang with the band, but it was wall to wall on the radio just now and she secretly loved it.

She meant every smoky word she sang to her intimate audience of one, the low-setting summer sun casting golden hues across her face. She opened her eyes for the final chorus and found Santo standing close by with his hand resting on the piano top, and the raw vulnerability on his face almost sent the lyrics clean out of her head.

"Did you mean it when you said you wanted to stay here forever?" he said.

"Yes?" she said. "No? I don't know. If every day could be like today, then yes, but that's not real life, is it?"

He rounded the piano and sat beside her on the stool, his face close to hers.

"But what if it was like this every day? You and me? I know you're supposed to leave for the rest of the tour, but you could stay here, we could make a real go of things maybe. I could make you gelato every day . . ."

She reached out and placed her hand on his cheek. "Santo, I . . . We don't —"

He leaned in and kissed his name out of her mouth. "Don't say another word," he whispered. "Think about it tonight?"

Viv allowed herself to momentarily imagine the life she could build here in New York. Would it work? Could she be happy working alongside Santo in the gelateria, settling herself down here, becoming part of his story? Or would she always wonder what might have happened if she'd stuck to her plan and followed her dreams? She'd spent her entire eighteen years clinging on to the edges of life by her fingertips, eating at other people's tables, sleeping in other people's beds, and she was, frankly, exhausted. The random meeting with Louis had finally set her free from having to depend on other people for the food in her belly or the roof over her head— giving up that hard-won freedom and fragile sense of security on the off-chance this thing with Santo became something more was a huge gamble. She'd fought so hard for this dream, and she wasn't sure she was ready to start on a new one just yet, as beautiful as Santo made it sound.

"I'll think about it tonight," she said, pressing her forehead against his. "I promise."

VIV CRAWLED INTO HER small bunk in the band's apartment an hour later, her head spinning with images of Santo, the painted glass door at Belotti's gelateria, and the evocative pull of being invited into a proper family. She'd lived her whole life alone, more or less—looking at the Belotti family history up on the wall in the gelateria had twisted her heart with envy. She closed her eyes and tried to see herself behind that counter alongside Santo in five years, then ten, then twenty. Would they go the distance? Have children, grow old together? Would his hair turn grey, her limbs soften with the fat of contentment? It felt like an impossible dream, not something that happened to people like Viv. And then she thought of the band, and Louis, and the string of gigs set up across America. She loved performing more than anything else in the world. Would she regret giving up this golden opportunity to make a name for herself? She spent the small hours of the morning turning the decision over in her head, wondering which path to walk, which to leave untrodden and wild. To have either would be once-in-a-lifetime precious.

4.

"WHAT AM I SUPPOSED TO DO HERE, BOBBY?"

Bobby places a coffee on the side table and sprawls on the blue velvet armchair opposite mine in his oak-floored penthouse. Bottles clank down below as bins are emptied on the early-morning city streets, sirens and horns, the sounds of New York being refreshed for another new day. I'm not feeling at all refreshed—I've seen almost every hour through the night and have brought my troubled conscience upstairs to Bobby.

"I'm literally the only person in the world who can help Belotti's right now," I say. "Isn't that bizarre?"

He reaches for his coffee cup. We're already on our second—he's listened to my long-winded story and looked at my mother's photo of Santo in her scrapbook, the most he's heard about my history since I've been here. It's credit to him that he answered my six-in-the-morning wake-up knock without grumble, and probably just as well that Robin is away on business. I'm super fond of Bobby's husband, but sharing my mother's secret with one person feels like an indiscretion; with two might have felt impossible. As it is, I'm grateful to have someone to share the load.

"The fact you even noticed that door at the festival is a

cosmic nudge." He mimes shoving me with both hands and raises his eyebrows. "You could just email them the recipe and never go back?"

"I've thought of that. But what would I say? I can't tell you how I know it, but here's your closely guarded secret recipe?" I throw in some jazz hands. "Because I don't for a second think that would be the end of it, do you?"

"They might just be so relieved that they don't ask any questions," Bobby says, although his face tells me he doesn't even believe that himself.

"Unlikely," I say. "They've traded on this top-secret family recipe story for the last hundred years—the fact it's known by someone on the outside would be a shock for them."

"Or . . . how about *I* send it to them?" he suggests. "I'll say, oh I don't know, I once knew this British chef who looked like Zooey Deschanel if you squinted and she made this fabulous gelato from a secret old Italian recipe she only ever shared with me to serve exclusively at my noodle restaurant, and just maybe, by some outlandish coincidence it's the exact same . . ."

I roll my eyes at his daily attempt at a recipe-grab.

"I'm serious, Bob. Santo was the young love of my mum's life, and now he's ill and I'm the only person who can save his family business."

Bobby looks at me over his steepled fingers, serious. "But would she want you to?"

It's the question that's kept me awake through the night. On the one hand, I'm absolutely certain she wouldn't want me to expose the fact that Santo shared his family secret. I don't know the Belotti family, but having scoured their website and been inside the gelateria, family loyalty and pride runs wild in their blood. And that gelato . . . it meant a great deal to me and my mother over the years, it sustained us through good and bad times. If it means that much to me, I can't imagine how much it means to the Belottis, how betrayed they would feel to discover someone else knows their secret too. But at the same time, the joy the recipe has brought me feels like a debt I should repay.

"They must have been so young," I say. "Santo must have lived all these years with the guilt of having shared the secret. Mum would hate the idea of breaking his confidence, I know that much. Keeping that secret was one of the only things I ever saw her take truly seriously."

"So don't say anything." Bobby splays his hands to the sides. "Forget you know anything about their current troubles and get on with your life."

I appreciate him playing devil's advocate.

"And let their business fold when I could have helped them save it?"

Bobby shrugs. "The old guy might remember the recipe tomorrow and all this soul-searching would be for nothing."

I nod. It would be the ideal scenario. And perhaps he might, but he might not remember it tomorrow, next week, next month, or before the spring deadline, if he ever remembers at all. I look up from my coffee as Bobby inhales sharply.

"You don't think this Santo guy's your daddy, do you? What if there's more than one secret that could come out?" he whispers, scandalized, then cracks up laughing.

"Piss off," I mutter, not offended because I know he's only trying to lighten my mood. I flick the pages of my mother's scrapbook to a picture of Charlie Raven mid-set, sweatband around his head, drumsticks raised. His grin is manic, the look of a guy high on the music he's making and probably something else too. "My father," I say, tapping the photo.

"She'd been on the road touring for two years by the time I was born," I say, just for clarity in Bobby's mind. "So definitely not. I could just post the recipe to Belotti's anonymously?" I throw it out there to gauge Bobby's opinion even though I've already pretty much discounted the idea.

He considers it.

"You could. And initially they'd be like, yay, we're saved! But then they'd start to wonder who, and how, and it would only take them a hot minute to realize that Santo must have given the recipe away. That, or they'd think his brother had been so careless as to let it end up with a stranger and it could start a whole new family rift." Bobby leans forward on his elbows. "But because Santo is the more likely candidate, and he has amnesia, he might not remember who he gave it to, and they all have to live forever wondering if Santo has a forgotten mistress or a mystery love child about to lay claim to their gelato empire or whatever. So it kind of seems like it would tear their family up either way."

I've thought all of these things, although in less colorful fashion, and ruled out sending an anonymous letter or email on the grounds of hurting the family. It would be kinder to let the business fold. Wouldn't it? I've turned this question around and looked at it from every angle for the last few hours, trying to find a perfect balance where nobody loses. I know instinctively that my mum would never reveal Santo's indiscretion, but equally, that she wouldn't have allowed his legendary family business to go under if it was within her power to save it. It isn't within her power, though. It's within mine. The Belotti family story has been invisibly connected with ours for as long as I can remember. The guy in the photo was the stuff of fairy tales when I was a child, the man who looked like a film star and made gelato for my mother. Theirs wasn't a sad, unrequited love story. *Forever* just wasn't written in their stars, she said. They were too young, her dreams with the band too big to be derailed by love. To me she was a pioneer, brave enough to let ambition take the driving seat, strong enough to follow her dreams rather than her heart.

Bobby reaches across and holds my hand. "Want me to come with you to Belotti's this morning? I can improvise, and I need to check out this guy's hands seeing as they got you so hot and bothered."

I should never have mentioned the hands thing to Bobby, he laughed for five minutes straight. I love him for offering to be my wingman, though.

"Yes, but no. You're the busiest man in New York." I put my shoulders back. "I think I need to do this on my own."

5.

IN PRACTICE, DOING IT ON MY OWN FEELS A LOT HARDER than it sounded. It's raining again, battleship-grey skies overhead as I approach Belotti's a couple of hours later. I've still got no clear plan what I'm going to say or do—I'm showing up because I said I would and because Gio looked like someone hanging on by a thread yesterday. I linger in the doorway, my hand resting on the brass handle. It's empty inside again, the stained-glass Tiffany lamps splashing red and green light pools across the floor, that same welcoming sense of timelessness. It probably looked almost the same back in the thirties, the fifties, and in the eighties when my mother came here. Different behind the scenes maybe, but the same holy decorating trinity of aged wood, polished brass, and oxblood leather up front. It's old school but not old-fashioned, the kind of place you might go when you need your nerves soothed and the security of knowing that some things will always stay the same. I'm sure it's different on a busy summer's day when they actually have gelato to sell, but today there's a library kind of calm when I push the door open and step inside.

"Iris, you came back."

Gio appears, summoned by the traditional brass bell

above the door. He doesn't look as if he slept any better than I did. Framed as he is by the gallery of family pictures behind him, I mentally add him to the list of timeless things about this place. Generations of dark-haired men flank him, all dressed in the same uniform of long-sleeved white shirt and black tie covered with a Belotti's apron, all similarly tall, ink-dark eyes staring straight into the camera. Gio's hair is longer, perhaps, and his shirt cut closer to his body, definitely, but the theme is strong.

"You didn't think I would?"

"I hoped you would," he says, coming round the counter. "Let me grab your coat."

I unwind my scarf and dump my huge, battered hobo bag on one of the leather bar seats, letting him take my rain-soaked jacket as I shrug out of it. He heads back behind the counter to hang it over a radiator, and I school myself to take it as a simple act of kindness rather than feeling as if my choice to easily leave has been taken away from me. I refuse to let shadows of my old life with Adam keep a grip on me here, but it's something I have to consciously remind myself of at times like this. An act of kindness can be simply that: kindness, without ulterior motive or underlying threat.

Gio wrangles with the coffee machine and I perch on the same bar seat as yesterday, lying my blue-striped bobble hat on the counter and unwinding a scrunchie from around my wrist to pull my damp hair back from my face.

"Did you have to come far?" he asks when he turns round, setting coffee down in front of me.

There it is again, the instinct to not reveal too much of myself. I push it down firmly. "No," I say. "Ten minutes walk."

He doesn't reply—in fact, I don't think he registered my words at all. He's frowning, his head slightly on one side, his gaze fixed on my hat. His expression is quizzical when he lifts his eyes to mine again.

"I knew we'd met somewhere before," he says.

I place a hand over my hat, unsure what he means.

"Logan's Bookstore? Valentine's Day?" he says.

My hand moves to my throat as dread settles low in my gut. *Oh jeez, no.*

"*Lapin,*" I mutter, as it all comes back to me in one hot panicky rush. I've done a good-enough job of trying to scour last Valentine's Day from existence that it's probably vanished off my kitchen wall calendar. I twitch just thinking about it.

"Did you ever read the book?" he says.

I pass my hand over my hot face. "No."

I bought a copy the following day, but I haven't even been able to open it since, and I really burned to read that damn thing. Every time I reach for it I'm reminded of the lie I told about my "dead husband," the shame I felt for snapping just to try and make someone feel bad, the embarrassment of having made an unnecessary exhibition of myself. And now I'm here with that same guy, telling yet another lie, even if this time it's because I'm trying to help him. I'd quite like the floor of the gelateria to open up and swallow me whole right now.

He winds a dish towel around in his hands. "Look, I'm sorry for putting my foot in it, about your husband, Iris, I really am. You kind of hit me in my weak spot when you mentioned my wife, I had no right to speak to you like that."

I flash back and see myself as I was that day, my furious eyes snagging on his wedding ring, his offended gaze bouncing to my mother's ring on my finger.

"Oh God. I should never have said —" I start, but he cuts across me.

"Please don't." He holds his hands up. "I understand. More than you know." He flicks his gaze toward the ceiling. "Penny, my wife . . . she died seven years ago."

My heart constricts at the measured way he delivers this information without meeting my eyes, at the flinch in his voice that tells me it hurts to even say the words out loud. I'm bereft of any words of my own, absolutely in hell. I can't believe I didn't place him as bookstore guy earlier. I didn't think I could be any more mortified about the lie I told that day, but knowing that he, a widower, thinks that a) I had a husband *and* b) he passed away has me absolutely shamefaced for so many more reasons than I can even process.

Gio watches me silently, then nods. "A pact to never speak about that day ever again?"

"Never," I agree hastily, taking the life raft he offers, unable to come up with a way to pull back my lie.

"Drink your coffee." He nudges my saucer toward me. "Then we can talk about gelato."

He looks over at the door as someone flings it open, and his face lights up. For my part, I feel saved by the bell.

"Sophia," he says. "You're late."

The library atmosphere in here dissipates with Sophia's arrival, a clatter of bangles as she battles to tame her inside-out umbrella.

"My dramatic youngest sister," he says, looking back to me.

She laughs as she slides behind the counter and drapes her wet coat beside mine over the radiator.

"And prettiest," she says. "And smartest. And not really his sister."

Gio rolls his eyes, obviously used to this line. "You might as well be," he says. "Sophia is Santo's youngest, noisiest, and most obnoxious daughter. The other three are much nicer."

Sophia is completely unfazed by the insult. There is palpable sibling warmth between them, their verbal sparring underscored with familiarity. "I've just talked to the hospital. No change. Although the nurse said he asked for cannoli so one of them brought him some from the festival last night."

Gio nods.

"This is Iris," he says.

Sophia's eyes slide to me, curious.

"She's a chef," he tells her. "She's going to try to help us with the recipe."

"Excellent," she says, hooking a Belotti's apron over her head. "We need all the help we can get."

"I don't know how much use I'm going to be," I say, anxious to play my role down.

"British?" she asks.

I nod.

"But you live here now, right, you're not just passing through on holiday or anything?"

"What is this, Soph? An interrogation?" Gio says.

"I live here now," I say. "A trainee New Yorker, if there is such a thing."

"Maybe you can convince Gio to add some new flavors to our range." She shoots him the side-eye as she speaks.

His expression stiffens and I see his shutters bang down, just as they did in the bookstore on Valentine's Day.

"What does our logo say?"

Sophia sighs. "*Vanilla forever.* I know all of that, but what if we never find it, Gio? What then? If we diversify now, we protect ourselves for the future."

His expression is unmoved. "We'll find the recipe."

"And if we don't?"

"We have time. We will."

They both look at me, and I hesitate to say anything because this is clearly a well-trodden argument.

"The others agree with me." Sophia folds her arms across her chest as she speaks, her expression every bit as obstinate as Gio's. I get the feeling sparks regularly fly between these two.

"Maria too?" he says.

Sophia doesn't reply. I'm guessing Santo's wife is of the same opinion as Gio.

"Exactly," he said. "Case closed."

"Good luck working with him." Sophia is speaking to me this time. "He's a massive pain in the ass."

He ignores the dig and looks at me. "Let's go to the kitchens where we can hear ourselves think."

"I've made a list of new flavor ideas, whenever you're ready," Sophia says, testy.

Gio doesn't bite, just turns away.

"This way," he says.

Sophia chucks me a grin behind his back, her corkscrew

dark curls bouncing around her face. I can't help but like Gio's spiky little sister. If the other three are anything like her, Belotti family parties must be a riot.

THE GELATERIA KITCHENS ARE cavernous, much bigger than the shopfront would have you believe, a curious mix of traditional and modern. Impressive stainless-steel industrial gelato machines line one wall—Gio runs me through how ingredients load into the top to heat and pasteurize and then pass down into the chilled bottom cylinder where they're churned with air to create gelato. It's a macro version of my micro process, super-slick and modern, which I somehow hadn't expected to find here.

"This is Santo's favorite," Gio says, leading me over to a much older machine, all ivory enamel curves and polished chrome. "He insists he can taste the difference between gelato made in this from that in the newer machines."

"Do you really think he can?" I say.

He places an affectionate hand on the side of the old machine. "I wouldn't bet against him," he says.

He leads me down to the far end of the kitchen, which, similarly to the store out front, looks untouched by time. A chunky, oblong mahogany workbench dominates the space backed by bespoke cupboards and open shelving. Two long rows of square drawers with pull stops and brass nameplates sit beneath the cupboards, all hand-labeled. The overall effect is of an upscale apothecary, a place where mixologist magic happens. Or gelato magic, as it is here. I'm enchanted.

"This place speaks right to my chef's soul." I breathe, running my fingers over the smooth, well-worn workbench.

How many generations of gelato makers have stood here, men and women, all working to recreate the same secret recipe? Seeing the history back here has helped me understand why Gio was so stubborn with Sophia earlier. The family have carved out a niche for themselves, they have a reputation to uphold.

"Santo and Maria had their first date right here," he says, smoothing a hand over the end of the worktable. "Pizza from across the street and gelato for dessert. They do it again every year on their wedding anniversary." He places both palms flat on the table, his arms braced as he sighs. "It kills him that he can't remember the date now."

I half smile, touched by the simple romance of the story.

"Tell me about the gelato," I say. "Tell me what makes it special."

"What makes it special?" He half huffs, half smiles, a faraway look gathering in his eyes. "So many things make it special. The taste, of course, but it's more than that. It's the connection, the memories, the way taste can trigger emotion."

His face comes alive as he speaks, and he expresses himself with his hands and his body as much as his words. He turns to open one of the drawers on the back wall, returning to the table with a handful of papers: letters and cards.

"See?" he says, fanning them out. "These are from customers. Thank you notes from people who've been back year in, year out on vacation, people who came here as kids and now bring their own children, like a rite of passage. This one is from a family who asked us to serve gelato at their father's funeral because it was the only thing he could eat in his final weeks."

We look through them, all of them really saying the same thing—thank you.

"It's not just gelato," he says, resolute. Stoic.

"I can see that," I say, gathering the papers carefully back into a pile. I understand more than I can possibly say—I could have written one of those letters myself.

"I owe Santo everything." He lays his hand on his chest. "He took me in as his own when I was five years old. Maria did too, even though she was five months pregnant with Francesca at the time. I've grown up behind the counter out there. I belong here." He picks up the letters and puts them back in the drawer. "My daughter belongs here."

I take a step back, surprised. "You have a daughter?"

"Bella." His expression changes when he says her name. Pride mingled with raw parental fear. "Fifteen going on twenty-five and thinks she knows everything there is to know about the world."

"Scary stuff," I say, mentally doing the maths. Bella can only have been eight or nine when her mother died, unfathomably young. I was thirty-one when my mother died and still wholly unprepared for the utter desolation. But then I was left alone in the world; at least Gio's daughter had the warmth of the Belotti clan to close ranks around her. Maybe things would have been different for me if I'd had people to lean on.

"Okay," I say, moving things carefully along. "So tell me what you know about the recipe."

He leans forward, resting his forearms on the table, palms pressed together. "Honestly? Beyond the basics, not much. Santo took—*takes* his role as the current custodian seriously, he really believes in keeping our family story alive. It probably seems bizarre to other people, and after all this I'll for sure be making some back-up plans when it's my turn, but tradition and loyalty matter to us. You'd understand if you knew Santo, he's spent his life behind this counter making sure we all get to benefit and prosper."

"He sounds like a special person," I say, doubling down on my commitment to never, ever tell these people that Santo shared their recipe with my mother. He's the head of this family and the poster boy for Belotti integrity; my mother would haunt me for the rest of my days if I did anything to damage that. And, in truth, it's not just about my mother anymore. I've only spent a small amount of time here, but I'm starting to feel a personal obligation too. This place and these people—I've never known what it's like to have roots, never understood what it means to be part of a family. These people don't just have roots. They're a mighty oak—or perhaps an aged Italian olive tree is a more fitting description—roots embedded deep beneath the streets of Little Italy, proud and secure because they take the time to nourish it. The carefully preserved glass painted door. The secret recipe. The family gallery displayed on the walls. Their strength comes from their unity, and the small glimpse I've had behind the curtain is enough for me to already be enamored.

"But none of that helps when it comes to the recipe," Gio says. "I know the general idea—sugar, milk, cream—no eggs, of course—but as for how to balance things or any other ingredients, I'm in the dark."

I look over at the industrial gelato machines, thinking. "If we're going to experiment, there's no point loading up big machines, it's a waste," I say. "Have you got anything smaller?"

Gio frowns. "Smaller?"

I swallow my smile. "You know, like people use in their own home, a domestic maker. No? I can see from your face that you haven't," I say hurriedly, because he looks mildly offended at the idea of people making gelato in their own kitchens rather than buying it from Belotti's. "I've got one, I can bring it with me tomorrow."

"I'll come by and fetch it if you like, save you hiking it around," he offers.

"It's no problem." I close his offer down, instinct making me keep myself to myself.

"You'll come again tomorrow, though?" he says, holding my gaze.

"Same time, if you'll have me," I say, swallowing hard.

"I'll be here," he says, same as yesterday.

I think about what he's told me about Santo's steadfastness, and I wonder if he realizes how much he exudes that same thing.

Sophia looks up from her magazine when I snag my jacket on the way out.

"Any luck?" She places a half-eaten apple down.

"Early days," I say.

She pushes her curls behind her ears, leaning forward to peer into the kitchen and make sure Gio is out of earshot.

"He *is* my brother, really. I mean, he isn't, but he is, in here." She rolls her eyes as she taps her heart, making light of her own sentimentality. "And he probably seems dull to you, but he isn't, he's just running scared. He spends too much of his time in here and not enough out there." She inclines her head toward the street.

I glance around the quiet gelateria. "Not a bad place to

spend your time," I say. I don't add that dull isn't a word that springs to mind about Gio, but then she doesn't know about our disastrous bookstore run-in.

"Oh, I love it," she says, that same protective gleam in her eyes as Gio when she speaks of Belotti's. "I just think we could get with the times a bit. Shake things up, you know?"

Gio appears from the kitchen and shoots her a long, knowing look, then opens that beautiful painted door for me.

"Tomorrow," he says.

I pull my striped bobble hat on and button my jacket. "Tomorrow."

6.

I KICK OFF MY BOOTS AND HEAD STRAIGHT FOR MY BED-
room when I'm home again, throwing off my coat and hat
and dragging the quilt over my head as I flop into bed. There's
so much about this morning to process, my guts feel like a
pressure cooker of anxiety. I curl up into as small a ball as
possible, warm and safe and alone. I guess it's one of the side
effects of being an only child—I crave solitude when the
world overloads me, and head first under the quilt has been
my preferred place since I was a small child.

So, Gio Belotti is the guy from the bookstore. The guy
who got under my skin on Valentine's Day. I don't know how
I didn't make the connection straightaway. We were bundled
in hats and scarves that day, maybe, distracted by all the Valentine's guff around us, possibly, our attention concentrated
on getting our hands on the book. And, of course, I've worked
hard to scour the incident from my memory banks. Too hard,
as it turned out. I should have realized—objectively speaking, Gio's a handsome guy. Tall, definitely over six foot, and
rangy, the kind of loose limbed you see on jeans campaigns.
Sophia might not be his blood sibling but she definitely had
her sister-goggles on when she called him dull, because he's a

striking man. I haven't seen him laugh yet; I find myself wondering how joy might change his face. Maybe by dull Sophia meant serious—I definitely get that vibe, but then he's a dad. Don't all parents lose their silliness veneer in the face of nappies and sleepless nights and algebra and report cards and Easter bonnet competitions? Not that I have much experience of most of those things. My mother home-schooled me by necessity as we spent most of my younger years traveling wherever her backing-singer career took us. I'm not complaining—she had a way of making all of our lessons seem magical, even if they were mostly held in the cold backseat classroom of our battered Vauxhall Viva.

Gio, though, he seems to be a person who does things by the book, someone who navigates life by trying to step carefully inside Santo's footsteps and a whole line of Belottis who came before him. I remember the ache on his face when he talked about his late wife, and I tuck my knees tighter into my chest and screw my eyes closed, full of dread.

He's a widower, and he remembers what I said on Valentine's Day about Adam. Knowing I blurted that horrible lie to Gio Belotti of all people makes me deeply, mortally ashamed. I don't know him well, but even so it wouldn't surprise me if honesty was his middle name. I absolutely cannot tell him that I lied about Adam, the thought makes my skin crawl. God, I hate that even now, nearly a year later and thousands of miles away, Adam still has the capacity to screw with my life. I force myself to breathe slowly, intentionally, counting my breaths in and slowly out again until my racing heart calms. It's okay, it's okay, it's okay. Except it isn't. I've told Gio one lie on top of another. I went to the gelateria to try to help, but right now it feels as if I'm in danger of doing the exact opposite.

"SORRY, BOBBY," I SAY, when he lands beside me on my sofa after midnight. "Gelato's off the menu, I've packed up my machine to take to Belotti's tomorrow."

He looks aghast. "Surely they have their own? How can they need ours?"

I lean against him and close my eyes, exhausted. "I've made such a massive mess of everything, Bob."

He puts his arm around my shoulders and tucks me into his body. "Come here," he says. "Tell your Uncle Bobby all about it."

I half laugh. "You know how creepy that sounds, right?"

He squeezes my shoulders. "Spill."

I couldn't have this conversation with anyone else, but over the months since I arrived here I've slowly shared some of the hideous details with Bobby about my past. He refers to Adam exclusively as "the asshole," and has made it very clear that should said asshole ever set foot in New York, he'll bust out his inner Liam Neeson, use his very particular set of skills to find him and, well . . . I don't think he'd kill him, exactly, but the intention to protect me is there and I love him for it.

Even so, I've kept what happened in the bookstore on Valentine's Day to myself, because I don't want him to think badly of me for it. I close my eyes as I tell him now, not wanting to see his face. I don't miss the way he mutters "if only" when I tell him I lied about Adam's death, nor his sharp intake of breath when I say that Gio Belotti has turned out to be none other than bookstore guy. When I go on to say that Gio is genuinely widowed, he twists to face me on the sofa with both hands clamped against his mouth, his dark eyes mortified on my behalf.

"This is very, very bad," he whispers.

"I know," I say, utterly miserable. "What am I going to do?"

He shakes his head very slowly, staring at me. It's not helpful. I wait.

"Okay," he says, laying one hand on my knee. "So you either fess up, which would be an unmitigated disaster and most probably scar you both for life, or just keep mum about the asshole being alive and stick to plan A: drip feed the recipe and run."

"I just feel so shoddy for lying," I say. "Of all the people in all the world, why did it have to be him?" Bobby looks alarmed by the uncontrollable shake in my voice.

"Don't even, Iris—God knows you're an ugly crier." He quickly tucks me back under his arm. I feel like a baby bird sheltering under its mamma's wing, and it makes me feel both better and worse. There are no words for how much I wish my mother was still here—she'd know exactly what to say and do. But then, if she was here, none of this would have happened. I wouldn't have been taken in by Adam, because I wouldn't have felt exposed and alone and desperate to be one of two again. I'd still be living and chefing in London now, maybe getting closer to my forever dream of seeing my name over the door of my own restaurant. My heart shivers at the thought of having never met Bobby, though, he's my silver lining. I slump into him when he plants a kiss on the top of my head, and finally untense my shoulders for the first time since walking out of Belotti's this morning.

"We'll figure everything out," he says, and because it's late and I'm knackered and it's Bobby, I tell myself to believe him.

MY GELATO MACHINE MIGHT not be heavy to carry across my matchbox kitchen, but it turns out that lugging it around the neighborhood is a lot more effort than I imagined. By the time I reach Belotti's I'm huffing like a carthorse, the box balanced in my arms, on the verge of hurling my bag in the nearest bin because it keeps sliding down my shoulder and dragging my scarf with it, almost strangling me.

I bump the door open with my backside and stumble in, depositing the box on the counter and my bag on the nearest stool, panting like an expectant mother.

"Help," I half shout. "I need coffee. And a defibrillator."

Gio comes through, flanked by Sophia, and then three more women follow in quick succession. They form a row behind the counter and smile at me; there is no question that these are the Belotti sisters, their similarity is striking. And intimidating.

"Francesca," says the one on the end.

"Elena," says the next one along.

"Viola," says the third.

"Sophia." Gio's youngest sister bobs a curtsy.

For his part, Gio looks testy, his jaw set stiff. "Contrary to what it might look like, we're not auditioning for *The Sound of Music*," he says. "My sisters were just leaving."

"Do you sing, Iris?" Sophia says, ignoring him. "You can be our new governess."

I laugh as I unwind my scarf. "I do, actually." I don't know why I admitted that. I haven't sung in years, not in front of people, anyway. I inherited my mother's voice as well as her blue eyes, but she was the performer in the family. "I'm afraid I'd be a terrible governess, though. I can't sew clothes from curtains or throw puppet shows. The only thing I'm any good at is cooking."

"Please let me apologize for my sisters," Gio says, his hand on his heart.

"Always so grumpy," Sophia mutters and, beside her, Viola looks at the floor to hide her laugh.

Francesca, on the far end, takes charge. "Enough, girls. Iris, I'm sorry if this looks like an ambush."

"Because that's exactly what it is," Gio says.

"We just came by on our way to the hospital," Francesca says, and they all nod, wide-eyed.

"Even though visiting hours don't start until noon and you all really ought to be at work?" Gio adds, earning himself dirty looks down the line from his sisters.

"This *is* my work," Sophia says, raising her hand as if she's in class. "I don't know what everyone else is doing here."

"That's it, Soph," Elena says, in the middle. "Throw us under the bus after you texted us all to say Gio's dating a dead ringer for Jess from *New Girl*. You know how much I loved that series."

Sophia throws her hands up, laughing. "Was I wrong, though?"

"You're wrong, and you're being rude," Gio says, cutting in. They all shrug, unapologetic, and he opens the door on to the street. "Out. All of you."

His sisters file out, murmuring variants of "nice to meet you" and "good luck putting up with him" as they pass me.

He snags Sophia's hood at the back of the line. "Not you. You work here, remember?"

"I thought you might prefer me to leave you to it," she says, smiling sweetly.

"And I thought you might prefer me to leave *you* to it," he says, pulling his apron over his head and handing it to her. "Iris, shall we? I have an idea."

I glance uncertainly at my beloved gelato maker on the counter.

"You can leave your tiny machine there, it's safe."

I pick up my bag and scarf. "Umm, okay. Lead the way."

7.

"Sorry, I just needed to get out of there," he says, steering me through the sidewalk cafés and busy last-day-of-festival preparations. "I swear, when they get together like that they're just . . ." He shakes his head, searching for the right words.

"A lot?" I suggest.

"Too much," he says. "Way, way too much."

We lapse into silence as we walk, awkward now we're alone and his sisters have thrown their spin on things.

"They were just kidding around," I say, trying to get us back on track. "Forget what they said. I will. In fact, I already have. I can't remember at all."

He glances down at me and I see the tenseness in his face ease. "Thank you," he says. "Because I'd hate for them to scare you away, you're the best hope I have." He pauses, and then hurriedly adds, "For the recipe, obviously. Not for anything . . . oh, for God's sake."

I press my lips together, because he's tying himself up in knots and making it worse. I veer into the nearest brightly lit store, feigning distraction as much to change the mood as anything else.

"Really?" he says, coming to an incredulous standstill.

I stand beside him, momentarily taken aback. It's a rainy autumn morning outside in New York, but in this place it's wall-to-wall, in-your-face, jolly-holly Christmas with jingle bells on.

"Oh my word," I say, backed up by the dulcet tones of Mariah Carey. "It's only September."

"Not in here," deadpans a passing store assistant wearing a "Christmas in New York!" T-shirt, his deely boppers flashing red and green.

"He doesn't seem that thrilled to be here," I say, still acclimatizing to the riot of glitter, revolving trees, and nodding reindeer heads on the walls. The store is huge and stuffed to the rafters with all things festive, like we took a wrong turn and ended up at the North Pole.

"Me neither," Gio says.

I can't lie—I love it. I don't think about gelato recipes or bookstore lies because I'm too busy trailing my fingers over rack after rack of glittering baubles, from homespun holly to tacky pink flamingos in sunhats and golden angels draped in the Stars and Stripes. I pause at a rack of cooking-related baubles, holding up a silver-glittered whisk.

"If it was December, I'd totally get this," I say, hanging it back with reluctance.

Gio trails beside me, much less enamored with the whole place than I am; but then I guess this is nothing new to him, the store is practically his neighbor.

"This place has my mother written all over it," I say, pausing to look at a huge Christmas village display. I watch the small steam train chug along its track around the illuminated houses and old-fashioned shops, remembering childhood

Christmases. It's testimony to my mum that all I really recall of those years is the hazy, nostalgic glow. There certainly wasn't much in the way of money for expensive presents, but it was homely and ours, just the two of us in our festive bubble. She was a charismatic person, exciting to be around, someone who could make any day, any occasion, any circumstance fun.

"Is she still in London?" Gio asks.

I look at him, blink a couple of times to shake the memories away and pull myself back to now.

"My mum? No. I lost her three years ago," I say. "No siblings either. Just me."

"I'm sorry," he says, placing his hand on my shoulder. "Your dad?"

Charlie Raven strolls through my mind, scraggy-haired, drumsticks in one hand, a beer in the other. "He died when I was much younger, but to be honest, he never really figured in my life even when he was alive." I shrug. "Just one of those things."

Gio picks up a snow globe and turns it over. "Families are complicated, huh?" He watches the snow settle as he places it back on the shelf. "My sisters this morning are a case in point."

"I like them," I say. "They scared the shit out of me, but I like them."

"They have their moments," he says. "Fran was born not long after Santo and Maria took me in. I went from a cold apartment to a warm home with Disney-level parents and a baby sister. And then another one. And then another one."

"And then another one?" I say.

"A particularly opinionated one," he says.

"Yeah, I noticed you two clash sometimes," I say.

"It's not that I don't have ambition for the business," he says, exasperated. "The mobile city carts were my idea, I'm not risk averse. Belotti's has changed with the times in every way but the flavor."

He takes a step back as he speaks and accidentally stands on the start button of a life-size singing snowman, and in his haste to move away manages to stumble and press two more. All three wheeze into loud, tinny life, swinging their arms as they sing "Last Christmas," an out-of-time chorus that is so ridiculous I start to really laugh. Gio looks at them in horror, and then at me, and then shakes his head and laughs too.

So that's what he looks like when he laughs, I think.

"That's definitely my cue to get out of here," he says.

Back on the street, he rolls his shoulders as if to shake off any traces of Christmas glitter. He glances in the direction of the gelateria, and then the other way.

"Let's try something out," he says, placing a hand on my elbow to guide me across the street between the stalls and generators. People know him here: they raise their hand as he passes, waylay him to ask how Santo is doing. It reminds me how embedded Belotti's is in this community, and I wonder if Gio appreciates what it means to hold a place within it. He's a crucial cog in his family machine, and they in turn are a founding cog in Little Italy. I'm not part of something like this. We moved too frequently when I was a child to be crucial anywhere.

Gio stops. "In here," he says.

I lean back and see we're at a gelateria, but any similarity to Belotti's ends there. This place is large and ultra-modern, and inside the glass display counter there are at least twenty different flavors of gelato, a parakeet display of color and drama.

"Wow," I murmur. "How do you ever choose?"

An immaculately made-up woman leans across the counter and kisses Gio's cheek, lingering for a second longer than a socially acceptable peck.

"Gio! It's been a while since we last saw you in here," she says. "What'll it be?" She glides her hands gracefully across the top of the glass and smiles. She somehow reminds me of a snake charmer.

"Vanilla," he says. "As it comes, no toppings, thanks."

She looks disappointed. "The blackberry is the best today."

He doesn't say anything, and she sighs as she reaches for a cup. "One of these days," she says, heaping it full of vanilla. I can't imagine she puts that much in everyone's serving, she'd be out of business in a week.

"Iris?" He turns to me. "For you?"

I look at the array of flavors and colors laid out before me, impressed. For the chef in me, this is better than a jeweler's shop window. And then I look at Gio watching me and I know what I'm going to choose.

"Same again, please. Vanilla." I look at the mountain of gelato in the cup on the counter for Gio. "Or, actually, can I just have a second spoon?"

He looks pleased, which is more than I can say for the woman behind the counter as she jabs another spoon into the cup, wobbling the precarious gelato tower. I'm not sure, but I think she might have imagined poking it in my eye.

"On the house," she says, when Gio reaches for his wallet. "I'll come by yours soon and you can return the favor."

We take a seat at one of the booths, the gelato on the table between us.

"Research?" I say.

He pushes it toward me. "Ladies first."

I pull out a neon green plastic spoon and swirl it in the gelato. "It's more yellow than Belotti's," I say, raising the spoon up to eye level to study it.

He doesn't touch his spoon, just watches me as I taste it. I find myself looking away from him as the cold gelato slides down my throat.

"It's heavier, I think?"

He reaches for the other spoon and tests it, one spoonful and then another.

"More cream, less milk," I say.

He nods. "This has a stronger vanilla flavor too."

He's right. There's a delicacy to Belotti's gelato compared to the intensity of this one.

"It's kind of custardy," I say.

"Yes," he says, pointing his spoon at me.

"There's no way I could eat this much of it," I say, waving my spoon over the piled-high cup.

Gio's gaze flickers toward the counter. "I think Priscilla was trying to make a point."

"I think she was blatantly coming on to you," I say, sliding my spoon back into gelato-mountain.

His eyebrows shoot up and he flushes as he looks away. "She thinks we would be a good partnership," he says after a pause. "In business."

I laugh under my breath. "Among other things. Maybe your sisters should be glancing across the street if they're trying to fix you up."

He sighs and lays his spoon down. "I don't need fixing up."

"From what I saw of them today, they probably just want to see you happy."

"I'm happy enough," he says, but his frown says something different.

"The fact you had to say enough at the end of that sentence tells me you're probably not, really," I say, and then I catch myself and wonder where that even came from. Did Priscilla sprinkle a little truth extract in with the vanilla?

He picks up his spoon again and slides it through the gelato, more for distraction than to eat it.

"I know you'll understand this better than most, Iris. Losing Penny . . . the world stopped turning. All of my plans, my hopes and dreams, gone, just like that." He pushes his spoon all the way into the gelato for emphasis and leaves it there. "Bella was the only reason I got out of bed in the morning. I'd lost my wife, but she'd lost her mamma, and I had to step up. God knows we were lucky to have family around us, but when I closed the door at night, it was still just the two of us walking around the edges of this gaping hole in our home. And you can't live like that forever, can you?" He shakes his head, his expression bleak. "Me and Bells . . . we found our way through the mess together, and by some miracle we managed to rebuild a solid floor beneath our feet." He looks up at me. "She's pretty terrific," he says.

"I'll bet," I say, thinking he is too.

"I'm not lonely," he says. I don't know if he's trying to convince me or himself. "I have Bells, my family, the gelateria. So when I say I'm happy 'enough,' what I probably mean is my world is turning again now, and having experienced what it feels like when it stops, that's something worth protecting. For Bella more than for me. My sisters think romance is the be-all and end-all because they're lucky and they're naive. I see it for what it is—fragile and unreliable, likely to blow a hole in your life when you least expect it."

It's clear from listening to him that his daughter is the center of his world.

"It sounds like you're a great dad," I say. "I grew up with just one parent too, so I know how that 'you and me against the world' feeling goes."

Gio huffs softly. "You and me against the world. Yeah, that's a good way to describe it."

As he repeats one of my mother's favorite phrases on a quiet breath, and he slowly lifts his gaze to meet mine, it feels for the briefest second as if he is talking to me. We look at each other across the table, a raw, vulnerable moment of connection that makes me want to reach across and slide my hands over his.

I don't though, I'm not brave enough. I bury my spoon in the gelato instead.

"Let's go back," I say. "I'll show you how mighty my tiny gelato machine is."

I don't miss his relieved half smile as he pushes his chair back, nor the evil eye from Priscilla as we leave.

8.

"PASS ME THE SPRING ONIONS?" I SAY, GESTURING TO the plate on the counter beside Bobby. He frowns, perplexed, and I quickly correct my English to American terminology. "Scallions."

It's Saturday night and we're slammed out front in the restaurant. We only seat eighteen, twenty at a tight push, but table turnover is high and Shen is calling orders through fast enough to make my head spin. She runs the place like a well-oiled machine out there, commanding a handful of student waiting staff to make sure people are fed and moved through with an efficiency Gordon Ramsay would be envious of. It's not the kind of place people come to linger—we're a "fill up and go, wipe down the Formica tables in between" kind of place, with last year's calendar still on the wall, an erratic cuckoo clock, and paper lanterns that have seen better days. There are no plans for change, though, it suits the diners who come here. There are other places for first dates and lingering over coffee.

Thankfully, we don't have an extensive menu. People come for our noodle specialities, dishes that are the work of minutes as long as the prep is done before we open. I love the high-octane energy of it, the buzz of turning out sizzling bowl after bowl, the all-consuming concentration required to keep up the pace when it's hectic.

Bobby is "helping" me out tonight as Robin's still away and our usual commis is sick, which in practical terms means I'm mostly flying solo. It's not really Bobby's fault; he loves to eat good food but I don't think his oven sees any action unless Robin is at the helm. Right now he's got his paper chef's cap on squiff and his T-shirt sleeves rolled up to his shoulders as if he's put in a twenty-hour shift instead of two hours not-very-hard graft in our tiny kitchen. He's keen on shouting "Service!" through the hatch at Shen every time he places bowls on the pass, and then spinning back to me and yelling "Three prawn, two duck!" or whatever he considers to be the next order in line. He nipped outside a few minutes ago to take a call and Shen stuck her head through the hatch and ordered me to kill him or else she would.

I glance up at the clock. Almost ten, just half an hour to go before we close up shop and I can collapse on the sofa. I don't care if it's lumpy. I just want to watch trash TV and sleep the sleep of the dead.

"I need your gelato more than life right now," Bobby says, pressing his cheek against the stainless-steel fridge. "It's hotter than a camel's hoof in here."

I open the fridge and he sways with it.

"Here. Cold water." I press the bottle against his other cheek. "You're not built for hot kitchens."

"And yet I hold the unofficial record for longest time in the Russian sauna," he says. "Go figure."

I drop a handful of noodles into the sizzling wok. "Chicken, bottom left of other fridge."

He groans as he peels himself off the door to get it for me. "You're so bossy when you cook," he says. "Are you like this at Belotti's?"

I've been going to the gelateria every morning for the last few weeks, spending a couple of hours with Gio, experimenting with ingredients. I'm finding it hard to balance saying enough with not saying too much too soon and causing suspicion. I'm just relieved it's cold out and demand is low so we have some time—the pressure would really be on if this had happened to them in the height of summer.

"No, because Gio listens to me."

Bobby peels the lid from the chicken container and holds it out to me. "Bring him over. I want to meet him."

"Gio? Why?"

"Because for the last nine months you've barely left this building, and now you're in and out more often than the cuckoo in that revolting clock out there."

The cuckoo in question pings out of the clock on a baggy spring whenever it feels like it, making a weird drunken hiccup-screech that makes nearby diners flinch. We tried taking it down but it left a stain on the wall so we hung it back again rather than have to redecorate. I don't appreciate the comparison and I turn to glance at Bobby, one hand on my hip, the other tossing noodles. I swear I must do that movement in my sleep.

"You know why I'm doing it," I say.

"Because he's got good hands?"

"Because I owe them." I lift the noodles high out of the pan with long tongs, twirling them into heaps as I lower them into waiting bowls.

"I don't, though, and I miss your gelato machine. Can it come home yet?"

"Stop being so needy," I say, handing him the dishes. "What's next?"

"I don't know," he says. "You leave me for the gelato people and never come home?" He bangs the dishes down on the pass, shoves his head through the hatch and shouts, "Service!"

When he turns back, I lay my cooking tools down and give him a quick hug.

"What was that for?"

"To say thank you for caring about me." I step back, my hands on his shoulders. "I'll always come home."

He presses his lips into a tight line, and for a second I think he's about to cry. "It's the gelato machine I really worry about," he says, and I hug him again, laughing.

I turn back to cook the final dishes of the night, more glad of Bobby than ever. He's reminded me tonight that while I may not be a well-established cog yet, I have a home of my own and a good friend, and that's more than I've had in a long time. In his own inimitable, roundabout way I see that he's trying to tell me to be careful, to keep a healthy distance between myself and the Belottis so I don't wind up getting hurt. It's good advice. I've started to feel dangerously familiar around Gio, and in all honesty I'm just blocking out the fact I lied to him about Adam, because opening the door on memories of my final two years in London sends me in on myself in a way I hate. I feel my shoulders lift and curve in, my head dip down, braced for impact. I can't breathe deeply enough or think straight, panic gets hold of me and tosses me around like a cat with a mouse. I'm not that mouse anymore. I'm not.

MONDAY ROLLS IN COLD, bright, and clear, a welcome relief after the rain-fest of a weekend. I spent yesterday cooking an elaborate three-course dinner to celebrate Robin's return from Chicago. I didn't go up there and eat with them. They asked me, of course, but it was more about the pleasure of creation than eating, for me at least. Besides, three's a crowd, they had some catching up to do. In all honesty, I was pretty glad to have the day to myself—no Belotti's, just me, my recipe books, and the rain on my windows. Smirnoff hung out with me, lured in by the kitchen smells, watching me flex my rusty culinary muscles as he hung around in the hope of scraps.

Mulberry Street is much quieter without the hubbub of the festival, a more leisurely pace of morning commuters and unjostled space on the sidewalk. I pause outside Belotti's to allow a couple of women in office suits and sneakers to pass by, both of them clutching steaming coffee cups and green-striped paper bags. I'm surprised to hear piano music when I step inside.

I smile at Sophia behind the counter and then turn my attention toward the piano, where someone has just stopped playing mid-tune to peer over the top of it at me.

"Bella, go again," Gio says, looking at her as he appears with a large drum of coffee beans in his hands, noticing me as he lowers it to the floor. "Oh, Iris, hello."

The jean-clad girl behind the piano slides off the stool and skips across to stand beside Sophia, her dark ponytail swinging as she goes. She's slight and swamped by her mustard hoodie, her eyes tracking me as I perch on one of the leather seats.

"Bells, this is Iris," Sophia says, her arm snaking around the girl's shoulders.

I meet Gio's daughter's eyes and smile, sensing her curiosity. I really hope she wasn't included in Sophia's text messages last week suggesting I'm here for anything but to help.

"I liked your piece," I say, nodding toward the piano.

She shoots me a reserved half smile. "Do you play?"

My mother struggled sometimes with home-schooling, particularly when it came to grappling with the trickier aspects of mathematics and scientific theories, but she was pretty magnificent when it came to music.

"I do. Well, I did. I haven't, for ages, but I used to love it."

Gio pushes a coffee toward me. "I didn't know that."

"She sings as well," Sophia says, obviously recalling our von Trapp conversation.

"Me too," Bella says, her smile widening. I see much of Gio in her; she has his eyes. "I was just practicing piano."

"She has an evaluation tomorrow," Gio says. "So maybe she could scoot her butt back on over to that stool and take it from the top again."

His comment earns him an exaggerated sigh, but she does as he asks all the same. I sip my coffee as she starts, halts, then starts again.

"You're making me nervous, all watching me," she grumbles, going pink.

I pick up my coffee and Gio inclines his head for me to follow him through to the kitchen. I look across at Bella, her head bowed in concentration, and I remember being that age with my mum alongside me on the stool. I was lucky to have her.

"I THINK THAT'S THE closest yet," Gio says, after testing this morning's batch of gelato. We've followed a recipe from an old cookbook he found in a secondhand bookstore at the weekend, and it's turned out well.

"Too sweet," Sophia says, when we take it out front for her to test.

I look across at Bella, who's doing a bad job of pretending she isn't more interested in the gelato than the piano. She's been practicing for the last couple of hours on and off. I found myself keeping an ear on her progress to see if she made it to the end of the piece without faltering or skimming her hands up the keys in frustration.

"Come on, then, you earned a break," Gio says, and she shoots across and grabs a spoon.

She tries it, screwing her nose up while she deliberates. "Not the same as Nonno's," she says, looking at her father. "It's nice, though. Can I finish it?"

"Will you practice some more if I say yes?"

She grins, knowing she's won, and takes the cup of gelato to add toppings. Belotti's might offer just one flavor, but they have an impressive collection of toppings arranged in glass jars behind the counter. Sprinkles, chocolate curls, sherbets, fudge cubes, pistachios, and amaretti biscuits sit alongside chocolate spreads and fruit sauces. Bella reaches down a big blue-and-white-patterned can, peeling off the plastic lid before lifting it to her face to inhale the scent.

"Amarena cherries," Gio tells me.

"Food of the gods," Sophia says, taking the can from her niece.

I watch Bella heap whipped cream and chocolate curls on top of her heavy-handed shake of cherries, noticing how she flicks a look beneath her dark lashes at Gio every now and then to see if he's going to stop her.

"I expect you to be note perfect after all that," he says, and she just nods, her eyes on the prize.

"Baby Leo's gonna be so excited when he can eat a sundae like this," she mutters, reaching for a long spoon.

It's disconcerting seeing Gio in his role as a father. I've become accustomed to him as a son and brother, someone his family stand alongside, rely on, and royally take the piss out of. As a father, he's subtly different. His daughter's eyes seek him out constantly, and in turn he keeps an eye and an ear on her too, gossamer-fine love threads between them, invisible to the human eye. I guess it comes from being a single-parent family—even with the cushion of the wider Belotti clan, it would inevitably have tightened the nuts and bolts of their unit in the same way I experienced myself. It must be tough as a parent trying to be all things for your child, no one to lean on or look to, and growing up I sometimes felt the weight of it too, exacerbated by being an only child.

I sit at the counter and watch Sophia and Gio wait on a couple of customers who've just ordered takeout, Gio at the coffee machine, Sophia sliding sugared pastries into green-striped paper Belotti bags. I know she bakes many of the shop's pastries herself; we've talked recipes over coffee most mornings I've been here. She's self-taught—or Maria-taught, to be more accurate—and full of ideas and ambition. I see her flinch as Bella falters with her piano piece at the exact same place as the last three run-throughs, and after a moment she takes a cannoli from the display case and passes it my way, the diamond stud in her nose glinting as she winks.

"It's a blatant bribe," she whispers. "Any chance you could help Bells out? I love her but if I have to listen to this for much longer . . ." Her eyes finish the sentence and I turn to look at Gio, but he's disappeared through to the kitchens.

"I can try?" I say, doubtful. I haven't felt like playing since my mother died, but I find myself sliding off my chair regardless.

I feel oddly nervous as I rest my arms on top of the piano. "You know, I used to find that playing something completely different helped me if I got stuck in a loop."

Bella raises her eyes and looks at me, miserable. "I'm going to fail the evaluation."

I chew the inside of my lip, thinking back. "What's your favorite piece to play?"

She teenage shrugs, not biting.

"Shall I show you mine?"

She flexes her fingers, probably aching from tension, and then shuffles across on the stool with a tiny nod. I round the piano and sit beside her, trying not to feel panicked by the run of black and white keys in front of me.

"It's been a while, I'm going to be rusty," I say, coughing as I rest my hands in place, hoping muscle memory kicks in. I'm crossing my fingers it's a piece she knows; it's a pupil staple back in the UK so there's a fair chance. I pick out the famous opening bars of "The Entertainer" with two fingers and glance at Bella, gaining myself the slightest eyebrow flick of recognition. Encouraged, I start to play, hesitant and then not so, elation glittering from my fingertips to my elbows to my shoulders to my heart as my body remembers this feeling, this joy. I've played the piano forever, beside my mother as a child watching her long, gold-ringed fingers, and this raucous gallop of a tune was always a beloved part of our repertoire.

I look at Bella and find she's smiling, and I nod toward the keys for her to join me. She bites her bottom lip, hovers her hands for a second then finds her place in the music with me.

I notice how slight her hands are, the span of her fragile fingers as she reaches for the notes, and I wonder if my mother noticed those same things about me on the countless occasions I joined her on the stool as a teenager. I can almost smell the stale smokiness of the working men's clubs and backstreet pubs we more often than not practiced in—any piano would do for us. She'd sing sometimes too, entertaining the handful of afternoon drinkers in there too early for her proper set later in the evening. Powerful memories kaleidoscope in my head as Bella and I play together, getting faster and faster, our hands racing to keep up with each other. Sophia claps in time as Bella gasps with laughter, and joy bursts behind my ribs as if the door of a birdcage full of songbirds has just flung open on its springs. I'd forgotten how good this feels, wild and magical music. I'm exhilarated, I'm free, I'm on top of the world.

"What's going on?"

Gio appears over the piano, staring at us, his tone harsher than I've ever heard it before. Sophia stops clapping, Bella hits all the wrong notes, and my fingers slow to nothing as I meet his dark, unreadable eyes.

"We were just messing around," Bella says, defensive.

"It was my fault," I say automatically, although I'm not quite sure what I've done wrong. "I thought it might help Bella to loosen up a bit, have some fun with a different piece."

"She already has an excellent teacher," he says, clipped.

"Dad, you're embarrassing me," Bella says under her breath, pulling her sleeves down over her hands.

"Enough for today," he says curtly, and turns away as the bell over the door rings. "These people haven't come in here to listen to this."

"But I always practice in here and you never . . ." Bella starts to answer back and then thinks better of it, probably because of the long warning look Gio gives her.

I find myself reminded of how I felt in that bookstore all those months ago, and I need to get out of here. Standing abruptly, I put a hand briefly on Bella's shoulder.

"Good luck tomorrow, just relax and you'll do great."

I can't look at Gio as I gather my bag and coat, because I'm aware my cheeks are burning and I'm swallowing down my emotions. Anger, confusion, humiliation. I absolutely refuse to cry in here. His sharp, unexpected change in demeanor has me shaken up, is taking me back to that horrible apartment in London with Adam, and I just want to leave. Nodding a quick goodbye to Sophia, I lift my head high and walk straight out of Belotti's.

9.

I'M NOT GOING BACK. NOT THIS MORNING, NOT TOMOR-
row, and maybe not again. I spent yesterday turning it over in
my head, running through the scant conversation to understand where things went wrong, why it felt so harsh, why I
reacted so strongly. I've felt worse in the last twenty-four
hours than I have in months with the reminder of my previous life, and logically *of course* I know Gio isn't Adam, nor is
he anything like him, thank God. These emotions are mine
to work through. It's just that he's the first person outside of
the Very Tasty Noodle House that I've allowed myself to get
to know in New York, and I guess I haven't taken the time to
see him, or anyone else at Belotti's, as whole people, with
their own complex emotions. I've defined them by who they
are to me and what they mean to my mother's story, and yesterday brought home to me the fact that they're people in
their own right with their own stories and their own baggage.
They're not the von Trapp family, all singing and dancing,
they're a real family. And while I think that makes them even
better, it also means I need to take a step back.

I'm secure here in the noodle house. This place is the
safety curtain to my life's stage; I step behind it with Bobby
and co and we are a well-oiled crew. Even Smirnoff knows

his role. Real life exists out on that stage beyond the safety curtain, and Gio and his family are the first people I've allowed to step on to it. I've painted their glass door into my set background, allowed Mulberry Street to become part of my production. I understand now that it's not a one-act performance. My set needs more buildings, it needs to be bigger, fuller, and richer, so while I'm not going to Belotti's this morning, I am going out. I'd become too accustomed to spending my mornings hiding behind the safety curtain before I saw that painted door, but I'm ready to step out from behind it now. New York is on my doorstep in all its messy, energetic glory—I'm taking myself out there to paint some new colors on my backdrop.

CLICHÉD AS IT MIGHT BE, I've decided to start at Katz's Deli. Not because Meg Ryan faked an orgasm there, but because I've got such fond memories of watching that movie with my mother. So actually, yes, maybe I *am* going because of Meg Ryan, in a roundabout way. I ducked in there when I first arrived in NY and pulled myself straight back out again; the place was jumping with an energy I didn't feel up to being part of. I don't expect it to be any different today, but *I'm* different, and hopefully that's enough. I haven't told Bobby what happened at Belotti's yesterday so I can't ask him to come with me, but that's okay. Part of painting my background set involves being assertive enough to do things alone, otherwise my background will always be someone else's take on life, and this needs to be mine.

It's one of those bright blue-sky days, the kind that looks warm through the window and then you get out there and find yourself in need of a warm jacket. And preferably a scarf. I have both of those things as I put my best foot forward and try to project New Yorker confidence, striding with my hands in my pockets and my head high. It's not much of a walk, twenty minutes or so, but it's wide, bustling streets and cluttered sidewalks, snatches of conversations, truck horns, street art, and kids on skateboards weaving either side of an old woman pulling a shopping trolley. It's alive, a sense of forward travel that gives me a low buzz of nervous excitement. I almost reach for my cellphone to video call Bobby just to show him where I am, and then I change my mind. I can tell him later. I see Katz's coming up on the corner in the distance and I instinctively twist the heart-shaped ring on my wedding finger for comfort. My mother gave it to me on my sixteenth birthday, sliding it from its forever spot on her hand to its forever spot on mine. She was a bit of a magpie for jewelry, the more bohemian the better, but the signet ring never left her hand until the day she gave it to me. All of her rings hold a special place in my heart, but this one is a little extra-special.

"Come on, Mum," I whisper. "Let's go in."

I queued to get inside the first time I came here, but when the guy in the entrance held out a ticket to me I lost my nerve and turned around. This time I smile as if I know what I'm doing. I don't, but I've looked it up enough to know it's going to be hectic and I need to hang on to my ticket as if it's made of pure gold. I hesitate once inside because, genuinely, it's kind of mind-blowing, especially on my own. I'm glad I'm early, at least: it's just before ten in the morning and, thankfully, quieter than the last time I was here. It's just how you know it's going to be inside, no frills, and neon, faded memorabilia and multiple queues, a sense of chaos and order running hand in hand. I follow the guy in front as he seems to know what he's doing and find myself in line at a cutter station. I don't mind the wait. The smell in here leans heavily toward savory; if a caveman ever found himself unexpectedly defrosted and in NYC this place would draw him in like catnip. I listen to the guy ahead of me rattle off his order and scan the menu quickly—if there's one thing that's valued here, it's knowing what you want when it's your turn upfront. I twist my signet ring again, repeating "half pastrami on club" until I'm there and say the words clear and loud, earning myself an efficient nod from the woman wielding the knife in front of me. The cutter stations are exactly that: places where the meat gets sliced and loaded on to bread — and, oh my sweet Lord, is there a lot of meat. She spears a sliver of pastrami for me to test as she builds my sandwich, her experienced hands a blur as she slices and fills my order. The pastrami is something else in my mouth as I wait, melting to nothing but flavor. And then I'm done and moved aside, tray in hand as I weave toward the back and find myself a table.

Coming here was never about the food for me, but now I'm actually sitting with this gigantic sandwich in front of me, it momentarily becomes so. I've worked in kitchens all of my adult life, but I've never been called upon to serve up a sandwich with proportions like this. I can't help myself snapping a shot of it for the food file in my phone, then I count the meat layers: eight, I think—there might even be a sneaky ninth. I don't think my mum ever actually came inside this place, and she certainly wouldn't have eaten anything of this magnitude. She floated barefoot through my childhood on a diet of Marlboro Lights and here-and-there meals, often sitting beside me and picking at my dinner plate rather than serving herself. As an adult looking back, I realize now how tight money was for her, and I wonder if she sometimes missed meals to make sure I didn't.

A woman sits alone at the table marked as the one used in *When Harry Met Sally*, and I wonder if she sat there purposely. She flicks the page of her book as she eats, absorbed in her story, and I find myself hoping she knows exactly which table she's sitting at and not giving a hot damn. I pick up my sandwich and people-watch, letting the hubbub move around me as I eat, soaking in the noise and the movements. As expected, the sandwich is as epic in deliciousness as it is in scale, and I take this moment alone to give myself a mental once-over. A year ago I felt hopeless, trapped in a controlling relationship, and going further back again, I was floundering around in the murky jaws of grief. Adam found me there and reached out his hand, and I clung on because someone, anyone, felt better than no one. I didn't realize how wrong I was until I was in way over my head and couldn't see a clear way out.

A nearby customer knocks an empty soda bottle on the floor, and the clank is enough to jolt me back from those unwelcome memories. I take a few deep, calming breaths and remind myself where I am now. I'm here in New York, sitting in the legendary Katz's Deli eating eight or nine layers of histrionically excellent pastrami, and I'm free to paint my background colors any which way I choose. I close my eyes for a second and mentally add a splash of Katz's red and biscuit beige. That's really what lies at the heart of my discontent yesterday: it reminded me how it feels when someone makes you feel as though you've done something wrong when you haven't, just to distract you from their own mistakes—a lesson I learned the hard way. Gio wasn't to know that, and of course I realize it wasn't his intention and I understand he has his own agenda and emotional flashpoints, but he will always have his family and Bella to turn to when he needs them. I don't have that kind of safety net, so I have to hold myself together instead.

WEDNESDAY MORNING FINDS RAIN battering my windows and me unwilling to leave the sanctuary of my bed, my get-up-and-go got-up-and-gone. I haven't heard from Gio, but then I haven't made contact either. He doesn't know my address, but Sophia has my cell number if she, or he, wanted to get in touch. I'm not surprised by the radio silence—I've been the one doing all the running, after all. It's been a really complicated few weeks, an emotionally draining merry-go-round. I feel as if I'm constantly trying to balance doing more good than harm to the Belotti family. It's so difficult being obscure with the truth regarding the recipe, but at the end of the day my loyalties lie firmly with my mother. I've squared it with myself by holding fast to the fact that I'm trying to honor her memory by helping Santo's family without compromising a secret that's stayed buried for more than thirty years. And that's felt okay, in the main. I've nudged Gio closer and closer to the recipe, but the more time I spend at the gelateria, the more compromised I feel on a personal level.

I hate, hate, *hate* the lie about Adam's death. I wish with all my heart I could rewind the clock and have a rerun at that bookstore encounter—I'd suck those words back in quick smart. Yes, I might sometimes, privately, inside my own head, tell myself that my ex is dead. It's an ugly admission to make, even silently, and I judge myself harshly for it. Not because it's wrong to wish harm on Adam—frankly, that man deserves whatever is coming to him. It's the detrimental effect on my own mental health that bothers me, that the only way to keep putting one foot in front of the other every day is to lie to myself and others about his demise. How could Gio even begin to understand that? There isn't a scenario where I can unpick that lie and come out of it with a shred of dignity or self-respect. Gio will hate me when—*if*—he ever finds out, and justifiably so—from his perspective, at least. Life has dealt him a very different set of cards and he will play his hand accordingly. I remind myself that I'm a decent human trying to do a decent thing, and then shove my head under my pillow and block the world out for a while.

10.

ONE OF THE NICEST THINGS ABOUT LIVING ON CHRYSTIE Street is the long, skinny park that stretches the length of it, a shimmering green line separating it from Forsyth Street on the other side. Bobby tells me it hasn't always been the safest place to hang out, but these days it's a shady refuge on hot city days and an oasis on any kind of day. Kids come for the playgrounds and basketball courts, green-fingered locals come for the community gardens. I don't feel much like it, but after my self-pity party yesterday I've pulled on my big-girl pants and hauled my ass outside to take a walk. I paint seasonal shade into my backdrop as I go—russets and burnt orange, evergreens and blackcurrant mauves, and the smoky, earthen scents of autumn. I feel . . . I don't know. Peaceful? I'm still undecided what to do about Belotti's, but after my strung-out morning yesterday I'm cutting myself some slack. I've got a home, friends, a job. Everything I had before I saw that door, I still have. All of the progress I've made since leaving London still shows.

Snatches of music catch my ear, and I follow them toward a busker who's set up a synthesizer on wobbly legs, a microphone in front of it. She's young, younger than me, and she's playing that small keyboard with some serious skill. I recognize the upbeat opening bars of "Don't Get Me Wrong" instantly—the Pretenders were a huge influence on my mother's musical style. Even in her later years she rocked a Chrissie Hynde fringe and heavy eyeliner. Other people linger to listen too, and I find myself sympathizing because the girl has the most beautiful tone but is clearly struggling with a throat infection. It's cold out here; she nods gratefully when someone throws a few coins in her upturned cap. It reaches deep inside me, reminding me of the way my mum would sell her soul to be out there performing. Music has always been my lifeblood too, so I sit for a while to show my appreciation to this girl for showing up even when she clearly feels like death.

When she plays the melancholy opening bars of "I'll Stand By You," all I can hear is my mother; it was one of her favorite songs to perform. I find a note and approach to put it in her hat, bending to tuck it inside the brim so it doesn't blow away with the autumn leaves. I'm singing with her as I straighten, as much in solidarity as anything, when her voice cracks. I see gratitude in her pale-green eyes and I smile in sympathy, but as I walk away she catches hold of my sleeve and nods toward the microphone. I falter, and although she keeps singing as best she can, it's clear she's not going to make it to the end of the track and is desperate enough to ask a stranger for help. Me. Can I? I'm paralyzed in the moment, wanting to help, not feeling able to. She holds my gaze, her fingers still around the sleeve of my jacket. My mother would have done it in a heartbeat. Did she ever come to this park? For all I know, she could even have busked here. I swallow, summon up what vestiges of courage I have, and for the woman I am now and the woman my mother was then, I step up and help this girl out in her hour of need.

"Okay," I whisper, pulling my bobble hat off and tucking my hair behind my ears.

She closes her eyes momentarily with sheer relief as she hands me the microphone, and I sense a ripple of anticipation among the people standing around. I'd be the same if I was watching this play out. I'd wonder if this random person was going to be able to hold a note or if it was going to be a bit of well-intended earache. *Please let it be the former*, I think. Singing in the shower is as good as it gets for me these days, and Smirnoff is an unreliable judge on my skills. Rolling my shoulders, I clear my throat and listen to the music. I know this song like the back of my hand.

"I'll stand by you . . ." I sing, picking the song up at the chorus, my eyes trained on the busker, her eyes watching me, a cocktail of hope and fear. She barely looks down as she plays the keys from memory and I hear my voice amplified in the park. Relief dissolves the fear from her eyes and a slow smile creeps across her face as she listens to me sing. An answering joy blooms in my chest as I find myself in the music and lose myself in the aching lyrics. *This.* Just as it was playing piano in Belotti's last week, making music is like watering my soul.

There's applause when the song comes to an end, and I can't quite believe I've just sung in public and that it felt so good.

The busker shrugs, laughing when I look her way. "More?"

I want to. I want to stand here and sing forever. She passes me her music book and I flick through it, pausing at a Pat Benatar track. "This one, and maybe this?"

She puts her fingers on the keyboard and bangs out the rocky opening chords of "Hit Me With Your Best Shot," and I'm away, riding shotgun with my mum in her old Vauxhall Viva, barreling along and singing at the top of our lungs in the dog days of summer. It's an anthem and I belt it out like one, a metaphorical middle finger to anyone who wants to come and try to take me down. I feel like I'm singing right into Adam's ear; how I wish the girl I was then could see me now. I slam a hand over my heart and sing for her. The words burst from me, strong and proud, and I dash away tears of elation from my cheeks. More people have joined the crowd now, and when my new friend rocks out the iconic opening beat of Joan Jett's "I Love Rock 'N' Roll," a guy at the front plays air guitar and people start clapping the beat, like a drum. We are in this together, a thirty-strong band, and it's actually electric. I'm singing, they're singing back at me, and by the time I'm belting the chorus out I feel as if I'm onstage in Madison Square Garden. People put more than another dime in the jukebox, they stuff money in the busker's hat until it's brimming, and it's like drinking champagne straight from the bottle. Oh Mum, was this why? Was this it? I've never been brave enough to sing in front of people, and I've somehow just brought this corner of this New York City park to a momentary standstill and it felt like pure, glittering magic. You know those scenes you see in the movies where the entire school canteen goes up, kids are on the tables, people spill on to the streets and dance on the roof of a line of yellow cabs? That's how it felt and, quite honestly, I think the last half an hour has changed me forever.

I hug the busker tight enough to crush her ribs, not giving

a damn if I catch her bug because she's just given me back something money can't buy: my confidence. I laughingly refuse the money she offers me and walk away, practically bouncing along the path until I'm out of sight of the scene. Hello, New York, I'm here, and I can't wait to spend a couple more hours spinning through this crazy, heart-pounding, life-affirming neighborhood I call home.

JUST AFTER MIDNIGHT, BOBBY bangs on my door.

"You can come in but there's still no gelato," I shout, not getting up from my spot on the sofa. It's been a busy night downstairs in the restaurant and I'm not moving unless the building's on fire.

He throws the door wide and stands in the frame with his phone in his hand turned toward me. It takes me a few seconds to realize that the video on his screen is from the park this morning, and that the sound coming from it is me giving the Pretenders a run for their money.

"What the ever-loving *God*, Iris!"

I groan and bury my face in my hands, shrinking into the corner of the sofa. This morning was pure spontaneity and joy, but seeing it recorded wasn't ever part of the deal.

"Where did you get that?"

"I'm sorry? How about where did you get that voice?" he says, slamming my door and landing on the sofa beside me. "You're more Chrissie Hynde than Chrissie Hynde is."

I pull myself up to sitting and sigh deeply. "She was my mother's favorite."

"And you're her doppelgänger," he says, shaking his head. "How have I missed this?"

"It was just something that happened this morning, it wasn't planned," I say, reaching out and turning the video off. "Who recorded it?"

He shrugs. "The guy from the coffee cart put it on the Buskers of New York page, tagged the park or something, I guess. It's popping up on local feeds, Robin saw it. This could go viral." He clutches my arm. "You'll be on *Oprah* by morning."

I roll my eyes and sigh.

"People want to know who this crazy talented gal is, Iris, and where they can see more of her."

I shake my head. "They can't."

"I mean, obviously the place they can see more of her is the Very Tasty Noodle House, NYC's newest music venue," he says, pointing downstairs with a look of "Yes, girl" on his face that I need to dispel asap.

"Absolutely not, Bob. Not here nor out there again." I gesture toward the window and the park beyond. "It was strictly a one-off."

He flops back against the sofa. "How did I know you were going to say that?"

"Because you know me better than anyone else in this city, and probably the entire world?"

"Maybe," he says, sighing. "Or at least I thought I did, until Robin sent me this and I was like, okay, hold my drink, I need to go home right now because Mariah's living in my building. I mean, I missed dessert for this."

I reach out and pat his hand. "And I don't even have gelato to give you."

"It's genuinely like you hate me right now," he says.

"You know I love you," I say.

"Will you sing to me?"

I can't give him my recipe, but I guess I can sing. "What do you want to hear?"

He leans against me, his head on my shoulder. "Surprise me."

I squeeze his hand and, after a moment's deliberation, I quietly sing "Golden Slumbers," because it was my mother's lullaby of choice when I was a small child in her arms. I feel Bobby's head grow heavy, and when I'm done I pull the blanket over us and close my eyes too.

11.

Dear Iris,
I'm sorry I was an idiot, please come back. We miss you,
*   I miss you.*

G x

THE TEXT COMES IN AS I BRUSH MY TEETH BEFORE BED.
I read it at least twenty times. "Dear Iris"—it's like an email
opener, isn't it? It's so like Gio to be formal. Most of my texts
are from Bobby or Robin, and they just launch straight in.
"Dear Iris" suggests someone who doesn't text often. As for
everything else he said, I'm moved by the simplicity, by the
apology without any attempt at mitigation. And "We miss
you, I miss you." I read it aloud, knowing what he means
because I feel the same. I miss them in general, the place,
Sophia, the gelato hunt . . . spending a few hours there each
morning fast became the highlight of my day. And then
there's Gio himself, an immovable rock steeped in tradition
and family, entrenched in that place as securely as those industrial machines in the back kitchen. It sometimes feels as if
he's lost touch with who he is among all that tradition, but
then when it's been just the two of us, I've glimpsed sparks of

the man beneath. I've been so wrapped up in being guarded about the recipe that these small unacknowledged moments have accumulated into a neglected pile.

Objectively, of course, I've acknowledged he's hot—he just is—but not in a boy-band way. He's coming on forty and exudes this air of, I don't know, being a man who knows stuff. He looks as if he could build me a bookshelf and mend his own car with those good hands of his, and is the sort of person you need around in a crisis. That doesn't really touch the sides of what I mean. It's the small things. The green-glass shards in his amber-brown eyes I've noticed sometimes when he looks directly at me, the edge of an unseen tattoo visible when his white shirtsleeves are folded back in the kitchens. It's the strength of character and grit that runs through him like a river, a seam of solid gold alongside the steel. There's vulnerability when he speaks of the people he loves, the woman he lost, the daughter he worries for. He's a complicated man embedded in a complicated life, and I'd be lying if I said I haven't missed all of those things about him in recent days. I've kept my life purposefully small here in New York, but that seemingly throwaway act of going to the festival with Bobby has opened the doors to new possibilities. My world is opening up. I'm singing Joan Jett songs to strangers, for God's sake, and I kind of love the new me. It's a fragile balance—I want to go back to Belotti's because I miss them, I miss him, but I don't want to feel as if the secrets I need to keep make me a bad person. I stare at myself in the bathroom mirror, toothbrush in hand, and I decide to text him back. It's a risk worth taking, and I promise the girl in the mirror that I'll watch her back.

———

GIO IS ALONE IN Belotti's when I push the door open. He turns at the sound of the bell and I pause, half in and half out, as nervous as the first day I came here. He lays his cloth down on the counter and is still too, and we take each other in for a moment before a slow smile lifts one corner of his mouth.

"You came back," he says, reminiscent again of that morning a few weeks ago.

"I couldn't leave my machine here," I say, but soften it with a smile of my own so he knows I'm joking.

He half laughs and looks down. "I thought as much. Coffee?"

It's really cold out this morning, the tip of my nose and my hands chilled from the short walk. "Yes, please," I say, taking off my coat and scarf. "A bucket."

He turns away and busies himself at the machine, and when he turns back he places a mug down in front of me.

"Not quite a bucket," he says.

Customers here all get the same small white cup and saucer, and I have too, up to now. This morning I have a forest-green mug, and when I reach for it I see it has my name on it in gold lettering.

"Oh," I say, unexpectedly touched. Gio and Sophia have the same ones—I've seen a rack of family mugs at the back of the kitchen. "I love it."

He looks pleased, and then puts his cloth over his shoulder with a small shrug. "I was ordering new ones, so."

And now I'm the one looking at the floor and feeling like a kid at the school disco. Our small but significant text exchange seems to have upset the balance between us. I think it's down to me to try to right it.

"I'm sorry," he says, rushed. "I was out of line last week."

Okay, maybe not down to me. I expected Gio to avoid talking about it, but here we are.

"It's okay," I say, neutral. "I didn't intend to overstep the mark with Bella."

He sighs and shakes his head, polishing the already spotless counter. "You didn't, Iris, you really didn't. It caught me off guard, that's all, and reminded me of what she's lost," he says, then brightens. "She passed her piano test, by the way."

"She did? I'm really glad," I say, biting the inside of my lip as I think about what he said just now. "Was her mum musical?"

His hands still. "Penny? No," he laughs. "Brilliant at so many things, but totally tone deaf."

I fold my hands around my mug and draw it in toward myself. "Bella's full of talent," I say. "Where does she get it from?"

"The Belottis are a giant bunch of show-offs," he says. "My sisters all play instruments and sing."

"And you?"

He frowns. "Guitar for a while as a moody teenager," he says. "Nothing these days."

I suddenly wonder if he's seen that video doing the rounds of me singing in the park, and change the subject, embarrassed.

"So, the gelato," I say. "How's it going?"

"I've been trying to get the hang of your machine," he says. His accompanying hand motions suggest it's about the size of a thimble rather than capable of turning out a perfectly respectable three pints.

"And?"

"I think it likes you better," he says.

I mentally high-five my good old gelato maker. "There's a knack to it."

The bell over the door rings.

"Oh my God, it's freezing this morning!" Sophia flings herself inside the warm gelateria and lights up when she spots me at the counter. I find myself hugged, her cheek cold against my warm one. "I'm hanging on to you to steal your warmth," she says, lingering.

"Maybe you could wear a coat?" Gio says what I was thinking.

She rolls her eyes. "Yeah, okay, *Dad*."

"Don't you start, one grouchy teenager is enough for anyone," he says, chucking Sophia's work apron at her before turning into the kitchens.

She pulls a face behind his retreating back and then leans into me.

"I saw the video of you singing," she stage whispers, her eyes dancing. "I was like 'I know her!' And no one believed me."

I don't know why I don't want Gio to see it, but I don't. "Oh God, Sophia, can we not talk about it?" I say, equally quiet. "It was just something that happened in the moment, I didn't know anyone filmed it."

"That's what makes it so cool," she says, clutching my arm. "It's obvious you didn't go there to sing, and then you shut the place down." She mimes dropping the mike.

"Don't show Gio?" I ask, not even sure why I don't want him to see it.

She narrows her eyes and then shrugs. "Okay, I won't. But don't be surprised if someone else does."

By someone else I suppose she means Bella. I can only cross my fingers and hope that a thirty-odd-year-old British woman randomly singing eighties power hits in the park will be of little interest to her.

Gio sticks his head around the kitchen door, looking for me. "Coming?"

I shoot Sophia a quick "thank you" as I pick up my personalized mug and follow him through.

I NUDGE GIO CLOSER to the recipe than I've dared to yet, even though the demand for gelato is at its lowest now the cold weather is coming in earnest. It's unseasonably chilly in New York this week, the first frost of the season evident on the sidewalk when I left the building this morning. All the same, I can't legitimize stringing things out too much: there are December weddings and corporate bookings over the holiday period that will be jeopardized if they can't get back into production.

We're standing around the corner of the wooden workbench, the gelato in front of us as he passes me one of two spoons.

"I've got a good feeling about this one," he says.

I swallow. "You try first."

"I'm worried I've forgotten exactly how it tastes," he says quietly, staring at the gelato in front of him.

"You'll know when it's right." I set my expression to steel. "You just will."

He nods and then tests it, not meeting my eye. He goes in a second time and then lays his spoon down carefully beside the dish.

"It's closer than most. It might even be our best yet, but it's not exactly right."

We've gotten into the habit of giving each new batch a score, recording the recipe in a blue leather journal Gio keeps in one of the drawers that line the back wall. I flick back through the pages.

"Our highest score up to now is seven point eight," I say, chewing the end of my pen. "What do you think for this one?"

He picks up his spoon and swirls it in the gelato. "Color and consistency excellent. Taste is good." He stops and tastes again and is about to give his verdict when the kitchen door opens.

"Mamma."

He breaks into a smile that changes his entire posture, his arms outstretched and welcoming.

"Come, come," he says, beckoning her toward us as she hesitates in the doorway. "Iris, this is my mamma, Maria."

I get to my feet, nervous out of nowhere. Maria is nothing short of fabulous, an older, curvier version of Sophia with a single thick grey streak through her otherwise raven-wing waves. She smells of expensive perfume counters and jewels glitter on her fingers and in her ears. Put together, I guess you'd say, but the hug she gives me is a bone crusher and the hand on my cheek unexpectedly welcoming. Fundamentally, to me, Maria married the man my mother thought might have been the love of her life, but I'm instantly drawn in by her aura and her presence.

"I've heard about you, Iris," she says as she sets me at arm's length, her soft accent a perfect match with her appearance.

"I've heard about you too," I say, smiling. "These guys talk about you and Santo all the time, it's so nice to meet you."

She looks at Gio. "They're moving him," she says. "To the rehabilitation center."

He frowns. "Is that a good thing?"

Maria nods slowly, resting on the stool beside me. "It's a step toward coming home," she says. "They can work harder on his mobility there, it's more specialized."

"And his memory?" Gio says.

Maria shrugs and shakes her head. "I don't know, Gio. They don't know either."

Gio sighs, and they share a look full of worry and uncertainty.

"Would you like to try our latest gelato attempt?" I nod toward the dish in front of us, because maybe a slight change of mood will help lift their spirits.

She nods and Gio passes her a spoon. I watch him watch her, his breath caught as she tests it.

We both know it isn't exactly right, but even so, Maria's verdict feels important.

She takes her time, studying it on the spoon and in her mouth before placing her spoon down and looking at Gio and then me.

"You are both trying so hard," she says, squeezing my hand. "Santo appreciates it, and I do. This is excellent gelato, but it's not Belotti's gelato."

"I know," Gio says, resigned. He looks at me. "Let's give it eight point one."

I scribble the score beside the recipe and close the notebook.

"I should go," I say. "Leave you guys to it."

Maria looks at Gio. "Have you asked Iris to Ognissanti?"

"I —" He breaks off and looks away, a flush crossing his cheeks.

"Oh for pity's sake, Gio." She flicks a dismissive hand toward him. "Iris, I'm having a family dinner on Sunday evening, please come."

It's my turn to falter, and I look at Gio for guidance. His face is impossible to read, which, frankly, is no help. I don't want to say yes and upset the fragile balance between us again, but Maria is like a force field all of her own and I feel compelled to accept her invitation. But, then . . . is it disloyal to my mother to feel so dazzled by this woman? I don't know if they ever met; instinct tells me not. I hold Gio's gaze and try to telegraph a silent message: *Help me out here, I need a steer.*

"Mamma's right, you should come to the dinner," he says finally. "I know Bella would like to see you again."

"Well, in that case, how could I say no?"

I notice how he doesn't include himself and wonder if he's feeling press-ganged into this. If Maria notices the omission she lets it slide as she claps her hands, the gold bangles around her wrists making music as she pulls me in close again.

"She's a hugger," Gio says, shaking his head as he catches my eye over her shoulder. It's clear from his face that he loves her and she drives him nuts. I hug her back, and it catches me unaware how good it feels to be gathered into her maternal embrace. I think of my mum, so different from Maria, yet similarly free with her emotions and always ready to throw her arms around someone and make everyone feel special: the girl in the cinema who upgraded our seats to the fancy recliners for a one-night-only showing of *Pretty Woman* the year before she died; the guy in the local market who gave me a huge burnished-sunshine peach from his stall for free, when I can't have been more than five or six; a policeman in Trafalgar Square, working while others danced and wheeled around him one crisp and clear New Year's Eve. I can almost smell her perfume as the memories crowd around me, so I say my goodbyes and get myself out on to the street, glad of the cold wind in my face to blow the memories back into their safe place. It's so difficult, this act of balancing my past with my now, trying to do a good thing alongside trying to feel like a good person. I daren't think about my mother too much while I'm at Belotti's, it brings the past too close to the surface. I push my head down against the crisp, cold wind and power walk home, anxious for some time alone.

12.

SUNDAY FINDS ME SICKLY NERVOUS. IT'S HALLOWEEN
out there for most people across New York tonight, but I can't
say I'm sad to be doing something that doesn't involve ghosts
and ghouls. I never liked Halloween much back in the UK,
possibly because it's one of those things that only really looks
fun with old friends and good neighbors. Tonight will be all
about Ognissanti instead, which I've googled in an attempt
not to appear totally ignorant. I now know it's an Italian na-
tional holiday where families get together and feast, and
that—thankfully—I don't need to buy a witch's hat to attend.

Maria and Santo live in Brooklyn Heights, which—
although it's only a few miles as the crow flies—is across
Brooklyn Bridge, and means leaving Manhattan Island. I
haven't done that more than a handful of times since arriving
in the United States, which would probably seem extraordi-
nary to some but has been right for me up to now. Gio offered
to call round for me this evening—he and Bella live in the
condo above the gelateria and it wouldn't be out of their
way—but as I climb into the Lyft I'm glad I insisted on making
my own way. Now it won't be strange when I travel back alone.

I wasn't sure what to wear tonight. My favorite washed-out jeans felt too casual, but my only decent black going-out dress felt too short and too formal. I ended up scouring local stores and found a green velvet blouse that is probably too trendy for me, but I like it anyway. Paired with skinny black jeans and heels, I hope it suggests "I've kept it low-key but made an effort," and that the huge bunch of flowers in my arms say "Thanks for asking me over."

I'm distracted by the city at night as we cross the Brooklyn Bridge. I'm a Londoner at heart but, even so, the scale and grandeur of the skyline here takes my breath, especially tonight as I travel across the illuminated bridge spanning the East River. I'm dazzled, nerves thrown out in favor of drinking it all in, the only sound in the van that of the female driver chatting quietly to someone in her earpiece. The nerves kick back in with a jolt as soon as the cab comes to a stop halfway along a street of elegant brownstones, each accessed by a flight of stone steps edged with black wrought-iron balustrades. Santo and Maria's has small pots on each step filled with winter flowers, and at the top grand wooden double doors in an ornate stone surround. It's stunning. Daunting, actually. So daunting I almost lose my nerve, but then one of the doors flings open and Sophia is pulling me inside.

"I saw you from the window," she says, hanging my coat on the stand in the wood-paneled hallway. "You okay?"

"Are you sure I'm not gatecrashing a family thing?" I say, chewing the inside of my lip as I take in the polished parquet, sweeping staircase and low chandelier.

"Mamma's excited to have you here, she wants to impress you with her cooking," she says, laughing as she points out the guest bathroom before leading me into the living room. I'm overawed by the old-school opulence: high ceilings, grand framed mirrors, and a magnificent, welcoming carved fireplace. Deep sofas face each other either side of a low coffee table, pools of lamplight bathing the scene in warmth and comfort. For all of that, it's not at all austere, and the family filling the space are not standing, or indeed sitting, on ceremony. The sofas are filled with Belotti sisters, and kids dash up to us, all of them come to have a look at the new person in their midst.

"You've met most of us," Sophia says, taking the flowers from me as her sisters jump up to hug me. It's a lot: so many people and so many hugs, too many kids' and partners' names being tossed out to have a hope of remembering any of them.

"Iris."

Maria appears in a cloud of expensive scent and subtle sophistication—it strikes me that her house reflects her style perfectly.

"The flowers are so pretty, thank you," she says, pressing a kiss against my cheek. "Gio is on the way, he called to say they're stuck in traffic." She looks down as a crawling child pulls himself up on her leg and she bends to lift the baby into her arms. "What is it, Leo? You want to say hello to Iris too?"

The child is frankly adorable, round-limbed and pink-cheeked, and I'm thrown completely off guard when he holds his arms out to me.

"He's a total ladies' man," Maria says, passing him over without a second thought. I feel a moment of pure panic—I don't have any practice with small children. No nieces or nephews, no friends asking me to be a godparent or babysit. I do my best to look as if I know what I'm doing with Leo, balancing him on my hip as Maria did, my arms around his small, robust body as he leans back to get a good look at me. I smile when he grins, showing me the two milk teeth that have just broken through his bottom gum. I'm caught unaware by the unexpected pleasure holding this child brings me, as if an age-old instinct awakens at the weight of an infant in my arms. I laugh as Leo clutches a great handful of my hair, and when I look up, Gio is leaning against the door frame watching me. He holds my gaze until I look away, flustered, and Bella appears behind him and bounces over to me, taking the baby as she showers him with kisses and shoots me a small smile.

"I hear you aced your piano test," I say.

"Concert pianist in the making," Maria says, her arm around her granddaughter's shoulders.

"Iris helped me," Bella says, bending to place the wriggling baby down. He shoots off toward the sofas on all fours with impressive speed, and a small, shaggy dog ambles up behind him. No one bats an eyelid as the dog sniffs the baby's foot, at which Leo scoots himself around until he's nose to nose with the pup.

"Bruno, poor old boy," Maria murmurs, as one of Gio's sisters leans over the arm of the sofa to fuss the dog's ears before scooping Leo up.

I stand among the Belottis as they chat and laugh and move around me, three loving generations, and I feel . . . I don't know, warmed? I always tend to feel a bit like a kid standing outside with my face pressed to the window among other people's families. My mother made sure my childhood was busy and I knew I was loved, but there was no escaping the fact that it was just the two of us. Losing anyone is devastating, but there must be some comfort to be drawn from shared memories and experiences with other people. I don't have that. No one else remembers my childhood, and if and when anything happens to me, no one will be able to share my mother's stories.

"Drink?" Gio says, coming to stand beside me.

I realize that this is the first time I've seen him out of the black-and-whites he always wears at the gelateria. His dark shirt is unbuttoned at the neck, and there's a grown-up spice to his cologne that makes me think of smoky woodland walks and late-night bourbon. I glance at other people's glasses, anxious to fit in.

"Wine would be good?" I say.

Before he can move, Sophia arrives at my other side and hands me a glass of red.

"Mamma has us well trained. You'll never be here more than five minutes without a drink in your hand," she says.

"Just wait until you leave," Gio says. "She'll insist you take half the contents of her fridge with you."

Maria claps her hands on the other side of the room, a glitter of jewels and a clatter of bangles.

"Now that everyone has arrived, let's eat!" she says, and her family get to their feet and follow her into the dining room. Gio smiles and places a light hand on the small of my back.

"After you."

I find myself seated between Gio and Sophia around a long, beautifully set table, and although it looks formal, the people around it make it anything but. Gio's sisters are a force to be reckoned with when they're together, each amplifying the other, and they all take delight in winding Gio up. You'd never guess he wasn't their biological brother. Partners and children make the numbers up to sixteen, plus me—I know because I do a discreet head count. I can't even fathom what it must be like to be a Belotti, to spend your good times and your bad ones inside a family like this. Is it claustrophobic? The noise around the table never lulls, multiple conversations overlaid with old family jokes and traditions, laughter and shouting from the kids. Maria often slips into fast Italian, the others too, occasionally. It's passionate and lyrical to my ear, their speech punctuated with hand gestures, whole arm gestures. They speak with their bodies as much as their tongues, Gio included—he's more animated tonight than I've ever seen. It's life, but not as I know it. I wonder what it was like around this table ten years ago, and twenty years ago, how the faces and fashions have matured but the people have stayed the same. I should think the room has stayed the same too: leather-spined books filling the cabinets that line one wall; another fireplace, this time filled with fresh flowers. A slender chandelier hangs over the length of the table, delicate glass droppers that bounce light around the walls. Everything about the room looks as if it's been this way forever, an unchanging backdrop for the Belottis to love, change, and grow in. And now Santo is absent from this tableau, a place still set for him at the far end, a glass filled for him, Gio's toast for his speedy return to health the most poignant part of the evening. Will I ever get to meet him, I wonder? I don't know if that's a good idea. Thinking of him reminds me that my place at this table is temporary, an unwelcome thought I press to the back of my mind tonight.

Maria's food is a feast, traditional dishes she tells me she learned from her mother back in Naples. She weaves stories of life in the shadow of Vesuvius with the flair of a natural storyteller, evoking the vibrancy and colors of the old city, the winding cobbled streets, the tall, golden stone townhouse she grew up in as the youngest of seven. She speaks to me in the language of food, of spices and herbs, of sweet pastries and bitter coffee, aware I'm sure that she has led me to safe culinary ground where I'm more comfortable.

"Limoncello time, I think," Francesca announces, standing up. Gio's eldest sister is very like her mother in both looks and style, glamorous and always on the edge of smiling. She produces a glass-stoppered bottle of spirits and holds it aloft. "Pascal made it this year, so apologies now for your headaches in the morning."

Everyone groans and her French husband shrugs benignly beside her and raises his wineglass, Leo on his lap. Maria shoos everyone back through to the living room, and I find myself beside Gio on the deep sofa in front of the fire. I have that three-glasses-in wine buzz and quietly decide to go light on the limoncello.

"Bruno," Gio says, plucking the small dog up on to his lap. He's some kind of terrier, I think, a small, scruffy furball with kind eyes who turns himself around a couple of times and then settles into a relieved ball on Gio's lap.

"He's fourteen," Gio says. "Missing Papa like crazy."

"I always wanted a dog," I say, giving Bruno's ears a scratch.

"Did you ever have one?"

I shake my head. "It was never the right time." I don't

add that our lives were always too transitory and finances too unreliable to add a third mouth that needed feeding to our tribe.

Francesca comes through balancing a tray of crystal shot glasses and places it carefully on the coffee table. She hands me one first, as their guest, and I sniff it as everyone else leans in and grabs a glass. Gio shoots Bella a warning glance when she shows interest and she rolls her eyes before sliding back into her spot on the floor by the fire. I pretend not to notice when Maria allows her granddaughter a sip from her own glass, and I'm pretty sure Gio turns the same blind eye.

"*Cazzo,*" Viola murmurs, spluttering on her drink.

"Viola!" Maria frowns.

I glance at Gio for clarification. "It means fuck," he says with a laugh.

"Gio!" Maria says.

"Sorry, it's just so strong," Viola says, going in for more even though her eyes are watering.

I can only agree—the limoncello is rocket fuel.

Sophia is curled into a deep-green leather button-back armchair, her feet tucked beneath her bum. "What do you think, Iris?"

I feel as if someone just turned a spotlight on me as all eyes swivel my way. "It's, umm . . ." I gesture toward my throat—"like drinking lemon fire."

They fall around laughing, and Pascal shrugs again, as if he cannot be held responsible for his own creation.

"You know what would be the perfect thing to show Iris right now, Mamma?" Sophia throws a subtle wink at Bella. "Some really embarrassing photos of Gio as a kid. You know, the ones of him wearing Fran's pink overalls after he peed himself at the park?"

"Gio was such a beautiful child," Maria says, ignoring the context. "You all were. Bella, pass me the album."

I don't miss the look of pure sibling insta-hate Gio shoots across the room at Sophia, or the absolute couldn't-care-less insta-joy on her face in return.

Maria balances the thick old photo album on her knees and opens it, one hand on her heart as she flicks through the first few pages. After a moment she passes it across to Gio, her emotions close to the surface.

"Here, you can show Iris."

The album is open on a spread of old birthday photographs: Gio's seventh birthday, going off the cake and the badge pinned to his Garfield T-shirt. It looks like countless other family parties, dated in the eighties by the clothes and hairstyles. Bella perches on the arm of the sofa to peer over her dad's shoulder.

"You looked like a girl," she says, laughing at Gio's curls.

"I couldn't bring myself to cut it," Maria says.

"Remember when you let me put it in pigtails?" Francesca says.

"I didn't let you, I lost a bet," Gio corrects her. "You know I've always been a man of my word."

He turns the pages: family days out at Coney Island, Christmas trees in the corner of this very room, countless pictures of the kids behind the counter in the gelateria, some of them too small to see over it. This is the first time I've seen any other photographs of Santo besides my mother's single shot. To me, he has forever been that cool guy frozen in the eighties, but of course he wasn't always. Here I see how his life played out. The lines that bracket his mouth, the receding hairline, and the family he built.

Gio turns the page again and the strangest of sensations slides over my bones, and it's nothing to do with the wine or the limoncello.

"That's my father, Felipe," Gio says, touching a black-and-white photo. "With Papa."

Felipe is standing with his arm slung over Santo's shoulders, both of them holding half-full pint glasses and laughing into the lens. Felipe has an electric guitar hung over his tall skinny body, and the sweaty sheen of someone who has been under the glare of stage lights.

Several small explosions happen in my head at once. I've seen Gio's biological father in photos before. He was in my mother's band. But it's not only that. The photo looks as if it was taken late at night in a club, and in the background, her face turned away from the camera, is my mother.

"Was he in a band?" I manage. I'm glad everyone has had a few drinks, because I'm struggling to process this and aware my voice sounds strained. Pieces begin to slot into place in my head as I sit there. This is how my mother is connected to the Belottis. This is how she met Santo.

"He was always in some band or other," Gio says. "Still is."

"He never really grew up," Maria says. There's no edge to her voice; it's clear she doesn't in any way resent Gio's presence as the son she'd never have otherwise had.

I'm suddenly sickly warm from the fire and over-full of food and wine, and just too damn blindsided to sit here for even a second longer.

"I need to nip to the bathroom," I say, getting unsteadily to my feet.

"Off the hall," Sophia reminds me.

I wait until I'm in the bathroom and I've locked the door, then sit down heavily on the closed loo and drop my head in my hands. I'm shaking. It was such a shock to see my mum in the Belotti family album, thank goodness her face was turned away—our likeness was always the first thing commented on by strangers as I grew up.

I wish I hadn't had that limoncello, I can't think straight. My mother barely told me anything about Santo, certainly not that his brother was the guitarist in her band. God. She was in their album. My mother is in Gio's family album. I feel like an imposter, a cuckoo in the nest, and I want to go home. I should never have agreed to come here. I stay in the loo as long as I dare, running myself through the breathing exercises I've used often since I left Adam, calming down, getting a grip so I don't go out there and blow it. If it wasn't terribly rude I'd grab my coat and let myself out without facing them all again, but because that would look ridiculous, I splash some cool water on my face and meet my own eyes in the mirror. My mother's blue eyes. *Oh Mum. I miss you so much, but you've got me into a right bloody mess here.* Straightening my shoulders, I head back into the living room.

Games have been fetched in my absence; Bella is setting up Monopoly and Pascal has cards.

I hesitate for a second, feeling like an outsider, and then Gio glances over and catches my eye.

"I think I'm going to call it a night," I say, one foot tucked awkwardly behind my other ankle. "I've had a migraine threatening all day, I should probably get home to bed."

It sounds stupid as I say it, and I'm certain they all know I'm lying.

"But I was going to let you be the top hat," Bella says, holding the small silver playing piece on her outstretched palm.

"She always insists on being the top hat," Gio tells me. "That's quite something."

I smile back. "I was always the boot."

Gio throws his hands out. "That's my piece."

"What can I say? We can never play Monopoly," I say, pulling my phone from the back pocket of my jeans. "I'm really sorry, Bella. Another time, I promise."

Gio gets to his feet. "Come on, Bells, we'll leave too—we're going the same way, we can give Iris a ride."

I see Bella's face fall and feel terrible.

"Let Bella stay over," Sophia interjects, lining up the banker's money on the table. "It's about time I beat her at this. Plus, if you go, I get to be the boot."

Bella sits back down at the table and pushes the silver boot toward Sophia, then looks up again at Gio as an afterthought.

"Is that okay, Dad? Please?"

He looks at her, frowning, as if he's unsure what to do.

"You stay too," I say quickly. "I'm fine going on my own. I'll just call a Lyft, it'll be here in a jiffy."

Maria laughs, resting her hands on Bella's shoulders. "In a jiffy! I like that. Now, Gio, you see Iris safely home, and I'll look forward to making pancakes for this one in the morning."

Bella leans back against her grandmother. "With cherries?"

Gio looks at me and shrugs. "I guess that's sorted, then," he says. "I'll grab our coats."

13.

THERE'S AN INTIMACY TO THE BACK OF A CAB LATE AT night, especially with alcohol warming our blood and the ballet of city lights blurring around us. Our mornings at Belotti's, we have assigned roles. Here we are free of such constraints, we're two people who have studiously ignored the spark between us in favor of getting on with the job at hand. I'm not even sure what that spark is. Gio draws out emotion in me, for sure. Frustrated rage on our first meeting in the bookstore, as it happened, but spending time with him at the gelateria has been like taking a deckchair outside and sitting in the sun. I've basked in his company. I like him so much. He laughed at something I said around the dinner table earlier and, honestly, it was as if he'd stuck a gold star on my chest. And now we're thigh to thigh in the darkness in this cab, and I don't know what the hell to say. Small talk has always been my nemesis.

"Thank you for coming tonight," he says, saving me from saying something stupid. "I was worried about how it would be without Papa at the table, and you being there helped take everyone's mind off of it."

I wish I could comment on how crazy it is to realize his

biological father and my mother were in the same band so we could marvel at the small world, but of course the truth is that it's no coincidence. I've engineered this in a roundabout way. Not that I ever intended to become as involved with the Belottis as I have.

"I enjoyed it a lot, your family are great," I say.

He glances away out of the window. "I'm sorry if it seems like they're reading too much into our friendship."

"Are they?"

He passes his hand over his jaw. "There just hasn't been anyone since Penny, you know?"

"No one at all?" I say, thinking of the glamorous, sharp-eyed woman in the gelateria across the street from Belotti's.

Gio shakes his head. "A couple of awkward lunches, a movie date. Nothing that ever mattered, because I didn't want to open the door to all those feelings again. So now that they see us spending time together, they are jumping to all kinds of crazy conclusions."

"Crazy," I say, feeling as if it isn't *that* crazy because I feel something between us that I can't put a name to. I'm wondering if I'm brave enough to put my hand on his arm when the driver catches Gio's eye in the mirror.

"Sorry, guys," he huffs. "Emergency construction this end of Chrystie tonight, burst pipe. I can go round but it's gonna take a while."

"We could walk from here?" I say.

"You sure?" Gio looks at me, checking if I'm just being polite on this cold Halloween evening.

The driver looks as if that's exactly what he hoped we'd

say, already slowing at the curb to total the fare and tick the job off on his cell.

IT'S SEE-YOUR-BREATH COLD WHEN we clamber out on the street, frost glittering on the sidewalk.

"Now I wish I had my Converse," I say, putting a steadying hand out as my heel slips.

Gio catches it and pulls me into his side, tucking my arm through his. "Here, hang on to me."

I cannot put into words how good it feels, just walking arm in arm at midnight with Gio Belotti.

"Will you always stay in New York?"

"Yes," he says, no hesitation. "As long as Bella is here for sure, but Belotti's is my life. Santo and Maria need me here."

"Do you mind that? The obligation, I mean?"

"I owe them everything," he says. "They gave me a home and their love—I lucked out when I was left with them. I'll never take that for granted, you know?"

"I get that," I say.

"And then after Penny . . . well, they held me and Bella together."

I'm glad he had the love of his family around him at the worst time of his life. My life has been so very different from his. My mother was my only person. I felt like a fragile dandelion when I lost her, as if all the pieces of me had been caught up on a cold wind and blown in every direction. Adam snatched those fragments from the air and shoved them in his pockets, crushing them in his palms, making them small. No. I won't let those memories in tonight, they have no place here. I've traveled too far and tried too hard to let him affect me anymore.

I slide on a frozen puddle and Gio catches me, his arm around my waist as he stops me from falling in a heap.

"God, I'm like Bambi," I mutter, almost going again.

"I can hoist you over my shoulder, if you like."

"I doubt it." I laugh. "I'm sturdier than I look."

"You did pack a hell of a lot of food away tonight," he says.

"Rude," I gasp and thump his arm. "I was just being polite to Maria."

He laughs, shrugs. "Sorry. I guess I'm rusty talking to women."

"Free tip—don't tell them they eat too much," I say, mock-offended.

"What should I say, then?"

"Are you asking me how to flirt?"

"I haven't flirted in twenty years," he says, then huffs. "God, that makes me sound old."

I side-eye him. "You're way too young to say stuff like that."

He shoots me a look. "That's flirting, right?"

"Just reminding you how it's done." I laugh softly as I do my best to stay on my feet.

"Got it," he says, smiling into the collar of his jacket. "Bella showed me the video of you singing, you know."

"Oh," I say, glad my cheeks are already pink from the cold. Aside from Sophia, I thought I'd gotten away with the rest of the Belottis not seeing that clip.

"She just needed someone to step in and I was there."

"You surprised me. It's like you're a different person when you sing."

"People used to say that about my mum," I say, remembering the way people sat up straighter in their seats whenever she took the mic.

"Are you a lot like her?"

"In some ways," I say, picturing us as bookends on the sofa watching *Sleepless in Seattle,* reaching over to pass the popcorn between us. "In looks, yes, and I sound a lot like her when I sing, but she was more . . . more effervescent, I guess? Always the first one on the dance floor, a life-and-soul kind of person, someone people naturally gravitated toward."

"And you don't see yourself that way?"

I sidestep a frozen puddle. "There's only room for one magpie in the family," I say, because I don't want to say that maybe I was more like that once, before life pressed me down.

"I don't know, my family is full of them," he says. "I see your shine, Iris. I mean, look at me—the guy who has locked himself behind the counter at the gelateria, according to my sisters, but here I am walking you home like a nervous teenager."

"I make you nervous, Belotti?"

"Stop fishing for compliments or you might just get one, and then where will we be?"

"So awkward," I say.

"Exactly."

By my reckoning, everyone gets a handful of movie-worthy moments in their lives. Some people would probably pick out their wedding day or the birth of their child for their showreel, but for most of us it's the unexpected moments life occasionally gifts our way that make for the best memories. This is one of my movie moments. To anyone looking at us, they'd see a man and a woman pressed together from shoulder to hip, her unsteady on her heels, his arm around her waist. The silver threads in her scarlet scarf catch the light of the streetlamps as they weave their way slowly along the frosted sidewalk, their conversation punctuated by hushed laughter whenever she slips and he stops her from falling. They look like lovers.

My feet slow as we approach the familiar sight of the noodle house. I've left a lamp on for myself upstairs, and there's a string of orange pumpkin lights up at Bobby and Robin's.

"This is me," I say. "Thanks for not letting me break any bones."

"It's the bare minimum you can expect from a date, right?" he says.

"To not end up in hospital." I nod. "Is that what this was, then? A date?"

He glances away and then back at me. "It didn't start out that way, but it feels kind of like it right this minute."

"Good flirting," I murmur, and he laughs.

"So if this *is* a date, what happens next?"

"I don't know, Gio," I say. And I honestly don't. There has been a shift between us tonight, but the road ahead is littered with obstacles he isn't aware of coming in the other direction. But I see them and, because I do, I know that the more involved we become the more I'm likely to hurt him and myself in the process.

"It's been a long night," I say quietly. "I should probably head inside."

I see his throat move as he swallows hard. "Okay." He reaches out and cups my jaw for a moment, uncertainty filling his dark eyes. "Goodnight, Iris."

I smile against the warmth of his palm. "Goodnight."

He holds my gaze and then nods and turns away, taking several paces before he turns and strides back to me, making my stomach drop with anticipation. He holds my face between his hands and lowers his head to mine, his breath warm in my mouth, his lips trembling when we touch. His whole body is tense, his shoulders raised, his eyes pressed tight closed. I wish I could tell him that I know what this means to him, the courage he's had to summon, the complicated emotions he's battling. I'm knocked sideways by the sudden intensity of him, by the deep longing for more it awakens in me as I pull him in closer. It's the swoon-worthy climax of our showreel moment, this beautiful, achingly sexy kiss, slow and electric, full of pure, vulnerable kiss-me-forever magic. My fingers curl into the neck of his winter jacket when his tongue brushes mine, his pulse racing beneath my knuckles as his hand slips into my hair, cradling my head. Nothing else and no one else matters as we stand here pressed together. I don't feel the weight of the secrets I keep, or the mistrust and fear that lives in my darkest corners. This is the best first kiss of my life. Of anyone's life.

"Was that flirting?" he whispers, his laugh shaky.

"World class," I breathe against his lips.

He rests his forehead against mine.

"Still got it," he says, and pulls me inside his jacket as he presses his mouth against my hair.

"Hot," I say, because it's taking everything I have not to drag him up the fire escape and ask him into my bed.

"I'll see you in the morning?" He catches my bottom lip with his teeth, laying his hand flat and hot against the small of my back.

"Yes." I turn my face into his neck, enjoying the rub of his thumb over my spine. He smells of the crisp night air and warmer, sultrier places, and I wonder how it would be to be his lover, to share his bed, his body, his life. It's such a seductive thought. How I wish I could send all those oncoming obstacles down a different road and leave us a free run at this, because I know there's a world out there where he and I could make each other happy. I sigh and press my lips to the pulse at the base of his throat, human and vital, primal and raw. If this can't be forever, I'm greedily taking every second of now. I don't know how long we stand locked together like this, neither of us ready to step away.

"Iris, do you have a cat?"

I open my eyes, startled. "Sort of. Why?"

"It's behind you and it's giving me the stink eye."

I half laugh and look over my shoulder at Smirnoff, who is sitting on the step outside my narrow red front door staring at us. If he had a watch and the ability to tap it, he would.

"I think he wants his dinner," I say.

Gio steps away from me, and the cold night air settles around me like ice. It takes Herculean willpower not to step back into his body heat.

"Go inside," he says. "So I know you're safe."

"I don't think anything's going to happen to me between here and there," I say, nodding toward the doorstep.

"Who knows in those heels," he says.

"They are lethal," I say, taking exaggerated care as I pick

my way over to stand beside Smirnoff. He glances up at me with disinterest.

"Absolutely," Gio says, his gaze locked on mine. It feels knife-edge between us: if he asked to come inside I'd say yes; if I suggested coffee he'd follow me upstairs. But I don't, and he doesn't. He turns and walks away, and this time he doesn't change his mind to come back and kiss me.

14.

THERE'S A NOTE PINNED TO MY DOOR WHEN I GO upstairs.

Come up, we just saw you outside KISSING!
We totally weren't watching out for you, before you ask,
I just thought I heard the cat. Coffee on, full debrief
required pronto!

All I really want to do is go inside my own apartment and crawl into bed, I need to process tonight step-by-step. There's no fighting it, though—if I don't go up, they'll come down, so we may as well debrief in luxury and spare Robin the horror of my lumpy couch. He's adorable but from wealthy stock—he gets bilious whenever his expensive trousers touch man-made fibers. The fact that they live here is testament to how much he adores Bobby and the proviso that he had free rein on decorating upstairs.

Smirnoff looks up at me, plaintive. If he could speak, I think he'd have a low, menacing drawl, and right now he'd be telling me to open the stupid door and find him some tuna before he tears the place up.

"Sorry, bud, we're going to Bobby's," I say, knowing he'll follow me upstairs, and that he's not likely to be allowed on the couch when he gets there. Or the bed. I don't feel bad for him, though—Robin bought him a fancy cat cushion for the window ledge so he can survey his kingdom in comfort. Besides, he takes absolute liberties in my place, so it's just as well that someone attempts to teach him manners.

Their door opens before I can knock, and Bobby's expression is so I-know-what-you've-been-doing smug that I turn toward the stairs again. He catches hold of my sleeve and yanks me inside, shooing Smirnoff in too with his foot as he closes the door.

Robin appears in the kitchen doorway. "Coffee or G&T?"

I've had enough alcohol already tonight. "Coffee. Def coffee. I'm freezing."

Bobby takes my coat and I crash in the corner of their huge leather sofa, feeling my muscles finally untense for the first time tonight. Bobby puts a chunky knitted blanket over my legs and Robin hands me coffee that smells decidedly of rum, then they sit and stare at me expectantly.

"So . . ." Bobby says, when I say nothing.

"Rum fell into your coffee." Robin scratches his cheek. "High shelf. It was unexpected."

"Accidents happen," I say, not grumbling because it's hot and calming.

We lapse into silence again, aside from Bobby fast-tapping one finger on the arm of his chair. They both know the uncomfortable silence will get me talking faster than anything.

"Okay," I say. "So, dinner was overwhelming. They're a big, noisy family, everyone talks at once. Food was excellent. House a Zillow addict's wet dream. Serious chandeliers." I motion with my arms stretched wide to demonstrate the size. "Cute babies and scraggy dogs."

"It sounds like a Sandra Bullock movie," Robin says.

"Love me some Sandy B," Bobby murmurs.

I nod. *Speed* earned a regular spot on my mother's movie-night list—it didn't strictly fit our romcom diet, but Sandra and Keanu? Off the chemistry scale.

Bobby makes move-it-on gestures, impatient because he knows there's juicier stuff than chandeliers and babies to come.

"And then —" I stop, because it feels disloyal to Gio to say more.

"Oh, *come on*." Bobby rolls his eyes. "We saw you through the window with your tongue down his throat, it's not like it's a secret."

I sigh, still kiss-drunk. "There isn't much more to tell. We caught a cab home together, got out and walked the last bit because of roadworks, and then we . . . well, you saw the rest."

Bobby shakes his head. "Oh no. No, no. You're not doing that." He turns toward Robin. "I told you she'd be coy. Didn't I predict she'd be coy right before she came up here?"

I look at Robin and he knocks his rum back before getting up to throw another log on the fire. "Don't involve me." He laughs as he takes Bobby's empty glass and heads for the kitchen, tapping the top of my head as he goes. "Everything I need to see is written all over your face," he says, smiling at me. "I'm heading up to bed." He frowns at his watch. "Alarm in five hours."

"I'll tell you everything later," Bobby says, sliding from his chair to the floor beside my sofa.

Robin sighs. "Oh, I know it."

Bobby watches him leave and I shake my head, quietly loving their double act.

"I'm not asking for the mechanics, although feel free to give me the blow-by-blow if you want," he says, turning his attention back to me. "Just give me the feels." He makes a heart shape with his fingers and winks to make me laugh.

I finish my coffee and lean forward to slide the empty mug onto the coffee table.

"It was . . . Gio was . . ." I cast around for words that feel like they do what happened out there justice. "He was just so different tonight. Light-hearted. Funny. His family love him so much, and he them."

Bobby pats my blanket-covered leg and waits for me to articulate my jumbled thoughts.

"I'm scared, Bob. We talked and we messed around, and that kiss out there was the most full-on, brain-melting kiss of my entire life. What am I supposed to do with that?"

He raises his eyebrows. "Do it again tomorrow?"

I rub my hands over my face, bone-tired. "That's just it, though. I want to. I really want to trust it, and even that is unexpected and out of the blue. I honestly didn't think I'd ever be able to trust these feelings again after Adam."

Sometimes at night I imagine taking a black marker pen and crossing him out of the story of my life, like a redacted police file. The relief would be immense.

"Not all men are assholes," Bobby says, leaning his head against my legs.

"Thank God." I shudder as Adam's face jack-in-the-boxes up in my head. It's a mental effort to force him back down again. "I know, because you and Robin prove it every day."

"Of all the noodle joints in all the towns in all the world . . ." he says.

"I'm glad I walked into yours," I finish. It's a comforting routine we regularly fall into, and I watch the fire as I search for the words to express myself.

"You and I both know that Gio Belotti is the one person I shouldn't go there with. I told him Adam died, for God's sake." I shuffle down until I'm lying on my side facing the fire, my head on one of Robin's fabulous fur pillows. "And now I'm lying to him again every damn day about the recipe, and about my mother, who incidentally was in the same bloody band as my father, Charlie, and Gio's real father, Felipe. That must have been how she met Santo in the first place."

Confusion crosses Bobby's face, and I explain about the photograph of my mother in the Belottis' album.

"For what it's worth, I'm proud of you," he says. "I know how hard it is for you to put yourself out there again. Don't overthink stuff, what happens happens."

I smooth his hair. "That's worth a lot to me, actually."

After a few moments he gets to his feet. "Stay here tonight?"

I'm more comfortable than I've been in as long as I can remember. Rum-warm and fire-drowsy. "Robin has to be up early," I say.

"You won't be in his way, he's up and out. Besides, he threw a log on to keep you warm, we'd already talked about it. Seriously, even Smirnoff thinks it's a good idea."

I contemplate my cold apartment below and can't find one reason to move a muscle.

"You guys are the best brothers I never had," I say, meaning Bobby and Robin, even though the cat takes it as invitation to join me on the sofa.

"I'll leave you to deal with him," Bobby says, clicking off the side lamp and pulling the blanket up to my shoulders. "Get some sleep now."

I lie and watch the fire for a while, the cat curled up behind my knees. *Don't overthink stuff, what happens happens.* It's as good a bit of advice as any right now.

15.

I DRAG MY FEET AS I NEAR BELOTTI'S FAMILIAR GREEN-
and-white awnings. I slept the sleep of the dead on Bobby's
sofa last night, but right now I feel as if I have a tennis ball
bouncing around my internal organs, and I consider turning
back and running for home. I could, there's still time. No one
has seen me yet.

"Morning!" Sophia comes barreling out of the gelateria,
dark curls jumping around her shoulders, her apron sticking
out beneath her puffa jacket. "Milk delivery didn't come. I'm
on the hunt to find some, we don't have enough to make it
through the day."

So sloping off isn't an option. That's okay. I'm not a slope-
off kind of gal. I'm here trying not to overthink it, tennis ball
or no tennis ball.

I spy Gio through the glass door, stacking pastries into
the display case. There's a woman at one of the tables sipping
coffee, and a guy reading a newspaper at another. I push the
door open and Gio looks up, a series of micro-expressions
crossing his face that tell me he's not sure how to navigate
things either.

"Morning," I say, dumping my bag on one of the counter
stools.

"Hey, you," he says.

Two words, and now I feel like the class nerd who made out with the cool guy at the school disco last night. If this was high school, I'd drop my bag about now and he'd come over and help me pick up my books. But it isn't high school. We're in our thirties and we've been around the relationship block enough to know this is a dangerous neighborhood and you'd be wise to guard your bag rather than let it spill out.

"Iris, I wanted to—"

He stops speaking when the door pushes open and a couple of women come in and hover near the counter.

"You guys go, I'm still thinking," I say, turning to wave them forward.

"Can we get everything in here?" One of them touches the display case, her eyes scanning the contents. "And"—she pauses to count on her fingers—"fifteen Americanos to go, please?"

Her friend sighs beside her. "Staff meeting, caterer let us down."

"Of course," Gio says, glancing at me.

"Can I help?" I say.

He hands me an apron, and for the next few minutes we work as a team, me boxing pastries, him making coffee, and it feels harmonious, last night's tension melting away as I tie string around the green-and-white-striped boxes.

The woman in front of me reads the customer notice on the counter and then looks at me.

"Will there be gelato again soon? I miss that stuff."

Gio turns from the machine with takeaway cups in his hands. "We hope so," he says. "It's a temporary glitch."

The customer nods, already moving on to a different conversation with her colleague.

A temporary glitch. His words knock around inside my head as we pack and stack the order to go. It's a good summary of us, we are a temporary glitch in each other's timeline.

It feels unnaturally quiet when they leave. The woman at the table has gone too, leaving just the guy behind his newspaper over by the window.

"I think we should —" I begin quietly and stop again, because Sophia returns, her arms full of milk cartons.

"Managed to bum these from Priscilla," she says, leaning forward over the counter to put them all down at once. "She said you can pay her back with lunch sometime."

I conjure Priscilla from memory, the woman in the gelateria across the street, and swallow down unnecessary needles of jealousy. Gio can have lunch with whoever he wants. As can I, of course. I layer the cartons in the fridge beneath the counter as Gio restocks the display case and Sophia hangs her coat.

"I've been thinking," she says. "About the gelato situation."

"Join the club," Gio says.

She pauses and squares her shoulders. "Hear me out here? I know you're working on the recipe, and I've every faith in you both, I do. But those machines back there are standing idle when they could be making us a profit, you know? How about if we schedule some guest flavors, make a big splash about it with publicity?"

"This again." Gio looks absolutely unconvinced. "*Vanilla for—*"

"*Forever*, I know," she cuts in. "But at the moment we've got nothing forever, and the way I see it, it's a chance to be creative."

"We'll get the recipe right, we're closer than ever," he says, stubborn.

I stay low and rearrange the milk cartons in order to keep myself out of the conversation, because I can see both sides. Gio is dead set on keeping things exactly as they are, Sophia is full of fire and ambition and ideas for change. We've had many conversations about flavors and pastry recipes—she's a self-taught cook who loves to experiment and she regularly tries out new twists on old pastry classics for Belotti's customers. And she's good. *Really* good. I can see so much merit in what she's saying.

"Say you'll think about it, at least? Small batches, unusual flavors, put the story out there that we've misplaced our recipe and, while we hunt it down, come try out our exciting guest flavors?" She ends with jazz hands and a wide smile.

"So you want to announce to our competitors that we've lost our family recipe, let them all know Papa can't remember it? Have you stopped for even one minute to think how that would make him feel?" Gio throws his hands out to the sides and glares at his sister.

"Well, let's just let New York forget we make gelato altogether then," Sophia spits back, slapping her hand down hard on the counter. "How do you think Papa would feel about that?"

They stare each other down, at an impasse, and the guy with the newspaper closes it and shoots me a rather-you-than-me look as he exits.

Gio breaks first, huffing as he turns on his heel and disappears into the kitchen.

"Talk to him for me? He might listen to you," Sophia says, rolling her eyes. "He's just so freakin' set in his ways."

I think about his comment last night, that his sisters all see him as locked in behind this counter, and I can understand how they all find security in playing their designated roles.

"Well, I can try," I say, non-committal.

"I don't get why he always has to be so damn stubborn," she says, and I wonder if she realizes she's just the same way. "I mean, I love him and everything, but his unbendability drives me up the wall sometimes."

"There are worse things he could be," I say, trying to soothe things.

"Are there? Because right now it doesn't feel that way."

"You're just going to have to trust me on that one, then," I say. "I guess he's grown used to having to hold things together on his own and it's a hard habit to break."

Sophia's expression softens. "I know," she says with a sigh. "But he isn't on his own. He never has been, even when Pen died. We've all been here beside him the whole time."

"And he's incredibly lucky to have that," I say. "But you can have all the support in the world and still feel alone when you turn the lights out at night and there's just you trying to work out how to get through tomorrow."

"Oh God, I'm sorry, Iris, I've put my foot in it without engaging my brain," Sophia says, her dark eyes full of concern as she puts her arm around my shoulders. It catches me by surprise, this sisterly tenderness, something that comes easy to her and that I've never known before. "You can tell me to shut up if you like, but I'm always here if you need to talk about stuff. About your husband, I mean. Gio told me."

I swallow hard, blindsided.

"Because I read about how to talk about grief after Penny died, about mentioning her loads, how it's good to know other people remember the person you've lost too," she says, rushing her words out in an even faster jumble than usual. "And I know you don't have that kind of support here, people who knew him, so if you want to talk about him, you can to me, okay?"

She turns to look at me, and I nod as my eyes well with tears at her kindness. She's referring to Adam, of course, but I feel her sentiment about the profound loss of my mother.

"What was he like?"

My insides go very still. "He . . . it . . . our relationship was complicated," I say. "I . . . I was frightened of him sometimes." The words leave me before I have a chance to think about them, because Sophia's arm around my shoulders has lowered my defenses.

Sophia's eyes scour my face, her brows low. "Shit, did he hurt you?"

I close my eyes and look away, wishing I could unburden the whole truth. "Not physically," I say, and she squeezes my shoulder, her grip firm and reassuring, "but he made me realize there are a lot of other ways a person can hurt you."

"Fuck," she says, under her breath.

I dash the back of my hand over my eyes. "Yeah," I say. "Like I say, complicated."

"Maybe stubborn isn't the worst thing Gio could be," she says after a few moments, and I lean into her and laugh softly, because the tension is broken.

"Definitely not the worst thing," I say. "Will you be okay if I go on through?"

She looks around the empty gelateria. "I think I can cope with things out here."

I FIND GIO STACKING ingredients on the kitchen work-bench, tension emanating from his precise movements and set jaw.

"Are you okay?" I say, trying to meet his eyes.

"Absolutely fine," he says, turning to get something from a drawer behind him.

Not absolutely fine at all, then. I wait for him to stop busy-ing himself and look at me.

"Shall we begin?" he says, clipped.

This is awful. Not like our usual mornings at all, and I don't know if it's what happened between us last night or what happened with Sophia just now. Either way, it's not what I expected and I'm on the backfoot as to how to handle it.

"Can we talk first?"

He lays his palms flat on the table and breathes out slowly. "I think it's clear from what happened out there just now that talking is not my strong point."

I sit on one of the tall stools beside the workbench, and after a few beats he sits too, his knee brushing mine.

"I don't know about that. You were pretty chatty last night," I say, remembering our rambling conversations as he walked me home.

He nods slowly, his gaze locked somewhere down by my boots.

"About last night," he says, and his sigh is lead heavy.

"You regret it," I say, trying to read him.

He lifts his eyes at last and looks at me. "Yes. And no. No, because how can I regret a kiss that made me feel like a teenager again? It reminded me that my heart still beats, Iris, that I'm not just a son and a father and a gelato maker. But yes too, because being a son and a father and a gelato maker is who I am now. It's enough for me."

"Gio, I understand," I say. "I've purposely filled my life up with everything so there's no room for romcom worthy kisses or big family dinners or singing in the park, but then I met you and those things are happening to me anyway and it honestly scares me shitless."

I've just spilled my metaphorical book bag at his feet, and now I wait to see if he picks the books up or acts like a jerk and leaves me scrabbling on the floor. It's a moment he doesn't even know is happening.

He puts his hands on my knees. "Romcom worthy, eh?"

"It *was* very Mark Darcy to fold me inside your coat," I say, letting my fingertips touch his.

"I won't pretend to know what you're talking about," he says, stroking his thumb over my knuckles.

I curl my fingers and catch his hands in mine, and the look in his eyes slides from frustration to something so hot it sucker-punches me. "We could just not overthink things and see what happens?" I say, my voice quiet in the cavernous kitchen.

His eyes scan my face. "My family can be a lot," he says. "And Bell's at this weird age, she takes everything to heart. I can't handle her getting too invested in something that might come to nothing, you know?"

"Are you asking me to be your dirty secret?" I tease.

"No." He laughs low in his throat. "Yes?"

"I think we've just veered away from romcoms toward the adult channel," I say.

He looks at me, really looks at me. "I can't make you any promises," he says.

"Me neither," I say. My knees are between his now, our bodies closer than when we first sat down.

I want to kiss him, and because I'm not overthinking things and letting what happens happen, I lean into the space between us and close my eyes. His mouth meets mine, gentle and full of longing, my fingers gripping his as lust lands heavy in my gut. Jeez, I genuinely don't know how the hell we've worked together over the last however many weeks without tearing each other's clothes off, because this is off-the-scale, take-me-now-or-lose-me-forever sexy. Finally he pulls back, and we stare at each other, like two drunks who just downed a bottle of vodka.

"That was . . ." I can't even finish my sentence and I know my cheeks are burning.

"Let's not do that in here again," he mutters, his eyes moving to the door, his breath coming in shallow bursts.

"But we'll do it again, right?" I say, because this need is suddenly so heavy in me I'll probably die if he says no.

He holds my jaw and drags his thumb across my lips. "My head wants to say let's take it slow and the rest of me wants to drag you upstairs to my bed, Iris, so yes, I think we should do it again."

"Gio," I gasp-laugh, wide-eyed, my hand over my heart. "I feel like I'm on drugs."

"I can't stand up for at least the next five minutes," he says.

We eye each other warily, and then I laugh again because this is crazy.

"Have you ever seen *Moonstruck*?" I say.

He shakes his head. I'm not surprised.

"Cher plays this straight-laced accountant and Nicolas Cage is her fiancé's brother, but there's this explosive chemistry between them, and at one point he yells, 'Loretta, come upstairs and Get. In. My. Bed.'" I deliver the line in the growly, unhinged, urgent way Nicolas Cage does and Gio starts to laugh, slightly alarmed.

"You reminded me of that movie just then," I say.

"And does she do as he asks?"

I don't blink. "Yes."

"I'll watch it sometime."

"Can I watch it with you?"

"It sounds like you've seen it already," he says.

"But not with you," I say.

"Fine," he says, sighing. "You can watch it with me."

"I work every night but Mondays," I say.

"I work every day there is," he says.

"Monday night, then?"

"That's tonight, Iris."

"Okay," I say. "I'll bring popcorn."

16.

I DUCK INTO A BODEGA ON MULBERRY STREET TO GRAB popcorn and red wine en route to Belotti's. I've spent the afternoon alone, some much needed me-time to drink tea and keep my own counsel. How can something feel so right and so wrong all in the same breath? I lay on the couch this afternoon and considered cancelling, but my fingers refused to type the message. I submerged myself under bathwater and willed myself to float away to a new, easier version of my life, but then found myself relieved when I broke the surface and saw the cat sitting on the sink observing me in my cubbyhole bathroom. I pored over my mother's scrapbook at my small kitchen table, wondering what advice she'd offer me. It saddened me greatly that I couldn't find her voice in my head. The only advice I have to draw on is Bobby's, so I'm making my way to the closed-up gelateria to drink wine with Gio Belotti and let what happens happen.

"I bought butter flavor and Cheddar."

I hold up the popcorn bags and realize how Baby Houseman felt when she said she carried a watermelon.

Gio looks from the popcorn to me and nods, leading me through the gelateria to the door at the back of the kitchens marked PRIVATE. I haven't been upstairs to Gio's home before, and it feels strange after so many mornings spent around the kitchen workbench. I glance over my shoulder toward my gelato machine sitting forlornly in the darkness, and then follow him up the stairs.

"Have you always lived here?" I wish I could suck the question back in when his face falls.

"No. Bella and I moved up here after Penny died. Too many reminders in our old apartment, you know?"

I nod, not trusting myself to reply. I moved continents to get away from reminders of Adam.

"You look nice," he says, taking my coat.

I did that classic thing earlier, pulled out the entire contents of my wardrobe before settling for jeans and the black sweater Bobby and Robin gave me for my birthday. It's the kind of expensive that clings in all the right places and slides off my shoulder. I've not had occasion to wear it before tonight, as it's definitely not something to toss noodles in.

Gio looks uncharacteristically nervous. "I wasn't sure whether I should cook?"

"Oh. No, I've eaten," I lie, because I was too nervous to face food earlier. "Is Bella here?"

He shakes his head. "Mamma's making far too much of a fuss over her for her to bother coming home tonight. My guess is she'll be there three days, at least. Maybe even a week."

"Those pancakes did sound amazing."

He digs in a kitchen cupboard for a popcorn bowl. "It's a win-win. Mamma gets someone to feed while Papa's away, and Bella's more than happy to be waited on hand and foot."

"Sounds like a good gig, to be fair."

We're doing that thing again, avoiding the elephant in the room. But even though I hate terrible small talk, I'm okay with it right now because unreasonable things happen in my head and body whenever he touches me.

"This place is super cool," I say, looking around, taking in his home. I don't know what I expected—more of what's downstairs, I suppose. Classic, traditional, a mini version of Maria and Santo's Brooklyn brownstone. It's not like that at all. Gio's apartment would probably be described on Zillow as rustic-luxe, bare brick walls and exposed beams, stripped floors and industrial furniture softened with battered leather sofas and warm-toned rugs. For all of that, it still feels welcoming and unpretentious, scattered with the hallmarks of a family home—Bella's sneakers by the door, schoolbooks on the coffee table, photos pinned to the fridge. Gio suits his home. He has the same established, comfortable-in-his-own-skin vibe about him tonight. Worn-in jeans, dark T-shirt with faded band graphics, yet another new version of him from the guy who works downstairs and the guy attending his family dinner. I would imagine this is as close to who he really is as it gets.

"It's an ongoing labor of love," he says. "Keeps me busy, anyway. Less time to think about stuff when you're sanding floors or knocking down walls."

An unbidden image of Gio in overalls saunters through my head, and I turn the mental hose on him and scoosh him away.

"So this movie," he says, reaching two wineglasses down from a shelf. "Tell me what I'm in for."

I shake my head. "Uh-uh. The joy is in not knowing. Besides, I wouldn't do it justice."

He cracks the wine seal. "You did a pretty good Nicolas Cage impression earlier."

"You'll know just how good when you see it," I laugh.

I follow him to the sofa and perch on one end, accepting the glass of wine he hands me. He takes the other end, puts the popcorn on the empty seat between us, then clicks the TV remote.

"Already cued up," I say as the movie graphic fills the screen. "Impressive."

"Did you think I'd try to get out of it?"

"The movie or . . ." I trail off, unsure whether to call this a date.

"The movie," he says. "Not this." He indicates between us with his hand. "Popcorn?"

"I have a no-popcorn-until-the-first-word's-been-spoken rule," I say. It was my mother's rule, and I find it impossible to break even now.

He raises his eyebrows but doesn't speak as he presses PLAY and dims the lights. He doesn't eat the popcorn either, which I like. Such is the excellence of the movie that I'm pulled straight into the story I already know so well, and surreptitious glances at Gio tell me he's engrossed too. It's a fast-talking, tempestuous, wise-cracking ensemble piece you have to really pay attention to, and I feel my nerves dissolving as the familiar faces fill the screen and the wine loosens my limbs. Gio moves to fetch the wine bottle halfway through, and when he returns he sits nearer to my end than before. I excuse myself to the loo a few minutes later, and when I come back I sit closer to the middle too, almost shoulder to shoulder beside him as if we're at the cinema. I take a gulp of wine, knowing that we're coming up to the Nicolas Cage line I quoted earlier. My hand collides with his when we both reach into the popcorn bowl wedged between us.

"You go," he says.

"No, you," I say.

On screen, Nicolas Cage tells Loretta he wants her in his bed, and I try to flick a look at Gio without making it obvious and find him turned toward me, watching me watch the movie.

"You'll miss the best bit," I say.

"*You* are the best bit," he says, and then he leans forward and touches his mouth to mine, the unhurried kind of at-last kiss made for slow dances and late nights on vacation. I turn my body into him and his arm slides around my shoulders, and there's that moment where you wonder if you're going to fit together or jar on each other's angles and curves. We don't jar. We meld.

"For the record, that was a really corny line," I say.

"I'm old," he says.

"You're thirty-nine."

"Watch the rest of your movie," he says, resting his fingers on the back of my neck. "Then I've got something to show you."

I throw him a look. "That isn't as suggestive as it sounds, is it?"

He reaches for some popcorn. "I think you'll like it."

I'm glad I've seen the film before, because however brilliant it is, I can't take the words in while he's drawing slow circles on my neck with his fingertip and it's so insanely sexual that I feel as if he's actually drawing circles on my cervix.

For the love of God, Cher, just get in Nic's bed already, will you? Gio Belotti has something to show me and I cannot wait to see what it is.

"UP HERE."

Gio handed me a blanket just now, and when he opens the door at the top of a skinny staircase I see why.

"You have a roof terrace?"

He shrugs. "Kind of. It's a roof, at least."

Cold night air hits me as I step outside, but I'm too dazzled to let it bother me. It's a tight space, just enough room for a garden sofa on a patterned outdoor rug, a few big planters dotted around to add a relaxed vibe. The main event, though, is definitely the breathtaking view.

"Come stand over here." Gio leads me to the chest-height walled edge. I rest my elbows on the stones and drink the city in: blurred red streaks of moving taillights, the glitter of the Brooklyn Bridge spanning the East River, the majesty of the Empire State Building towering over the illuminated skyline. And then, of course, there's the three-quarter moon, hanging up there like the lead actor on the stage accepting his encore.

"I've never seen it from above like this," I say. "There's so much life."

He wraps the blanket around my shoulders and points over toward Brooklyn. "Over there, about three miles or so in that direction, is Cranberry Street."

I look sideways at him, not sure of the relevance.

"You say you love that movie, and you didn't pick up on the reference to Cranberry Street? Shame on you, Iris."

I smile and follow the direction of his finger. I'm living inside all of my mother's beloved movies—Katz's Deli, and now here I am a stone's throw away from Loretta's house.

"My mother would get such a kick out of this," I say.

He puts his arm around my shoulders. "You miss her a lot, huh?"

"Every day," I say. "She was a special kind of person. Addictive, people used to say."

"Like mother, like daughter," he says, turning me into his arms.

"You're getting better at this flirting stuff," I say.

"I've been practicing in the mirror," he says.

"You haven't."

"No, I haven't," he laughs, and then he isn't laughing anymore, he's looking at me all serious eyes and slightly parted lips.

"Wait." I put a hand up when he leans in to kiss me, shuffling us around ninety degrees.

"Are we dancing?"

"No," I smile. "I want the view behind you when you kiss me."

"Jeez, you're demanding," he says, half smiling as he lowers his face to mine. His kiss, when it comes, is so hot and sure it knocks the breath from my lungs. I stand on tiptoe so the skyline frames him, and I add new colors to my background: glimmers of gold, blurred streaks of red, a wash of midnight blue.

He bites my lip and then lifts his head, his hand around the back of my neck.

"Iris, get down the Goddamn stairs and into my bed."

I crease up laughing. "Gio, that was horrible. Try again without swearing."

"Okay." He kisses my neck. "Give me a minute."

I arch into him when his fingers slide inside the back of my sweater, warm against my spine.

"Iris," he murmurs, smoky and low, "will you come to bed with me?"

GIO LEADS ME BY the hand into his bedroom, his thumb brushing the pulse at my wrist.

"I'm nervous," I say, and he turns to me in the low lamp-light. The decor in here follows the same theme as the living room, pared back, exposed brick, the huge carved bed with simple white bedding the focus of the room.

"Can I tell you something?" he says, sitting on the edge of the bed. "I'm nervous too. More than nervous."

I sit beside him and he picks my hand up, playing with my fingers. "I haven't been with anyone since Pen. Truth be told, I haven't been looking, I kind of just thought that part of my life was done with." His eyes fixed on our hands. "And then . . . you came along. There's something about you that's just like pure fuckin' sunshine."

His words move me. "I think that might be the best thing anyone has ever said to me."

I look at Gio, and the naked vulnerability and want in his eyes embolden me. I stand in front of him and take off my sweater, then put my knees either side of his hips and sit down in his lap. His arms circle around me as I settle.

"I think we should take our clothes off and bask in that sunshine for a while," I whisper, and he leans into me and trails his mouth over my breasts.

"It does feel suddenly hot in here," he says.

I reach behind me and unhook my bra, and he slides the straps down my arms.

"I almost can't look at you," he says. "You're that fuckin' beautiful."

"I like that you do sexy swearing," I say, moving in his lap in a way I know full well is turning him on. His mouth is on me, his hands on my ass and my body, molding and cupping, low moans in his throat. I gasp when he slides his hand between my thighs, unsure if I'm about to insta-orgasm even through two layers of clothes.

"Stop," I say, thinking I should wait for him to catch up, then I say, "God, don't stop," and he laughs and bites my shoulder, increasing the friction below until I drop my head against his neck and start to shake.

"In a different life, that would be embarrassing," I mutter afterward.

"In this one, it was crazy hot," he says, flipping me flat beneath him and kissing me slow and hard. "And we're only just getting started."

I kind of lose it when his T-shirt comes off, there's just so much smooth skin and bunched muscle, and the shock of his body against mine makes me need to skip to the good bit and get naked. I reach between us for his buttons and pop them one by one, and he stares down into my eyes and bites his lip.

"I might be a little rusty at this," he says.

"Trust me, you're not rusty," I say. "Get your jeans off."

He lifts away from me enough to shed his clothes, and then he unzips my jeans and sits back to pull them off too. He leaves my black lace panties on, and I cover my face with both hands when he moves them aside with gentle fingers and lowers his head.

I know it's greedy to have two orgasms before he's even had one, but he splays one hand on the inside of my thigh and takes his sweet time, and he says my name like a quiet prayer and tells me there's no rush, and then there's a sudden almighty rush in me. He knows it and holds me there, his other hand flat on my stomach, and in all of my days I don't think I'll ever feel anything so bone-wrackingly, violently sexy again.

He slides up my body, his knee between mine, and I wrap my leg around his thigh.

"I told myself to take it slow tonight," he says.

"You can do that next time," I say, rocking my hips. "Condom?"

He nods with a smile and reaches into his nightstand, settling the matter.

I watch his face as he pulls me back to him, see him trying not to lose control too soon. "Let go, Gio," I breathe, my hand on his jaw. "It's okay, you can let go."

And he does. He lets go, sinks into me and we wrap around each other, holding, gasping, slow and then not slow. His breath quickens and he murmurs what sound like urgent Italian curse words, and I feel as if I'm tangled in my torrid lover's bed on a long, hot night in Rome. It's sultry and intimate, and then the judder of his body is so carnal that I clutch him against me, hard. We're tender with each other afterward. The drift of his mouth over my closed eyes, the smooth of my hand over his hair. We stay like that for some time, recovering, and I find myself inexplicably close to tears from the sheer animal beauty of it all.

"Not rusty," I say.

"Slower next time," he says.

"As long as there's a next time."

He raises his head enough to look at the bedside clock. "Give me an hour."

I laugh into his shoulder. "Three orgasms. I think you earned some sleep."

"I set that bar too high," he says.

"And all that Italian stuff," I say with a sigh. "So hot."

I feel rather than hear his laugh.

"What was it you said to me?"

He shakes his head. "I don't know. I wasn't exactly thinking straight."

"It was magic to my ears. Shall we do this every Monday?"

"You mean like a sex date? Are you propositioning me?"

I nod. "We can do all of the things we normally do every morning so no one else knows, and then on Monday nights—boom." I make fireworks in the air with my hands. "You whisper unspeakably filthy things to me in Italian and I have three orgasms."

"I don't know if I can keep my hands off you all week," he says. "You've woken something in me I thought was long dead and now it's all I can think about."

I pause, because something about the cadence of his words wasn't quite natural. "Are you role-playing *Moonstruck*?"

"Yes," he says, turning on his side to face me, smoothing my hair back from my face.

"It was very convincing." I roll on to my back. "This doesn't even feel like my life."

He rolls on his back too. "Mine either. I'm the guy too stuck in his ways to experience this."

"And I'm the noodle chef afraid of her own shadow."

Gio raises himself on one arm, his head resting on his hand as he looks down at me.

"Why are you afraid?"

I've exposed too much of myself. How I wish I could tell him the truth, that I didn't think I'd ever feel safe with anyone again, that my being here is a testament to the undeniable goodness that radiates from his bones. I sigh and shake my head, not wanting to burst this bubble between us.

"I don't know. Life just knocks you around sometimes, doesn't it?"

He doesn't push for more, just slides his arm under my shoulders and pulls the quilt over us. He curves his body around my smaller one, my back against his chest, his knees behind mine, his arm over my body.

"*Cucchiaino*," he says.

"What does that mean?"

He strokes his thumb along the underside of my breast. "Little spoon."

"How do you say big spoon?"

"*Grande cucchiaino*."

I smile. "It sounds better in Italian."

"Everything does."

His breath fans my neck, his hand splayed on my ribcage as I close my eyes.

"How do you say bliss?"

"*Beatitudine*."

"So many syllables," I murmur, pressing my back into his chest.

And that's how we stay until we fall asleep. *Beatitudine*.

17.

"Don't be mad, but i've made something for you to test."

We've been downstairs for an hour or so by the time Sophia arrives for her morning shift, going about our usual business so as not to make it obvious I've spent the night here. But she's so preoccupied with the silver thermos in her hands, the squat kind you usually carry soup in, that I don't think she'd have noticed if she'd walked in on us kissing.

She takes a seat at the counter and opens it, shooting a "help me" look my way as she pushes it toward us. I can't help my chef's curiosity, so I lean forward to have a look inside.

"Great color," I say. "Blackberry?"

"And blood orange," she says, unable to keep the gleam of excitement from her eyes or her voice.

She grabs two disposable spoons from the customer pot and slides them toward us.

Gio doesn't react so I take the lead, and my tastebuds burst alive with dark fruit and citrus.

"Wow, it's punchy," I say, trying it again. I can see that my opinion matters to her, so I don't just pay it lip service, I take a third spoonful and mentally sift the flavor profile for what might be missing.

"It's delicious as it is," I say, "but I'm wondering if adding a touch of something sweet in the background, honey or maybe a hint of almond, might make it pop even more."

She reaches for a spoon and tastes it herself, her eyes narrowed as she considers my suggestion.

"Oh my God, yes, you might be right," she says, her eyes bright with an anticipation I well understand—the need to make a dish sing. "Almond could be interesting. I'll do another batch."

Gio still hasn't said a word, so we both turn to him. I think for a second that he's going to refuse to even taste it, and watch his eyes and see him consider that option seriously. Then he squares his shoulders and reaches for the spoon. Sophia's eyes widen a fraction and she bites her bottom lip, uncharacteristically nervous for one usually so full of beans. I'm nervous for her as Gio studies the deep-purple gelato on the spoon. We stand in tense silence as he slides it into his mouth, and I have to look away because I can't help but remember all the places on my body that mouth touched last night. He lays the spoon carefully down and lowers his gaze, the sweep of his impossibly dark lashes hiding his eyes from us as he considers his verdict. Sophia flicks me an anxious look, and I do a tiny shrug because I don't know any better than she does.

"Okay," Gio says.

Sophia leans in a little. "Okay you like it, okay you hate it, or . . . ?"

"Okay we'll try it your way," he says. "You can make your guest flavors, on the understanding that we go back to vanilla when we have the recipe again."

It's almost funny to watch Sophia fast forward through such a wide range of emotions, from battle ready to incredulous to euphoric happy dancing on the spot.

"Oh my God, Gio! I promise you won't regret this, I have so many ideas for flavors," she says, talking too fast as she opens her bag and pulls out a notebook.

"But, Sophia, there is to be no public mention of losing the recipe," he says, serious. "For Papa's sake."

"*Sì, sì.*" She draws an imaginary zip across her lips. "Not a word."

He nods, then turns on his heel and disappears into the kitchen. Once he's gone, she checks the door has closed and leans her back against it, laughing with exhilaration.

"I can't actually believe he said yes," she whispers. "You heard him too though, right? I didn't just dream that?"

"It's seriously good gelato," I say.

She grins, her shoulders coming up around her ears. "Isn't it, though?"

She opens her notebook and runs me through some of her other flavor ideas, noting down any suggestions I make as we chat between customers. It's one of the nicest half-hours I can remember, trading flavor options, discarding one idea for another, unearthing my knowledge of food and lifting it into the light for a while. Menu planning used to be one of my greatest joys, picking through the best of what was in season to create new flavor combinations, testing, tweaking, honing dishes on instinct until they were worthy of a place on a menu.

"Do you miss it, working with fine food?" she says.

I laugh. "I'll have you know I make a mighty fine bowl of noodles."

"Oh, I'm sure you do," she says, smiling. "But watching you just now, it's pretty obvious that you love being creative," she says. "And it's also obvious how much you know."

For a few seconds I remember the ambitious woman I was before Adam, before my mother's illness, powering my way through noisy, high-energy hotel kitchens, thriving on the pressure, living for the pleasure of preparing dishes to wow our customers. That woman feels a long way from who I am today, but I like to think she's still in there somewhere.

"I do miss it sometimes," I admit, surprising even myself. "I had to take a step back when my mother was ill, and then after she died . . ." I shrug. "I don't know, it's a tough industry to get back into." I don't mention Adam, and I'm grateful Sophia doesn't push me.

"No finer city than New York to dip your toes in again," she says. "If you want to, that is."

"Maybe one day," I say. "I'm happy with what I've got for now."

Sophia closes her notebook. "But you'll help me perfect these flavors?"

I nod. That I can happily get on board with. "I should go through," I say, glancing toward the kitchen door.

"Don't rush that vanilla recipe too soon," she says, then screws her nose up. "I don't mean that, obviously. It's just, you know. This is exciting."

"I get that," I say, and then I head for the kitchen, and Gio.

"SOPHIA WANTS TO KNOW if aliens have taken over your body," I say, standing beside Gio at the kitchen workbench.

"Did you tell her yes?" he says.

His eyes linger on me, the lightest brush of the back of his hand against mine.

"I think you've done the right thing," I say. "It'll create a new buzz."

"I hope so," he says. "Sophia works hard, she deserves recognition for her place here."

"Do any of your other sisters ever work here?"

"We all worked as kids during the summer and as teens for pocket money, but as adults, no." He shrugs. "It's not for everyone. Fran and Pascal have a deli in Brooklyn, and Elena teaches math at Bella's high school. Viola has just made junior partner in a veterinary practice in Queens—she cut open pretty much every teddy bear she ever owned. Sophia and me, though . . . it's always been about this place for us."

"You make a good team when you're not going for each other's throats."

"We're Italian, it's how we love." He throws his hands up and laughs.

I might be giving myself way more credit than I'm due, but it seems to me that Gio laughs more now than he did when I first started to come here. Or perhaps he just keeps the good stuff for people he knows, and it's taken a while to become one of his inner circle.

"The more I know you, the more I like you," I say. I wouldn't have said that before last night, but the boundaries between us have fallen down.

"Me or my family?" He puts his arm around me, his hand flat on my shoulder blade.

"Oh, I like your family a lot," I say, enjoying the way he's massaging my aching muscles. "But I like you in particular."

"I like you in particular too," he says. "I want to kiss you again right now."

"Not in here," I say, wildly turned on by his words and the touch of his hand. "We agreed, remember?"

"Oh, I remember. But that doesn't stop me wanting to," he says. "Or telling you that I want to."

"I'm not sure I can think straight this morning," I say. "I might need a gelato rain check."

"Don't go, *cucchiaino*," he whispers.

"How can you make little spoon sound so sexy?" I say.

He laughs against my hair. "Go home, before I do something I regret."

BELLA SKIPS INTO BELOTTI'S just as I'm leaving, having made headache excuses to Sophia.

"Iris, I hoped you'd be here."

"I was just on the way out," I say, although that's evident from my winter coat and scarf.

"I need to ask you something," she says, unhooking her backpack from her shoulders. Her cheeks are pink from the cold outside and her hair plaited either side of her head, more student-ish than when I saw her last at Maria's dinner.

"Will you sing with me at my school's Thanksgiving showcase?" she says. "Please? We all have to give a performance and I hate doing them because I feel like everyone's watching me, but if I play piano and you sing, everyone will be so wowed by you that they won't even look at me."

My gut reaction is dread and I glance at Gio for guidance.

"Bells, Iris is a busy woman," he says. "I don't think she'd have time . . ."

"Please?" Bella puts her hands together like a child at

prayer, her determined eyes round and fixed on me. "Please say yes, Iris, please? I promise it won't take up much of your time. We'll do a song you already know so you won't need to practice much and my school isn't far. Ellen Connelly keeps going on all the time about how she's the big star of the show, and she'll be so pissed if I bring you as my surprise guest after you went viral singing in the park."

"Language, Bella," Gio mutters.

"Ellen Connelly *is* a giant pain in the ass, to be fair." Sophia rolls her eyes. "I know her older sister, she was just the same, all jazz hands and everyone look at me."

I consider it. It's just one song at a local school performance. Something about it sits badly with me, but I can't think of a way to say no without looking—and feeling—like a jerk, so I relent and say yes. Bella crushes me in a hug, and over her shoulder I meet Gio's eye and shrug. What harm can it do?

IT'S FUR-LINED-BOOTS-AND-BOBBLE-HATS CENTRAL AS I make my way home to Chrystie Street, but I feel insulated from the inside out as I remember last night. My emotions are like a tangled ball of wool, knotted and difficult to make sense of. My original mission was clear. Linear. Help Belotti's on behalf of my mother, and out of personal gratitude for everything their recipe has represented for me over the course of my life. But somewhere along the way that straight line splintered into different threads, and now they're all overlapping and messy. The Belotti family are a passionate force to be reckoned with—even being on their fringes is seductive. Sophia is my culinary kindred spirit. Bella wants me to sing at her showcase. And Gio. Gio is my lover. Flashes of last night flicker across my prefrontal cortex and I'm glad of the chill wind to cool my face down. It's almost a relief being away from them all for a while—I'm someone who needs to turn their light off sometimes and just sit in the dark. I'm going to go home and wallow in the bath, and then later I'll toss noodles and try to recalibrate my brain.

18.

I FEEL AS IF SOMEONE HAS TURNED MY LIFE-DIAL UP from its safe, predictable setting to high-voltage, scream-if-you-want-to-go-faster. The last few weeks have been both physically exhilarating and mentally exhausting, because keeping what's happening between me and Gio secret isn't as easy as it seemed in principle. The last thing I need in my life is an extra layer of subterfuge, I've got enough of that already around my relationship with the Belottis. I feel like two people inhabiting one body and, to be honest, it's not the most robust machine to demand double duty of. My mornings have been spent gelato-making, stealing moments alone with Gio and helping Sophia with her experimental flavors before I hotfoot it home and become the girl who tosses noodles, glad of the *Groundhog Day* sameness of work to keep me stabilized.

Gio came to mine last Monday as Bella was home, and Bobby made sure to conveniently leave something in my apartment that he just had to call in and collect. He spent five minutes attempting to give off big-brother vibes and then another thirty just plain old schmoozing before I unsubtly sent him back upstairs. Seeing Gio in the confines of my apart-

ment was strange—it was just too poky and plain to house
such a gorgeous creature. Not that it mattered once he kissed
me, we could have been in a broom cupboard or a five-star
suite. The week-long tension between us overspilled its banks
and submerged us for several spine-tingling hours. Something incredible happens when we're alone: it's as if Gio allows himself to wear his heart on the outside of his skin for a
little while. He's quick to smile, able to slay me with the slow,
trembling emotion of his kiss. He's buried this part of himself
so thoroughly that no one gets to see it, and I find it deeply
sexy that he allows me close enough that I do. There is
strength in his vulnerability.

Tuesday found me steamrollered, sleeping in until after
ten, unwilling to get up even though Gio had left just after
one in the morning so as not to leave Bella alone all night. It
was a lot to process—his head had been on my pillows, his
body tangled in my sheets—and then I had to find a way out
of my dream life and back into my real life.

"I'M GOING TO CANCEL the holiday bookings this afternoon." Gio passes coffee to Sophia and me. "We are going to
risk giving ourselves a bad name if we leave it too late."

I've been dreading him saying this—I know the upcom-
ing Christmas party orders have been on his mind. He fears
damaging the gelateria's reputation with commercial customers by canceling and has been holding off in the hope of us
landing on the recipe in the nick of time.

"Yesterday's test batch was really strong," Sophia says.

"But not right," he says.

"Delicious, though," I say. I've slowly steered him really quite near to the exact recipe, and both Sophia and Gio had to test yesterday's effort twice before being sure it wasn't right.

"We could speak to them about shaking things up a bit with the guest flavors instead?" Sophia says. She didn't waste any time taking Gio at his word with her experimental flavors, and to give credit where it's due, they've proved to be something of a hit. It's not really gelato weather, but even so, she's sold out every day and it's created enough buzz to have the till ringing with customers checking back in to see what today's flavor is.

Gio sighs. "We've been booked for our vanilla," he says.

"Would it be so bad to use the recipe from yesterday's batch?" I say. "It was really excellent stuff."

I can see from his expression that the answer is no.

"People will notice the difference."

"Ah, come on, Gio." Exasperation sharpens Sophia's tone. "We're talking about work parties and weddings, everyone will have taken advantage of the free bar by the time dessert comes out. No one will know."

The atmosphere in the room chills to below gelato temperature.

"No one will know? I'll know. You'll know. And Papa would know. He might not know the recipe right now, but he'd know the taste."

"But, Gio, Papa isn't going to know a damn thing about it!" She slams her hand down on the glass counter. "We fulfill our orders, our customers will be happy, and Papa returns to business as usual when he's good and ready."

"More than a hundred years trading in this city, and you don't think our recipe is distinctive enough for people to recognize when it changes? How many other shops do you know that only need one flavor to be successful?" Gio throws his hands up, and his ancestors behind him on the wall seem to do the same.

I sip my coffee and stay out of it. This is between them. It's about the recipe, for sure, but it's also about their fiery love for the family business and their overriding fear for Santo's health. They're an anxious family just now, and their stress spills from them in the form of heated clashes of opinion. Thankfully, I've also seen the flip side of the coin and they're good at rebuilding the bridges they've blown up, quick to apologize and pull together again. It's not a dynamic I've ever really witnessed before—they're like a dangerous but beautiful box of fireworks.

"That's not what I'm saying and you damn well know it," she says.

He folds his arms over his chest, and she juts her chin in the air and does the same.

Gio looks at me. "What would you do, Iris?"

I sigh inwardly. So much for staying out of it.

"Well," I say, playing for time as they both stare at me and expect me to take their side. "Obviously, the ideal thing would be to have the exact recipe." I try not to see my mother's ripped napkin with Santo's handwriting across it.

They both nod.

"And protecting the Belotti brand is paramount."

They wait, and I cast around for a diplomatic answer. God, I'd never make a politician. My eyes fall on the Thanksgiving closure notice.

"Given that everywhere is closing for Thanksgiving in less than a week, I'd maybe leave things until afterward before making a decision. I mean, who wants a problem thrown in their lap right before shutting up shop for a few days, right? You'd pretty much be doing them a favor by waiting, and there's always the outside chance something might change here in the meantime." I glance from one to the other, trying to encourage them to lay their swords down on the middle ground I've created for them.

Sophia throws a sidelong look at Gio, who narrows his eyes, thinking. They may be equally passionate about the business, but he's Santo's second-in-command.

He shrugs, and she drops her arms and mutters in Italian.

"Fine," he concedes. "But the minute we open that door again after the break, I'm making those calls."

I feel a sense of having temporarily staved off the inevitable. The only person who can truly resolve this problem is me. My eyes linger on the closure notice, dully aware that it's putting the clock on me to call time on the recipe hunt too. I don't know what I'll do without my gelato experiment mornings, but this has gone on long enough.

19.

"I THINK WE'VE NAILED IT," I SAY, HIGH-FIVING MY phone screen. "You played out of your skin that time."

Bella grins and flexes her fingers. She's on her lunch break at school, her phone propped on the music department piano so we can remotely rehearse for her performance.

"I've practiced loads."

"I can tell. Just do it exactly like that on Wednesday. You've totally got this," I say.

"I can't wait to see Ellen Connelly's face," she says, then after a beat adds, "and my dad's."

A bell sounds in the background and Bella shoves her books into her backpack. "See you on Wednesday," she whispers. "You won't be late, will you?"

"Promise not," I say, because I can hear her nerves from several miles away.

I let the supportive smile fall from my face when she clicks "end call" and flop onto the sofa with my arm over my eyes. I didn't realize when I initially agreed to sing that family would be able to attend the performance too. I'd imagined a small school assembly in my mind, but it sounds like a bigger affair altogether. Gio is going to be in the audience with Maria and Sophia in tow, possibly his other sisters too. As a rule, I greatly admire the Belottis united front as a family, but in this case I'm feeling sickly with pressure and wish it was Thursday morning already.

"LORD, BELLA, IT'S HUGE. Elton John will have sung this to smaller crowds," I mutter, casting my eye around for the fire exit in case all else fails and I need to make a run for it. "Your school hall is bigger than some theaters in England."

My heart is ping-ponging around inside my torso, ricocheting off my ribs, glancing off my lungs, making it hard for me to draw breath.

"I've never seen it so packed," Bella whispers, not helpful at all.

We're backstage at her school performance, ten minutes to the seven P.M. curtain up, and I genuinely think I might be about to lose my lunch. Why did I ever say yes to this? People teem everywhere, mostly overexcited teenagers and anxious-faced teachers trying to corral them into some kind of order. Typically, we're last on the list of performances, so plenty of time for my nerves to build.

"Couldn't they have gone alphabetical?" I say to Bella.

"Why would you want to be first?" she says, turning her wide, nervous eyes to me.

We can hear the buzz of chatter from the crowd out in the hall, the scrape of chairs and rise and fall of hundreds of small conversations underscored by the school orchestra tuning up in the pits. What kind of high school hall has actual orchestra pits? And a balcony? My mother would have loved this, but I am not my mother. She probably wouldn't have chosen an Elton John track either, but "Your Song" is exactly right for us to perform tonight. It brings Bella's piano skills into the limelight, and is universally known across the various generations gathered in the hall this evening. I'm hoping its popular appeal goes in our favor.

"Tell me how you felt when you sang in the park?" Bella asks, pulling her hoodie sleeves down over her hands.

We perch on a table at the back of the busy scene and I pull in a long breath. "Not as nervous as this," I say. "But then I didn't have time to think about it or rehearse because it happened on the spur of the moment."

"That's Ellen Connelly," she says, nodding toward a tall girl holding court in the center of things. "She's on first. Of course."

"Of course." I nod, twisting my ring around on my finger. "It's going to be fine, you know the piece inside out," I say, because I really need to be a grown-up shoulder to lean on. "Being last means the crowd will be really warmed up, they're going to love you."

"Us," Bella says. "Love us."

I nod and give her shoulders a squeeze. "Yes, us. You're not on your own out there."

Bella sits on her hands and twists to look at me. "Will you stop coming to see us when you find the recipe?"

Gosh. I wish she'd asked Gio that question rather than me.

"Um, I hadn't really thought about it, Bells," I say. "I don't think so, though, I'm only a few blocks away and I like you all too much. Besides, I think I'll be due a lifetime supply of gelato if I ever find the recipe, so I'll have to come by sometimes to claim it."

I feel her body relax beside mine. "Dad likes you," she says.

"I like him too," I say, then modify with, "I mean, I like all of you."

It feels as if we're speaking in code. I don't know if she's trying to tell me she knows about Gio and me, or if she's fishing because she has her suspicions and doesn't want to ask her father directly. Or even if she hopes it's nothing like that at all, and she's looking for reassurances that I'll disappear in a puff of smoke once my mission has been accomplished.

An expectant hush falls out in the hall and we hear the principal run through her welcome spiel to the crowd. Ellen Connelly stands in the wings smoothing her pale-blue ballet tutu, her hair high on her head in a tight blonde bun.

"She's probably just as nervous as you are," I say, as we watch her run through warm-up exercises while she waits to be announced.

"You think?"

"Nerves can be useful," I say, remembering my mother's words on the morning of my driving test. She'd taught me herself, doing things her own way as usual. I took my test in her dinged-up Vauxhall, and from the moment I passed I designated myself as the family driver. She was terrific at so many things, but her driving always had me clutching my seat with clammy hands. She drove like she sang: full throttle. "The trick is to channel the nerves into your performance. You'll see. You'll get out there and feel like you're flying."

I'll give it to Bella's high school, they know how to put on a show. If I'd been out in the audience I think I'd have had a really entertaining time, but as we move slowly toward the front of the line backstage I find it harder and harder to enjoy what we can hear of the performances.

"It's taking forever," Bella says, drumming her fingernails against each other. "Everyone will have gone home by the time we get out there."

"I doubt it, your family bought almost a whole row of tickets. They'll sit there till midnight if needs be."

She shakes her head. "So embarrassing."

I throw her a wink as I nod toward the exits. "Shall we skip it? Make a run for the fire door?"

A harassed teacher appears, headset clamped on and red pen in hand. She looks as if she'd like to trade her clipboard for a stiff drink. "Bella, you're next up. In the wings, please, and shush." She puts a finger to her lips for emphasis.

Sheer, waxy panic freezes Bella's features so I square my shoulders and grab her hand. "Come on, Bells, let's go show these guys how it's done." I lean into her as the principal announces her name and people in the hall begin to clap.

"Easy as pie," I whisper.

"Easy as pie," she repeats, and steps in front of me when I gesture for her to lead the way. The applause is much louder out here and I daren't look at the faces in the front rows in case I see Gio. I keep my eyes on Bella as she sits down at the piano and places her sheet music just so, and then she looks up and gives me a quick nod to tell me she's ready. I turn to the audience and smile, surreptitiously wiping my clammy hands on my jeans. It's on Bella to decide when to start, and after a few seconds silence I fear she's lost her nerve so shoot her a tiny you've-got-this smile. It's pin-drop silent in the hall. I know she can do this, she just needs to get going. I fleetingly wonder if I should go perch beside her and play the opening bars together, but then she places her fingers on the keys, takes a shuddering breath, and begins to play. I close my eyes with relief and raise my hands to the microphone, trying to ignore the devil on my shoulder suggesting I've forgotten all the words. *I won't go blank, Bella, I promise.* I blink, almost blinded by the glare of the stage lights, but then my eyes find Sophia in the crowd and she chucks me a quick double thumbs-up and it's enough. I know this song, Bella knows this song.

I hear the wobble behind my first couple of notes and work to get my breathing under control, consciously relaxing my shoulders as I let the words float and then soar from my body. My mother told me once that she imagined gilded musical notes flying out of her mouth over the heads of her audience, and I see those notes shimmering everywhere in the hall now as I find my full voice for the chorus. It may not be the kind of song my mother would have performed, but the tone she gave me suits it well. I look at Bella and she's grinning, almost laughing with pure joy as she runs the back of her hand up the piano keys, building her performance pace for pace with mine. She plays out of her skin, elation on her face every time I steal a look at her, and we feed off each other because we know damn well we're knocking this thing out of the ballpark. It's such a gift of a song; the entire audience knows it and is with us. I feel the music, I am the music. Bella and I are afloat on our sea of musical notes and I never want the song to end because this high is so heady. By the time we reach the last line, I know for sure I'm not going to miss that big note, and I throw my arms out to the sides to create enough space in my lungs.

And then it's done. It's over, and Bella hurtles across the stage to me and crushes my ribs with her hug. I'm momentarily disorientated, but then I'm back in the room with Bella and aware of thunderous applause. Bells and I hold hands and take a deep bow, laughing, and then another because it goes on and on. The Belotti family are on their feet, Maria swiping her eyes with a handkerchief, Sophia cheering as if her favorite team just hit a home run, all of Gio's sisters clapping. And then there's Gio, statue still beside Maria with his hand splayed over his heart, pride shining from him brighter than the footlights lining the stage. It's pride in Bella, of course, and I bask in the glow too for my part in helping her get here to take her bows.

"We did it," I say, when she looks at me and shrugs, laughing and incredulous.

The next few minutes are a blur of backstage congratulations and Bella is quickly swamped by other kids, so I take a seat out of the way and watch the hubbub. I never had this. I used to watch TV shows set in high schools with green-eyed envy, even though most kids trudging to school every day would probably have swapped with me too. For a while, at least. They'd have loved the freedom and unpredictability of my days, but how I yearned for the support network and friendships of theirs.

"Iris!" Bella swings round and calls out to me. "Come over here."

Her friends turn too, so I slide off the table and join them. I'm thirty-four years old and rendered shy by this gaggle of teenage girls. I'm relieved when I hear my name called again and see Sophia heading our way, bouncing several steps ahead of the rest of the Belotti clan.

"Eat your heart out, Lady Gaga," she half shouts, pulling Bella close as she grabs my hand in hers. "You two fucking killed it!"

A teacher spins around and frowns at her, and Bella's

friends dissolve into laughter. I catch Gio's eye and can't work his expression out, so after a second I glance away.

"Dad, is it okay if I go back to Ruby's? Her mom said she'll bring me home later."

Gio isn't the kind of father to burst his shiny-eyed daughter's bubble with a no.

"You better get used to that," Maria says softly, noticing his face after Bella walks away with her friends without glancing back. "Five of you, and it never got any easier."

Someone has finally opened those fire doors and we make our way outside, hit by the chill as we spill from the stuffy, overexcited school hall to the bitingly cold car park.

"Walk you home?" Gio says, Bella's school bag slung over his shoulder.

"Sure," I say, as his family say their goodnights and scatter into various Brooklyn-bound vehicles.

"Do you need me to tell you how good you were tonight?"

I consider his question as we make our way out onto the street. Objectively, I know we did well. I felt it, that same lit-from-within freedom as busking in the park.

"I guess I'd rather know what you thought," I say.

We're far enough from school to be clear of prying eyes, so he puts his arm around my shoulders as we walk.

"I thought a lot of things," he says. "I watched Bells up there tonight and it got me right here." He touches his heart. "Pen would have been so damn proud."

I've learned since losing my mother that there is always a missing piece at any festivity or celebration. Other things and other people do not fill in that space, the river simply flows around it.

"And then I looked down the line at my family's faces, and they were all so caught up in the moment, not worrying about Papa or all the other stuff, so that was a gift for them as much as for me."

Gio told me this morning that preparations are being put in place for Santo to come home in time for Christmas, and they have all been buoyed by this news. Maria has gone into overdrive making adaptations at home; he isn't fully recovered by any means, and it's going to be a physical challenge as much as a mental one. He hasn't recovered his missing memories yet either, but it's going to mean so much to them all to have him in his rightful place at the head of the dinner table at Christmas.

"And then there was you up there onstage too," he says. "I saw how you made room for Bella. Your voice . . . you could so easily steal the show, but you didn't. I noticed all the moments where you held back to let her shine. I went to watch my daughter, but I couldn't take my eyes off you."

I don't think I've ever felt as seen, and it moves me beyond words as we walk the quiet streets back through Little Italy. Belotti's striped awnings beckon us, and when we reach the doorway he tugs me in and presses me against the wall with his body weight, the glass door in shadow beside us.

His kiss says thank you for tonight, and then the inevitable fire between us takes hold and his kiss tells me he doesn't know how to handle this heat. I don't either. My kiss tells him that I can't control how much I want him, that it's always like this when he touches me. He drops Bella's school bag and pushes his hands into my hair, tipping my head back to slide his mouth down my neck. I don't feel trapped. I feel desired, and outrageously turned on.

"If I was twenty years younger I'd unfasten your jeans right here," he whispers, breath hot against my ear.

"What would the neighbors say," I reply, half laughing, half gasping when his cold hand slips inside my sweater.

He stops just long enough to open the door and tug me out of the way of prying eyes, and then we throw our coats off, he tips me back over the nearest table and, as promised, unfastens my jeans.

We clutch each other afterward, breathless and spent, and I know I'll never walk through that door again without looking at this table and remembering tonight.

"Bella asked me if I'll stop coming here once we find the recipe," I say.

He strokes my hair and sighs.

"Am I a selfish man, *amore?* I've allowed her to love you a little, because I do, and now I risk her marshmallow heart."

There is so much to unpack in that sentence that I have to pause to drink it all in. He called me *amore,* and it fell from his lips so naturally that it almost went unnoticed. He said his daughter loves me a little, and that he does too. A little is not nothing. It's a conversation we'll have another day, because right now his concerns are for Bella.

"Marshmallow heart?"

He shifts me into the crook of his arm, his palm resting on my hair.

"You know how it is at that age," he says. "So tender. My heart is nearly forty years old, and it's not a pretty sight. It's been through catastrophe and magic, chunks missing and given away, a mangled thing held together by gelato and tradition and *famiglia*. But Bella . . . her heart is still soft, unprotected, no shell. I know it can't stay that way forever, that there will be"—he pauses, grimaces as if he just sipped acid—"boys." He fills the word with such darkness that I fear for those future boys. "But I don't want to be the one who puts the first crack there, and I'm afraid that the closer she gets to you—that *I* get to you—the more possibility there is that she will be hurt."

I appreciate his honesty. I think he's asking me what the future holds, and is standing guard for Bella and himself because they've been through something catastrophic. He's right to be wary. I don't have a crystal ball, but if I did, I think I'd see us walking blindly toward oncoming traffic, the secrets I'm holding on to flashing their lights at us to get out of the way before it's too late. He asked me just now if he's a selfish man. He isn't. I'm the selfish one. I stepped through that glass door and tumbled into the Belotti universe, a place so seductive and all-encompassing that I'm finding it almost impossible to walk back out of the door for good.

WE WALK HAND IN hand to the noodle house, quiet, caught up in our own thoughts. He lingers outside my front door, pulling me into his arms.

"Thank you for tonight, *cucchiaino*," he says, his voice rough in his throat. "You sing like a fuckin' angel."

"Stop already with the sexy swearing, you know what it does to me," I whisper, and he laughs under his breath before he kisses me, slow and searching. I press my fingers against the imprint of his lips on mine as he walks away, and I watch him until he's swallowed by the darkness.

———

I THINK ABOUT GIO'S marshmallow heart analogy as I go through the motions to prepare for bed, of his heart glued together by family and gelato. He's been both terribly unlucky and terribly fortunate, the Belotti safety net always stretched out beneath him to ensure he doesn't injure himself irreparably. My life has been more precarious. My mother was my only safety net, and without her I fell so far and so hard that I almost lost myself completely. That I didn't is on me. I remembered whose daughter I was just in the nick of time, and found the strength from somewhere to claw myself up out of the well and run away. The real miracles in my story are that I kept running as far as Chrystie Street and that I found Bobby, who picked my trampled self-worth up from that damp sidewalk and held it when I couldn't. So, yeah. My heart isn't marshmallow either. We share that much in common, at least.

20.

MARIA HAS INVITED ME TO SPEND THANKSGIVING WITH them, but I find myself relieved to have to politely decline. I've had long-standing plans to eat with Bobby and Robin, who are excited to be hosting a fancy dinner for Robin's family. I offered to cook, and Robin almost successfully hid his horror behind assurances that he'd hired in caterers. "You spend every night behind the stove," he said. "Enjoy the gift of time off feeding people." I chose to accept his offer gracefully, but in truth I'd love to have cooked dinner. I've had so little opportunity to use my finer culinary skills here, I miss the adrenaline rush of creating food for people to feast on. This will be my first experience of Thanksgiving. The effort of keeping secrets from the Belottis weighs heavy on my shoulders, a constant reminder that I don't truly fit in. It's a depressing thought. My entire life I've felt that way, never settling anywhere long enough to feel part of the landscape. Until Bobby, that is, so I'll put on my nicest clothes and head upstairs to eat turkey I haven't cooked myself with them later and thank my lucky stars for the noodle house on Chrystie Street.

————

ROBIN'S FAMILY TROOPED PAST my door a few minutes ago, so I hang back to give them time to say their hellos and settle in before I show my face. I've bought a decent bottle of red I know Robin will hide at the back of the cupboard and I've made them a batch of cinnamon rolls—if I can't contribute to dinner, they'll at least have something to nibble on in the morning. I'm sitting on the sofa browsing recipes on my phone to pass the time when a message alert scrolls over the top of my screen. I glance at it and go cold, all fingers and thumbs as I fumble to open it, hoping I misread the sender. I didn't.

Adam Bronson.

Just his name is enough to make me sick. What does he want? How does he have this number? I close my eyes and try to slow my panicky breathing. I could just delete it, not look. But then I'd wonder and worry, create even worse scenarios in my head than the real one. I don't want him in this life I've built. I don't want to see his name on my screen, or to allow him any space in my head, but I have to read it right now.

> *New York, New York, someone's a dark horse! Who knew you could sing, little mouse? Your Song, my song. @BellsyB16 was more than happy to send your info on to an old friend who might be passing through soon to pay you a surprise visit.*

I throw the phone across the sofa, my eyes scalded by the incendiary words. Fuck. *Fuck.* I lean over and grab it again, stabbing at the screen. Bella sent me a link earlier to a video posted on her school YouTube channel of our performance last week and, sure enough, she's supplied my full name for the description. Oh, *Bella*. Why? I know why, of course. Because she's fifteen and naive, because she's proud of us and doesn't see the danger, because I've lied to them all and she doesn't know any better. And now Adam knows I'm in New York, and can fairly accurately pinpoint me to within a few streets. And he contacted Bella, for Christ's sake. My skin is literally crawling off my flesh with shame that I've exposed Gio's daughter to the nightmare that is Adam, a man willing to exploit the kindness of her marshmallow heart. I can't breathe. I sit down with my head in my hands, and the rage that boils up in me has no exit but hot, angry tears and clenched fists pounded against the sofa.

Bobby texts to say come up and save him from Robin's mother, and I push my face into a cushion and scream. I can't go upstairs. I can't pretend this hasn't happened. *Little mouse*. Today is supposed to be about gratitude and thankfulness, but right now all I feel is ugly hate and humiliation.

I make excuses in the form of period cramps, and one look at me through the crack of the door is enough to convince Bobby I'm not lying. My brilliant friend taps lightly on my door half an hour later and leaves a plate piled high and a hot-water bottle, and I add Bobby to the list of people I lie to now.

I don't know what to do. I've worked so hard over the last year to build this new life, and in the space of a few scant lines Adam has set a ticking bomb underneath it. Why did I write my real surname on the cast sheet at the school? Have I learned nothing? It just never entered my head that it would leap from that simple sheet of paper on to the internet, a hop, skip, and a jump away from anyone who might tap my name into a search engine. Do I reply? Ask him what he wants? Or do I ignore it and pretend it never happened? Both feel like the same level of risk.

I pull my duvet onto the sofa and climb underneath it, shivering, set back to the crumpled woman I was when I arrived here all those months ago. *Little mouse.* I long for my gelato machine. I want the therapy of loading the familiar recipe into the top, of spooning it into my mother's pink melamine bowl, of savoring the lifelong taste of home in my mouth. I cry my hollow, grey heart out, painful sobs that wrack my body. I want my mum.

"IRIS?"

Bobby taps the door, his voice low and soothing. I heard Robin's family leave an hour or so ago, it's pretty late now and I was just about to drag my quilt from the sofa to bed. I contemplate ignoring him, but he deserves better than that so I open the door and try to raise a smile. I fail, feel my mouth tremble, and he instinctively holds out his arms for me to walk into.

"What is it?" he says, closing the door and ushering me back to the sofa.

I know I look pathetic. I feel pathetic, as if I've shriveled in on myself over the hours since I read Adam's message. I pick up my phone and open it for Bobby to read for himself, and after a couple of read-throughs he turns the screen off and lays it face down on the floor.

"So, if he turns up here, I'll kill him, and Robin will dispose of him. Dissolve him in a suitcase and chuck him in the Hudson."

I pull a watery smile out of my boots, because Bobby is so vain about their screamingly expensive luggage collection. "Not the Vuitton, he isn't worth it."

"You are, though," he says, staunch, and I know there is no greater love than a man who is prepared to sacrifice his monogrammed carry-on for me. It steadies my nerve.

"What should I do?" I say.

He turns his head to look at me. "Absolutely nothing. DNR. Do not respond."

"Just carry on as normal? I don't think I can, Bobby. What if it makes him angry and he turns up here or messages Bella again? I can't risk that." I try to keep a lid on my escalating fear but it's running away with me again. "God, Gio is going to really hate me, isn't he? Not only is my ex not dead and not ever my husband, but he's also a vicious snake coiling itself around his daughter."

"Iris, stop it." Bobby sits up straight and holds my hands, his eyes locked on mine. "None of this is your fault. You have not caused this, okay?"

I squeeze his fingers, not really believing him.

"Adam won't come to New York, it's an empty threat. We'll sit here and come up with a cover story you can tell Bella to stop her from responding to him if he contacts her again, which he won't. It's going to be just fine, I absolutely promise you." He ducks his head to keep eye contact when I look down. "Okay?"

I nod, exhausted. "Or I could just tell Gio the truth."

"You could," he says. "And you should when you're ready, but not because you've been backed into a corner by some asshole."

I slump against him and close my eyes.

"How was your dinner?"

"Oh, predictable," he says. "Robin's mother brought her own turkey in case we tried to serve an alternative Thanksgiving dinner. His father brought Japanese whiskey in an attempt to give me something culturally appropriate."

"Yet wildly inaccurate," I marvel.

Bobby sighs. "He tried, I guess. And they turned up, which, let's face it, wasn't a given. His grandmother even arrived with her own cushion to sit on. Go figure."

Robin's old-money family are ambivalent at best toward Bobby. An apartment over a noodle house, however tasteful the decor, just doesn't make any sense to them for their son.

"Maybe she's having continence issues," I say, just to make him laugh.

His face is reward enough. He isn't good with bodily fluids.

"You really think ignoring this is the right thing?"

He holds my hand. "You didn't tell Gio that the asshole was dead for no reason. It was self-preservation. So now you hold the line. Don't acknowledge he exists."

I know he's right, but the idea of Adam contacting Bella again is abhorrent. Now that I know there's even a one percent chance he could do it again, I'm not sure I can live with myself if I don't safeguard her against him.

I just don't know how to do that yet.

Hey cucchiaino, how was your thanksgiving dinner? Everyone missed you here, me most of all. Call me if you're still awake. G x

The message lights up my dark bedroom just before midnight, and I press the screen against my body and curl up in a ball. I missed him too. I missed them all, but on Monday morning I'm going to give them their recipe and walk out of that door for the final time. It's the only decent thing I can do now.

21.

Drinking rule number one: step away from messaging people when you've got alcohol in your system, you'll either embarrass yourself or say something you'll regret when you're sober. I know this rule perfectly well, yet here I am, my blood diluted by a bottle of red and my finger hovering over the send button. It's been forty-eight hours since Adam's message arrived and I've thought of nothing else. I'm consumed by it. How dare he try to firebomb my life? And as for messaging Bella . . . he crossed so many lines there that I cannot just sit on my hands and ignore it. I can't. I've tried, and much as I know Bobby is right, the fear of doing nothing and something happening is worse than the fear of doing something and something happening. So I'm here at one in the morning with my laptop on my knees, re-reading the reply I've just written to Adam to make sure I've hit the right tone.

> *Do not attempt to contact me again, nor anyone else in order to obtain information about me. I've moved on with my life and am no longer associated with you in any way. I suggest you do the same.*

I think it's enough. It's bald, to the point, and at least this way I don't feel as if he's in the driving seat. I read it once more and press SEND, then close my laptop and reach for my wineglass. There. It's done. It's Sunday tomorrow, the last day of the holiday, and I intend to spend it cleaning my apartment and wallowing in the bath. I'm desperate to wash away this greasy film of distaste that's coating my body, to bleach all traces of my vicious ex from my home. Just having his words in the room feels like a violation. And then, on Monday morning, I'm going to go to Belotti's one last time and get the recipe right. It will be a celebration for them, and a goodbye for me.

I'M FURIOUS AS I walk between the noodle house and the gelateria, stomping so hard it hurts the soles of my feet. It's bitingly cold; there was the buzz of potential snow excitement in the radio forecast this morning. I've yet to witness real New York snow. It stayed unseasonably mild throughout the winter season last year, just the occasional flurry here and there that dissolved on impact with the busy city streets. I'm dreading getting to Belotti's. I've lied to Gio this last couple of days about being unwell; I know he's probably seen my flimsy excuses for what they are. I don't know if I'm more angry with Adam or myself: him for rearing up just when I was starting to get myself together, or me for allowing him to pull my strings from across the Atlantic. Bobby is adamant that I'm doing the wrong thing, we came as close to a row as we've ever been when I told him what I'm doing this morning. I haven't told him I replied to Adam. I still don't feel sure it was the right thing but it's done now, so that's that.

I come to a stop a few steps from the painted gelateria door, pause to draw in a steadying breath. I can see Sophia inside with her back turned as she wrangles with the coffee machine, and a couple of customers too by the looks of it. No matter. My business is with Gio. I'm going to fire up my old gelato machine, load it with their secret recipe and pray he believes me when I pass it off as sheer dumb luck. We've skated pretty close to it already, it's not so much of a stretch to be completely implausible.

"Iris."

Someone says my name as I step into the warmth of the gelateria, the smell of fresh coffee and the sweetness of baking in the air. It literally couldn't be more welcoming unless they filled the place with armchairs and a library of well-thumbed books.

I turn toward the voice and see Maria rising from a nearby table to greet me. She catches me by surprise, gathering me into her arms and kissing both my cheeks.

"*Bambina*, you're feeling better?"

I bite the inside of my lip to stop it from trembling as I raise a smile. "I am, thank you. It's so nice to see you."

I look up as Gio appears from the kitchens. If he has any reservations about my apparent illness, he makes a good job of not showing it on his face. His smile is genuine and relief registers in his eyes. He's carrying a bowl of gelato.

"Mamma," he says, placing it down on the counter.

Maria takes a seat on one of the high stools and reaches for a spoon.

Sophia looks at me and raises her eyebrows, then shrugs in a way that suggests she has no more clue what's happening than I do.

Maria takes her time over tasting the gelato, several spoons, her eyes closed each time. Has Gio somehow stumbled on the recipe? Has Santo remembered it?

She places the spoon down with care and then nods at Gio, moving around to stand beside him. Sophia opens the door so the only customer in the shop can leave, and then closes it and leans her back against it.

"What's going on?" she says, looking between her mother and her brother. "Do we have the recipe at last?"

Maria looks at Gio to reply.

"Mamma and I have decided to use the most recent test recipe for the holiday orders," he says. "It's not exact, but with Papa coming home soon there's a decent chance he might recover his missing memories once he's back in his familiar environments. He's excited to try, anyway."

Sophia picks up a spoon and tastes the gelato.

"We agree that the best thing to do in the meantime for Papa's health is to keep the business going without disruption, so this"—Gio gestures at the gelato bowl—"is the recipe we will put into production, effective today."

There is a clear sense of unity between Gio and Maria. This is a decision they've reached together, a done deal in order to protect Belotti's and give Santo the best chance of rediscovering his old memories once he can get back in the kitchen again.

Maria looks at me, her face full of compassion.

"You have tried so hard, Iris, more than anyone could be expected to. We couldn't have come this far without you."

Sophia has eaten half a bowlful. "I think it's absolutely the right decision," she says. It's testimony to her respect for Gio that she doesn't say "I told you so."

I'm blindsided. I can't give them their recipe now that Santo has pinned his hopes on the idea that returning to his kitchen will jump-start his memory banks. I hope they're right for all their sakes, I really do, but what do I do now? I feel redundant and at a loss.

Maria is buttoning her camel winter coat.

"I have to go to the market," she says, raising an eyebrow at Gio. "A certain little bird is coming to stay with me tonight, if I'm not mistaken?"

Gio makes pretense of being offended. "You feed her too well, Mamma, she takes advantage."

"The house is too quiet without Santo." She's already on her way out of the door on a cloud of expensive scent and the jangle of bangles. "She's good company."

"Mamma, wait up. I'll walk over with you, I need some ingredients," Sophia says, then glances at Gio. "As long as I'm still making my flavors? Because they're selling so well and I still want to—"

He raises a hand to stop her mid-flow. "Yes."

"Cool." She grins as she bobs after Maria, shoving her arms into her coat as she goes.

There's a hush once they're gone. On a usual day Gio and I would head to the kitchen by now, but there will be no gelato-making today. Or there might be, but it'll be the big industrial machines that rumble back into action rather than my little machine.

"Coffee?"

I nod, unsure how to play things, whether to sit or stand, what to say.

"Let's sit," he says, carrying our drinks to the table in the window.

I stir in milk and sugar, thinking. In some ways this has made things easier for me. Logistically, I am no longer needed here. They've made a plan to keep the business operational, in the short term at least. They will need their recipe by the spring but that's a few months away—hopefully Santo will recover his memories and that will be that. And if he doesn't, then maybe I can say I've been working on it too, at home, and hit on it. I don't really know. It all feels unnecessary this morning, too far down the line to think about when what I really need to say is goodbye.

"You've been avoiding me over the holiday," he says, quiet.

Gosh, that was direct. "I've been under the weather," I say, knowing it sounds like the lie it is and hating myself for it.

"Is there something wrong?"

I can't drink my coffee, my throat feels swollen with the effort of not crying. I'm so distressed at the way things have turned out for us. In a different place and time, I really do think Gio and I have what it takes to make each other happy. It probably makes me a weak person that I cannot bring myself to tell him the truth about Adam. I'm the first person he's emotionally invested in since his wife died seven years ago. What would it do to him to know I've lied through my teeth from the very first time we met? Will he lose faith in his own judgment, retreat to his place behind the counter forever more? He deserves better than that. He deserves better than a relationship based on secrets and lies. I just need to find the words to walk away, words that feel as if they don't exist in the English language, because how do you end things when every fiber of your being wants to stay? But . . . Bella. Adam.

The recipe. I've been ostriching over the lies and keeping my head in the sand because being with Gio feels so separate, so safe, like an island we visit where only we exist and everything is about us, but that's not real life, is it? The island is surrounded by shark-infested waters, and if I just do nothing, it will sink with us both on it. I don't have to let that happen. I can wade into the water and battle the sharks—maybe I'll survive and maybe I won't, but at least Gio won't get a mauling in the process. Bella needs her dad, and the Belottis need him to be the rock he's always been. So I look him in the eyes and take a deep breath, my hands around the mug with my name on.

"I lied about feeling unwell," I say, miserable.

He doesn't say anything, just waits.

"And now there's no need for me to come here anymore. For the recipe, I mean."

He looks at me levelly. "Is that all you come for?"

"In the beginning, yes." I swallow. "But then things got out of hand between us . . ."

He nods slowly. I can see his expression setting like fresh plaster. "Out of hand?"

I look at Mulberry Street outside, Christmas lights strung from streetlamp to streetlamp, pretty even on this frosty morning.

"It's just all happened so quickly," I say. "I can't separate being with you from being with your family, and Bella too. The last thing I want is for anything to hurt her."

"She's my worry," he says, a coldness inching into his voice that feels like snow on my heart.

"I think now is the right time for me to not come here

anymore," I say, walking around the edges of saying it's the right time for us to not see each other anymore.

"I don't understand," he says. "I thought you felt the same way I do about us."

I can't look at him. "What we do when we're alone . . . it's been good, Gio. It made us forget the rest of the world for a while, but the truth is we both have real lives and it's threatening to spill over into them, and neither of us want that to happen."

He leans in and covers my hands with his. "What if I do? What if I say I'm ready for everyone to know, that Bella will be thrilled, that my family have probably guessed already and are just waiting for us to say something?"

Oh, how I would love it to be that easy. I close my eyes and allow myself to imagine it, vivid and piercingly sweet, like a five-second montage from the Hallmark Channel. There's a tree, and Christmas jumpers, and Bublé on in the background. I can almost smell the hot chocolate and pine needles, feel the warmth of the fire crackling in the hearth. Those movies usually come with a heavy dose of sugar and a problem that's resolvable with a sensible chat and the belief that love conquers all. That isn't going to cut it here. I don't see a world where Gio and I have a sensible chat about the fact my ex isn't dead after all, and how I'm only here because my mother and his de facto father had a love affair and he divulged their closely guarded family secret. That's not a sensible chat, it's a flood of problems for a family who don't deserve it.

"I'm not ready for that, Gio," I say, little more than a whisper. "I just don't think we're a good idea anymore."

"Oh."

He fills that one tiny word with a million others, and I see the shutters slowly roll down over his face, the stiff brace of his shoulders, the lean of his body away from the table. Away from me.

We look at each other in hurt, disbelieving silence. There isn't a single thing I can say that will make this easier, so I stand up from my chair and leave the gelateria without looking back, the glass door rattling behind me for the last time.

Vivien

...

THE DOOR HANDLE WAS ALREADY SUN-WARM WHEN SHE pushed the painted glass door open the following morning. Santo sat at the same table he'd sat at the previous night, his smile pensive, his eyes saying *I'm so glad you came* as she slipped into the chair opposite his and held his hands on the tabletop.

"I can't stay here," she said. "A big part of me wants to, but I can't."

His gaze fell to their clasped hands. "I wouldn't let you down, Viv."

Painful tears constricted Viv's throat—no one had ever promised her that before. "I know you wouldn't," she said. "But I'd always wonder what might have been, and I've pictured myself watching the band leave without me and all I can feel is panic. I have to be on that bus at midday."

As she said the words, the sight of Santo's tear-filled eyes as he looked away toward the street made her flinch with sorrow.

He huffed softly, shaking his head. "I knew it was a crazy thing to ask. I guess I was kidding myself thinking a girl like you would stick around for a guy like me."

"Santo, no! It's not that way at all," she said as she gripped his hands tight, hurting for him even more than for herself. "I just need to see where this thing with the band takes me, you know? It's my chance to *be* something, to be someone people can't forget; I've never had that before and I'm terrified I'll never get it again. What if I stay and you don't love me once you get to know me? No one else has ever loved me, why should you? I've always been a bit too much for people—too competitive, too opinionated, too difficult."

She'd had it drummed into her many times over the years, both as a child and as a teenager, that she needed to hide her spiked edges to make people want her. She'd learned early not to expect much of people, and for the most part she'd been proved right. Until now. Until Santo Belotti.

"We could stay in touch," she said, and she desperately meant it. "Long distance, you know? I can call you, we could write . . ."

He looked at her, really studied her as he held her hands, and she saw a whole storyboard of emotions play across his face.

"My life is here, Viv," he said. "It's always going to be here, in this small gelateria on Mulberry Street. It's what I want. Let's say the band makes it big—are you seriously going to walk away from it all to come back here to be with me? Come on, you and I both know the answer. And if that's the dream you want, then I want that for you, even though, selfishly, I want you to stay here."

She looked down at his hands around hers, strong and dependable, his thumbs stroking her wrists. He was right, of course. She was trying to have her cake and eat it too . . .

"Listen," he said, his voice gentle in the quiet gelateria. "You're too talented to stay here with me. I probably wouldn't have let you even if you'd said yes. But so you know, you're just about the most electric person I've ever met, and no one could ever, ever forget you. I know I won't. I've only known you two days and I love you already. All of those things you said about yourself? I love all those things about you, and if you were to stay, I'd love all the other parts you think make you imperfect too."

Hot, fast tears tumbled down Viv's cheeks.

"I'll stay," she said, panicked at the thought of leaving him behind. "I'm going to stay here with you, Santo. I am. No one will ever love me like you again."

He laughed as he shook his head. "You're such an idiot," he said. "The whole damn world's gonna love you as much as I do."

She envied his rose-tinted view of the world. "They haven't so far."

"Trust me," he said, resolute.

Viv could feel herself splitting in two, wanting to leave and wanting to stay, both choices terrifying her in different ways. "I wish I could, I want to, but I don't trust anyone. And no one trusts me," she muttered.

"I trust you," he said, steadfast.

"I wish I could believe you," she whispered, pushing her chair backward. "I should probably go."

He lifted his gaze to hers and held it steady, then suddenly stood and grabbed her hand. "I'll show you," he said, tugging her across to the counter. He tore a mint-green Belotti's napkin in half and grabbed a pen, and she watched as he wrote across it in bold blue ink, then handed it to her.

"That's how much I trust you," he said.

She scanned it, her breath caught in her throat.

"No one outside my family has ever seen that," he said. "If my family ever knew I'd given it to you, hell, I don't know what they'd do. Disown me or something, probably. But I trust you, Viv. I trust you to keep it safe. You can go out there and be brilliant now because we're connected, always. And every time you look at that napkin, I want you to remember that I'm right here on Mulberry Street if you ever need me."

He pulled her into his arms and hugged her harder than anyone had ever hugged her before.

"I'll bring it back," she whispered, the napkin pressed against her wildly beating heart. "I'll bring it back one day, I promise. I'll give it back to you because I won't need it anymore, because after that day you'll be there to make the gelato for me. I won't need the recipe to remember you by because you'll be in my life again."

"I look forward to that day," he said, pressing a kiss against her hair.

She stepped back and wiped her eyes, picking up a photograph propped against the cash register.

"Can I take this?" she said, looking at the picture of Santo leaning against the shop window, his hand raised to shield his eyes from the summer sun.

He nodded, then made a picture frame with his hands and looked at her through it.

"What are you doing?" she asked.

"Taking a photo of you with my mind," he said. "Keep still."

She raised a trembling smile for Santo's imaginary shot, then slid the photo and napkin inside her shirt for safekeeping.

"I'll be seeing you," she said, and he touched his fingers to his forehead in silent salute.

They didn't say another word. He crossed the black-and-white checkerboard gelateria floor and opened the glass painted door, and she nodded and walked out into the hot July morning, her head high.

Santo watched her until she disappeared in the distance, flexing his fingers at his sides, aware of the forever scorch from temporarily holding on to lightning.

22.

WALK AIMLESSLY, SNATCHES OF CHRISTMAS MUSIC REACH-
ing me from open shop doors. It feels as if New York has
pirouetted seamlessly from Thanksgiving straight into holiday festivities, easy as changing from pumpkin latte to cinnamon spice. I think I just royally screwed up. I mean, I'm
walking away single and off the hook about the recipe, so I
guess you could objectively call that a win, but it certainly
doesn't feel like one. I'm heartbroken—and worse, Gio is
too.

I don't want to go home, I don't know what to do with my
Monday. I'm ghost-walking without really seeing where I'm
going until raised voices in a side alley pull my attention back
outside of myself. A girl, seventeen or eighteen at most, and a
guy who looks a little older snatching her phone from her,
shoving the screen in her frightened face, close enough for
her to have to jerk her head backward against the wall. He's
mad about some message she's received, demanding details,
calling her names no one should be called. Nobody else has
noticed, or if they have they're not willing to intervene. I
pause, feeling sick as I'm mentally thrown straight back into
life with Adam. How I wish someone had intervened for me.

I see the guy step uncomfortably close to her, his forearm in front of him across her shoulders, pinning her to the wall.

"Get your hands off her right now."

The words bark out of me on instinct, and they both turn my way as I stalk toward them in the alley, unwilling to let him see my fear. He rocks his upper body back and throws his arms out to the sides as if to question who the hell I think I am, and she shakes her head, a tiny movement designed to send me on my way, telling me not to involve myself. I know that look all too well, and cobra-like fury rears up inside me, swallowing the fear.

"Mind your business, grandma," he says, his chin coming up, all bravado and laughing. "Nothing to see here, is there, Jade?"

I step closer and a single tear rolls down her cheek as she shakes her head.

"Nothing. Honestly, it's fine," she whispers. "You can go."

"Give her her phone back and get lost," I hiss. "Or I'll call the police. You choose." I pull my cellphone from my back pocket. "You've got exactly ten seconds."

He stares at me, desperate not to do as he's told by a woman twice his age and a good foot shorter, but I don't flinch a muscle. *I've dealt with worse than you, shithead,* I think, crossing my arms over my chest.

"Seven. Eight." I tap my phone screen into life and stare him down.

He all but growls as he bares his teeth and chucks the girl's phone on the ground as he shoulders past me.

"Stupid bitch," he says, right down my ear.

"Eat glass," I spit back, watching him leave.

I push my cellphone back into my pocket and turn to the girl. "Jade, right?" I pick up her phone and wipe it on my jeans before handing it back to her.

"Thanks," she says. "I was all right, you didn't need to do that."

"Oh, I really did," I say, matter-of-fact. She passes her hand down her face and I see she's shaking. My heart rages.

"Let's sit for a minute, give him time to bugger off." I nod toward a couple of concrete steps leading to the side entrance of one of the stores.

"Can I tell you something?" I say, sitting alongside her.

She shrugs, hunched forward, hands clasped around her phone.

"Is it to dump him?"

"Oh God, yes. Drop him like a stone," I say, no hesitation. "Because he won't change. He'll only get worse, and you'll get more and more isolated."

She takes a slow breath. "He doesn't hit me, if that's what you're thinking."

I nod. "My ex didn't hit me either. Violence isn't the only form of abuse. How long have you been together?"

She sits back and sighs, resting her head against the door. "Seven months. Maybe eight." She slants a look at me. "He isn't like that with anyone else."

"Let me guess," I say. "Everyone thinks he's a right laugh."

She nods.

"And he doesn't like your friends, so it's easier to just not see them." I don't phrase it as a question, saving her the bother of trying to defend the indefensible.

"My ex took everything from me. For the last year we

were together I didn't have a cellphone, or a bank card, or a door key. He dismantled my entire life, made me doubt myself, and I blamed myself for the way he treated me. He called me his little mouse, because I spent my days and my nights scurrying around the place trying not to do or say the wrong thing, desperate not to make him angry."

Jade finally looks at me properly, and I can see she's listening and, in parts, relating. Hopefully she's too young to have gone too far down this black hole, and maybe she's also too young to hear some of my unvarnished truths, but I can see her teetering on the edge of real trouble and I feel like it's my job to stand guard.

"Jade, this will not get better," I say. "I stayed with my ex for two years, and the truth is I'm still looking over my shoulder. I finally left him on Christmas Day, threw all my most precious belongings into a suitcase while he was passed out from vodka."

"And you're all right now?"

I lift one shoulder. "I'm working on it. Challenging assholes in alleyways, that sort of thing."

She rolls her eyes. "You made a good Marvel superhero."

I suppose I did, looking back. "Next time you see him, look him square in the eye and tell him—"

"To eat glass?" she cuts across me, wide-eyed, and half laughs.

"*Schitt's Creek* inspired," I say.

I discovered *Schitt's Creek* not long after arriving in New York. The beloved Rose family felt like a safe gang to hang out with until I was strong enough to face the world again. Sometimes I'd leave it on low all night in the background, just so I'd see familiar faces if I woke up in a cold sweat.

"My mom watches that," she says.

Way to make me feel ancient, Jade, I think. Coupled with her jerk boyfriend calling me "grandma," I might need to invest in a decent night cream.

"Does she know what's been going on?"

She shakes her head. "She's a nurse. She doesn't need my shit on top of everything else she has to deal with."

What I hear is that Jade loves her mum and I want to tell her to talk to her, to make the most of their time together while she can, but I think I've handed out enough unsolicited advice for one day.

"Want me to walk with you?" I say, sensing she's ready to go.

She shakes her head. "I'm good."

Back on the sidewalk, she lingers before walking away. "Thank you for . . . you know. For stopping."

"That's okay," I say.

She nods and walks off, quickly swallowed by the day, and I duck into a quiet café. I hope I made a difference. I hope I've altered the course of events for Jade, and that in time she might pay it forward and do the same for someone else, who in turn might form another link in the chain.

There wasn't a have-a-go superhero around when I needed one. I did it alone, and I see now that all of the effort I've put in from that day to this one will be for nothing if I'm unable to take my own advice. Am I *really* prepared to allow Adam to sit thousands of miles away and pull the strings of my life for his own perverse kicks? I know how his mind works. He'll have been keeping a regular eye out for me online, sure that I was flailing miserably somewhere in London. He must have been boiling in a vat of his own vitriolic piss

when he found me performing onstage in New York. Bobby
was right, I should never have responded to his message, but
the added complication of Bella backed me into a corner,
cowed. I'm not cowed anymore. I pull my phone out and open
messages.

> *Hey Bells! Great to see the video has so many
> views—in your face, Ellen Connelly! By the way,
> someone contacted me through you—a guy, he's
> trying to organize a school reunion, bleurgh! I'm
> going to say no—so glad I'm in a different country
> as a good excuse. I'm sorry he messaged you, he
> was always a bit random! If he messages you again,
> could you do me a big favor and just ignore it? He
> probably won't, but just in case—block and delete!
> See you soon xx*

There. Another link in the chain soldered into place. Eat
glass, Adam Bronson.

23.

ROBIN HAS WHISKED BOBBY AWAY ON AN OVERNIGHT surprise. It's the first time I've been properly alone in the building and it feels kind of weird. Even the cat's deserted me. I've splashed out on a decent steak and a bottle of red, an impulse buy on the way back from my stint as a superhero earlier. I'm just about to warm the griddle pan when someone presses the buzzer down on the street. I go perfectly still. *Is he here? Has he jumped straight on a plane and tracked me down?* I tiptoe to the rain-spattered window and peer around the edge of the frame, hoping he won't look up as I look down. He does, and I almost slump against the glass in relief. *Gio.* I pull up the sash.

"Special delivery," he shouts, his face turned up into the rain. He's holding a box in his arms. "Can I come up?"

I slam the window shut and buzz him in.

"You must have some serious muscles to have carried this thing to the gelateria," he says, rainwater spiking his dark lashes as he stands in my doorway. "It weighs a ton."

My gelato maker has come home at last.

"I'm stronger than I look," I say, a glass of wine down and full of bravado.

"Can I come in?"

"Oh. Yes, yes." I step aside to let him put the box on the kitchen work surface.

He looks at me, hands shoved deep in his pockets, shoulders lifted high around his ears. "Look, you can tell me I'm wrong here if you want, Iris, but I don't think you meant the things you said this morning."

I bite my lip because all I want to do is tell him how right he is, and he fills my silence with words.

"Monday nights and all my mornings will be too lonely without you." He reaches into the box and pulls out a paper bag. "I got you something."

I'm so entirely charmed by this man. I take the bag and look inside.

"You went back to the Christmas store," I say softly, dangling the glittered silver whisk ornament from my fingers.

"And you know how much I hated it in there," he says.

"I remember."

"Don't end this," he says, his eyes urgent on mine. "If you don't want to be more, I understand, but I don't want to lose what we have."

I step onto the island of us and hold my hand out to him, pulling him close. "You're wet," I say, even though I couldn't care less.

"Rain," he murmurs. "It's filthy out there."

"You better stay here tonight," I whisper against his mouth.

"I really should get out of these clothes," he says, holding my face.

"I'll run you a bath," I say, and he sighs into my mouth as he kisses me.

"It's been a real long time since anyone did that for me."

He talks me into getting into the bath with him, which is never going to go well as it's a small, old-fashioned tub with large, bulbous taps, absolutely not made for two people.

"This isn't as romantic as it was in my head," he says, exasperated when he shifts to give me space and traps my knee against the side, making me yelp.

"This is every bit as romantic as it was in my head," I say, when he sweeps me up and carries me to my bedroom a few minutes later.

"My back disagrees," he says, laughing as he tumbles us both onto the bed in a heap.

WE SHARE THE SINGLE steak on one plate a while later, sitting pressed together at the chipped kitchen table. My wineglass from earlier becomes our wineglass, and we don't care at all because this is the best steak anyone ever tasted and the wine is nectar in our mouths.

"I'm imagining that we're on a desert island," I say. "We've checked into the only place on the island, and it only has one room."

"Ocean view?"

I nod and slice a sliver of steak. "One of those wraparound porches with sunchairs, uninterrupted turquoise as far as the eye can see."

"Sunshine?"

"Sunglasses every damn day."

"What's it called, this place?"

"The Monday Night Motel," I say.

"I mean, I meant the island, but I kind of like that now you've said it."

"Service is a bit shit, though," I say, tapping our empty wineglass.

He looks over my shoulder. "I'll try to catch someone's eye."

"Forget it, I'll do it myself," I say, topping us up.

"We should complain to management," he says, taking a sip of wine.

"Better not," I say. "We might come again next Monday."

"Let's take our drink through to the bar," he says, when we're done eating.

I follow him to the sofa, lying with my head in his lap when he sprawls in the corner seat, his arm flung out across the cushions.

"This is turning out to be a pretty fine vacation," he says, resting his head back and closing his eyes.

"An easy five stars on Tripadvisor," I say, my legs propped on the back of the sofa.

"Oh no, let's not tell anyone else about this place," he says, looking down at me.

"You're so right," I say. "We don't want word getting out."

He strokes his index finger down the bridge of my nose. "You look peaceful," he says.

I find I can't easily answer. It's been a tumultuous day, and I didn't expect it to end with Gio. I move up the sofa into his lap and lay my head on his chest, relieved he didn't take me at my word this morning. He pulls the blanket from the back of the sofa and settles it over us, then closes his arms around me so I'm warm and held and safe. I listen to his breathing as he strokes my hair, and it's the dictionary definition of bliss. I haven't felt this depth of peace for as long as I can remember. Maybe ever.

24.

My MOTHER TOOK ME TO SEE *LOVE ACTUALLY* FOR MY sixteenth birthday, popcorn smuggled in from the discount store. A trip to the movies was a high-days-and-holidays-level treat on our roster. Every time I catch the film on TV I remember my mother laughing beside me at Hugh Grant's terrible dancing and the pin-drop silent audience heartbreak for Emma Thompson when she cried in her bedroom. My mother sang Joni Mitchell songs as part of her set for a while afterward, a heaven-sent match with the melancholy smoke of her voice.

Bella is sixteen in a few days. There's to be a surprise party at the gelateria after closing time tomorrow and I offered to make the cake. It's been pure joy to flex my baking muscles again, especially in the gleaming kitchens at Belotti's—the temperamental stove at my apartment is far too risky for something as special as a sixteenth birthday cake. The temperature dial is more a request at home, it's a moody old beast that burns on a whim.

Gift-buying was a whole new world of angst for me. I've no clue what sixteen-year-old girls are into, so I've picked out a simple silver trace chain bracelet with a tiny piano charm. I'm trying to strike the right note for "family friend who's also Dad's girlfriend, of sorts," if there is such a category. There probably isn't, it's fairly niche.

Gio and I have paid another visit to the Monday Night Motel of Dreams, trying to pack enough into one night to see us through the week ahead since we're no longer "working" on the recipe together. It's a little like a long-distance love affair, a long week punctuated by one bone-meltingly good interlude. He calls me sometimes after midnight when Bella has gone to bed, hushed conversations in the dark, my phone on my pillow where I wish his head could be. And then I close my eyes to sleep alone, dully aware of the ever-present coil of tension in my gut, the low, insistent tick of a clock I'm ignoring at my peril. It breaks through into my dreams, changing them to nightmares where Gio turns to me in the coffee shop but it's Adam wearing a Belotti's apron, or the ripped napkin with their recipe across it falls from my pocket onto Maria's polished mahogany floorboards. I wake in a hot panic, always with a sickly dread of having let them all down, cast out of the painted gelateria door surrounded by the shoddiness of my lies.

Are you sure Shen can cover my shift tomorrow?

I press SEND on my message to Bobby, hoping he's remembered to make the arrangements. His reply comes back unsurprisingly fast—the man's phone is in his hand at all times.

Green light, songbird.

I smile, relieved. I don't see enough of him at the moment, he's caught up in the whirlwind of opening a new Very Tasty

Noodle House location and preliminary plans for another in Queens. Even so, he never lets me down.

"IS SHE TOO OLD for a surprise party?"

Gio looks at me and Sophia, doubt all over his face.

"No way," I say.

"You're never too old for a surprise party," Sophia says.

"Maybe it's just that I don't like surprises," he says, checking his phone.

I file that information away for examination when I'm alone later. All of Gio's sisters and their various partners and children are packed into the gelateria, plus Maria of course, all waiting for the guest of honor.

"She's coming," he says loudly so everyone hears. "Quiet!"

Sophia knocks off the lights and a hush falls over the jittery gathering, excited whispers from the smallest family members. Gio's hand finds mine in the dark, a momentary connection.

"Shush," someone says, as we see Bella's silhouette move into the doorway and hear her key in the door. Sophia flicks the lights on as the door swings open and everyone leaps from their place, shouts of surprise and "Happy Birthday!" filling the gelateria with noise and excitement. Bella's double-take makes everyone's clandestine effort worth it: she lights up like the star on top of the Rockefeller tree when she realizes this is all for her.

This is family, I think. *This is what it's like.*

The kids break into a rendition of "Happy Birthday" and the family join in, English with a smattering of Italian, and

Gio moves forward to hug his daughter so tight that her feet leave the ground. She's laughing as he sets her down and pulls her bobble hat off, and for a moment they are a bubble of two contained within the snow globe of their family.

"Let her through, we all need a hug," Maria says, a prettily wrapped parcel clutched in her hands.

There's holiday music on the radio in the background and the gelateria has been decorated for Christmas, white fairy lights glowing around the family gallery on the wall, a festive wreath on the kitchen door. It feels as much like a holiday party as a birthday, until someone shouts for cake and Sophia cranes her neck to look for me. I follow her into the kitchen where the cake stands ready to go. The family left the design up to me, and after much deliberation I went for a huge, double-layered rich chocolate cake laced with Bella's favorite cherry filling skimmed with white chocolate frosting. I've piled chocolate truffles and plump fresh black cherries high on top with a dusting of gold glitter for the birthday girl.

I am pretty pleased with it, and nervous too now it's time to carry it out to the waiting family. We lift the board between us and someone dims the lights as we crab carefully sideways to place it down on the counter, resplendent with its lit candles.

The family sing again, and I feel Gio's eyes on me as everyone exclaims at the sight of the blazing cake.

"*Buon compleanno, mia nipote,*" Maria says, her arm around her granddaughter's shoulders. The candles illuminate Bella's face as she holds her curls back to lean forward and blow out all the candles on one long breath, earning herself a ripple of applause, and Sophia's phone flashes as she captures the moment.

"Iris made the cake," she says. "Isn't it amazing?"

I feel heat creeping up my neck as everyone looks at me.

"I like to cook," I say, shrugging away their effusive praise. My mother would be deeply unimpressed to hear me reduce my years of training and kitchen experience to "I like to cook," but here it's accepted on face value.

"I like to cook too but it never turns out like that," Francesca says, her eyes on the cake.

Pascal, her husband, nods sagely but doesn't dare say a word.

A knife appears, the cake is cut, and champagne flutes are found and filled. There's a groan of horror when Pascal produces a bottle of his lethal limoncello, but he just smiles and shrugs, nonchalant as he tips a little into everyone's champagne.

I find myself beside Bella, and I reach down into my bag and dig out the small gift-wrapped box.

"Happy birthday," I say, and she grins, excited.

"You shouldn't have," she says, pulling the string bow open. "But I'm glad you did!"

I chew the inside of my bottom lip as she unwraps it, hoping I've got it right. I know I have when she opens the box and touches her fingertip lightly against the little silver piano charm.

"I love it," she whispers, lifting the silver link bracelet from the box.

I help her fasten it and she holds her wrist out for us to admire it.

"Perfect," I say.

She looks at me, and then back at the bracelet and smiles. She's about to say something when one of the kids starts banging the piano keys, a discordant, out-of-tune clatter that makes people wince.

"Bella, stop them, I beg you," Pascal says. "Play something for us?"

She looks wrong-footed. "I don't—"

"Something Christmassy?" Maria chips in, overhearing.

Sophia helps her niece out. "I'll sing if you play. And you too, Iris?"

I sensed that was coming and knock back half of my lemon-laced champagne for courage. "Of course."

Bella lifts one shoulder and sighs, but the sparkle in her eyes suggests she's actually quite happy to be in musical demand. She takes a seat on the piano stool and tucks herself in, then glances up at Sophia and me.

"Umm, I played 'Jingle Bells' for the school concert a few years ago?" she says, the upward inflection at the end of her sentence turning the statement into a question.

Sophia looks at me and laughs, and I pull up the lyrics on my phone. "Got it."

Bella begins to play, her quick fingers conjuring instant Christmas spirit with the chirpy introduction. Sophia's voice is every bit as clear and confident as she is when she starts to sing, and I find myself happy to join in, because I'm not the only one. Everyone knows the words and joins in to more or less a degree. Enthusiasm from the little ones, a shoulder jiggle from Maria, and Gio's sisters have the kind of blend to their voices that only comes from decades of singing together. Gio has his back braced against the wall nearest to the door, and for a second I catch his eye among the noisy bonhomie and he gives me a look that whisks me straight to the Monday

Night Motel. It sears me. And then he looks away, distracted by movement outside the glass door. Most people don't notice that there's someone out there in the doorway, but I do and panic ices over my vocal cords. I'm singing but there's no sound coming out, because there's a hooded guy outside and Gio is frowning as he unlocks the door. *Don't open it. Please, Gio, don't open the door.* I put a hand out on a nearby table to steady myself, unsure how everyone else is still singing with this happening, how Bella's speed is getting quicker and quicker to make the children laugh, a crazy spinning-top whirling faster and faster. I want to scream at everyone to shut up because it's all white noise as Gio takes a surprised step backward and the stranger walks into the gelateria and throws his fur-lined parka hood back.

Bella's hands go still on the keys and the singing dies out as everyone realizes there's someone new in the room.

"I didn't expect a welcome party!"

My breath slams back in, as if I've been choking on a piece of meat and someone just thumped me hard on the back and dislodged it. It's not Adam. It's not Adam. I don't know who it is, but it's not Adam Bronson.

"*Dad?*"

Gio is staring at the newcomer, incredulous, and Maria rushes forward, her arms out in an embrace.

"Felipe, this is a real surprise!"

Everyone springs back into action, the moment of inertia broken. Someone takes the new arrival's coat, babies are placed in his arms, champagne glasses are refilled, the birthday party a reunion party too now. Gio's bronzed, globe-trotting father is swamped, and I hang back, watching the scene from the edges. Now that I know who he is, he's recognizable from my mother's photograph album, black-and-white stills from high-energy gigs, electricity leaping from the images. He's considerably older, of course, but he has that Peter Pan kind of wiriness that refuses to age and a head of steel-grey hair. I thread my way toward the kitchen door and watch him, transfixed.

"Tell me I'm nothing like him."

Gio is behind me, he must have ducked into the kitchen for something. His fingers curve around my hip, and he quietly tugs me into the kitchen and closes the door.

"Are you okay?" I say, touching his face. "That must have been a shock for you."

"He always does that. Appears out of thin air like a genie out of a bottle." He shakes his head, a resigned lift of his brows as he puts his hand against the door over my shoulder and leans into me.

"I'm so glad you're here, *cucchiaino*," he whispers.

The term of endearment takes me back to our first night together upstairs, to the movie, to the rooftop, to his bed. I stand on tiptoe to kiss him and straightaway it's how it always is between us, a lit fuse on dynamite. He takes it up a notch further, urgent, trying to escape the reality happening on the other side of the door.

"We should stop," I say, wishing with every fiber of my being that we didn't have to.

He rests his forehead on mine. "I know. I just needed to be with you for a moment."

"I have a lot of moments like that," I say, unguarded, and he pulls his head back and looks me in the eyes. He doesn't say anything, just cups my face and strokes his thumb over my cheek. I look at him, and he looks at me, and there in the kitchen with his entire family on the other side of the door, we say things with our eyes that we can't say with our mouths. His breath fans my lips as I silently tell him of the darkness I hold inside me, and his heart beats beneath my palm as his eyes tell me he longs for me, for the magic that happens when we touch.

"Better now?" I say.

He nods. "Better now."

I busy myself covering the half-eaten cake while he heads back through to the party, and after a few calming minutes I slip back in there and find myself collared by Sophia.

"Iris, come meet my rock-star uncle," she says, limoncello-tipsy.

I nod and paint on a wide smile. "Hello," I say, sticking my hand out for something to do and immediately wishing I hadn't.

He studies my hand for a few seconds, surprised, and then shakes it because it would be rude not to. He locks eyes with me and I feel his handshake slow and see his brow furrow.

"Have we met before?" he says, his head on one side.

I shake my head. "I don't think so," I say, hoping it's not a lie. I was a toddler when my mother moved us to London from L.A., and I don't know if she ever saw Felipe Belotti in the interim years. Not that he'd recognize me personally, of course, but there are echoes of my mother all over my face.

I'm glad Sophia has had enough champagne to not think anything of the slightly odd exchange, and Pascal looms with booze to top up everyone's glass. I use the distraction to move away, gathering my jacket from the coat stand. I can't see Gio anywhere, so I take one last glance around and let myself quietly out into the crisp, cold night air on Mulberry Street.

> *Hey you, have called it a night before Pascal can catch me again with that limoncello, I can already feel it going to my head. Call me later when things have calmed down. Xx*

It's a lame excuse to not say goodbye but the best I can come up with as I walk briskly away from the gelateria, safer with every step I put between me and Felipe Belotti.

25.

"WHAT AM I GOING TO DO, SMIRNOFF?"

The cat was waiting for me on the noodle house step, a grumpy doorman in need of tuna to restore his mood. He's now well fed and sitting on my windowsill giving his paws the once-over, thoroughly disinterested in my conversation.

"The thing is, I don't know if Felipe is going to realize why he thinks we might have met before."

I have my mother's scrapbook open on my knees, a monochrome shot of a young Felipe back-to-back with my mother onstage, electric guitar slung across his body, microphone in her raised hand. Her head is tipped back on his shoulder, her mouth open mid-song. She's in a black vest and jeans, he's in faded jeans and a sweat dampened T-shirt, tattoos running riot down his arms, a joint behind his ear. It looks like an eighties album cover. Her hair is cut in choppy bangs not unlike mine, her profile so similar to my own. She's probably nineteen or so, frighteningly young now I have Bella to compare against, as close to a child as a woman. She fell pregnant within a year of this photo, and there's a whole swathe of her life I know barely anything about. I close the album and put my hands on it, my guts churning with anxiety. There's only one thing I can think of to help my mood right now, my childish fail-safe. It's turned ten already and my gelato machine takes a while, but even the action of loading the ingredients is soothing.

I jump when my cellphone pings.

Midnight gelato date?

I sigh with relief. Bobby.

You have the ears of a bat.

He sends me back a string of emojis, bats and ice creams and love hearts, and I pull the two pink melamine bowls from the back of the cupboard and line them up in readiness.

"FUUUUUCK," BOBBY SAYS, his eyes widening as I regale him with the earlier events of the evening.

We're either end of the sofa with our bowls in our hands, the blanket spread between us, the scrapbook open to the image of Felipe and my mother.

"What's he like now?"

"Felipe?" I frown. "He has a nomadic look about him, as if all the places he's visited have grafted layers onto who he is. Faded tattoos, leather bracelets, that sort of thing. He's skinny, and still quite a lot like he is in these photos, just more . . ."

"More . . . ?"

I cast around for an appropriate word to describe him. "I don't know. Walnutty?"

Bobby choke-laughs on his gelato. "Walnutty?"

I screw my nose up. "I mean he looks as if he's sat in the

sun for years without sun cream, weathered and lined, you know? Yet still boyish somehow, which is weird."

"Lack of responsibility." Bobby flares his nostrils as he scrapes his spoon around his bowl. Loyalty is engrained in his soul, it's one of the things I love about him, and it means he's deeply unimpressed with the idea of a man leaving his brother to raise his child in order to skip off around the world playing guitar.

"God, I've missed this stuff." He gets up and pulls the silver gelato pail from the freezer. "More?"

I nod. It's definitely a double serving kind of night.

"I don't know what to do, Bob," I say. It feels inevitable that Felipe is going to piece together who I am.

"The man's in his sixties and lived a crazy life, chances are he'll have forgotten all about you by morning," Bobby says, handing me my refilled bowl. "I mean, I'm thirty-seven and my memory's already shot, what chance does he have?"

"You're thirty-eight."

"Like hell I am." He pauses, affronted, spoon midway to his mouth. "Oh God, I am." He shrugs and points his spoon at me. "Which just illustrates my point. He's a pickled walnut. Not making assumptions, but am guessing he's probably had more than his fair share of the old giggle smoke over the years." He mimes smoking a joint, inhaling and blowing smoke rings.

"You really think so?"

Bobby is still watching his imaginary smoke rings. "Felipe sounds like a rolling stone. He won't stick around for long. Just avoid him until he hits the road again."

I stir my melting gelato, casting a long glance at the photo of Felipe and my mother. In different circumstances I'd love to talk to him about her, he'd be a rare glimpse back into that world I know so little of.

"Seriously, Iris, do not let this be another reason to dump that delectable man. He might believe you and not come back next time."

I can only hope Bobby's right and that, like the genie in the lamp, Felipe will disappear in a puff of smoke.

26.

"IRIS, THERE'S A GUY OUT FRONT ASKING FOR YOU."

I whip around from the stove and stare at Shen, panicked. She's seen Gio, she'd have said if it was him. The Adam Bronson dread that's becoming all too constant swills over me like foul water.

"What does he look like?" I whisper.

Shen's mouth twists. "Way too old to be wearing a shark tooth necklace and mirrored sunglasses even though it's been dark for"—she glances at the clock—"like, six hours?"

It's half past ten, a whisker away from closing up. I peep through the gap in the door to the restaurant beyond and see Felipe nursing a shot glass, his face turned toward the shadowed street.

"So much for being a rolling stone," I mutter, stepping back from the door. It's been twenty-four hours since Bella's birthday party and, unfortunately, it appears that Felipe's memory is not the magic roundabout Bobby predicted.

"I can tell him you're not here if you like?"

I shake my head, knowing this isn't something I can avoid. Better he speaks to me now than to Gio first.

"Just ask him to wait, I need ten minutes to finish up in here."

She doesn't come back so I assume Felipe has agreed, and when I'm done in the kitchen I head front of house.

"Go on home, Shen, I'll lock up," I say.

She shoots a frown toward Felipe and then a questioning look at me, and I nod a silent yes, it's okay to leave me here alone with that guy. I wait while she gathers her coat and I see her out, locking the door behind her.

"Another?" I say, looking at Felipe's empty glass.

He nods and leans back in his chair, watching me as I get myself a tumbler and take the bottle of Jack Daniel's back to the table with me. He's silent as I pour us both a drink, screwing the cap on slowly as I wait for him to speak first.

"Listen, let me save us both some time here," he says eventually. "You are without doubt Vivien and Charlie's daughter. You look like her, you sound like her—oh, I've seen the videos—and," he touches my hand across the table, "you're wearing her ring."

Instinctively, I twist the signet ring on my wedding finger and he knocks his drink back in one.

"And now you've turned up here and settled yourself nicely into the middle of my family. I may be getting on in years, but that's no coincidence, is it?"

He makes it sound cold and premeditated, as if I'm trying to exploit the Belottis, and it stings. I don't know how much of the truth Felipe deserves. I hear the accusatory tone in his voice and it feels both chastising and unjust, because from what I know of him he's been almost entirely absent from his son's life and is hardly entitled to walk in and play the protective father card.

I touch the bottle. "More?"

"I'd prefer answers," he says, but pushes his glass toward me regardless.

"Okay," I say, topping him up. "You're right, I'm Vivien's daughter."

"Did she put you up to this?"

I'm offended on her behalf, but of course he doesn't know. "My mother died a few years ago." I sit with the pain of saying the words aloud, a wound that never heals.

To give him his dues, he looks genuinely shocked, deep furrows channeling his brow.

"But she would still have been so young," he says, shaking his head.

"Yes," I say. "She was fifty-two."

We sit in silence as he digests the news.

"I'm very sorry to hear that," he says, stiff.

"Thank you," I say, equally clipped, even though the floor is still mine. Regardless of the news about my mother, I still need to provide him with answers to his questions.

"Things were difficult after she died," I say. "I came to New York for a fresh start. My mother's best memories were made here, it seemed as good a place to start again as any. I went to Katz's Deli—she used to tell me about the time she sang —"

"Just down the street from there," he says, cutting me off. "The cops moved us in the end. I can still see one of them picking your mother up, even as she sang." He shakes his head and huffs. "Still singing when they put her in the back of the cop car too."

I didn't know that last detail. I sit for a second and allow it to embroider itself onto the story in my head.

"I came here because I had nowhere else to go. I wanted to see her reference points, to stand in the places she'd stood, experience the city she'd loved. I had this crazy feeling that I'd feel closer to her here than anywhere else."

I don't tell him that I've brought her ashes to New York to scatter one day when I feel strong enough to let her go.

"And so I walked, and I saw a 'chef wanted' sign in the window here, and that was that. I had no clue that Belotti's gelateria existed until . . ." It'll be easier to show him than tell him. "Wait there."

I leave him in the closed-up restaurant while I run upstairs for my mother's scrapbook, pausing to carefully remove the torn napkin first. That secret belongs to Santo and my mother, an indiscretion that's not for Felipe's eyes.

"This was my mother's," I say, laying the scrapbook on the table when I sit back down. It's open to the photograph of Santo, the glass door behind him in the background.

"She told me he was the only man she thought she ever truly loved, but never spoke his surname or told me where the photo was taken."

Felipe finally removes his mirrored sunnies to study the photo, tapping it lightly with his index finger.

"Always the hero," he murmurs, a story between brothers for another day. The Santo in the photograph is eighties cool and unencumbered, unaware that in years to come he'll raise his brother's son.

"It was the glass door," I say. "The photo could have been taken anywhere, but I walked past that door on Mulberry Street and I knew straightaway that this was another echo from my mother's story. I couldn't not see inside. It was as straightforward as that. No agenda or plan, I just walked through the door and met Gio and Sophia and everyone else, and that's where my mother's story ended and mine began."

"And no one knows about your mother's connection to Santo?"

"*I* don't know about my mother's connection to him, besides this single photo," I say. "Her history led me through the door, but what has happened since has had nothing to do with the past."

I think of the photo of my mother in the Belotti family album, her face turned away from the camera.

"You have to tell them," he says. "Our family doesn't stand for secrets like this."

Childish defiance grips me. *Why? Why should I tell them? What good will it do?* I don't ask him the questions that thunder through my head.

"Is there something between you and Gio?"

My defiance turns to desperation. I look into the depths of my drink because I don't want to tell Felipe the truth. I know Gio and I cannot stay forever at the Monday Night Motel, but it seems grossly unfair that this man who is never here should be the reason why it ends.

Felipe reads my silence for what it is and sighs.

"Look, some might say I don't have a right to steamroll in given how little I've been around, but the family seem to genuinely like you and that concerns me. I'm sure you're a decent kid, but they've been through enough already, with Santo. It was a long time ago, but your mother did a number on him, and the shock of seeing your face, given his condition now, worries me. And Maria—she doesn't deserve to feel like the consolation prize . . ." He swallows his drink and reaches for the bottle to refill his own glass. I wonder if it's irresponsible of me not to stop him, but then I think of the photo of him with my mother and realize he's more than aware of his own limits.

"I haven't been any kind of father to Gio," he says. "Maybe this is my one chance to watch his back." He eyeballs me across the table. "You tell him yourself what brought you through our family's door or I'm going to have to." He swills the whiskey around in his glass. "It's not an ultimatum, Iris, I'm not having a *Godfather* moment. I'm just trying to do right by my kid for once."

I expect he can see how much this speech has winded me, and he reaches across the table and pats my hand.

"You can take your time," he says. "I can see it's not easy, but I'm sticking around for a while." He clears his throat and flips into a heavy New York accent. "Thought I'd spend the holidays in New York with the family, see the ball drop, *capisce?*"

I look up and see the rogue twinkle in his eye. In other circumstances I'd probably quite like him. I mean, I'd hate to have to rely on him in an emergency, but he seems to be someone who thinks of life as a merry jig, a party he's always invited to. My mother was much the same way.

"That was quite menacing," I say with a half smile.

He picks up his fedora from the seat beside him and places it on his head. Jaunty angle, of course.

"Blood's thicker than water," he says.

"Again, menacing," I say, getting up to let him out.

I lock up and pour myself another drink, the scrapbook still open in front of me. Blood is thicker than water, Felipe said, an offhand, overused phrase that I feel the accuracy of like a knife between my ribs tonight. Belotti blood is thick

and rich, the binding agent that holds them all together, even
Felipe. And I understand it well, because even though there
was just me and my mother in our family unit, the bond that
glued us together sustains me. I'm alone in the world, but
never entirely, because her love shields me even now.

She didn't have a family of her own. Abandoned on some
town hall steps at three days old with nothing but a blanket
and a gold signet ring, she was a product of the 1960s London
care system, passed from foster home to foster home until she
left for America. Her voice saved her. It saved us. It was her
currency when she was broke, her identity in the absence of a
birth certificate or a loving home. She was a motherless child,
and because of her own experience she held me closer, loved
me harder.

I twist my mother's signet ring on my finger again, a
heavy conviction in my heart that I must do the right thing. I
appreciate that Felipe has given me some grace in terms of
schedule, and it's not as if I ever thought I'd be able to keep
the balls in the air indefinitely: Adam; the recipe; my mother;
Gio. *Gio.* Much as I like to tell myself that what's happening
between us is separate and private from the rest of the world,
it isn't really. We are all concentric circles, not desert islands.
I don't have much time left with Gio before I'm going to
have to draw the blinds for the last time, because if I know
anything about Gio Belotti, it's that he values honesty and
loyalty above all. I've compromised both of those things to be
with him and, once he knows, I don't think there's going to
be any more to our story.

Life is just so damn complicated, isn't it, a series of random coincidences and chance meetings that add up to a lifetime. Perhaps in coming here the symmetry between my

mother's life and my own has become too linear. There's probably a cosmic scraping sound every time our tracks unexpectedly overlap, a shower of dangerous iron filaments sparking through the ether.

I pour myself another generous measure of whiskey in the darkness of the noodle house and sit alone, recalling how Felipe mentioned the ball drop. I watched it alone on my small TV last year, Times Square ablaze with technicolor billboards and overexcited people in razzmatazz party hats and puffa jackets, their eyes on that huge faceted ball as they shouted the countdown to midnight. I'd planned on going to bed early and missing it altogether, but as the New Year flashed up in huge block numbers and the presenters waltzed to the sentimental sound of "Auld Lang Syne," I wrapped my arms around a cushion and let the tears stream down my face. But then they changed tempo in Times Square to Sinatra's "New York, New York" and showered the crowd with glittered confetti, and I lowered my cushion and watched, my tears drying to mascara tracks on my cheeks. I found myself mumbling the words, and then sitting up and singing the words, my voice trembling but gathering strength, because if I can make it in New York, I can make it anywhere. And I have. I've made lifelong friends in Bobby and Robin, I have a job and a home and part-time custody of a reluctant cat. Those things matter, and they were enough until I saw that painted glass door.

Sitting alone in the dark noodle house, I count how many days there are until New Year's Eve. Nineteen, I think. Three of them are Mondays, including tomorrow, but the holidays will probably mean Gio's busy with family stuff. Felipe didn't expressly set a New Year's deadline, but I understood him well enough—don't dangle my son's heart on a string. Impending exclusion isn't a new feeling for me, but I guess I'd hoped I'd left it behind me. No such luck. I'm about to be that lonesome kid again, the one with her face pressed against the window, on the outside looking in.

I wish I could turn the clock back to the Feast of San Gennaro festival and guide myself past Belotti's without a sideways glance. I didn't notice the heat from the shower of sparks when the tracks of the past and present touched that day, but I feel them tonight, hot filings scattergunned across my chest. They really fucking hurt.

27.

Wrap up warm tonight, I'm taking you somewhere
I think you'll like.

Gio's text arrives as I'm staring into the depressingly empty fridge trying to decide.

Or you could just come over and roleplay Moonstruck again?
Masterful Gio turned me on something terrible.

I press SEND and my cell bips again after a couple of minutes. I drop the gone-soft cereal in the bin as I reach for my phone.

Put your coat on or freeze, we're going out whether
you like it or not.

My eyes round, startled, and I laugh sharply in my quiet apartment even as my phone bips for a third time.

For the record, I really didn't want to send that text.

And that, right there, is why I feel so safe with this man. I crack eggs into a bowl as I text with my other hand.

Don't ruin it now, I was just about to call you for phone sex.

> *Great. Am about to go into a meeting with Bella's teacher and now all I can think of is you naked.*

You're so welcome.

> *And you're so . . . and the teacher's here. Be ready at 7, I'll pick you up.*

I flick the gas on beneath the pan and tip the eggs in.

Damn it, and I'd just unhooked my bra. Saved by the bell, Belotti x

I make the omelet on autopilot, tired even though it's barely half past nine. Last night's heavy-handed serving of Jack Daniel's sent me to sleep but didn't keep me there—I woke up anxious a little after four and ended up at the kitchen table drinking coffee. I can't expect Felipe to keep my secrets indefinitely and it isn't fair to ask it of him. It's good of him to allow me to handle things in my own time. I came to a conclusion of sorts in the small hours. I'm going to live my life strictly in the here and now until the ball drops in Times Square, and then I'll tell Gio everything. Oh, I'm well aware that, as plans go, this one is akin to driving headlong at a solid brick wall with my foot flat to the floor. There's nothing else I can do, though, because the thing I privately acknowledged this morning is that I'm uncontrollably, intoxicatingly, ferociously in love with Gio Belotti.

———

I HEAR A CAR HORN rather than my door buzzer, and cross to look out of the window, surprised. It's just before seven and, as requested, I'm bundled into my winter coat and bobble hat, gloves shoved in my pocket, scarf on the table to pick up on my way out.

Gio is outside, not in a cab as I expected, but standing in the road beside a long, low-slung retro black car.

I scrape the window up and lean out into the see-your-breath cold evening.

"Have you ever seen *Pretty Woman*?"

He rests his arm on the open driver's door and looks up at me. "Not that I remember."

"Richard Gere pulls up in a fancy car and climbs the fire escape," I call down.

My mother always liked to say she was named after Vivian from *Pretty Woman,* even though she was born more than twenty years before its release. Gio eyes the rickety ladder zigzagging the front of our building and shakes his head, and I laugh and slam the window shut.

Down on the sidewalk, I stand and gaze at the imposing muscle car. It's gleaming black and chrome, long, low, *Saturday Night Fever* kind of cool.

"Did you borrow it from John Travolta?"

He grins and bangs the roof. "It's a 1972 Cadillac Sedan Deville, and it's Papa's pride and joy. He asked me to drive it sometimes and keep it oiled for when he can use it again."

"It's big enough to have its own zip code," I say as Gio gets in and leans across to open my door.

"Oh my God," I groan, because I'm enveloped by cherry-red leather. The car smells just as you'd hope it would, of nourished leather and wood polish, of age and distinction, definite gentleman's club vibes.

"Can I live in here? This is way more comfortable than my couch."

I stroke my hand over the teak dashboard. I wouldn't be surprised to see a button marked "bourbon over ice"—and I'd press it too. It's a drive-in movies kind of ride, a deep, button-back bench seat in the front with an armrest pulled down between us.

"Pretty cool, huh?" Gio says, gunning the engine.

"Where are we going?"

"Not far," he says. "It's a surprise."

I settle in, surreptitiously watching Gio out of the corner of my eye. "You look sexy driving this."

He shoots me a look. "Don't ask me to talk dirty again," he says. "You got me in enough trouble this morning."

"You liked it," I say, laughing into my scarf.

He doesn't deny it. "You didn't really take your bra off, did you?"

I contemplate a lie. "No, I was making an omelet."

He laughs, shaking his head as he turns the radio on. "You're a real bad influence on me, Iris."

I look out of my window, trying to stay in the moment rather than let his off-the-cuff words spiral me into thinking exactly how bad I am for Gio, jumping forward to the New Year when his opinion of me will hit the floor. The idea of him thinking badly of me is lead in my heart, so I tune my ear into the Christmas songs on the radio and hum along instead.

———

TRUE TO HIS WORD, our journey isn't a long one, but it's one I hope to remember forever. The combination of the car, the man driving it, and the glittering city lights as we drove across Brooklyn Bridge was the kind of perfect snapshot you can't hope to capture on your cellphone camera. I've captured it in my head instead and filed it away to look back at in the days and years to come, in much the same way my mother spun a million love stories around that single photograph of Santo.

"Here should do it," Gio says, pulling the car up curbside in a quiet residential street.

"Is it a restaurant?" I say, hoping not because Bobby and Robin called me upstairs to share pizza earlier.

Gio shakes his head as he gets out and locks the car.

"A bar?"

He shakes his head again and links his arm through mine.

"You're not going to tell me, are you?"

"You'll see," he says.

The farther we walk, the more people there are on the streets too, obviously headed the same place as us. Couples, families with little kids, everyone bundled up in winter coats and hats.

We round a corner and I gasp, coming to a surprised standstill.

"Worth the suspense?"

The road ahead is a blaze of color, every house almost obscured by Christmas lights and ornaments. Huge golden snowflakes, life-size snowmen, illuminated Santas climbing down chimneys. This is the America of my childhood movie-spun fantasies, Disney-bold and brashly beautiful.

"What is this place?" I breathe.

"Dyker Heights," he says. "They've done this every year since the eighties, it goes on for another twenty blocks or so."

We join the throngs of sightseers walking slowly through the illuminated streets, and honestly, I feel as if someone scooped me up and dropped me on a holiday movie set. Every house seems to be more ornately decorated than the last. Candy canes and dancing elves fill the front lawns, shimmering presents line the porch steps, starlight nets cover trees and shrubs.

"You can probably see this from space," I say, blown away by the sheer scale and spectacle.

We pause outside a huge old house guarded by a battalion of ten-foot-tall nutcrackers, their brass uniform buttons flashing gold as Christmas music pumps from hidden speakers. Angels dance between the trees, and a life-size nativity scene takes up most of the lawn.

"Wow," is all I can say. "How do they even do this every year? They must need another house just to store all the decorations."

"It's companies mostly these days," Gio says. "Big business."

"Oh, I quite fancy that job," I say, taken with the idea. "Professional elf."

We buy hot chocolate from a vending van, because this scene isn't quite festive enough already, and Gio produces a hip flask of brandy and hands it to me.

"You think of everything," I say, sloshing some into my cup.

He slides the bottle back inside his jacket and I realize he's brought it just for me, just for this hot chocolate, and I link my arm through his as we wander from house to house, bedazzled.

I stop to admire a vintage metal sleigh that rivals Santo's Cadillac in length, metallic scarlet and big enough for us to climb aboard. We don't, though—the front seat is already taken by a Coca-Cola-worthy Santa Claus holding on to the reins of eight reindeer in flight across the lawn, all of them aglow with hundreds of golden pinprick lights. I check, and of course the one up front has a red nose.

"For a guy who doesn't like the Christmas store, this is a big step," I say.

He drops his arm across my shoulders. "This is different. We came here every year as kids."

I see the Belottis in my mind's eye, a gaggle of overexcited little girls and Gio, dark-haired and serious-eyed, tagging along behind them.

"We come from very different lives," I say with a soft sigh. "My mother was a huge Christmas fan, but we never amassed a collection of family decorations or yearly traditions, we moved around too much. If it didn't fit in the backseat of the Vauxhall it didn't come with us, and it was nothing like the size of Santo's Cadillac, let me tell you."

He squeezes my shoulders. "Come spend the holiday with us this year?" Christmas lights reflect gold and green in his eyes as he looks down at me. "Unless you have other plans?"

I don't have other plans. Bobby has been furious this entire year straight that he and Robin are committed to spending the holidays on a cruise with Robin's family because Robin's eldest sister has decided to get married while everyone is together. Up until today, my vague plan has been turkey for one plus Smirnoff, gelato on tap, and the TV on. I haven't actually been depressed about the idea, it's felt simple and unfussy. I've been eyeing up new pajamas and saving a bottle of champagne just for the big day.

But what now? Gio has offered me a seat at the Belotti dinner table. I don't need to be the little kid with her face pressed against the window this time, or even the woman telling herself her lonesome Christmas is stylish and independent. I long to say yes, to experience a real family Christmas Day.

"I'd love to," I say, and I do an internal double-take at myself for blurting the words out before my head and my heart have had at least a ten-minute ruck about it. "Only if you're sure? You can change your mind, I won't be offended."

His laugh comes easy and warms my cold cheeks. "I won't change my mind."

Okay, then. Christmas with the Belottis it is. It sounds like a movie I'd queue to see, and I stand there in the middle of the over-the-top lights of Dyker Heights and try to remind myself that Christmas Day falls before my New Year's Day deadline, and to get a grip and soak in this temporary joy.

"THAT WAS BONKERS," I say, back in the cherry-leather comfort of the Cadillac with the heaters on full. "Fabulous, but bonkers."

"Bonkers," he says.

The word sounds ridiculous in his accent.

"You know, crazy but fabulous," I say.

"I know what the word means," he says.

He pulls out into the slow-moving traffic and I settle back in my seat, my elbow on the armrest between us.

"I'm buying myself one of these," I say, the brandy warm in my bloodstream. "I'll roll grandly around New York in it every night." I close my eyes and smile, my head tipped back against the seat. "I'll take Smirnoff with me for the ride, and we'll become infamous as that eccentric English woman and her standoffish cat. We'll wear sunglasses in the summer and matching knitted scarves in wintertime."

He doesn't reply, and I open one eye and find him pulled up at a red light and looking at me.

"You're a sight for my sore eyes," he says, and then he puts his hand on my knee and leaves it there when he pulls away from the light.

I remember back to confessing to Bobby about Gio's good hands, and here we are a few months later with that very same hand resting on my knee. I cover it with my smaller one in the darkness of the car, and the only word I can put to how I feel is content. It's not precisely the right word. Ideally I'd like something that combines content with a side order of the need to climb Gio Belotti like a tree, but he's driving and this is one precious vehicle, so content will have to be enough for now.

"Where are we going?"

"Wait and see."

I squeeze his hand. "Another surprise?"

"Yes."

"Will I need more brandy?"

"You might."

"You don't like surprises," I say. "You said so the other day."

"I did?"

I nod. "To Sophia."

"I probably used to like surprises, as a kid." He keeps his eyes on the road. "These days, not so much."

Shop facades and illuminated street signs throw colors across his profile as we move through the dark streets, electric blues, strobes of red. His thumb strokes my kneecap, a steady back and forth.

"You're a very grown-up grown-up," I say, with the tongue-loosening benefits of brandy.

He shoots me a look out the corner of his eye. "I guess I've had to be."

I nod. I get that. I've no one else to be responsible for but myself, and I'm not all that great at that sometimes. Gio has the weight of caring for Bella and his family on his shoulders.

"You don't have to feel responsible for me," I say.

"What do you mean?"

He's frowning as he drives, and I search my head for better words.

"I just meant that you already have a lot of people relying on you," I say. "You don't have to add me to the list of people you need to worry about. In fact, let *me* be the one with the list, and you on it."

He makes a left turn on to a parking lot, and I squint into the darkness beyond the windscreen.

"Is that the sea?"

"The Atlantic Ocean," he says. It doesn't feel like a correction, more a wistful observation.

"We're at the beach?"

"Coney Island."

"As in the amusement park?"

"The rides are closed up for winter, but yeah. Shall we walk a while?"

The air outside is brisk, salty on my lips as we head for the wooden boardwalk.

"It's so packed here on a summer's day you can hardly move," Gio says.

It's certainly not like that right now. There's barely a handful of people out on the wooden boardwalk tonight, a couple of dog walkers and the occasional hardy runner. We have the place pretty much to ourselves, and I feel eighteen again when Gio takes my hand as we stroll, roller coasters silhouetted on one side of us, the ocean on the other. I haven't walked hand in hand with anyone in . . . I don't honestly know how long. Adam wasn't a PDA kind of man, even in the early days.

"We can grab some food if you're hungry?"

"Maybe in a while," I say, because I'd be happy to just walk like this until we run out of earth.

He passes me the brandy and I take a nip, my eyes on the outline of the big wheel. The cars have all been removed and mothballed for the winter, leaving just the spoked steel wheel arcing against the skyline.

"Bella was so scared on that one she cried all the way around," he says, following my gaze. "She was only this high." He indicates with his hand by his hip. "Stamped her feet to go on and then couldn't wait to get off."

It reminds me that his whole life history is wrapped around this city; tonight has been new to me but a trip down memory lane for him.

"My mother took me to a version of this as a kid," I say, recalling the occasional Southend trip. "It was smaller, of course, but it has this same ramshackle beachside thing going on." I laugh softly at an unexpected memory of my mother's red fifties-style sundress. It was entirely inappropriate for roller coasters—not that it stopped her for one moment. "Fish and chips, bumper cars, bucket-and-spade days."

"It's Nathan's hot dogs here," he says.

We walk on a little farther, each absorbed in our own thoughts, and I take a good slug of brandy to ward off the chill. It's good stuff—however cold it is tonight, I am fire inside.

"Penny for your thoughts," I say.

I catch the micro-wince as he looks my way, and I beat myself up for not choosing more careful words. "Gio, I'm sorry, of all the phrases I could have picked . . ."

"Hey, it's fine." He squeezes my hand. "You can say her name without it being awkward."

I nod, swallow hard, squeeze his hand back and still wish I'd said anything but that.

"Iris, can I say something?" He draws to a stop and turns me toward him. "Your loss is more recent than mine. If this is all going too fast, just say the word and we can slow it right down." He reaches out and adjusts my hat so it covers my ears properly. "I get it if Christmas is too much of an ask, okay?"

Cold tears gather on my eyelashes. I fight the need to spill the ugly truth out into the iced air between us, let the sulfurous wind carry it out over the ocean and sink it fathoms deep where it can't trouble either of us.

"Adam . . . my partner . . . he wasn't always a very nice

person," I say, because I cannot and will not add to the lie. Gio had a good relationship that ended too soon. I had a terrible relationship that should never have happened at all.

I watch my words land on Gio's face. His expression falters, his thumb strokes my jaw.

"It's brave to be so honest," he says, his eyes searching my face. "Don't feel guilty for remembering the bad stuff as well as the good, people don't become saints just because they die."

There's a full-on burning ball of pain in my throat, because Gio is just too damn decent for his own good.

"You will." I choke on my stupid self-indulgent brandy tears. "You'll get trumpets and medals and your own swat team of cupids and angels."

"I think you've had enough brandy." He holds my face between his hands. "Just so you know, I'm not thinking saintly thoughts right now."

I gulp-laugh, overwrought, and he pulls me in close and lowers his head to mine. Our kiss is laced with salt and heavy with longing.

"Can we make out in the back of the car?"

He laughs into my mouth. "You fucking bet we can."

My stomach dips, and I want to tell him that he's just hit my perfect *Moonstruck* sweet spot between taking charge and overbearing, but I don't, because he kisses the thought straight out of my head.

I feel like a teenager as we head back across the deserted car lot, pausing twice for the fevered kind of kisses that feel as necessary for survival as oxygen, and we need to make it to the car alive to rip each other's clothes off. Gio's fumbling in his pocket for the keys, his mouth hot on mine, sexy-cursing in Italian because the big old beast of a Cadillac has to be manually unlocked. I half laugh and half groan when he drops the keys in his haste, and then I make a sound that feels animal in my throat when he picks up the keys and stays bent low to move his mouth up my inner thigh. I look down at his dark head and he raises his eyes to meet mine, and it's so devastatingly sexy that I genuinely have to lean on the car to hold myself up.

He slides up my body, pressing me against the cold metal, and I gulp and reach for the keys.

"Give them to me," I say, taking them from him in case he drops them again, and I turn toward the car, reaching for the lock.

He leans his weight against my back, his breath warm on my neck. I'm momentarily pressed between man and machine, and when his hand slides up under my jumper to my breast I lean my head back on his shoulder and groan.

"We need to get inside this damn car," he mutters.

"Do we?" I say, because he's just pulled the lace cup of my bra down and I've found my happy place.

"Either that or we're gonna land up in a cell for indecent exposure," he says, taking the keys and jamming them into the lock beside my hip. We both gasp with relief when we hear the locks pop, and Gio hauls the rear door open and practically shoves me inside. He slams the door as he lands on top of me and I'm suddenly aware of how cold it was outside now that we're out of the weather.

"For a big car, this suddenly feels like a small space," I say, my back pressed against the padded red leather bench seat.

"I think I might be too old for this," he says, raising himself on his elbows in an effort not to squash me.

"Press me down," I say, pulling him back by the collars of his coat. "I like it."

He half laughs, his mouth a kiss away from mine as his hand slides under my jumper again. "Me too."

"Your hands are cold," I whisper.

"Your body's hot," he says, and then pauses, frowns and adds, "temperature wise, I mean, not . . ."

I raise my eyebrows, enjoying the way he's tying himself up in knots. "You don't think my body's hot?"

"No. I mean, God, yes. Yes I do." He unhooks my bra and I yank my jumper over my head so I'm naked from the waist up.

"Hot as hell," he murmurs, trailing his mouth between my collarbones. "Like touching the surface of the goddamn sun."

"Good save," I murmur, aching for more. "I've never had sex in the backseat of a car before. Nor the front seat, for that matter."

"Me either," he says, kissing me hard on the mouth as he flicks the button of my jeans open. He kisses me some more as he eases the zip down, and then some more, slow and deep, as his hand moves inside my jeans and underwear, his fingers no longer cold as they slide into me.

"This might be the best moment of my life," I gasp, and I feel his smile against my mouth.

"It's pretty high on my list too," he says as I unbutton his jeans and push them down. He sucks in a sharp gasp of air and closes his eyes when my hand closes around him, and we're frustrated because my jeans are too high up my thighs and his are restricting his movement. He's making it both worse and better by cursing in Italian, and I'm laughing and gasping as I wriggle around to shove my jeans below my knees until at last he can settle between my legs and push himself inside me.

"Thank fucking God," he mutters, and I swallow hard and nod, delirious with relief and shocking, eye-watering pleasure.

"I take it back," I say. "This is the best moment."

And then he slows everything down, his mouth gentle over my face, his hand smoothing my hair away from my forehead, his eyes intense on mine as his breath hitches in his throat. I move under him, pushing my knee out against the leather seat so I can lift my hips and hold him closer, and he sighs my name and bites his bottom lip. I wouldn't have imagined backseat sex could feel tender, but this does. We're in our own world right now, a Cadillac of dreams, and we take our sweet time over each other.

"Welcome to Coney Island," he says afterward, his forehead resting on mine.

"Every bit as thrilling as the guidebooks claim," I say, my heart banging against his.

"You should see it in summer," he says.

"I think I prefer it in winter," I say.

He kisses me, unhurried and satisfied. "Yeah, me too."

"Shall we stay here like this all night?"

He huffs. "I'd never walk again."

I laugh. "I think I might have dislocated my hip, but it was worth it."

He eases away from me, and we shuffle-drag our clothes back into place and flop side by side, as if we've just crossed the marathon finish line. I'm grateful when he reaches into his coat and silently hands me the brandy.

"You're like a Saint Bernard," I say, pressing the flask to my lips. "Always rescuing me."

He frowns and shakes his head, but I see the smile behind his expression and I lean my head on his shoulder and smile too. So much quiet joy in the man. So much love.

28.

TUESDAY MORNING DAWNS BITTER COLD, AND I LIE IN bed remembering the night before. Did I say something about Saint Bernards and a swat team of angels? It's hazy, but what I'm left with is a glow that has nothing to do with celestial beings and everything to do with what happened on the backseat of the Cadillac. My early romance experiences were not terribly exciting, I was too busy rushing about in steamy kitchens every night to fool around. Last night classed as A-star, top-grade fooling around. It was hands-down the most thrilling sex of my entire life. I don't think either of us expected to be so deliriously turned on by the whole deserted car lot thing—maybe we're both overdue a little excitement in our lives.

I pull my phone from beneath my pillow when it buzzes.

> *I've def put my back out.*

I pull the quilt over my shoulders and curl on my side, warm and comfortable.

> *That's what happens when you seduce girls in the back of cars.*

I'm pretty sure it was your idea . . .

I laugh as I close my eyes and think back. Brandy. Trumpets. Let's make out in the backseat. Yep, guilty as charged. My phone beeps again before I can formulate a response, and I'm still smiling as I check it. It's not from Gio.

> *Oh little mouse, now you've gone and hurt my feelings. Maybe I should head on out to see you and smooth things over, deliver your Christmas gift in person. You can show me the sights, make me some of your ice cream. You like the sound of that?*

I feel blistered, as if someone tipped a boiling kettle over me. It's too swift a gear change for my brain to handle, from the heaven of last night to the hell of Adam Bronson. It's as if he's reared right up out of my cellphone into the safety and stillness of my bedroom. My phone vibrates again, another new message, and I curl into a tight ball and screw my eyes shut, too frightened to look. It vibrates again and again, until I hurl it at the wall and lurch for the bathroom on shaky legs to retch my guts up.

I STAND UNDER THE hot shower and try to let the water sluice away my panic. I practice the breathing exercises that got me through those early days after I walked out on Adam. *He won't come to New York. He won't come to New York. He won't come to New York.* I repeat it like a mantra, knowing that it's most probably true. Adam Bronson is a small-town manipulator, he's spitting tacks that I'm thriving and he's trying to exercise power he no longer has. Bobby would tell me all of those things if I showed him the latest text, but I'm not going to because I should never have replied to the first one. I hate this feeling of being sucked into the vortex of Adam's whirlpool. The water is dark and rancid and filling my mouth. It's in my hair, coating my skin, hard to scrub off even though I have the shower turned to its hottest setting.

I sit at the kitchen table a little while later, cold even though I'm bundled into my dressing gown with a towel around my hair and coffee in front of me. I put a hand on my left thigh, aware my leg is trembling. It hasn't done that for a long time, an involuntary reaction I thought was in my past. I don't know what to do. I'm not going to reply. I know that's what he wants—to feel sure his message has landed, that I'm cowering. I try to summon my inner superhero from a couple of weeks ago in that alley, but she's deserted me. I'm anxious and on my own. Perhaps this is how things are always going to be for me. It's a depressing thought, one I don't want to give credence to because it's exactly how Adam kept me small—make her feel powerless and beholden, don't let her see there are other people and other places. Except I have. I've gone the full ten rounds in a boxing ring to get myself here, black and blue with effort. Did I do all of that to allow him to snatch the win, a late knockout from a lucky punch?

I close my eyes and force myself to breathe slowly, to see that boxing ring, to imagine my arm being lifted in the air, victorious, Adam slumping to the canvas in defeat. I hear the crowd roar and I look to my corner and see my people fist-pumping the air. My mother's cornflower-blue eyes, Sophia's bouncing curls, Gio's strong shoulders. I glimpse someone else too, fleetingly. I barely catch her face as she turns to leave but she looked a heck of a lot like me, and I think there might have been a glint of triumph in her small smile. There wasn't a cape or superhero boots, but it brings me comfort to know she's close by.

29.

SHEN COMES INTO THE KITCHEN WITH A STACK OF DIRTY plates in her hands. "Hate to say it but that old dude is back again."

I sigh. Felipe. It's been three days since Adam's text arrived and I've barely slept or thought of anything else. I think I've pulled it together just enough to avoid ringing alarm bells with Gio when we've spoken or texted, and Bobby is rushed off his feet with work, but I'm having a silent and painful internal crisis. Shen looks at me and frowns, then puts her hand on my shoulder.

"You okay?"

It's not the right question to ask someone in my state. I buffer it with a painted-on smile and move away to pull something from the fridge so it doesn't seem as if I'm shaking her hand off.

"I'm fine," I say. "Tired, I think, stayed up too late watching a horror movie."

The lie comes easy and she nods, accepting it.

"Tell him I'll be out in a sec," I say, glancing at the clock. It's just turned eight, I don't really have time to talk, but I can't send him away.

He's hovering near the kitchen door when I flick off the gas burner and step into the restaurant.

"Iris," he says, taking his hat off and pressing the rim against the breast of his heavy woolen coat. "I won't keep you long, I can see you're busy."

"Can I get you something to eat?"

He shakes his head and lays his other hand over his stomach. "Maria has me well fed. The woman can't cook for less than a dozen even when there's only two of us at the table."

I nod, tuck one foot behind my other ankle and wait.

"I found some things you might like to look over. From back in the day, from when your mother was around."

He gestures with both hands as he speaks, awkward, and I understand that he's offering a kindness in recompense for his ultimatum.

"I'd really like that," I say, and there it is again, that ever-present lump in my throat. I'm not usually someone who wears their emotions so close to the surface, it's exhausting.

His shoulders drop, relieved. "I have a storage unit a few blocks away." He hands me a slip of paper with spidery writing across it. "Tomorrow morning?"

"Okay."

He looks for a second as if he might have something else he wants to say, and then he decides better of it and puts his hat back on to leave.

"Thank you," I say, folding the address and slipping it in the back pocket of my jeans.

He touches the rim of his hat as he walks away, and I head back into the sanctuary of my kitchen and lean against the door, massaging the bridge of my nose as I cycle through the familiarity of one of my breathing exercises.

———

TRUE TO HIS WORD, it's not far to the address on Felipe's scrap of paper. I've bundled up warm against the harsh December wind, and soon enough I see him loitering on the street outside a double-glass-windowed building covered in self-storage signs.

"I brought coffee," he says, holding up a silver thermos. "Maria made it, actually."

I yank my bobble hat off, sweat prickling in my hairline. "You haven't told her about my mum, have you?"

He swats my concern away. "I told her I was catching up with an old friend, which, in a roundabout way, I am."

There's a spring in his step as I follow him into the building. I think he might be rather enjoying himself. For my part, I'm intrigued, and glad of the mental respite from thinking about Adam. We're in one of those places that has sprung up everywhere, warehouses converted into small rental units for people to store their clutter and crap, an elevator ride up to a maze of identical white roller-shuttered doors.

Felipe pauses and looks around us to get his bearings, then heads off down one of the hallways. He has a small key on a plastic tag in his hand, and when he eventually stops he holds it out to me to look at.

"Three-five-nine, right?"

I nod. "My mother resisted reading glasses too," I say lightly, and he huffs as he works the key into the padlock on the unit.

He rolls the door up with a showman's flourish.

"I was here yesterday, thought I'd take a look for that damn recipe," he says. "No such luck."

I'm surprised by the interior of the unit. I was expecting disorganized boxes piled high, but it's relatively tidy and there's a leather chesterfield sofa set against one wall.

"This is kind of cozy," I say, watching him fiddle with the switches on a blow heater.

He flicks on a lamp and grins. "Stick with me, kid."

"Don't they worry people will live in these places?"

He ushers me inside and pulls the shutter down. "They charge daily for an electricity upgrade to stop people from running refrigerators full of beer. Party poopers."

"And their TVs," I say pointedly, eyeing the portable TV on a stand.

"That too," he says. "Have a seat."

I unwind my scarf and unzip my coat as I perch on the sofa, feeling slightly bizarre. No one knows I'm here, yet I don't feel any sense of danger. For one, Felipe is a Belotti, and secondly, he's Gio's father. Most importantly, though, I know he's trying to do something decent for me out of respect for my mother—I suspect he's made quite an effort to spruce this place up for today.

"You don't look so good," he says, pouring me coffee into a plastic cup.

I obviously need to up my makeup game—I thought I'd made a good job of hiding the dark circles under my eyes.

"I'm not sleeping very well." I shrug. "It'll pass, it always does."

He sighs heavily as he sits down and reaches a large brown envelope up from the side of the sofa.

"I found these in a box," he says. "I figured they might mean more to you than me at this stage of life."

I put my coffee on the floor and rest the envelope on my knees.

"Just so you know, I'll probably cry, but don't feel bad about it because it seems I cry at least three times a day, at the moment anyway. I think I might actually have a fault with my eye ducts or something."

He rubs his chin, watching me. "Your mother used to say odd things too."

I consider being offended, but then decide to focus on whatever's inside the envelope instead. It's quite bulky. I pull out a bundle of newspapers and photographs and lay them on my lap.

"I don't remember keeping them, truth told," he says. "They must have been left behind by Louis." He can obviously read from my expression that I don't have a clue who Louis is. "Our manager at the time. He dropped us when things got sticky, bigger fish to fry."

All of this is news to me. I wish I had a pen to write it all down so I never forget. I content myself with looking at the photograph on top of the pile instead.

"There's one very similar to this in my mother's scrapbook," I say, looking at the staged shot of the band grouped around Charlie Raven's drum kit. He's perched on the stool with his drumsticks in his hands, nervous energy radiating from his tall, rangy pose.

"My father," I say, touching the photo lightly.

"I was sorry to hear how he died," Felipe says.

"We weren't in touch," I say.

Felipe makes a gruff sound low in his throat. "He made the same choice I did. Be a father or hit the road."

"My mother had that choice too," I say, looking at her picture.

"She picked you," he says. "The band hit the skids pretty much as soon as she found out you were on the way. She got sick most days, Charlie got scared. They couldn't be in the same room, let alone the same band."

I hang on to Felipe's every word as I set the photograph aside to look through the others. Some of them I've seen before but many are new to me; it's such an unexpected gift to see her again.

Felipe does his best to supply locations and anecdotes as I work my way through them, and after a few minutes he passes me a box of tissues.

"It's the ducts," I mumble.

"You said."

I smooth out a rolled-up poster for a gig in some downtown L.A. club, a silhouetted outline shot of my mother onstage. It captures her essence so well that a small noise escapes my throat, and I cough a couple of times to clear it.

"She found out she was pregnant the day that was taken," he says. "I can see her now, shoving the test in her back pocket as she ran out onto the stage."

I study the poster closely, and sure enough you can just about make out the white tip of the plastic test sticking out of her pocket. I turn to Felipe, knowing I must be a mascara-streaked mess.

"I'm in this picture," I whisper. "Right there, probably no bigger than a grain of rice, but I'm there."

I demonstrate the minuscule rice size with my thumb and finger, and he puts his arm around my shoulders and pulls another tissue from the box for me. I've never seen any photographs of my mother during her pregnancy, this is a precious first.

"I'm going to frame it." I blow my nose. "Hang it on my wall forever."

He pats my shoulder.

"There's something else, but given your . . . ducts," he gestures toward my face, "I don't know if we should hold off for another day. Tomorrow, maybe."

I dash my hands over my face and stare at him. "No. No way, I need to see it all now. Felipe, please, I'm okay, honestly I am."

He lifts one shoulder and sighs. "If you say so. Drink some coffee first at least."

I put the papers and photos carefully back into the envelope and lay them to one side.

"Thank you," I say, reaching for my cup. "For all of this."

He lifts his eyebrows. "Viv was one hell of a girl," he says.

I hesitate to ask my next question, not wanting to be insensitive. "Do you know much about what happened between her and Santo?"

He casts his eyes to the ceiling and laughs softly. "We were all a little bit in love with your mother back then, but we were chopped liver as soon as she laid her baby blues on my brother." He shakes his head. "He came by for a few beers before a gig one night and that was that. For the next two days they were love's young dream. I hardly recognized Santo, he was so entranced by your mother."

He speaks slow and low, remembering in his own time.

"And then it was time for us to hit the road. Gigs lined up

across the country, heading toward L.A. and the big time, if Louis was to be believed. In truth, I wasn't so sure she was going to go. Thought she'd pick my brother over us."

"But she didn't," I say, because this is the one part of the story I know.

"It was touch and go," Felipe says. "The bus waited five minutes, then ten, before she came running around the corner and got in, tear ducts overflowing just like yours are now." He waves his hand toward my face. "Didn't speak to a soul the whole way, she just slunk to the back of the bus like a wounded animal."

We sit in contemplative silence, punctuated by my tearful sniffs. I'm so incredibly saddened to think of my mother caught between love and ambition, far too young and fragile to make such life-changing decisions. Yet she didn't hesitate for a moment when she found out she was pregnant, Felipe said. She always told me that the day she discovered she was expecting was the happiest of her life, because she'd finally have someone to love forever. It's beautiful and heartbreaking, especially now I have all this new knowledge of how much she gave up to be a mother. She must have gone out on to that stage full of swirling emotions. Perhaps that's why the photograph seems to capture so much of who she was—she was literally caught between her old life and her new one.

"You said you had something else to show me?"

Felipe scrubs his hand over his bristled cheek and then gets up and crosses to the television. I watch him, perplexed, until I notice the VHS slot beneath the screen.

"Felipe . . ." I say, my hand over the base of my throat. "Is there film?"

He turns back to look at me. "You sure you want to do this?"

I'm breathless, my eyes nailed to the screen, unable to believe I might be about to see my mother.

"Yes," I whisper.

"It's our highlights reel." Felipe leans back and squints to read the buttons on the machine. "Brought back some memories for me watching this yesterday, let me tell you."

"Highlight reel," I murmur, as if he's speaking a completely different language. My heart is banging so hard I might not be able to hear the film.

"That's got it," he says, sitting back down as the screen flickers. "Give it a minute."

I'm so nervous that my palms are sweating, terrified that the old player is going to chew the tape.

"Why is it taking so long?" I mutter, looking between Felipe and the screen.

"Just wait . . ." He bats his hand toward me. "It's an old machine, takes a bit of time to get going."

I grip the edge of the sofa when the screen fills with a still of the band's logo and one of their tracks crackles from the speakers.

"Bit dusty," Felipe says, but I don't care, because the logo disappears and the band bursts onto the screen, a recording of a live performance to a packed, sweaty crowd. It's a bit dark and the sound isn't perfect, but it's my living and breathing mother as I've never seen her before and I'm entranced. I watched her perform countless times across my life, but this . . . this is electric. She's so young but so damn powerful, holding every single person in that club in the palm of her hand.

"She was a proper superstar, wasn't she?" I whisper, swiping fat tears from my lashes so I can see.

"Dynamite," Felipe says.

The performance ends and the film fades to black, then fades back in again to a Q and A with the band. They're answering banal questions in the main, but it doesn't matter to me because she's chatting and laughing. Her voice is lost music to my ears, her laughter a bell calling me closer to the TV. I'm off the sofa now and kneeling in front of the screen, and I reach out to touch her face when she looks down the camera and laughs. It's as if she's looking directly at me, and I laugh and cry with sheer wonder because it feels as if she's fleetingly here, as if by some miracle we can see each other for just this brief, tiny moment of connection.

"Mum," I murmur, my mouth full of salty tears. I'm not just crying, I'm sobbing, hot therapeutic tears, my body shaking because the last few days have been so horrific and it feels as if she's found a way to reach out and tell me I'm going to be okay. "I miss you so much," I whisper, still touching the screen as it fades and credits roll.

Felipe puts his hand on my shoulder, and when I get to my feet he holds his arms out for me to stumble into.

"It's okay, kiddo," he says, patting my back. "It's okay. I got ya."

He steers me back to the sofa and passes me more tissues, patting my knee while I pull myself together.

"Sorry," I gulp. "That was a real shock."

"I'm sorry you lost your mother," he says. "I know how wonderful she was."

I hear emotion thicken his voice and try to raise a watery smile for his benefit, because he didn't have to do this and I don't have words special enough to express what it means to me. I didn't really know what to expect when I came here this morning. Not this. Not to feel as if my mother has reached through the ether between worlds to hold my hand and remind me exactly whose daughter I am.

"Can we watch it again?"

Felipe presses rewind, and we sit alongside each other and watch it twice more, then he ejects it and hands it to me.

"Keep it. I was there, it's all in here." He taps the side of his head as he buttons his coat. "Sometimes it's the letting go of things that sets you free, Iris."

I clutch the warm chunk of plastic as if it's precious metal. This tape, the poster taken on the day my mother discovered she was pregnant . . . they're gold dust for me. How strange that they've sat forgotten in this lock-up all these years, as if they were waiting for the exact moment to reveal themselves when I needed them most of all. I'm not a superstitious person as a rule—I'll walk under ladders and much prefer grumpy orange cats to lucky black ones—but there's an undeniable feeling of cosmic interference here, as if Felipe's crackly old TV set was a temporary conduit between realms. I finish my coffee and realize I'm finally warm for the first time in days. I put my hand on my left thigh and it isn't shaking anymore.

30.

I'VE DELETED ADAM'S TEXTS AND BLOCKED HIS NUMBER. He's become a phantom lurking in every shadow in recent weeks, but I came home from my morning with Felipe and knew exactly what I needed to do. Block. Ignore. Decide he's dead to me and really believe it this time, because I didn't claw myself away from him just to let him become my own personal Voldemort. I'm a New Yorker now. What happened to me in London does not define me here.

I've spent the weekend working, either downstairs in the noodle house or up here sprucing the place up for Christmas. I've draped my mother's string of golden fir cones over the mirror and tacked warm white fairy lights around the window frame. It was a cold, crystal-clear London morning when we foraged for those fir cones, gilding our fingers with the gold paint afterward. They've faded significantly over the years, but they still lend Christmas cheer to this icy Monday morning. The breakfast radio weather guy seemed certain about imminent snow, but he's had me fooled before so I'll believe it when I see it.

Something spatters my window—a spray of small stones, I think—and I dash across the room to check the sidewalk, my heart in my mouth.

"Saw this outside the bodega and thought of you," Gio shouts, shielding his eyes with his hand as he looks up. He's standing beside a Christmas tree that comes up to his shoulder, his hand out supporting the top of the trunk. I shake my head, laughing as I throw my hands up in the air at him.

I run out on to the landing as he hauls it up the communal staircase, standing it up outside my front door with a flourish and a grin that makes him look about eighteen years old.

"I wasn't planning on getting a tree," I say.

"Yeah, you said," he says. "But where will you hang your whisk if you don't have a tree?"

I gesture toward the corner as he shuffles it into my apartment, and we both stand back to look at it once it's in place.

"It looked smaller outside," he concedes.

"You don't say."

"Maybe if we turn it around?" He has a quick go, but it's so bushy that whichever way round it is the bottom branches flop over the arm of the sofa.

I slide behind it and sit down, parting the branches to look at Gio.

"I feel like I'm staking someone out," I say.

He pushes the sofa along with me still sitting on it until it's clear of the tree's reach. It's wedged up against the breakfast bar at the other end, but at least I won't feel like I'm part of a nature documentary every time I sit down.

"Perfect fit," he says.

I get up and stand beside him. "You know what? It is."

This is the first real tree I've had in years. Adam had a small, sparse pre-lit plastic one from before we met, which he wouldn't hear of replacing, a woebegone object that somehow managed to make the room even more dispiriting than usual. No baubles, and certainly no gifts piled beneath it.

"Lights?" Gio looks at me and I shake my head. The only string of lights I have is pinned around the window.

"Ornaments?"

I fetch the whisk and hang it on the tree, then step back. It spins slowly, catching the daylight, a solitary splash of color on the mountain of greenery.

"You know what this means," I say.

He groans. "Please don't say we have to go back to the Christmas store."

"We have to go back to the Christmas store." I rub my hands together like an excited child. "I'll get my coat."

MY LIFE FEELS LIKE a Coney Island roller coaster at the moment, a series of euphoric highs and stomach-plummeting lows. Today I'm flying high, sweet as you like, because Gio and I have spent the afternoon dressing the tree and eating panettone from a little bakery he knows over on Mulberry. I had a moment as we walked back home weighed down with Christmas bags. Gio was a few steps ahead of me on the sidewalk, hunkered inside his navy reefer jacket, panettone wrapped with brown paper and string dangling from one hand, Christmas decorations from the other, and the weatherman finally made good on his promise of snow. Gio turned back to look at me, fat white flakes settling on his shoulders as he cast his eyes toward the skies, and I clicked the shutter on my internal camera to save the scene forever.

"It looks like you bought everything in the shop and

threw it at the tree," he says, when I finally declare it to be perfect.

"I love it," I say. "It's the best tree in the history of Christmas trees ever."

It looks insanely festive, a blaze of vintage-colored lights—pinpricks of rose pink, apple green, candy apple reds. I completely lost my head in the Christmas store earlier, bought far too many tree ornaments, and I'm not one bit sorry, because my tree looks like something from a child's drawing. From my own wistful childhood drawings.

I cook pasta for dinner, and afterward we lie on the sofa and bask in the fairy-light glow, the TV on low and snow falling steadily outside.

"Heavy snow at the Monday Night Motel," he says.

I adjust my head on his chest. "Maybe we'll get snowed in."

"Maybe," he says, even though we both know it's coming up to the time for him to leave. Bella's at the cinema, and he's walking over to meet her at ten to make sure she gets home safe in this weather.

"It feels like Christmas already," I say.

"You do have the best tree in the neighborhood," he says.

"Thanks to you."

I'm deeply comfortable in Gio's arms, even though I'm always subconsciously aware of a quiet ticking clock in my head. It was there long before my New Year's cut-off date. It's there when I'm awake and features in my dreams when I sleep, eerie dreams where I stand and stare at the clock face and realize that the quarter-hour markers have been replaced with words. LIAR in black capitals at quarter past, SECRET printed at the half-hour point. Adam's name marks quarter to, and a tiny faceted ball sits ready to drop at midnight. The hands spin in both directions, fast and out of control. It wouldn't take a psychiatrist to analyze the meaning behind my dreams, the portent of danger that runs like the San Andreas Fault beneath my precarious life.

Before Gio leaves, we make love—and it is love even if we haven't said the words aloud—on the sofa by the haze of the tree. I used to grumble about this sofa, but if Bobby ever asks me if I need it replaced, I'll say no, because it's the keeper of my secrets and the custodian of some of my best memories now. This one in particular.

SNOW CHANGES EVERYTHING, doesn't it? The Narnian view from the windows, the muffled sound of the world, the conversation on the streets. New York has become an even more magical place for me this week. I went to the park across the street this morning to make fresh footprints in the overnight snowfall. I stopped to listen to the busker for a while; she's in fine voice these days and reached out to touch hands when I dropped some money in her plastic tub. It's too wet out there for upturned hats this weather.

I spent a couple of hours at the gelateria yesterday morning, helping Sophia out behind the counter. I go every now and then, not for the recipe anymore, as there's little call for gelato while the city dithers under this deep freeze and the family waits for Santo. I go because I love being there, because Sophia has become one of my favorite people, because the Belottis make me feel as if I belong. I have a coffee mug with my name on it. Maria sometimes sends recipes she thinks

I'll appreciate. Bella played the piano yesterday, Christmas carols that rendered the atmosphere almost unbearably sweet as Sophia, Gio, and I slid homemade cannoli and tender sugar-glazed Italian cookies into green-and-white-striped paper bags. An illicit tray of small shots of Pascal's limoncello sat on the counter for the customers as they waited in line, designed to keep tempers calm and the till ringing.

I'm sure the Belottis suspect there's something happening between Gio and me, and I appreciate that none of them have asked directly, although there have been moments when Sophia has seemed as if she's bursting to. They know Gio well enough to understand that he's someone who needs to do things to his own timescale, and for my part I'm relieved to just keep things in precarious balance for as long as possible. I wish with all of my heart that this was an uncomplicated love affair, but it isn't. Gio has his baggage, and I drag my invisible suitcase of secrets behind me like a lead weight. It's going to burst open one day and spill my dirty underwear in the street for everyone to see, but for now I just want to take joy from the simple things as the calendar flips from day to day. Tomorrow will take care of itself.

31.

"ALL I WANT FOR CHRISTMAS IS YOUR GELATO RECIPE," Bobby says, handing me a glass of wine. It's Christmas in three days and the noodle house has officially closed until after the holiday, so I've come upstairs to say goodbye before they head off to rendezvous with Robin's family at some ungodly hour of the morning. Their Vuitton luggage stands packed and ready by the door and the apartment is spick-and-span, more Robin's organizational skills than Bobby's, I suspect. They've generously given me a key and free use of their place over the holidays, but I think I might find it hard to leave my own apartment now the tree is there. I get a thrill every time I flick it on, like my own mini light switch-on ceremony. I don't do a countdown, but I totally could.

"You're still going to Gio's family for Christmas, right?" Robin says, lifting Smirnoff onto his window seat.

"Don't worry, I promise I won't spend the day alone with the cat," I say, watching the ginger furball turn circles on his cushion before folding himself down.

"He's terrible company," Robin says, fussing Smirnoff's ear and getting his hand batted for his trouble.

Bobby sits beside me on the sofa and I reach out and touch his leg. "Are you wearing leather trousers?"

He rolls his eyes as he swats my fingers. "Pants, for the millionth time, and yes, one hundred percent lambskin."

"Are you testing them as uniform for the waitstaff?"

Bobby looks horrified. "They're Balmain, Iris. Your eye for quality is disturbingly inaccurate."

"Wipe clean, anyway," I say, catching Robin's eye with a subtle wink. "Practical."

"Jesus, I'm not going hiking in them," Bobby says. "Talk to me about fashion when you don't buy your clothes at the grocery store. Bacon and a sweater. Who does that?"

I laugh into my wineglass because he's right. "It's not my fault if my boss doesn't pay me Balmain wages."

"I heard he's awful to work for," Robin says, always happy to tag team with me when it comes to rinsing Bobby. "You should probably report him."

"They'd never catch him to arrest him," I say. "He's like the Scarlet Pimpernel."

"Okay, I have no idea who that even is, but I hope he has a better handle on fashion than either of you," Bobby says.

"He was a swashbuckling hero," I say. "Definitely wore leather trousers."

Bobby looks slightly mollified. "You're going to miss us," he says.

"What he means is he's going to miss you." Robin raises his glass to me from his armchair by the fire. "Because he's being forced to spend the holidays in Bermuda with my family."

"I don't like boats," Bobby says.

"Or my mother," Robin says, and they both laugh, because Robin's mother is incredibly hard work.

"I'll miss you both," I say. "Text me every day."

Bobby puts his hand on my arm. "Call us if there's an emergency. Make one up if you have to."

I rest my head on his shoulder and watch the fire for a while.

"You'll be back by New Year's Eve?" I say, checking even though I know the answer.

"Home before the ball drops," Robin says.

I finish my wine, relieved I'm going to have my friends around me come the New Year.

"I CAN'T BELIEVE IT'S Christmas Eve tomorrow," Sophia says. She's wearing an elf hat, a bell on the end that jangles every time she speaks. "I'm so ready for some time off, not thinking about anything but food."

"How's things at home?"

Santo finally came home a few days ago, and from what Gio has told me, it's been a big change for everyone. His mobility on a stick is good enough for him to get around independently, especially with the subtle adaptations Maria has put in place to make sure he still feels like the vital head of the Belotti household rather than someone who needs taking care of. He does, of course, but they've made careful plans and surreptitious rotas to make sure Santo never feels less than the strong, respected man he's always been.

Sophia rolls her shoulders, making her bell jingle. "Not too bad. Everyone's thrilled to have Papa home, of course, but Mamma's routines have all had to go out of the window, you know? She's cooking for Christmas, Felipe is there a lot of the time . . . I think it's all driving her a little crazy but you

know what she's like, always calm and collected on the outside. I'm glad to be out of the way for a while."

Sophia has her own apartment a couple of blocks away but
she's been staying at the family home to help her parents for
the last week or so and I know she's been finding it stressful.
She's had me drinking mini shots of limoncello at ten in the
morning, a tiny plastic glass of Christmas sanity.

"Papa's coming here later," she says, biting the side of her
fingernail.

I nod, putting a hand up to steady the reindeer antlers Sophia has me wearing. "Gio said."

They're all quietly worried about Santo's return to the
gelateria, more for his health's sake than the forgotten gelato
recipe. There's a weight of expectation, pressure mostly ap-
plied by Santo himself. He's coming over with Maria later
once the shop's closed up for the afternoon. Everyone is hopeful that Santo's memory will be jolted by his return to the
kitchens, even if the doctors have said it's a long shot.

"Will you be okay here if I nip down to the market?" she
says. "I promised Mamma I'd grab a few things for tomorrow
night's dinner."

"Sure, carry on," I say.

Gio's out this morning too, last-minute Christmas shopping, but business has all but dried up now so I'm not overly
worried. Sophia replaces the elf hat with her coat and bobble
hat before dashing out, and I stand behind the counter with
just the festive radio for company. I wipe the coffee machine
down, buff the glass counter to a shine, line up the few remaining cookies in the cabinet. This is the first time I've been
completely alone in the gelateria and it's an unexpectedly
strange feeling, as if the photographs of the Belotti ancestors

are holding an emergency meeting as they scrutinize me from the walls.

I pour myself a glass of water and try to tune my ear into the quiz on the radio but I just can't shake the discombobulated feeling. I empty the dishwasher for something to do, my back turned to the door as I stack the clean cups on the shelf beside the coffee machine, studiously avoiding the Belotti eyes on the walls. Had I been facing the other way I might have spotted the yellow cab pulling up outside, and the two men climbing carefully out and stepping into the doorway. I'm humming along to "White Christmas," oblivious until the bell over the door jangles and I turn around and find myself face-to-face with Santo Belotti.

Felipe is behind him, both of them in heavy cashmere coats and fedoras, Santo leaning heavily on a wooden walking stick.

I don't know what to do. He isn't supposed to be here for hours. I've been dreading this moment ever since Felipe put the pieces of my identity together so easily. Panicky, I surreptitiously remove my mother's ring from my finger and push it into the pocket of my jeans.

Santo is absolutely still, leaning on his stick as he stares at me.

I wish I wasn't wearing a Belotti's apron, I feel like a fraud.

Felipe touches his brother's arm. "Santo?"

Still he doesn't speak, still he doesn't move, so Felipe pulls out a chair at the nearest table and guides his brother into it.

"Coffee," Felipe nods to me, and I spring into action, all fingers and thumbs.

"Everyone's out," I say. "But they'll be back soon, I'm sure, one of them will anyway. Both of them probably, in fact. Any minute, I shouldn't wonder." I'm aware I'm gabbling but I can't seem to stop the words frothing from me.

I close my eyes for a second and lean my forehead against the coffee machine as it brews, desperately trying to gather myself together. I'd hoped that Santo wouldn't find the same familiarities as Felipe—he won't have heard me sing and my mother's ring isn't on my finger. I swallow hard as I carry the hot coffee to their table, the cups shaky in their saucers as I set them down. Santo catches hold of my hand and stares up into my eyes.

"Vivien." His voice is barely more than a whisper.

I sit down beside him at the table.

"You weren't supposed to be here until later," I say, stalling as I try to think of the right things to say.

"Santo wanted to give it a try without any fanfare—you know how Maria fusses," Felipe says, watching his brother closely.

Felipe and I hold this logistics conversation without looking at each other, because Santo's dark eyes are searching my face and he's still holding my hand.

"Vivien," he says again, stronger this time.

"I'm Iris, her daughter," I say, as steadily as I can.

He's shaking his head slowly, as if he's seen a ghost. I wait, give him the time he needs.

"Is she here?" I can't decide if the expression in his eyes is hope or fear.

I glance at Felipe, who just shrugs his shoulders and gazes down at his coffee. I reach across the table and hold Santo's other hand too, which for two people who've only just met, feels strangely right.

I steel myself and look him straight in the eyes, keeping my voice as steady and calm as I'm able. "She isn't. I'm sorry to tell you this, Santo, but my mother, Vivien . . . she died three years ago."

His hands tighten in mine as he takes a sharp intake of breath, his eyes misting with tears.

"Cancer," I say. "She was fifty-two."

He lets go of my hands and pulls a cotton handkerchief from his pocket to dab his eyes. He takes a few sips of his coffee as he steadies himself, and I can only imagine the thoughts that must be racing through his mind.

"I came to New York to see the places she loved," I say, trying to make my story as simple as possible.

"Do they all know who you are? Maria?"

Felipe puts his hand on Santo's shoulder. "No one knows anything, brother."

Santo nods. "And you work here now?"

I smooth my clammy hands on my apron. "I've been helping out some mornings, here and there."

He falls quiet again, making sense of things.

"It was all so long ago," he says.

"A lifetime," Felipe agrees.

"So similar," Santo says. "Uncanny."

Felipe pulls a hip flask from his inside pocket and tips a nip of whiskey in each of their coffees.

"My tablets," Santo says, but reaches for the cup anyway.

"I'm sorry I shocked you," I say, feeling terrible for the distress I've caused. It's the last thing my mother would have wanted. "I didn't mean to upset you. Shall I go? I can lock the door on my way out, Gio or Sophia will be back soon."

"Stay." Santo reaches for my hand. "You have her eyes."

"You should hear her sing," Felipe says. "It feels like a time machine."

The two brothers sit across the table from me drinking their whiskey-laced coffee, and I feel as if I'm waiting for them to make a decision.

"There's more," Felipe says, grave. "Gio loves her."

I open my mouth and close it again. Gio hasn't used the word himself, it's an assumption on Felipe's part. Santo huffs softly and shakes his head.

"Of course he does." He absorbs his brother's words, and then adds, "Does he know about Vivien?"

We both shake our heads.

"I'll tell him," I say. "Please? He should hear it from me."

Santo swallows, staring at me, and I belatedly remember I'm wearing flashing reindeer antlers.

"I'll make up a reason not to come for Christmas, and then once it's all over I'll tell him, I promise."

Felipe frowns and looks at Santo, and they share a quick-fire Italian exchange. I don't feel excluded, it just feels as if they find it easier to express themselves in their mother tongue, so I look at my lap and pull at a loose thread on my apron.

"Come for Christmas," Santo says eventually.

"We both think you should," Felipe says.

"For Vivien," Santo says, resolute. "Her child is welcome at my table."

"And then, for everyone's sake, you have to tell Gio. We

can't keep this secret from our family," Felipe says, though Santo looks nervous.

"I know," I say. I'd neither want nor expect it any other way. I know better than anyone how wearing secrets are on your soul.

We all glance up as Sophia bursts through the door, weighed down with shopping bags. She lowers them to the floor as soon as she catches sight of Santo.

"Papa!" She flings her arms around his neck from behind and presses her cold cheek against her father's. "You're too early!"

"Don't fuss, Sophia, and for the love of God don't call your mother," he says, patting her hand.

I get up from the table and untie my apron.

"I'll leave you guys to it," I say, grabbing my coat off the stand.

"You can't wait for Gio? He shouldn't be long," Sophia says, glancing at the clock.

"Something I need to do," I say quickly. "Tell him I'll call him later?"

Sophia pulls me into a quick hug and I cling to her, wishing she was anything but a Belotti so I could confide in her. I'm completely alone without Bobby and Robin. Smirnoff is a great secret keeper but not much use when it comes to sage advice.

"I'll see you on the big day," she says as she lets me go. "Come hungry, Mamma always makes enough food for a block party."

"She's Italian," Santo huffs.

"I'll be there," I say, and then I make my quick farewells

and leave, because I don't think I can handle seeing Gio just now. I'm breathing heavily into my scarf as I push my way through the snowy streets toward home, the inevitable tears stinging my eyes because I'm unable to shake the feeling that this is the beginning of the end.

Vivien

...

VIVIEN ADJUSTED THE SUNSHADE ON THE THRIFT-STORE stroller to shield her baby daughter from the late Sunday afternoon sun.

"I'm nervous, Iris," she whispered, safe in the knowledge that her nearly two-year-old child didn't have the faintest idea what she was talking about. "What if he isn't here anymore?"

But, in her heart, she knew Santo would be here. He'd said he'd be there forever. They hadn't spoken a word since the day she'd walked out of the gelateria four years ago, her head too full of starry-eyed ambition to realize that she was walking away from her best chance at forever happiness. She knew it now, though, and she could only hope she wasn't too late. Life on the road hadn't quite panned out the way she'd expected: too many late nights and smoky backstreet clubs, the occasional brush with stardom that could so easily have sent them stratospheric yet somehow didn't. Getting pregnant with Charlie Raven's child didn't feature anywhere in

Viv's life plan, yet there wasn't a single moment when she regretted bringing her child into the world.

"My baby" quickly became her favorite words in the English language, closely followed by "my daughter." Being a mother turned out to be more important than being a singer in a band, eclipsing everything and everyone, even when she found herself alone in L.A. trying to scrape together enough money to buy baby milk. As usual, her voice saved her—the cute busker with an even cuter baby strapped to her front was hard to pass by without dropping a few coins in her upturned hat.

"He might not even recognize me," she whispered to Iris, who laughed, delighted as she waved her beloved plastic giraffe in the air. Viv couldn't help but grin back; her daughter's joy was infectious.

"I hope your life is always this simple," she said, swallowing hard as Belotti's familiar green-and-white awnings loomed up ahead. "What am I even going to say?" she muttered, tucking herself into a doorway a few stores down to catch her breath. "Hi there, Santo, remember me, the girl who you gave your secret family recipe to? Anyway, I brought it back—I said you could trust me. I know it's been a few years but I've been kind of wondering if you still love me because I'm ready now? He might tell me to piss off. I would. I totally would, especially turning up with a kid in tow." She glanced down at Iris and immediately felt regretful. "Sorry, baby, it's not your fault."

She leaned down and brushed her hand over Iris's wild dark curls, so very like her own, and as she straightened a young woman stepped out of the gelateria pushing a baby around the same age as Iris in a stroller, a small dark-haired boy in shorts and a Spider-Man T-shirt skipping a few steps ahead. The woman called out to the boy to wait up then turned back toward Belotti's, and a joltingly familiar guy stepped out and joined them. Viv froze as she watched the idyllic scene unfold, a slick of panic sliding over her bones as she saw Santo bend to pull silly faces at the laughing child in the stroller. Jamming her cap down hurriedly over her face, she unzipped the baby bag hanging on the back of the stroller and rummaged inside it for something to do rather than look up, distracting herself enough to miss the fact that Iris had dropped her giraffe on the floor until she yelled.

"Shushhh," Viv said, urgent and fast, but before she could reach it the small boy in the Spider-Man T-shirt dashed over and picked it up. Viv scanned his serious little face and instinctively smiled, and he blinked as he held the giraffe out to Iris.

Iris beamed, thrilled to have her favorite thing back, and for a second the two children studied each other curiously.

"Gio, come on," the woman called, and the boy gave Iris a shy smile before turning on his heel and running back to his family. Viv kept her head down, surreptitiously watching the small family turn and walk away from the gelateria in the other direction. Once she was sure Santo hadn't spotted her, she raised her head, tortured as he slung his arm around the woman's shoulders and hoisted the small boy on his hip.

"They look really happy, don't they?" she whispered, half to Iris, more to herself. She'd imagined herself coming back here many times over the years, and now she'd finally plucked up the courage only to find she'd left it too late. She bore Santo no ill will. They hadn't made each other promises to wait, and she could hardly think badly of him when she'd had Iris.

Acute loneliness settled over her as Santo and his family disappeared out of sight. She'd always held on to the idea of him as her security blanket; letting him fall from her shoulders left her shivering now, even on the warm New York afternoon. Glancing down, she saw that Iris had fallen asleep, her giraffe clutched tight in her chubby hands.

"Just you and me against the world, baby," she whispered. She'd never experienced so much as a single second of regret over becoming a mother; when it came to the choice between baby or band, there was no decision to make. She'd struggled through a difficult, sickly pregnancy in a bedsit in L.A., some days eating only Santo's gelato, which she made from memory now. But the moment her small, red-faced daughter was laid on her chest would always stand out as the most significant of her life. She would never be alone again, because she was a mother.

Sighing heavily, Viv took one long last look at Belotti's green-and-white awnings, and then she let that particular happy-ever-after dream float away like a balloon released on the warm breeze. She'd tried. She'd come to the United States on a wing and a prayer, and she really had given it her all, but she didn't belong here. It was time to go.

32.

WHEN I WAS A LITTLE GIRL MY MOTHER AND I SPENT our Christmases in various provincial towns and cities up and down the country. She'd made quite a name for herself on the pantomime circuit, always in demand because she looked the part and her Joni Mitchell-ish voice helped carry the less vocally gifted stars of the show, usually soap actors and comedians. She never made the posters or the big bucks, but it gave us a secure income and a place to hang our hats for a few weeks over the holidays. The cast became my temporary family. I was the child helping out backstage or studying at my table and chair in the corner, they'd blow me kisses as they dashed past for a whirlwind costume change and the ensemble would mill around swapping gossip and heel plasters. They answered my math problems and told me stories that were wildly inappropriate for my young ears, but those frenetic weeks were always my favorite time of year. Christmas Day was the only day the theater closed, a precious few hours together in whichever digs we'd been given. My mother didn't subscribe to the turkey tradition on account of the fact she was a terrible cook, but it was festive on our own terms. We'd have fairy lights and golden fir cones, tins of sweets and gelato, and we'd crash on the sofa or the hotel bed and watch

Christmas TV. It wasn't grand scale or full of annual traditions, but it was ours and we loved it.

I woke this morning and thought about those Christmases, made myself a coffee and touched the fir cones around the mirror as I passed them.

Today is going to be my first experience of a big, traditional family Christmas. I'm nervous, even though I know everyone will go the extra mile to make me feel welcome and included. I'm relieved to have met Santo in advance, at least, so there shouldn't be any surprises there. I've made truffles and bought small gifts for everyone to say thank you, wrapped them prettily and put them beneath my tree ready for today. My outfit is hanging on my wardrobe door, a green dress threaded with silver that catches the light, high heels and a vintage holly hair clip I spotted in a thrift-store window and fell in love with, my mother's magpie genes coming out. My cab is booked for midday. I'm organized, on the outside, at least. On the inside, though, I'm a jumble of emotions. I let them run riot through me as I shower and dry my hair, acknowledge all of my fears as I apply a thankfully perfect cat's-eye flick. I feel all of those worries and nerves now, in the hope that if I let them have my morning, they might let me have one afternoon of peace and joy. I allow the devil on my shoulder to whisper that I'm a terrible, selfish person, and the snake in my gut to coil around my fragile happiness and attempt to squeeze the life out of it. Adam Bronson manifests in my living room and orders me to spend the day here with him instead, sneers and asks me who I think I am pretending I belong somewhere. And then I smooth out the poster of my mother with her pregnancy test in her pocket and look at it until the devil on my shoulder pops like a soap bubble, until the snake realizes he's not feasting today, until Adam Bronson eats glass instead of roast turkey. *Enough, all of you.* I put on my dress and slide the clip into my hair, let my high heels and fake fur coat lend me confidence, and by the time the cab horn sounds on the street outside, I'm ready.

WHITE LIGHTS AND GARLANDS line the steps up to the Belotti family brownstone, a huge fresh holly wreath hanging on the double doors.

"Iris, you look so pretty," Bella says, throwing the door wide before I can ring the bell. A scurry of kids fill the hall around her and she shoos them away so I can step inside with my bag of presents. Maria's house has taken on Disney-esque holiday glamour, the kind of dressing that must have come from one of those specialist companies Gio told me about because it would have taken a normal person weeks to achieve this look on their own. The staircase garlands, the lights, the baubles, the fireplace . . . it's glitzy but tasteful, homey but sophisticated. Whoever did it has matched the holiday decor to the homeowner seamlessly—it's Maria to a tee, and I love it.

"This place looks . . ." I gaze up at the giant tree in the hallway, lost for words.

"I know, right?" Bella grins. She's wearing a Minnie at Christmas sweatshirt and has red glittery mouse ears on her head.

"I like your ears," I laugh, and she touches them, self-conscious.

"Sophia made me do it," she says. "She has some for you too."

"I should hope so," I say as she leads me into the grand, twinkling living room.

It's exactly as I'd imagined it would be. Fire crackling in the hearth, everyone dressed to impress, Santo in his armchair with one of his grandkids on his knee. He didn't have any success with remembering the recipe when he spent time at the gelateria the other morning; they plan to try again after Christmas, maybe load some ingredients into his favorite old machine to see if going through the motions helps. That's a worry for another day, though, not on anyone's mind right now. The Belotti women seem to have cornered the market in red lipstick—I chew my rose-glossed lower lip and wish I'd thought of it because it looks so festive. I'm hugged, passed around like a long-lost family member, and finally I reach Gio, who has been leaning in the kitchen doorway watching me.

"You look nice," he says, kissing me on both cheeks. He smells so good when he leans in close, of warm spice and familiarity, and I long for him to hold me in his arms. I sense the family watching us expectantly and step away to hand my present bag to Sophia.

"Ears, non-negotiable," she says, taking the bag in exchange for a set of glittered ruby Minnie ears. She must have cleared the shelf of them because all of her sisters have them, plus Maria, of course, and I laugh and put them on my head as Felipe appears wearing some too.

"Better than cracker hats," I say.

Sophia frowns. "Cracker hats?"

"You know, Christmas crackers?" I glance at the dining table. "Are they not a thing here? You pull them and they go bang, and a paper hat flies out with a terrible joke and a tacky gift?"

They're looking at me as if I'm speaking a different language as I make the motion of pulling an imaginary cracker, and I wish I'd never mentioned it because the glitter ears are so much nicer anyway.

"Billy's brother told me a funny joke last week." One of the kids skids across the wooden floor in his Christmas socks, unintentionally coming to my rescue. "But it has a curse in it so I'm not allowed to say."

Felipe rubs his hands together and bends down, almost losing his mouse ears. "Whisper it to me, it sounds like my kind of joke."

"I don't think so," Maria says, bustling everyone out of the way to hug me. It breaks the moment, as she no doubt knew it would, and someone presses a glass of champagne into my hand. I catch Santo's eye and he gives me a nod, the ghost of a complicated smile. I know it must be strange for him to have me here. I'd like to spend a few quiet minutes with him this afternoon if I get the chance—there's something I'd like to give him back.

I let myself be absorbed into the family atmosphere, and I don't feel awkward as gifts are given or as if there are in-jokes I don't understand, because they include me easily in everything. Bella hands my gifts out and I'm given pretty things in return: a turquoise bracelet from Maria and Santo, a vintage champagne saucer from Sophia. It's overwhelming, really, sitting among them as they give and receive, watching the kids rip paper from new toys and the dog mosey around everyone. Gio is beside me on the sofa, and the urge to touch him is so strong it hurts my fingers to not curl them around his. My glass seems to refill itself, and I'm . . . I'm really, truly happy.

Lunch is a slowly savored feast: antipasto platters heaving with cured meats and wooden boards laden with Italian cheeses, briny stuffed olives and marinated mushrooms, slippery peppers alongside braised artichoke hearts—and that was just the beginning. Gio has been seated beside me with calligraphed name plates, Sophia on my other side, Santo at the head of the table.

Maria's pasta is featherlight and her beef ragù tastes as if she's been simmering it for the last week straight, rich with Barolo and so delicious I tell her I could eat it every day for the rest of my life and not get bored.

"*Salute!*" Santo raises his glass when the roast is placed center-stage, and Felipe springs from his seat beside his brother and reaches for the carving knife and fork.

"Would you mind, Santo?" he says, gamely brandishing the implements. "I've never carved for the family before."

He makes it sound as if his brother is bestowing the favor by allowing him the honor of carving, a simple act of generosity that I find I have to look away from.

"So much food," I murmur as the meat is surrounded by all manner of vegetables and roast potatoes, and beneath the table Gio puts his hand briefly on my knee. I cover it with my own, a fleeting moment of connection, of us, within this busy festive scene.

"Do you miss London, Iris?" I look up as Francesca spoons garlic-coated green beans onto her son's plate while she chats to me across the table.

"I don't anymore, really," I say, picking through the bones of my previous life to find something positive to say. Without mentioning my mother, there's nothing. "I'm pretty settled here now and I've barely scratched the surface of New York."

"I miss Paris," Pascal says, mournful, but I could have kissed him for the ease with which he has rerouted the conversation from London Underground to Paris Metro in one swift stop.

Francesca rolls her eyes. "We were just there, Pascal."

The conversation ebbs and flows around the table as plates are filled and refilled, gravy boats replenished and wineglasses topped up. There's no hurry, no sense of anyone wanting to move proceedings along. Felipe has many stories to tell of far-flung places, and he doesn't seem to have any particular guilt about the way he's chosen to live his life. Equally, there seems no animosity from the family toward him; Gio is a gift bestowed upon Santo and Maria, their only and much-beloved boy. How fortunate he is to have so many people who adore him—but then, as I've learned in recent months, he is an incredibly easy person to love.

"I don't think I've ever eaten this much in my life," I say, laying down my cutlery. "I'm admitting defeat."

"There's still dessert," Maria says, and everyone around the table slides a little farther down in their seats and groans. Sophia was right about Maria cooking enough to feed the block. There's been enough food on this table today to feed most of Brooklyn. I help clear the table, glad of the excuse to stretch, enjoying the experience of milling around the kitchen with Gio's sisters. The conversation is easy, wine-fueled, and funny, and I'm still laughing when I excuse myself from proceedings to go to the bathroom. Gio is nowhere to be seen, but as I stand in the grand hallway Felipe comes in the front door.

"Sneaky cigar with Santo," he says, tapping the side of his nose as he shrugs his coat off. "Don't tell Maria."

"Is he still outside?" I say.

He nods, tucking his half-smoked cigar behind his ear.

"Do you think he'd mind if I go out and join him for a few minutes?"

"I shouldn't think so," Felipe says.

I'm nervous at the thought of talking to Santo alone, chewing the inside of my lip as I reach for my coat and slip out through the double doors. It's snowing lightly, and I find Santo sheltering beneath the porch overhang in his heavy coat, pulling on his cigar as he surveys the neighborhood.

"Mind if I join you? I could do with a breather."

He looks at me as I stand beside him out of the snow.

"Thank you for letting me come today," I say.

He nods in acknowledgment.

"He's had enough heartbreak in his life already," he says, clearly talking about Gio. "I see him with you and he's alive again. Seven years, and now he's alive again."

I don't know what to say. Nothing perhaps, so I just listen.

"But to not say anything about you, to not tell him who you are to me . . . it's gonna eat me alive, and you too, and the more it eats, the more damage it does. Like dry rot. You cannot have dry rot in your house and expect the place not to fall down around your ears, Iris."

I nod, miserable because I know it's true.

"My Maria," he says, prayer-like, looking to the skies for guidance as he shakes his head. "Your mother's name is not part of my family story. I was a stupid young fool. I made mistakes. But they've stayed in here"—he taps his chest—"and in here"—he taps his head, and his eyes tell me how hard he's labored to keep his secrets all of these years. "And then I walk into my gelateria and there you are, with her cornflower-blue eyes, and it's a judgment on me, because of what I did. I gave my family secret away and so now it's been taken away from me, blown straight out of my head." He makes a hand gesture toward his head, like a small bomb exploding. "Some kind of judgment, huh?"

I reach into my coat pocket.

"And now I'm giving it back to you," I say, and I hold out the torn mint-green napkin.

He looks at it in silence without taking it from me.

"She treasured it," I say. "She made this gelato for me my entire life. She made me swear to never share the recipe with a living soul, but somehow I don't think that promise included you." I place it in his hand, even though letting go of it is like letting a piece of her go too. "Please, take it. It's always been yours."

He studies his own youthful handwriting for a few seconds, then tucks it away inside the chest pocket of his overcoat. I can see he's moved, so I watch the snow fall and wait.

"Your mother . . . it was like trying to hold on to lightning. Too bright, too hot. I loved her, but I got burned."

I think of how she was in Felipe's video, and I see how easy she must have been to fall for.

"What is it they say, lightning doesn't strike twice? It felt like it did when I saw you standing there, only it's Gio who's going to lose this time and he's lost too much already."

My heart twists.

"The question I've been asking myself over and over is how to do right by my family. For Gio. For Maria. For my girls. *La mia famiglia*."

The way Santo says "my girls," how the phrase encompasses every woman in the house behind us but me, reinforces my position as the interloper. I'm the kid on the outside again, as always. My heart has a go at anger, tries to rally, to ask what about me, but it's too hard.

"What are you asking me to do, Santo?"

He looks down. "I see you, Vivien's girl, and my old heart wants to help you, you know? I know Felipe thinks you should tell Gio your connection, your history. But the price is too high. If Gio knows, then Maria will know. This family you love, your place in it is built on a lie, on a betrayal. My betrayal, yes, but yours too. To welcome you in is to let all of the rabbits out of the hats."

He takes a long drag on his cigar, and I hate that this is the way things are playing out between us.

"I got over your mother. She left, and I let go of her in time. You know what I learned from that? A clean break heals easiest."

I look at the picture-perfect snow scene in front of me, and I feel the chill all the way through to my bones. He's telling me to go, to be my mother's daughter and leave town. I can't pull myself together enough to form words.

"He won't forgive you for deceiving him. So why tell him? Just to hurt him? To hurt us? Just go. He'll be all right, you have my word," Santo says eventually. "He's my boy, and he has his family."

And he is. Gio Belotti is their boy, even though for a while it's felt like he's mine. Every word that Santo has said out on this step tonight is true. Blood is thicker than water. I stand beside him, the only man my mother ever loved, and feel wretched. The Belottis have their recipe back. Order has been restored to the family, and now it's time for me to leave.

———

I DON'T KNOW HOW I got through the last two hours. I stepped back inside the house and walked straight into the bathroom, locked the door and sat on the edge of the tub with my head in my hands. Santo has told me to leave. Or asked me to, I guess, but he made himself crystal clear. I wanted to scream and shout, to punch the walls until my knuckles bled, but I didn't do any of those things. I splashed cool water on my face and cycled through breathing exercises, and then I stepped outside and painted a smile on my face. I hugged Maria, thanked everyone for the best afternoon ever, packed the boxes of leftovers already set aside for me. I fake-groaned when Pascal winked as he slid a bottle of limoncello in my bag. I accepted sticky kisses from the kids and lipstick ones from Gio's sisters, and hugged Bella so hard she laughed and said she couldn't breathe. I did all of those things. I kissed Felipe, who slipped a Christmas card into my coat pocket, and then I kissed Santo, who couldn't meet my eyes, and then I lied and said I had a call coming from family back in London and better get home because they could talk for hours.

When my cab arrived, Gio carried my bags out onto the sidewalk and loaded them in, then pulled me in for a hug.

"I'd kiss you but I get the feeling we're probably being watched by most of my family," he whispered, laughing. "I think we should tell them soon, they all love you."

I took a step back.

"New Year's Eve?" he suggested, his eyes trying to read mine.

I couldn't speak, I didn't know how to say goodbye.

His fingers brushed mine, the briefest of touches. I wanted

to cling on, to tell him I loved him, to pull him into the cab and make him understand, but I didn't.

"When the ball drops," I said, and he smiled his heart-breaker smile.

"I didn't get you alone to give you your gift," he said.

"I have yours too," I said, thinking of the only gift still wrapped beneath my tree.

"Iris, I—" he said, but the cabdriver slid his window down and asked us to hurry things along, so I'll never know what he was going to say. Perhaps he was going to say he'll call me later, or maybe he was going to tell me he loves me. I hope not.

I climbed into the car and he closed the door for me, and I laid my hand against the cold glass as we moved away from the curb.

"Chrystie Street?" the driver said, meeting my eye in the mirror.

I nodded and gave him the address of the noodle house, then laid my head against the window and closed my eyes, exhausted.

33.

COULD I HAVE DONE THINGS DIFFERENTLY? I COULD have not lied about Adam in the first place. God, how I wish I could change what happened in that bookstore, that I hadn't spoken so impulsively. I'm so tired of shaming myself for it. I've hung my green dress back in the wardrobe and scrubbed my face clean of makeup. I haven't turned the tree lights on, because I've never felt less celebratory in my life. It's too hard, being in love, like jumping from a plane without a parachute and trusting someone to catch you. I'm in terrible distress.

When I lost my mother, I had time to acknowledge her illness, I knew she was going to leave me. It didn't make it any less devastating, but at least there was a process, it followed the expected downward curve.

When I left Adam, I was at rock-bottom, on my uppers in every possible sense, but it didn't come as a bolt out of the blue. There was a downward spiral, an erosion, a build-up of pressure until I finally found the strength to end things.

And now I've lost Gio. There is to be no gentle goodbye, no attempt at an explanation that might soften the blow, no slim chance that he'll understand, because, as Santo said, a clean break heals easiest. Part of me—a big part of me—

wants to push back, because this is my life, and Gio's life, maybe even our forever if we were lucky enough to have that. And I would push back, if I wasn't so held down by the guilt of my own lies. What good would explaining myself do? Make myself feel better? Whichever way it happens, the end result is going to be the same, so perhaps Santo is right. A clean break will mend soonest—not for me, but for Gio, at least. He is at the center of all this, the person Santo is trying to protect, the person I'd rather hack my own heart out of my chest with a rusty knife for than cause even a second's pain. But I'm going to, either way, so the only decision that's mine to make is how. Santo doesn't want me to tell him anything about my mother or the recipe, doesn't want his son to see him as less than perfect. I'm more than a little wounded that he has scrubbed my mum out of his story completely, when there are so few people left who knew her. Oh, I get it. He picked himself up and went on to build his strong, solid family, built a beautiful relationship with Maria. Of all the women in all the world, I'm probably the last one he'd choose for Gio. And I understand that. I do. If I was him, I might even try to do the same thing, anything to steady the Belotti ship. But I'm not him. I'm the one over here losing everything—not just Gio, but all of them, all of this life I've built in New York.

I can't stay here, living a few blocks over from the gelateria. That isn't anyone's idea of a clean break. It's a messy, vicious one where I'll be forced to look him in the eyes and tell him even more lies, to steel myself against him. Sophia would come, and Bella would come, and Maria would come, because they would all see him struggle and need to understand why I would do that to him. I can't fathom it. I don't know what to do, but I know I can't wait here in my apartment to be looked for and found. So I don't spend my Christmas night watching crap TV or drinking champagne or playing board games. I spend it folding clothes into the same suitcase I dragged away from Adam's house exactly one year ago today, too numb to cry as I pack toiletries. I drag the box with my gelato maker in over to the doorway, and then I turn back to take a long last look around. It's as I found it really, no extra cushions or ornaments to feather the nest. My nomadic roots run deep after all, it seems. I turn out the lights and lock the door, then drag my suitcase downstairs to the sidewalk.

SMIRNOFF SITS ON THE noodle house step watching me pile my belongings up out of the snow with a disinterested eye. I lay a saucer of food on the back corner of the step for him and risk my fingers to give his ears a scratch.

"Bye, buddy," I whisper, hunkering down beside him. I've texted Shen to ask if she'd mind taking care of him for a few days until Bobby gets back; she sent me back a string of emojis that suggest she's fine with it.

"I'll miss you," I add, and he lifts his face out of his dinner to glare slowly sideways at me. If he could speak I think he'd be saying he won't miss me a bit as long as someone puts his tuna down, and I'm glad, because he's one living being I don't have to feel guilt over.

I pull Felipe's Christmas card from my pocket as I wait for the cab and read it again.

From one rolling stone to another, I thought you might need somewhere you won't be disturbed to hang your hat for a few days while you get yourself together.

I've paid the electricity up to New Year's Eve,
consider it an apology.

   Good luck, kiddo, I know it's tough. Florida's warm
this time of year.

                                                        F

I put the key to unit 359 back inside the card with a heavy sigh. The cabdriver pulls as close as he can to the sidewalk in the snow, and I heave my things into the back and ask him to take me to Belotti's. He waits while I slide an envelope under the painted glass door, then I get back in and give him the address of Easy Self Storage.

34.

Dear Gio,

Before I say what I need to say, please know that these last few months with you have been the happiest days of my life. You're the best human I'll ever know, even if I live to be a hundred.

I have to tell you something. My heart is heavy as I write this, I'm so sorry not to tell you myself, to your face. Truth is, I can't. I just can't bring myself to say the words out loud and watch you hate me, so I'm taking the coward's way out and writing them down.

I lied to you, Gio. My ex isn't dead, and we were never married. Adam Bronson is an awful, manipulative, abusive man who I ran away from on Christmas Day last year. I got into the habit of telling myself he was dead to try to stop myself from looking over my shoulder all the time, but I should never have said it out loud to you. I should have corrected you when you assumed I was married that day in the bookstore.

I don't have any excuses for it. Finding out you're a widower made it impossible to walk back from that stupid, horrible lie, but I just can't go on with it any longer.

*What kind of a person tells a lie like that? I'm so
ashamed. You deserve so much better than that, than me.*

*There's something else you should know about this too.
Adam found the video of me singing at Bella's school and
messaged her for my number. I don't believe he'll come to
New York, and even if he does he absolutely isn't a physically violent threat to Bella, but I need you to know so
you can be watchful, just in case. I'm so desperately sorry
to bring that to your door.*

*I'm leaving New York and I won't be coming back this
way again, so this is goodbye. Thank you, Gio. Thank
you for the Monday nights and the safety of your arms,
for the Christmas tree and the mug with my name on,
and for not being able to say horrible things to me, even
as a joke. I've never felt I belonged anywhere the way I do
with you, and with your family. Tell them I'm sorry too?
It's really quite something to be a Belotti.*

*Be happy, Gio. Your heart is too full of love to keep it
all locked inside you.*

*Love,
Iris x*

35.

As CHRISTMAS NIGHT GOES, FINDING MYSELF HOMELESS
and sleeping in a storage unit is only my second worst on
record, which speaks volumes about my life with Adam
Bronson. I've brought a pillow and blanket from my apartment, although it's quite warm in here now thanks to Felipe's
space heater. I have warmth and light from the lamp in
the corner, and no one is likely to trouble me. You'd have to
pay someone a fair amount to sit in that sterile reception
downstairs over the holidays and, unsurprisingly, no one is
around depositing junk in their units either. I have this soul-
less place to myself. I'm relieved to find there's a toilet at the
end of the corridor; that's one embarrassment dealt with, at
least.

I've run my phone battery down on purpose, because I
can't face the barrage of messages that will no doubt shotgun
in once my letter is discovered. I bury my face down into my
pillow and close my eyes at the thought of the letter, the truths
I've told, the bridges I've set ablaze. There is a hollow, miserable peace to be had in finally telling Gio the truth about
Adam. I should have done it face-to-face. I should have done
it months ago. I know both of those things.

I sigh heavily and put the video of my mother into the machine, and then I close my eyes and, just like when I was seven years old, I let her sing me to sleep.

I FEEL LIKE AN animal in a lair. I washed my face and brushed my teeth in the tiny cloakroom sink this morning, but I feel crumpled and stiff, half alive. I've been out for supplies, skulking around like a fugitive even though the place is still deserted. The street outside was too, just a dog walker in sight when I ventured across to the bodega on the corner early this morning. Their bacon, egg, and cheese roll was my breakfast, and I've stocked up on enough to get me through for a day or two. I know I can't stay here any real length of time, but I don't seem to be able to form a plan. My brain feels as if it's surrounded with cotton wool, muffled and unable to think beyond the next half an hour. I've been sleeping, or trying to, and I've been remembering, or trying not to. Florida doesn't appeal, despite Felipe's recommendation. L.A. doesn't appeal either—my mother didn't find any happiness there and I've no reason to imagine I would either. I'm definitely not going back to London, I know that much. For today, and maybe for tomorrow, I'll lie low here and hope my mind unfogs enough to work something out. I feel like a person on the cusp of falling. I see how homelessness can happen, how easily people can fall through the cracks when they don't have other people around them to watch their backs. I'm not going to be homeless, I won't let myself fall that low, but I understand the downward plummet, how easy it is to feel transient, and it's sobering.

———

IT'S BEEN ANOTHER DAY and another night, according to my watch and my aching bones. I have to get out of this place today. I've decided to leave behind the things I can't easily carry, my gelato maker and other bits I won't need immediately, and then try to contact Felipe when I get myself set up somewhere and have him send them on to me. I hate the thought of leaving my stuff, my gelato machine most of all, but it's the only way I can face getting myself moving today. I feel at my lowest ebb, physically incapable of lugging my things through the snow.

I hear the lift doors out in the main hallway rumble open and sit perfectly still, even though there isn't a realistic chance of anyone having discovered I'm here and coming to turf me out for breaking the rules. My heart pounds all the same as I hear heavy footfalls, and then I suck in a sharp breath because someone is shouting my name and banging on random doors.

"Iris! Iris, where are you?"

A key fumbles in the lock of my door and then it's yanked up, and Gio stands framed in the opening and stares at me. I feel so many emotions crash over my head, I want to put my hands up as a cage to hold them off. Humiliated by the state of me. Embarrassed that I've been sleeping in a storage unit. Full of self-hatred for the letter I wrote him, and frightened. Not of him. I'm frightened *for* him, because he looks like hell.

"Gio." I say his name because it's all I'm capable of, and he shakes his head and holds his hand up to stop me speaking.

"I don't believe this," he mutters, his eyes running all over the unit, taking in my temporary home. "This stops right now, do you hear me?"

We stare at each other, and a tear of temper rolls down his face and breaks my heart.

"I'm sorry," I say, realizing I'm crying too when I taste salt. "I'm so sorry."

"Just get your stuff," he says, and when I don't move, can't move, he does it instead, grabbing my things and shoving them into bags. "I mean it, Iris, get your stuff. Is this yours?" He holds up my pillow. "This?"

I've never seen anyone contain so much tension in their body. He looks in pain from it.

He picks things up at random, Felipe's clothes, I think, and I shake my head, mortified, not knowing what to do or say.

"There's a cab outside and you're going to get in it. It's going to take you back to the noodle house, where you're going to unpack your stuff and sleep in your own bed like a grown-up, do you hear me?" He dashes a hand over his eyes, furious at his own tears, and at me.

"You'll have a fridge and running water and you'll be safe." He turns away from me as he chokes the last word out and thumps the metal shutters hard, a harsh noise that reverberates around the quiet building.

I stand up and go to him, put my hand on his rigid shoulder.

"Gio," I say, my mouth trembling with tears. "Gio."

He turns to me and he's in such a mess that we just hold each other, hard, and rock each other, because we're so very wounded.

"I'm sorry, I'm sorry," I whisper.

"Stop apologizing," he says. "Just stop. I can't hear it today."

He grips me by the shoulders and stares down at me. "You never have to run from me," he says, his voice raw and ragged. "Do you get that? I'm so fucking mad at you I can't think straight, but I'd never hurt a hair on your stupid, stubborn, beautiful head."

He lets go of me and pushes his hands through his hair and then sits down heavily on the sofa. I sit on the other end, my hands pressed hard against my mouth, trying to pull myself together.

"I've spent the past two days thinking about you, and about Penny, and about Bella . . ." He looks sideways at me, still struggling to speak. "My daughter. For fuck's sake, Iris. She should never have been caught up in this shit."

There isn't anything I can say to make it okay. I feel empty of any words anyway.

"Just go home," he says, weary. "I can't sleep unless I know you're safe. Go home and get some proper rest."

He picks my bags up and waits while I put my coat on and turn everything off, then we catch the elevator down onto the sidewalk, too exhausted to speak to each other. There's a cab, just as he said, and he puts my stuff in and then turns to me, his expression bleak.

"If this thing between us is over, then we say goodbye properly." He swallows hard and looks away down the deserted, cold street. "Take a few days. Look after yourself better than this." He gestures toward the storage building and sighs. "I need some time to get my head straight, okay? I'll come to your apartment on New Year's Eve, and we'll treat each other kindly, because I care about you too damn much for it to end on a sidewalk like this."

I nod and get into the car, because I don't know how to say goodbye properly to Gio Belotti. Not on this sidewalk today, in my apartment on New Year's Eve, or ever.

36.

I DO AS HE'S ASKED. I LET MYSELF BACK INTO MY APART-
ment and drop my bags by the front door, and I stand in the
quiet cold space I didn't think I'd see again. I don't know if it
feels like failure or reprieve. I make tea and put the heating on,
and I let the cat in when he appears on the fire escape. I go
through the motions until I strip off and stand under the hot
shower, and then it finally gets me. All of it. My mother's death.
Adam. The Belottis. Gio. I sit on the floor and wrap my arms
around my knees, and the last three years swirl around me as
if I'm surrounded by IMAX screens. Words and memories.
Black dresses at funerals, kisses on rooftops, painted glass doors,
Moonstruck Monday nights, vacuuming the same room three
times, terrified I'd missed something, singing in the park, Maria's perfume, Sophia's curls, Bella's fragile hands on piano keys,
streets full of houses covered in Christmas lights, my mother
looking into my eyes as she laughs down the lens. They all slide
and clash against each other, jumbled and discordant, and I
close my eyes and lay my forehead on my knees, battle weary.

I'M SITTING AT THE table with a cold cup of coffee in front
of me. I slept deeply as soon as my head touched the pillow

last night, yet I still feel as if I've been hit by a bus this morning. I jolt inside my dressing gown when the buzzer goes. I sit still, hoping it's a mailman who'll decide he's out of luck, but it goes again, insistent, and I sigh when I look outside and see bouncing black curls.

I open my door as Sophia runs up the stairs with grocery bags in her hands, and she steps inside and puts them on the kitchen surface.

"I brought you some things," she says quietly, putting milk and ham in the fridge, bread beside the kettle. "Why don't you go and put some clothes on while I make us some fresh coffee?"

I do it, because it's almost a relief to have someone tell me what to do.

"I saw your letter," she says, passing me a mug when I walk back to the kitchen. "He didn't want to show me, I made him."

I sit down at the kitchen table and try to raise a half smile out of my boots, because it's kind of Sophia to come here and I can well imagine her not taking no for an answer. She sits down in the chair next to mine and shuffles it until she's as close to me as the table allows.

"You could have told me about him," she says, covering my hands with hers. "I'd have listened."

"I didn't have the words," I say, pushing my hair out of my face as I lift my eyes to hers. "Is Gio okay?"

"He will be. I promise." She unwinds a hairband from around her wrist. "Will you?"

I shrug, because I have no idea how I'm going to be, or where. She gets up and stands behind me, gently finger combing my hair back into a ponytail. She puts her hands on my shoulders and squeezes, warm and reassuring, and I reach up and hold them. We stay like that for a while, connected, and I think about how, actual brother and sister or not, Gio and Sophia Belotti share the same big beautiful heart.

"Don't leave New York," she says. "I don't want you to go."

"I can't stay here," I say. "It's too much. I need to be somewhere else, find myself a fresh start, somewhere without baggage."

"Baggage," she says, almost scathing. "Jesus, Iris, everyone has baggage. You do. Gio does. You guys have enough baggage between you to fill a goddamn carousel at JFK, but isn't that kind of the point of love, that you help each other carry the bags? Fresh starts are for Hallmark movies, not real life."

She slides back into the chair next to mine and looks me in the eyes.

"You've done the worst part. Gio knows the truth now, he'll make his peace with it, I'm sure he will. Stay here. Stay for him. Stay for me."

She makes it sound so easy, so seductive, this life she's laid out before me. I wish with all my heart that it could be so easy, but she only knows what she sees. She doesn't know her father has asked me to leave New York in order to protect the secret he's kept for decades.

"I can't, Sophia. Please don't ask me again, because I honestly can't."

She sits with her knees touching mine and rests her forehead against my head.

"Who am I going to talk gelato flavors with when you're gone?"

I close my eyes. *"Vanilla forever."*

"You know it."

She laughs softly, and a tear falls from her cheek onto our clutched hands.

IT'S NEW YEAR'S EVE tomorrow, which makes today my last full day here. This time there will be no moonlight flits or sleeping in storage units. I'll welcome Bobby and Robin home, and I'll wait for Gio to come, and then I've booked myself a ticket out to Toronto in the small hours of January first.

New year, new country, yet another new start. I'm not sure I have it in me to reinvent myself all over again, but I looked up where *Schitt's Creek* was filmed and let that be my guide. It's about one percent more targeted than throwing a dart at a map, but it's going to have to do.

So this is it. Officially my last full day in New York, and there's something I have to do before I leave. I pull on my snow boots and my winter coat, then hook my backpack carefully over my shoulders and head out into the cold, clear morning.

I'm not going far. Just to the park across the street, in fact. I've walked there countless times over my year as a temporary New Yorker, and today I'm going there to scatter my mother's ashes. I may be leaving the city tomorrow, but leaving her here feels like the right thing to do. I'm glad when I hear the familiar tones of the busker, serenading passersby with Christmas favorites. I hope they're giving generously, she deserves it. She sees me and raises her hand, and I make my way across and stand to the side as she finishes the final minute or two of "White Christmas." And it really has been. There's still quite a lot of standing snow around, I'm so glad I got to see New York like this.

"Are you taking requests?" I say, giving her a quick hug when she reaches behind her speaker for a bottle of water once the song's over.

She grins. "For you, yes."

"Do you know 'River'?" I say.

"Joni Mitchell? Of course," she says, like it's a no-brainer.

It was one of my mother's favorites, she used to sing it at the end of late-night sets in smoky clubs. The melancholy Christmas lyrics feel as if they were written for today, the minor chord treatment of the opening bars turning "Jingle Bells" from a lilt to a lament. I've asked to hear it for my mother and for me, because it's a song about things coming to an end, about leaving, and about the pain of causing the people you love distress. For all that, it's beautiful, and I find it uplifting because it reminds me of my mother at her happiest—singing for an audience.

"In a while, though, yes?" I say. "Not straightaway."

She nods, giving me a thoughtful look. "You got it."

I make my way over to a broad-trunked old oak tree I've developed a fondness for. I've sat beneath it with my back turned against its trunk on warm summer days, and I've sometimes paused on a walk to lay my hands against the bark just to draw strength from its solid presence. My mother was an unabashed tree-hugger and I know she'd have appreciated this oak even more than I do. I'm relieved to see that the overhanging branches have sheltered the ground beneath it from the worst of the snow, and there aren't many people around on this midwinter's morning. I can hear kids farther down braving the icy basketball courts, and I kind of like their noise, their shouts, and their laughter. It's real life, always moving.

I place my backpack down against the base of the tree and take my mother's ashes from it, a simple silver urn. I've carried this with me since she died; it's disconcerting to think of finally letting her go. Maybe I should think of it as letting her stay here, instead.

I rest my backside on my bag and lean against the tree, the urn pressed tight against my chest. There's no rush. I suspect the busker understands what this is for me.

I close my eyes so I can recall my mother's face, screw up my nose to try to bring the scent she always wore close to my memory. I saved her almost empty last bottle, and cried silently in the bathroom when Adam binned it without asking me.

"This is it, then," I say, opening our final imaginary conversation. "Is this place okay? I don't know if you ever came here. I hope so. You'd have hugged this tree for sure." I lean my head back against it, my eyes open, miles away from here in my mind. I'm a round-limbed child coloring pictures backstage at one of her shows, I'm a grouchy teenager sharing popcorn at the cinema beside her, I'm a frightened daughter holding her dying mother's hand.

"I've made such a mess of everything, Mum," I say. "But they have their recipe back now. I managed that much, at least."

I look at the silver urn in my hands. It doesn't feel as if she's really in there. I guess she isn't, really. She's everywhere. She's in the perfect pitch of an unexpected Joni Mitchell song on the radio, in the rose-gold streaks of the best holiday sunsets, in the catch of her favorite perfume on a stranger as they pass by. She's in every pink melamine bowl of gelato. She'll always be with me, whether I'm in London, or New York, or Toronto. Leaving her ashes in New York doesn't change that.

I cast a look toward the busker and find her watching me, and I give her a small, forever grateful smile as she plays the opening bars of "River" for me and my magnificent, bohemian, lightning-bolt mother. I don't feel the expected rush of dread when I unscrew the lid. I listen to the poignant words as I slowly tip the urn, and I smile through my tears as her ashes catch on the cold New York wind. I blow her a kiss as she scatters and flies and dances, disappearing slowly out of sight like a balloon released from a child's fingers. I look toward the busker and see she's crying as she sings.

37.

NEW YEAR'S EVE DAWNS CRYSTAL CLEAR, A BLUE-SKIES sub-zero last day of the year. I've been up since long before sunrise, taking my time to pack things carefully away. I've sorted stuff I'm going to need over the next couple of weeks into my suitcase, and I'm going to speak to Bobby about getting the rest mailed when I know what I'm doing. I know he won't mind, and I feel easier about leaving my gelato maker here than in the storage lock-up. He and Robin are due back from their vacation today. They should have been getting back right about now, in fact, but he messaged earlier to say they've been delayed so he'll see me later.

I'm dreading telling him that I'm leaving New York this evening, but at least this way I get to do it properly rather than just disappear. I sigh, thinking about Gio's phrase. *Say goodbye properly.* How does anyone do that, really, especially when it's to people you love and are leaving behind? I'm comforted by the idea that at least I'll be able to stay in contact with Bobby and Robin. Maybe they'll even come and see me when I'm more sorted, and of course there's always video calling. I don't have to completely lose them from my life.

It's a different story with the Belottis. Santo made his thoughts clear—a clean break is the kindest thing for Gio.

Even if he could get past the lie about Adam—and I suspect he probably would understand, in time—there isn't a happy ending written in the stars for us.

Santo's history with my mother is exactly that—history, in the past. She broke his heart, he compromised the family secret, and despite both of those things he went on to build a strong, wonderful family. For me to stay, everyone involved would have to know all of this. Gio, Maria, Sophia, and his other sisters. Family loyalty and tradition are Belotti corner-stones, which is why Santo has kept this part of his life locked safely inside for over thirty years. Who am I to force him to bring it all into the light now? My mother certainly wouldn't want me to cause him that kind of distress, especially given his recent health.

Besides, what good would knowing all of this be to Gio? He'd realize I've known their recipe all along, that I could have solved his problem on day one. He'd know that I've been part of his life for months without saying a word about the connection between our families, that the woman in his family album with her face turned from the camera is my mother. It feels like one betrayal after another. I can see how it looks from the outside, but only I know how it is on the inside. That curiosity propelled me through their painted glass door, and that I only ever wanted to help without com-promising my mother's memory or Santo's confidence. I didn't plan on falling in love with Gio, or with the rest of the Belotti family either, for that matter.

There's an undeniable part of me that wants to tell Gio everything, to throw it all out there and let him be the judge, because surely this is about our lives now, not my mother and

Santo's lives more than thirty years ago? But then I hear my mother whispering in my ear to never tell another living soul, and I hear Santo asking me to make a clean break, and I hear Felipe telling me blood is thicker than water. And that's the crux of things, really. Blood *is* thicker than water, Belotti blood most of all. Gio is first, foremost, and forever a Belotti. He would always want what's best for them, and he'll get over this because he has them.

I wish it was tomorrow, that the goodbyes were behind me and Canada in front of me. I know nothing about Toronto beyond the name of the airport. I don't have any of the plans or preconceptions I had when I flew to New York, none of my mother's steps to retrace. I'm going to be completely on my own there, and there isn't a single part of me that's looking forward to it.

I'M CLOCK-WATCHING, WAITING FOR Gio, missing him desperately and sick at the thought of this being the last time I'll see him. He sent a text to say he'll come by around one, and it's almost twenty past twelve now and he's never late. My hands are clammy. I wipe them on my jeans as I turn the kettle on to make coffee and then turn it off again because I know I won't drink it anyway. I sit on the sofa, change my mind and sit at the kitchen table so I'm closer to the door, ready to let him in. I've nothing in my stomach. I couldn't face food this morning, yet still my guts churn like my gelato machine.

The buzzer goes loud and shocking in my quiet apartment and I freeze like a kid playing statues. He's here. I almost run to the buzzer and press it several times in case it doesn't work

and he leaves. I take steadying breaths as I listen to his footsteps on the stairs, and then he finally taps my door and I
brace myself and open it wide.

"You stopped replying to my messages, little mouse.
Upset me so much I've come all this way to check up on you
in person."

38.

I LURCH BACKWARD, SICK WITH PANIC AT THE SIGHT OF Adam Bronson. I've promised myself so many times he isn't lurking in the New York shadows, reassured myself that he would never go so far as to turn up here. And now he's inside my apartment, closing my front door, smiling broadly as if I should be rolling out the welcome mat.

"What are you doing here?" I say, holding my nerve.

His eyes move slowly over the apartment, taking everything in. "So this is where you went."

I don't say anything else. I'm shaking violently inside; I don't trust my voice not to betray my fear. He ambles across the room toward the sofa, picking things up to inspect them as he goes. A letter from the bank. A store receipt. Insignificant pieces of my life that I resent him touching.

"Well now," he says. "How are you, Adam, would you like a cup of coffee, Adam, how was your flight, Adam?" He sits down and crosses his legs, throwing his upturned hands out to the sides. "Take your pick. Or shall I just answer all three, save you the bother? Yes, I'd like coffee, you know how I take it." He ticks it off on one finger. "My flight was fucking long and expensive, and no, I'm not doing so well, seeing as you ask. I lost my job and then my little mouse blocked my number."

I stare at him. "I don't have any milk."

He looks at me and raises his eyebrows, then gets up and crosses to the kitchenette, opening the fridge.

"Oh, look. You do."

He puts the carton down on the counter next to me, slow and deliberate, and I swallow back vomit, bilious when his distinctive aftershave clogs my air space.

"I'm not making you coffee. I want you to leave. Right now."

He laughs lightly, as if I made a joke, and bitter, furious tears sting the back of my eyes.

"I missed you, mouse," he says, putting his arm around my shoulders.

I shrug him off and half run to swing my front door open. "Get out."

He looks at me like I'm a child trying his patience, and it sends a cold shiver of recognition down my spine. I've seen that glance so often before, and I know the unpredictable snap into rage that can follow it.

"I'm not frightened of you," I say, raising my chin.

"Why would you be?" He laughs. "I've never laid so much as a finger on you. Not one you weren't gagging for, anyway." He wriggles his eyebrows up and down suggestively, and I watch them in disgust, like two slugs crawling into his hairline.

"If you don't go, I'll call the police," I say. "The station is right round the corner."

"And say what? My boyfriend came to visit and asked for

a cup of coffee?" He holds his wrists out in front of him. "Cuff me, officer, it's a fair cop."

"Ex-boyfriend," I say through gritted teeth.

He gives me that warning look again, and I swallow, trying not to let him see how much he's getting to me. The buzzer goes, and he watches me with interest.

"Expecting anyone?"

Oh shit, no. No, Gio, no. I shake my head, stringing words together out of nowhere and hoping they make sense. "It'll be the mailman. He buzzes to let me know if he's left a parcel."

Adam nods slowly, then crosses to the window and checks. "Doesn't look like the mailman."

Someone bangs on the front door when I don't buzz it open. "Iris!"

It isn't Gio. It's Sophia.

"Friends of yours?"

"Just someone I work with."

"Iris, open up!"

Adam puts his head on one side as he peeps outside again and then looks back at me with a scandalized expression that tells me he's thoroughly enjoying himself.

"Please, we need to speak with you."

I close my eyes and swallow hard, because that was Maria's raised voice, not Sophia's. I want them as far away from this place as possible, but the fact that they're both here instead of Gio spikes fear through me in case something terrible has happened to him.

"I really need to go and talk to them," I say quickly, hating my own lack of volume. "Please, Adam, just wait here."

He folds his arms. "You want me to leave, you want me to stay, you won't make me coffee, you threaten me with the cops, and now you want to run off and chat to your friends. This isn't going how I thought it would at all, mouse, and I don't think I like it."

He frowns and turns back to the window at the sound of car doors slamming.

"Oh good, more people. It's turning into a street party."

I can hear the commotion and I'm desperate to go and see, but he's by the window and he screws up his face in disgust when Smirnoff appears on the fire escape the other side of the glass. Adam detests cats. Dogs too, for that matter. He's not an animal person generally, which, thinking back, should have been a major red flag.

"Vermin," he mutters, and I gasp as I hear the front door downstairs open even though I haven't buzzed anyone in.

"Iris, honey, there's a line of glamorous people out on the sidewalk waiting for you. Get your butt down these stairs pronto!"

Bobby.

I look at Adam, and he stares back at me, and then I dash out of my open apartment door to the top of the stairwell. Robin is down there wheeling their Vuitton luggage inside, and Bobby is standing with his hands on his leather-trousered hips, a huge fur-trapper hat on his head. I sense rather than see Adam move to stand close beside me, and I try not to visibly flinch when he puts his arm around my shoulders, his grip digging into my upper arm.

"You're being rude, mouse, introduce me to your friends."

I walk stiffly down the stairs as Sophia and Maria crowd into the small hallway behind Robin, and I'm mortified to see

Santo and Felipe are with them too. I pause on the bottom step and feel Adam beside me again, and I close my eyes for a horrified second when his hand lands on my shoulder, pulling me in tight against him.

Bobby yanks his hat off his head, frowning as he tries to get a measure on the situation. It's silent for a few seconds, everyone watching everyone else.

"I'm Adam Bronson. If I knew you were coming I'd have baked a cake!"

He laughs, that hideous, forced jovial laugh that makes me shudder, and Bobby shakes his head, muttering "Oh I don't fucking think so" as he hurls his fur hat on the floor and launches himself bodily at Adam.

"*Madonna santa,*" Maria breathes, stepping back quickly as Adam unbalances and hits the deck, Bobby straddled on top of him like a feral cat. Adam shoves him off easily and stumbles to his feet, swearing, swinging round to stare at me.

"Maybe you should call the police on this dickhead, not me," he says, dusting himself off. "I'll come back later. This isn't my kind of party."

He elbows Sophia out of the way to get past and she shoulder-checks him right back, almost unbalancing him again.

"Asshole," she spits.

Adam leers toward her in reply and every Belotti in the place steps forward and starts shouting and shoving him at once, some in English, some in furious Italian, and then he's suddenly yanked backward by the scruff of the neck and dragged straight out into the street. I didn't see Gio arrive but he's here now and I gulp, frantic with relief that at least his family haven't come en masse to deliver terrible news.

Everyone tumbles out into the street as Adam sprawls on his ass in the snow.

"Get up," Gio says, standing over him.

Adam slides around on the ice as he hauls himself to his feet, undignified. He stares between Gio and me for a few seconds and then starts to laugh.

"Oh, I get it now," he says, gesturing between us as if he finds the idea hilarious. "I wouldn't bother, mate, she's dull as fuck."

Gio glances at the sky and sighs, then smacks his fist hard into Adam's jaw, sending him sprawling across the sidewalk into a heap of black bin sacks from the fish restaurant two doors down. Adam crawls forward, wiping stinking food waste from his clothes. Smirnoff, God bless that cat, appears from nowhere at the scent of fish and swipes his claws over Adam's hand a second before Gio lifts him back on to his feet by his lapels.

"You want her, you come through me," he says, right up close in Adam's face.

A sudden and unexpected sensation of inner strength powers through me, like a shower of metallic lightning bolts firing themselves around my bloodstream. I step forward and lay my hand on Gio's arm, because much as I appreciate the protective ring everyone has instinctively thrown around me, it's time for me to be my mother's daughter. Adam is my demon to dispel, I have to do this for myself.

"Stop. Gio, please, I don't need you to fight this battle for me."

He looks sideways at me, breathing hard, and I see all of the Italian passion and fury burning bright behind his beautiful dark eyes. I hold his gaze steady, willing him to listen to me, and after a beat he does as I've asked, letting Adam go with a small shove. I nod, grateful that even in this moment of true anger, Gio is a man who is prepared to listen to the needs of others. I think he understands how important it is for me to finish this on my terms.

"You shouldn't have come here." I draw myself up to my full height as I turn to look Adam square in the face. "New York is my home now. I'm never coming back to London, nor to you. I'm not scared of you anymore, I'm done letting you be the monster under my bed. You're a nobody, a miserable, pathetic excuse for a man who gets his kicks from manipulating people when they're at their lowest. Well, newsflash, Adam. I'm not at my lowest anymore, and I'm not your mouse. I'm not your anything, in fact, and I never will be, so get the hell out of this city and never set so much as a foot near it again, do you hear me?"

Adam smirks down at me, his lip swollen and ugly. "Big talk," he says. "You'll come crawling back."

"I promise you I won't. These people have taken me into their lives and into their family—" I begin.

His sharp bark of laughter cuts across me. "Family? You're nobody's family, mouse." He pouts his split bottom lip at me in fake sympathy, and I note his flinch of pain with satisfaction.

Behind me, Gio makes a sound somewhere close to a growl and takes a step toward us, but Santo raises his hand and moves in front of his son. A temporary stillness falls over proceedings at the older man's intervention; even Adam seems to defer to his authority.

"Iris is *my* family," Santo says, leaning heavily on his cane.

Maria steps up beside her husband. "And mine."

Sophia takes her place in the line. "And mine."

Felipe moves beside his brother. "And mine."

On the front step of the noodle house, Robin and Bobby stand side by side. "And you better fucking believe she's our family too," Robin half shouts, looking mutinous.

Adam glares at them all. "Bunch of fucking losers," he mutters, blood dripping from his lip, stark against the snow.

I gaze around at each and every one of them, proud and overwrought. "Bunch of fucking heroes," I say.

And then I walk right up close to my ex, liberated, all fear gone. I smell his stomach-churning cologne for the last time as I think about the living hell he put me through, and I quietly acknowledge the strength it took to leave him when I was at my lowest ebb. I think about the girl I met in the alley a few weeks ago, and on behalf of every woman living in fear of a controlling man, I raise my chin and stare that bastard down one last time. I deserve to have the final word.

"Eat glass, Adam Bronson."

39.

WE ALL STAND IN THE STREET, MY NEW YORK FAMILY and I, until Adam finally disappears from view, and then they close in around me. I don't really understand what just happened, why they're even here, but all I know in that moment is that they *are* here and it's overwhelming in the best way. Gio stands back and waits for his family to finish passing me around for hugs, and then finally he's holding me in his arms and I start to cry. He pulls me closer still, really tight, the kind of hug designed to make someone feel held and safe.

"I've got you," he says, stroking my hair. "I've got you."

I look up at him, and he gazes down at me, and then he lowers his face and kisses me slowly. I hear Sophia's sigh, and Maria is crying, and Bobby and Robin usher everyone around us up to their apartment for a stiff drink.

We stay exactly where we are until there is just us and Smirnoff left on the sidewalk. Gio smooths my hair back with both hands and looks at me, serious-eyed.

"You okay?" he whispers, holding my face.

"I am now," I say, and I mean it. "You?"

"Not even close," he says, stepping back. "This whole thing, Iris, it's . . ."

He reaches into his coat and pulls something from his inside pocket. I look down and see the familiar mint-green torn napkin from my mother's scrapbook. Santo's writing. Their beloved family recipe.

"Papa told us everything," he says. "And Felipe filled in the gaps."

I stare at the napkin. "I've wanted to tell you every single day," I say.

He looks at me. "All those mornings together at the gelateria, and you knew the recipe all along."

"It wasn't my secret to share," I whisper. "I just wanted to help, not cause any discord in your family."

"You should have trusted me sooner," he says.

"It was never about trust," I say. "It was about loyalty to my mother, at first, at least. And then to Santo too, because the more you told me about him the more I understood how big a deal what's written on this napkin was. And the lie I told you about Adam . . . it made my skin crawl with shame. I just dug myself a hole I had no idea how to get out of. I'm so sorry."

Gio stares at the napkin. "Mamma has told me to give this back to you."

My heart aches at the memory of Maria just now, taking her place in the line to defend me. "How is she?"

Gio sighs softly. "She's been amazing, as always. They've been through too much together over the years for this to break them. Too much history. Too much love. This was a long time ago and, in the end, I think she's grateful it brought you to us, recipe and all."

"But she has every right to hate me," I say, miserable at the thought because Maria's warmth and generosity of spirit has wrapped itself around me like a winter coat.

"But she doesn't," Gio says. "Mamma has a heart the size of a lioness and, like it or not, you're one of her own now."

One of her own. I felt like one of her own today, protected in a way that's been missing from my life since my mother died.

"And Santo?" I say. "Is he okay?"

Gio glances up toward Bobby's apartment. "Stoic, as usual. A little relieved, a little ashamed, I think."

"He has nothing to feel ashamed about," I rush in. "They were little more than kids. Shall I try to say something to make things better? This is all my fault."

"It's not your fault," Gio says. "He's lived with the weight of his choices from back then, you just tried to put things right. This is private, between them now. They need to deal with things in their own way, and they will."

I understand what he's saying. It's not my narrative to control from here on in.

He kisses my forehead. "You tried your best. What's done is done now, everything is out in the open where it belongs."

I feel the weight of the last few months lift from my shoulders, lead into feathers. He knows everything. He knows about Adam, and about my mother, and about the recipe. He knows all of my secrets and he's still standing here.

"Iris," he says, his hand warm on the back of my neck when I look into his eyes.

"I love you," I say, because after everything that's happened, I want to be the one to say it first. "I love you so much, Gio."

He slides his thumb over my bottom lip as I say it. "*Ti amo.*"

I smile and say it back, and the sounds feel new and precious in my mouth.

"She speaks Italian," he murmurs, and I hear the choke of emotion in his throat.

Smirnoff grumbles on the front step. It could be appreciation of my new foreign language skills, or it could be a threat of impending violence, it's difficult to tell. Either way, he's getting a whole can of tuna today. I might even serve it in a pink melamine bowl.

THERE'S A PARTY ATMOSPHERE going on in Bobby and Robin's apartment when we finally head inside. They might be fresh back from holiday with their cases lined up in the hallway, but they've slipped straight into consummate host mode and cracked open the champagne. There's crooner music on in the background, chosen for Santo's pleasure I suspect, and Sophia and Bobby are laughing at something on the sofa, already thick as thieves.

"I feel as if I've walked into a Christmas card," I murmur. Smirnoff shoots past my ankles as everyone turns to look our way.

Sophia jumps up and hugs us both tight, pressing the back of her hand against my cheek. "You're freezing," she says. "Come and get by the fire."

"I'm fine." I hold on to her fingers until she looks at me. "Thank you for everything," I whisper. "You were bloody brilliant."

"Oh, I just wish I'd landed a punch on him," she says.

"Not worth breaking your nails over," I say, making light of the heaviest thing I've carried in my heart.

Sophia glances at Gio. "I've never seen him quite like that," she says, love and admiration for her brother written all over her face. I glance at Gio and remember the way he stood up to protect me, but also the way he stepped back to allow me the space to stand up for myself.

Bobby joins us and holds his hand out to Gio. I see the look of acknowledgment and respect pass between them as they shake hands, Gio's other hand resting on Bobby's shoulder.

"Just so you know, I'd pretty much got the situation under control by the time you arrived," Bobby preens. "I had the asshole on the floor."

"I heard about that," Gio says. "Iris said you were heroic."

Bobby looks my way, his eyes suspiciously watery as he mouths the word "heroic."

"Iron Man has nothing on you," I say, kissing his cheek, deliberately choosing his favorite superhero for maximum effect.

Robin comes over and ushers us farther into the living room, and we are enveloped by warmth and Belotti love. I kiss Maria and hug Santo and Felipe, and then I sit on the sofa between Sophia and Gio and hold their hands.

I close my eyes and listen to Frank Sinatra croon his famous love song to New York, and I smile because I know that somewhere, somehow, my mother put in this special request just for me.

I came to New York in search of a fresh start, alone and unsure if I'd be able to make it here. I'm not unsure anymore. This heart-racingly wonderful, chaotic, neon city is my forever home, if it'll have me.

I'm not alone anymore either. I've been invisibly connected to the Belotti family my entire life, by a painted glass
door and a torn green napkin and endless bowls of comforting vanilla gelato. How lucky I am to have somehow, miracu-
lously, joined the dots, that the stars aligned and led me to
that exact same glass door. It's wishful thinking to imagine
my mother has somehow had a guiding hand—but if such
things were possible, I know she would have moved heaven
and earth to lead me to Belotti's. The gelateria on Mulberry
Street was her safe place here in this city, and now, three decades later, it has become mine.

Back then, she had the choice to stay and she didn't. We
were similar in so many ways, my mother and I, but my New
York story ends differently, and that's not because of fate or
the stars or even because of my mother. It's because of me. It's
because of the strength I found to get myself on a plane to
New York with just my beloved gelato maker and a battered
suitcase. At the time I felt as if I was running away, but now,
with the benefit of hindsight, I can finally see the whole
messy, beautiful picture.

I was coming home.

Epilogue

...

"I THINK I JUST SAW ONE," I SAY, POINTING AT THE SKY. "Right there."

Gio follows the arc of my finger and then looks sideways at me. "You did not."

I laugh under my breath. "No, I did not. It's too cloudy. But you went to all this effort, so I'm going to lie and say I saw a shooting star and you're going to smile and pretend you believe me."

"I'll never stand straight again after this," he says, shifting his shoulders against the ridged metal floor of the open-back pickup truck he moved mountains to hire as a Valentine surprise. He's driven us upstate for most of the day so we can lie out under big dark skies to look for shooting stars, but the weather is not being kind to us.

"I should have got an inflatable mattress," he grumbles.

I shake my head. "It had to be a checked blanket, or dinner on top of the Empire State Building."

"Or some other equally trite shite," he says, in the same

terrible English accent he used on our initial bookshop encounter twelve months ago. I couldn't believe he'd remembered what I said that day, nor could I believe the effort he'd
made to surprise me with this echo of our first meeting, a
checked blanket in the bed of a truck under the stars.

I land a punch on his arm and smile into the darkness. I
can think back on that day now without the accompanying
feelings of dread and shame, because it triggered a chain of
events that led me here with the love of my life.

Gio rolls on his side and gazes down at me. "I don't think
we should make this our annual tradition," he says.

"Definitely a one-off," I say. "My turn to plan Valentine's
next year."

"Can it be somewhere inside, with a bed?"

I nod. "Deal."

I sit up cross-legged and pull my rucksack toward me. "I
got you something," I say, lifting a gift-wrapped parcel out of
my bag. I hand it to him, and he reaches under the blanket
and produces a gift for me too.

"Swap," he says.

"Open yours first," I say.

He pulls the ribbon and opens the box, and his laugh is
quiet as he looks at the two silver spoons lying there.

"One big, one little," I say.

"*Cucchiaino*," he says, massaging my knee.

I turn the gift he's given me over in my hands.

"I know what it is," I say.

"Open it anyway," he says.

I unwrap the book and trace my fingers over the intricate
cover design. It's a special edition hardback with golden
sprayed edges, not at all reminiscent of the paperback we ar-

gued over last Valentine's Day. I'm glad; perhaps I'll be able to read this copy without any lingering feelings of shame and regret.

"*Coniglio,*" he says.

"No clue what it means but say it again," I say, because he knows full well it does something to my brain when he speaks Italian.

"Rabbit," he says. "It means rabbit."

"Smartass." I spot the hidden rabbit on the cover and then lie down again and prop myself on one elbow. "Think that sky is going to clear?"

"Not a chance," he says.

"I don't care," I say. "It's all about the truck and the blanket for me anyway."

"You could have said that before I drove five hours straight to get here," he says, winding a strand of my hair around his fingers.

"It was romantic. I love you for trying."

I lean over to kiss him and he rolls me on to my back beneath him.

"You're right about this truck, though," I say as my shoulder blades jar against the metal.

"I love this truck right now," he says, putting his hand inside my sweater. "I might buy it."

"Not too cold to make out?" I whisper, when he kisses my neck and says something I hope is unspeakably dirty in Italian.

I open my eyes and, honest to God, I see stars.

ACKNOWLEDGMENTS

THANK YOU TO MY WONDER AGENT, NELLE ANDREWS, AND my UK and U.S. editors, Harriet Bourton and Hilary Teeman. I will forever appreciate your extra-mile kindness and unflinching support while I worked on this book.

Special thanks to all at Notarianni Ice Cream in Blackpool for providing the initial spark of inspiration for the story via a segment on *The Hairy Bikers*—all of my hours spent idly surfing cooking shows are not in vain!

Thanks as always to everyone at Viking and Penguin UK and the rights team for your continued brilliance, I feel fortunate to be in your hands.

Huge thanks to everyone at the mighty team Dell. I'm so thankful for our continued relationship and the thoughtful way you share my stories with the U.S. audience.

Much gratitude to all of my overseas publishers; it's amazing to think of my books in the hands of readers in distant corners of the world.

Love to the Bob girls for the many, many years of friendship and cheerleading, and to Emily Blackledge in particular for your wise singing advice.

And last but never least, love and thanks to my lovely family and friends. As always, you are my favorites and my best.

A
WINTER
IN
NEW YORK

JOSIE SILVER

RANDOM HOUSE

BOOK CLUB

AN AUTHOR'S
INSPIRATION

...

M Y INSPIRATION COMES FROM LOTS OF DIFFERENT places, and this particular story began late one night as I lay on the sofa surfing TV channels. We have a cookery show in the UK called *The Hairy Bikers*, I don't know if it's made it over to the United States? It's a cookery show, and in this particular episode the two guys, who unsurprisingly are hairy bikers who love to cook, visited Notarianni's iconic ice cream shop in Blackpool, a coastal town in the north of England.

I listened to the segment about the proud history of this legendary ice cream shop stretching back over more than ninety years, and about the Notarianni family who have run it for all of that time—the story of their secret family recipe really stopped me in my tracks. They spoke about how only two family members are allowed to know their recipe at any given time—they even fly separately just in case!

I found myself rewinding the TV to listen to the piece a second time, and the romance of the family history and their story stuck itself somewhere in my head. That was a couple of years ago now, and it's been percolating like a good cup of Belotti's coffee ever since.

I'm super grateful to the Notarianni family for allowing

me to use their wonderful family history as the spark for *A Winter in New York*, which is of course entirely fictional. I hope they love reading about Iris and Gio, and that they get a kick from knowing these characters wouldn't have made it onto the page without them. ♥

A Q&A WITH
JOSIE SILVER

...

Q: Thanks so much for telling us about the Notarianni family and how they inspired *A Winter in New York*! Do you always have some kind of specific inspiration for your novels, or do you find that inspiration comes in a different way every time you sit down to write a novel?

A: I often see something mentioned on TV or in a magazine that will set off a train of what-if thoughts in my head, as was the case with *A Winter in New York*. Music inspires me too, sometimes it can even be just the way someone's voice sounds when they deliver a particular line. I'm a bit of a country music fan—those guys really know how to deliver a line with emotion, don't they?

I keep a notebook of my story ideas, but I don't always have it with me if I'm out and about. I've been known to come home with random ideas scrawled over the back of store receipts, or failing everything else, on the back of my hand. I have to write things down when I think of them or they're gone!

Q: We were shocked to hear that you wrote this book without ever actually having been to New York, especially since you capture the spirit and the vibrancy of the city so perfectly! What references did you use to create the city?

A: Ideally, I'd love to have visited New York, but this story actually started out life set in the UK. It relocated to the United States as I started to get words down on paper and realized it would work so much better if I moved it to New York City, by which time I was on deadline and needed to stay put with the story.

Not having been to the specific locations in the story put me on the back foot; all I can say is thank goodness for the internet! I spent countless hours watching New York walking tours, talking to friends, and reading travel blogs for individual experiences. I'm lucky to have a fabulous U.S. editor too. I knew she'd be on hand to go through it with a red pen to make sure the details were accurate and authentic.

All those hours of research and immersion have left me more desperate than ever to experience New York for myself soon, and I'll be sure to time my visit to coincide with the San Gennaro Feast that Bobby takes Iris to at the beginning of the story!

Q: Iris and Vivien are huge romcom fans (as are many of us!)—are you a big fan as well? What romantic movies are your favorites?

A: Am I a huge romcom fan? Oh, absolutely and emphatically yes! I loved being able to include *Moonstruck* in the story as it's one of my all-time favorite movies, but if pushed, I think I might choose *Crazy, Stupid, Love* as my ultimate favorite romcom.

But then . . . *Bridget Jones's Diary* will always have my heart, *Four Weddings and a Funeral* is a must-watch at least once a year, and Christmas just isn't Christmas without *The Holiday,* is it?

Q: All of your novels feature characters who not only go on relationship journeys, but on personal journeys as well—it's one of the things readers love most about your books! Why do you think you are drawn to writing characters who are struggling with larger themes like grief or self-acceptance or healing as they find love?

A: Great question! I guess because I've been married for a fair while and we have teenage kids, life is often complicated and messy and sprawling. It's not all date nights and flowers, it's busy and hilarious and sometimes heartbreaking, and I find that comes out on the page whether I plan things that way or not. I find real joy in writing ensemble casts, especially multi-generational characters and families. It's just real life, isn't it? Romance doesn't happen in isolation, it's influenced and shaped by all of the other important people in our lives. I like to lean into that to deepen and enrich the story.

Q: What does your writing process look like? Are you an author who likes a lot of structure to your writing days, or an author who writes whenever the mood strikes?

A: I would love to say I'm organized, that I make charts and plans and tick off my days in a methodical manner, but I'm afraid that's not how I work best. I tend to go fairly steady and slow in the beginning stages of a manuscript, gather pace as I hit the middle, and then write really intensively toward the end. It's not an easy way to do it—I find the later stages stressful, but in an exhilarating way I strangely kind of love!

I've learned to accept that this is the process that works for me and not to give myself grief over it.

Q: And last but not least, we'd be remiss if we didn't ask who your dream cast would be if *A Winter in New York* was made into a classic romcom movie! Is there anyone that comes to mind?

A: Ah! This question is the one I love and loathe the most! I often dream-cast characters in my head as I write—I find it helps with dialogue to have a specific person I can imagine delivering the lines, down to their mannerisms and the way their body moves. Strangely though, I haven't nailed it down for this book. I can see them all, but they're not fully formed— I'm sort of side-eyeing them in my head all the time. I can see Iris's blunt cut bangs, the way Gio's shirt skims his body when he turns to the machine to make coffee, and the bounce of Sophia's curls as she moves. I see the jauntiness of Felipe's walk and the slightness of Bella's hands, and the cloud of expensive perfume that envelops the room whenever Maria walks in. I just can't see their faces. It's a fun game though, isn't it!

QUESTIONS AND TOPICS
FOR DISCUSSION

...

1. What did you think of Iris and Gio's initial meet-cute at the bookstore? Has there ever been a book in your life that you'd have fended off a stranger in order to get ahold of? If so, what was it?

2. The first real relationship Iris forms after moving to New York is with Bobby, her best friend/neighbor/boss. Have you ever had a friend like that, who has helped pick you up when you were down?

3. We soon come to learn of the secret gelato recipe that Iris's mother passed down to her, and their tradition of eating it from pink melamine bowls, often while watching old New York–set movies. What family recipes or family traditions have been passed down in your family?

4. New York City is its very own character in this novel, especially the neighborhood of Little Italy. Did the setting make you want to visit the city? If you've visited before, did it make you want to return?

5. What did you think of Iris's plan once she realizes where her mother's gelato recipe must have come from? Do you agree that it's the most sensitive way to handle the special circumstances? Why or why not?

6. As we come to know the Belottis, we learn that they are lively and loving and absolutely wonderful—did you also wish you could have spent time with them at the holidays or at the gelato shop?

7. Both Iris and Gio have reasons that they have avoided relationships and opening up to new people—what was the moment that you started to see this changing for them? What do you think was the first moment they really started to trust each other?

8. The Monday Night Motel is a space that Gio and Iris created just for themselves, to be a little bubble of escape from the world. Have you ever created a space or ritual like that for yourself, with or without a partner? If not, what would you want your ideal little escape to be?

9. How did you feel when Santo issued his stern request to Iris? Could you see where he was coming from, or do you think he should have been happy for Iris and Gio and been more understanding instead?

10. What did you think about the climax of the novel, when all of our characters come together in one big scene? Did you laugh or cry? Were you angry or happy? Or did you feel all of those things by turn?

11. By the end of the novel, we've seen Iris and Gio go on personal journeys as well as a journey together. What did you think of their character and relationship arcs? Do you think they are stronger for it?

A VERY NEW YORK
MUST-WATCH ROMCOM LIST

...

INSPIRED BY IRIS AND HER MOTHER'S TRADITION OF watching New York–set romcoms, we've curated the ultimate watchlist for every kind of romcom lover!

For those who like their romcoms a little more vintage, we've got some oldies but goodies:

Barefoot in the Park
That Touch of Mink
Sabrina
An Affair to Remember
Breakfast at Tiffany's

For the strongest Iris and Vivien vibes, we've got their favorite romcoms:

When Harry Met Sally
Moonstruck
Working Girl
Sleepless in Seattle
You've Got Mail
Splash

And for those who love how the romcom tradition has carried on:

Maid in Manhattan
How to Lose a Guy in 10 Days
Serendipity
Two Weeks Notice
Kate & Leopold

A TASTY VANILLA
GELATO RECIPE

...

AND OF COURSE, NO ROMCOM MARATHON IS COMPLETE without vanilla gelato! (Okay, it might not be the super-secret Belotti family recipe, but we encourage you to experiment with this recipe and make it your own family tradition!)

INGREDIENTS:

4 egg yolks
¾ cup granulated sugar
1½ cups whole milk
1 cup cold heavy cream
Vanilla extract to taste

METHOD:

Whip the egg yolks and sugar until the mixture is soft and creamy. Bring the milk to almost a boil and keep it simmering at 185°F, making sure it does not boil. Slowly add the egg mixture, stirring the entire time. Simmer the mixture for another few minutes, then add the cold heavy cream, stirring as you go and mixing well. Transfer into a gelato machine and follow the instructions for your device.

ABOUT THE AUTHOR

JOSIE SILVER is an unabashed romantic who met her husband when she stepped on his foot on his twenty-first birthday. She lives with him, their two sons, and their cats in England. She is the #1 *New York Times* bestselling author of *One Day in December, The Two Lives of Lydia Bird,* and *One Night on the Island.*